MEROVIN—
THE WORLD
THAT C.J. CHERRYH BUILT!

It all began with ANGEL WITH THE SWORD, C.J. Cherryh's acclaimed novel about the world of Merovin and the people, abandoned Terran colonists, who dwelt in the canal city of Merovingen. So real did Merovingen seem, so filled with life and adventurous possibility, that it fired the imaginations of many of C.J.'s fellow writers. And so this series, MEROVINGEN NIGHTS, was born.

So welcome now to FESTIVAL MOON, the first volume of MEROVINGEN NIGHTS tales. And join C.J. Cherryh, Robert Asprin, Lynn Abbey, Janet and Chris Morris, and other top writers as they set their own characters loose to pole the dark waterways and prowl the high bridges, form unexpected alliances, fight battles for survival and mastery, and pit their cunning and quickness against one another and against the many perils of that most dangerous and intricate of cities—Merovingen.

MEROVINGEN NIGHTS
FESTIVAL MOON

C.J. CHERRYH

DAW BOOKS, INC.
DONALD A. WOLLHEIM, PUBLISHER

1633 Broadway, New York, NY 10019

DAW Book Collectors No. 704.

First Printing, April 1987

1 2 3 4 5 6 7 8 9

PRINTED IN THE U.S.A.

This book is dedicated to all these people, who Did Something to make the dream of spaceflight a reality.

Isaac Asimov,
Real and Muff Musgrave,
Roger Zelazny,
Robert E. Vardeman,
Mildred Downey Broxon,
Poul & Karen Anderson,
Donald A. Wollheim,
Elsie B. Wollheim,
Betsy Wollheim,
Peter Stampfel,
Arthur L. Rubin,
Stephen R. & Stephanie Donaldson,
Dave Wixon & Ann Layman Chancellor,
Gordon R. Dickson,
David & Joanne Drake,
Robert A. Heinlein,
Jack Williamson,
David Brin,
Benjamin M. Yalow,
Bob Goodwin,
Kurt Baty and Michelle Doty,
Donald and Jill Eastlake,
Tony & Suford Lewis,
Grover C. Farrish MD,
Bob & Susie Galyon,
Charles Sheffield,
Edward L. Ferman,
Bill Kerby,
James P. Poon,
Richard Curtis,
Frederick Wamsley,
Philip José Farmer,

Lorena S & Jack C Haldeman (III), & Vol & Lori & Joe & Gay Haldeman,
Michael J. Lowrey & C.K. Hinchliffe & T.M. Cason,
Milwaukee Science Fiction Fans,
Ellen A. Asher,
Virginia Kidd,
Eric and Vicky Webb,
Phoenix SF Society of Atlanta Ga,
Rivercon SF Convention of Louisville KY,
Robert Asprin & Lynn Abbey,
Michael Swanwick & Marianne C. Porter,
Teresa Minambres,
David B. Mattingly,
Barry B. Longyear,
Nashua Association for Space Awareness,
Ad Astra SF Society of Toronto,
Algis Budrys,
Nancy C. Asire,
Tom Doherty Associates Inc.,
Martin Caidin,
L-5 Society National,
OKon and members of Starbase Tulsa,

Los Angeles Science
 Fantasy Society Inc.,
Christopher S.
 Claremont,
Esther Friesner,
Ben Bova,
National Space Society
 [NSS],
Richard & Wendy Pini,
Ronald M. Sharrow;
 Atty.,
Dr. Dean R. Lambe,
Andrew Unangst,
Janet Morris,
Chris Morris,
Peter Straub,
Michael Resnick,
Eleanor Wood,
Analog Science Fiction
 Science Fact
 Magazine,
Rodman A. Frates,
Frontiers of Science
 Foundation of
 Oklahoma Inc.,
Darwin Bromley &
 Anne Elliott,
Mayfair Games Inc.,
Isaac Asimov's Science
 Fiction Magazine,
Stephen King,
Kirby McCauley,
American Astronautical
 Society [AAS],
James Baen,
Donning-Starblaze,
Robert Adams,
Kristy Alberty,
Roger Allen,
Arizona State U.
 Planetary Science
 Researchers,
Jack B. & Evelyn M.
 Asire,

Mark W. Bailey & Gail
 E Mathews-Bailey,
Stanley C. Baker,
Greg Bear & Astrid
 Anderson Bear,
Mary Martha Berry,
Curtis W. & Marilyn &
 Lisa Berry,
Jackie Bielowicz,
Betty & David H.
 Bigelow,
Mark Bishop,
Sue A. Blom,
Glen A. Boettcher,
George S. Brickner,
Robert Briggs,
Ann Broomhead,
Donna Buchanan,
Kathleen Buckley,
Larry D. Bunge,
Gerald Burton,
Wm. A. Buthod,
Ritchie & Delia Calvin,
Johanna Cantor &
 Edward C &
 Edward H &
 John H Hitchcock,
David Cantor,
Elisabeth Carey,
Lillian Stewart Carl,
Jeffrey A. Carver,
David Caswell,
David A. Cherry,
Emory Churness,
Mary Coffee,
Gary Cone,
John C. Connolly Jr.,
Juanita & Buck Coulson,
David Crockett,
Barbara Jane Cross,
Charles Crumm,
Dallas/Fort Worth L-5
 Chapter,
Ned Danieley,

Scott Davis,
Dan DePalma,
Salvatore di Maria,
Carrington B. Dixon, Jr.,
Ann Doan,
Dennis Drew,
Douglas E. Drummond,
Rosemarie D. Eierman,
Marji Ellers,
William D. Evans,
Charles E. Fallen,
Allen Fancher,
Lynn Fancher,
Jane Fancher,
Randy Farran,
Bill Fawcett,
Jan Howard Finder,
Leah J. Fisher,
George P. Flynn,
William R. & Marilyn H. Forstchen,
Richard Foss,
Timothy & Donna Elaine Frayser,
Frank Kelly Freas & Polly Freas,
Giovanna E. Fregni,
Pamela D. Fremon,
Michael Jan Friedman,
Tom Galloway,
Lisa Gannon,
Richard Garrett Sr.
Marie Garrettt,
Barbara H. Geraud,
Glenn Glazer,
David Govaker,
Roland J.Green & Frieda A. Murray,
Jeanette Gugler,
James E. Gunn,
Casey Hamilton,
Cynthia Hanley,

Herbert A. Hansen & Nancy Melcher,
Steven & Susan Herold,
Elaine M. Hinman,
Charles J. Hitchcock,
Arthur D. Hlavaty,
J. Eric Holcomb,
Ben Hopkins,
William & Phyllis Hubeny,
Thomas Huffman Jr.,
Mark Hyde,
Aron & Merle Insinga,
David Jacobs,
Carol Johnson,
Danny Gene Johnson,
George Jones,
Joyce Jones,
Jack Jones,
Emma & Joyce & Susan Joyce,
Rick Katze,
Lee & Pat Killough,
Lynn Kingsley,
Oscar Kirzner,
Jean-Cristophe Komorowski,
Tim Kozinski,
Karen Kugler,
Mercedes Lackey,
Devra Michele Langsam,
Alexis Layton,
Lon Levy,
Bob Lidral,
Paula Lieberman,
Susan J. Lindell,
Peter Little,
Serge Mailloux,
Laura Mallard,
Jim & Laurie Mann,
Frank Manning,
Ed Martin,
Tim McGrain,
Loretta McKibben,

Morgaine McKibben,
Kevin T. McLaughlin,
David Means,
Scott Merritt,
Margaret & Morris
  Middleton,
Sandra L. Miesel,
Nancy E. Mildebrandt,
Craig Miller,
Tera Mitchel,
Elizabeth L. Mitchell,
Samuel Mize,
Therri Moore,
Cheryl Morisette,
Francine & Latisha
  Mullen,
Peter Nielson,
David C. Newkirk,
Andre Norton,
Michael S. & Marsha G.
  Oberg,
Off Centaur Publications,
Wanda Olson,
Mark L. Olson,
Frank Olynyk,
Christina Oseland,
Paula Oseland,
Ric Overley,
Jack Palmer,
Karen Pauli,
Scott H. Paulson,
Joan Phillips,
Mark Poliner,
Jeffrey J. Rebholz,
Jim Reidmann,
Raul Reyes,
Frank Richards,
Robert Richer,
Walter Rickel,
Ambria M. Ridenow,
Callinda MacAran
  Ridenow,
Barb and Dave Riedel,
Kay Riffle,

Doris T. Robin,
Steve K. Rockwell,
James Salyers,
Kurt Sauer,
Lee Schneider,
Ed Schoenfeld,
Edward John
  Schoenfeld,
Science Fiction
  Chronicle,
Mark Sharpe,
Barbara Shell,
Dr. Susan Shwartz,
Gary Skibicki,
Robert Sloan,
Laura Spiess,
Reginald Sprecher,
Starbase Kansas City,
Claire F. Stephens,
John E. Stith,
Andrew Strassmann,
Tim Strum,
Paul Sullivan,
Sunrise Book Review,
Lawrence D. Tagrin &
  Darla Malone Tagrin,
Susan Rae Tallmadge,
Shannon Taylor,
Peter Thiesen,
Greg Thokar,
Dana Thomas,
Caryl Thompson,
Van Faulkner Consortium,
Michael J. Vandebunt,
Mary L. & Charles T.
  Wallbank,
Alan B. Wasser,
Robert Weissinger,
Sheryl L. Williams,
Janny Wurts,
Jane Yolen,
Candace E. Young,
Timothy & Anna Zahn,
Kevin Zellmer,

MEROVINGEN NIGHTS
FESTIVAL MOON

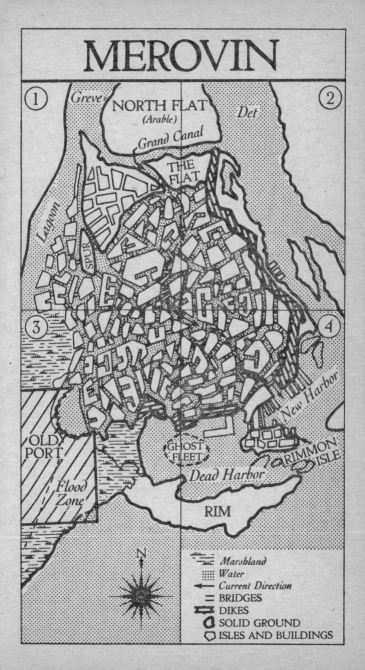

CONTENTS

FESTIVAL MOON

C.J. Cherryh

There was solemn celebration coming to Merovingen,
the 24th of Harvest. The greater bridges all up and
down the webwork of canals were already decked
with the red and gray ribbons of the Festival of the
Scouring, and solemn and somber banners already
hung from windows on the greater and the lesser
Isles (of which there were one hundred forty and
nine in sinking Merovingen, in this city of wood and
spires and lofty bridges and dark tangled waterways)
—for on 24 Harvest six hundred years ago, fire had
cut through the skies, the alien sharrh had scoured
the world they had reclaimed from human government, and as inexplicably departed, leaving human
survivors.

That was the beginning of Merovingen on its canals, from spaceport (sunken, the domain of crazies)
to wooden city of bridges; and the world had seen
six hundred forty-odd such solemn commemorations
of the attack since. The world muddled along, thank
you, in spite of the sharrh (who might return) and
the rest of humanity (who never returned). It was
modest (it could build tech, but who could say
whether the sharrh might not be provoked again
should humanity get ambitious). It waited for the
Retribution, when victorious humankind would sweep
down from the stars, put the sharrh to rout and

gather up its forgotten brothers and sisters of Merovin to fly to the technological paradise of human territories.

So Adventists believed. The 24 Harvest reminded the devout of this hope of deliverance; and even the most relapsed Adventist turned at this season to contemplate his connections with the starfaring Ancestors, and to wonder whether the golden Angel who stood on Hanging Bridge had advanced his sword any further from its sheath—for the Angel RETRIBUTION stood guard and sentinel over the world of Merovin and especially Merovingen, and reminded humankind in their workaday business, that elsewhere humankind flew free among the stars and dreaded nothing.

Revenantists had other opinions: the great Isle of the Revenant College up on Archangel Canal was hung with banners too in this predominantly Revenantist city, banners which reminded Revenantists of every degree that they were justly damned and doomed to Merovin for the sins of their Ancestors, and that only virtue and pious acts and the purchase of appropriate posthumous rites would ensure a rebirth to a wealthier life on Merovin, or even to a rebirth (it was every devout Revenantist's golden dream) somewhere on a free human world far from Merovin and sharrh, a world where the virtuous were reborn forever in glorious cities enriched by humanity's inventive genius—where electrics were a universal birthright and from which great spacefaring ships launched out among the stars. The Angel of Merovingen proclaimed, to Revenantists, not so much the Retribution, which hope Revenantists did not entirely deny in the long term, but the stability of the world and the order: the name of the Angel, Revenantists said, was MICHAEL, and his sword was half-drawn, half-sheathed, signifying the potential of destruction and renewal, the sword alternately advancing from its sheath and returning according as the weight of good and evil in the world tipped one way or the other. As long as the Angel stood on that span, Merovingen would survive its quakes, its floods, its seasonal storms. And the Retribution if it came, when that sword should fly from its sheath with lightnings and terror, would come when the whole world had achieved righteousness and the last human soul had been reborn elsewhere.

There were other ways of thinking on the matter, of course. Merovin had a multitude of cults and religions, from the Janes to the New Worlders; and even furtive sharrists, who looked for salvation by imitating the elusive, faceless aliens themselves. The very nature of the world was diversity. And this was, be it noted, the center of the world, oldest and first city—Merovingen of the sunlit towers and the dark waterways, where the great Det rolled down to the Sundance Sea; the city of two harbors (one living, one dead); the indomitable survivor of flood and Scouring and earthquake.

That history was truly what Merovingians commemorated together on the 24 Harvest: the city's own many-minded persistence against adversity.

The days leading up to the Festival were a prosperous time: the heart of the Festival was solemn, but the days before were riotous, frugality went the way of sobriety and the city banged drums and marched in processions and drank and slept-up with partners planned and unplanned. The abstinent sort of Revenantist was rare and the abstinent Adventist was non-existent.

And if Altair Jones was a little more concerned with the barrels of beer she freighted to Moghi's Tavern on Ventani Isle, or to Cooper's over on Petri and Prosperity's on Turk, than with the current state of her Adventist soul or the nearness of the Retribution, well, she was seventeen (or sixteen, a canaler might forget a thing like that), she ran her own boat, and she was enjoying the best run of business she had ever had. Being sole owner of the blunt-bowed skip she poled about the winding waterways, and being nowadays respected in the Trade . . . well, at least canalers knew her name, the way they had known her mother's, and knew that that name meant fair dealing for fair dealing, and a deal of trouble when crossed.

There were whispers, of course, that Jones had connections, connections which went right up to the great houses. But that was not a thing to bandy about. Canalers were a reticent lot; and the great families were even more so, and defended their business with money and poison. So no one talked aloud about Jones' unaccustomed and unexplained prosperity—how a ragged orphan of a skip-freighter who had always looked a little starved and no end desperate had suddenly turned up with a new sweater, new breeches, and a full tank of fuel and a can to spare.

Jones smiled a great deal lately, the flash of white teeth in a brown, tanned face, startling sight to those who had known the sullen, knife-fingering Jones of hungrier days. She wore her battered river-runner's cap tilted back on her short, straight hair, she worked her skip solitary still, but with a cheerfulness which left discreet whispers in her wake among canalsiders; and left discreet little gestures and pursings of mouths behind her among canalers, who had languages more than one.

On this particular evening she made a delivery to Moghi's at what on any ordinary evening would be closing-time; and walked up from the loading slip by Fishmarket Bridge Stairs, to Moghi's itself when she had done and the barrels were off down the back alley to Moghi's back door. Moghi's wooden porch, up a few steps, was lit with lanterns; the double doors were still wide open, the Festival customers coming and going to the poleboats which were moored off that porch on the left like a school of black fish, and drunken, happy landers clumping off down the walk toward Hanging Bridge, some few *not* clumping along in wood-soled shoes, but having a reckless look of money about them. The black water of the Grand Canal lapped and danced with lantern lights out of Moghi's, and lights showed in windows high up on Bogar Isle and Fishmarket across the water. From Moghi's and elsewhere the tinny sounds of sithers and the deeper tones of gitars wafted out across the canal and echoed up against tall Fishmarket

Bridge. It was her world. It stank and it rarely saw the sun or the stars because of the webby tangle of bridges which laced back and forth between the Isles at every opportunity. In night it was very black and in sunlight it was shadowed; and it smelled always of water and old wood and old rope and tar, and smelled of places like Moghi's, which drew her to its lantern-lit heart, amid other smells of sawdust on wooden floors, and the aromas of Hafiz' best beer and smuggled whiskey, and Jep's unnameable stew.

Moghi also prospered, since the infamous day of the Poisoning. The tavern had, earlier in this new prosperity, suffered an influx of uptowners seeking thrills—till a young uptowner found one he had not expected, and they found him floating.

Merovingen-below never changed. And the laws in hell never did.

" 'Lo," she said to Jep, all the while her eye scanned the accustomed corner; and caught sight of an unlikely riverman, a tall man with fair skin, dark blue sweater, dark blue watch cap with pale blond hair curling out from under it. The man saw her; she gave a delighted wink and paid quick attention to Jep, who had his hand out for the tally sheet from Hafiz's and the count from the dockboys. She pulled both from her pocket, her own reckoning bold and clean and on real paper just like Hafiz'.

"Feller's been real edgy," Jep said, and gave an unshaven grin. "You want ter settle 'im down, eh?"

"Shut your mouth, Jep. Mark the damn sheet."

"Hey," Jep said, and the grin was wicked. "You do 'er, all right." But he shut right up then, Moghi's office door being open and Moghi himself suddenly looming up in the doorway, as great a block of a man as Jep was a lank graying wisp—Moghi was solid, even to his large gut; his jowls disappeared into a bull neck and that neck into shoulders that could heft a full barrel without a hook. Moghi was not one to smile, but there was halfway pleasantness in his dour snatch of the paper from Jep's hands—it *must* have been a good day.

"Old Hafiz ain't tried to put off the old stuff on me, has he?"

"Hey," Altair said, "is he going to try that with me?"

"Huh." Moghi's jowls doubled and he hooked a thumb at Jep and Ali the sweep, who was hanging about with broom in hand and ears pricked. "Get back there and help with them barrels. I tend the bar.—Want your pay on the tab?" he asked Jones.

"Yey, just gimme a silverbit, I got some supplies t'buy."

Moghi fished into his pocket, flipped it her way and she snatched it deftly on the fly and favored him with a grin.

"Thanks, Moghi." She walked back to the man at the table, back into the darkest corner Moghi owned.

Mondragon, this man's name was. And his face when he looked at her was the Angel's face. Her heart always did a curious skip-beat when she met him, when she looked at him again and discovered it was not just memory, how fine he was. And her nothing but a canal-rat, born and bred; with the canals in her speech, a canaler's roll in her walk, and she was *not* that wonderful to look at, with her callused hands and her flat nose with that break in it a pole had made when she was twelve and first on her own with the skip. She was nothing special. He was. And he was hers. He looked up at her with the candle-light turning his skin to ivory and his hair to finest gold, and there was no finer or more wonderful man in all the governor's court.

He kicked out the other chair for her. And Moghi's new boy was already bringing over two glasses of Hafiz' best whiskey. They lived high at Moghi's place, they did, on Mondragon's coin, which kept Moghi happy. And if that coin came from uptown and from places Moghi had no wish to know about, they did not burden him with explanations.

Or with Mondragon's real business. In that, Mondragon was different than every other client Moghi had.

Jones sat down and took the whiskey the boy set

past her shoulder. She lifted it as Mondragon got his, and she sipped it with a sigh. The warmth spread from throat to stomach to weary legs and back and arms, and she felt a vast contentment, thinking of the upstairs room and a hot bath waiting. And him involved in both.

"Heavy load tonight," she said, and sighed again, gazing into his eyes.

Then the whiskey warmth gave way to a little prickle of warning. Mondragon had a worry-look.

"I can't stay long," he said.

"What d'ye mean, ye can't stay long?" Hurt welled up; Festival began tomorrow and it was a long-planned special night. But panic chased after the hurt, quickening her pulse. Mondragon's associations were no dockside kind of trouble, that a barrelhook could deal with.

"We'll talk about it." His eyes drifted in a gesture up, meaning: in the Room; and then centered on her again. "Business, Jones."

She took another drink of the whiskey, a healthy one. Mondragon's sat untouched. "Damn—"

"I'm sorry."

"That ain't what I'm damning." The boy was back again, this time with two bowls of Jep's stew, and fresh bread on the side. She shut down and kept her face placidly pleasant while the boy served, went so far as to give Mondragon a smile with the mouth only, which was: *You can damn well bet we got to talk about it;* and: *You'd better tell the truth.*

He gave a look back which was: *Don't get in my way, Jones.*

And all the while the boy fussed about setting the bowls down unspilled and setting the bread down proper, and the spoons and the knives being just so, while Will the gitar-player over in the canalside corner launched into a lively clog. A handful of canalers shoved back chairs and went to dancing, barefoot as canalers worked, which nonsense evidently spread to the porch as well, a couple of canalsiders joining in with a thunderous whump of wooden shoes on the planks.

Festival. Sober shopkeepers drunk as rivermen on a spree. Jones curled her bare toes and picked up a piece of bread, dipped it in the stew and munched the corner of it. There was a lump in her throat and a flatness about the taste. Across from her, Mondragon took up his spoon and ate a bite or two.

"Are you mad?" he asked.

"Hell, no, I ain't mad. Are-n't mad." Mondragon was teaching her uptown talk. She tried it to please him, though privately she knew what she would look like if ever Mondragon dressed her up in velvet and lace and took her on the high bridges to the fancy places he belonged in.

But he was so gentle and earnest about it: *Teach me how to talk canalsider; I'll teach you uptown.* At one of those moments in bed when she had no sense at all. He was always doing that to her. And because it was a bargain she had made, she kept trying, and feeling the fool.

"Am't," she said now she had thought about the *aren't.* And frustration welled up in her which had nothing to do with lessons. "Dammit to hell. Are you in trouble?"

"Nothing I can't handle," he said. "I figured I owed you more than a note. I'm sorry. I'll make it up to you."

"I ain't worrying. Why should I worry?"

He felt *that* slice along the skin, and flinched. His eyes flickered in that peculiar misery of a clever man constrained by secrecy not to argue, and she spooned stew into her mouth to save herself even looking at him.

Man goes and breaks appointments.

Break my damn arms hurrying to get here and what do I get?

O Lord, what *is* it, Mondragon? What do I got to do to get the truth out of you? You'll lie to me, you got an eel's ways and you ain't got to tell me none of it, I know you too damn well, I do.

"Stew's fine." She looked up in triumph, having landed on the word. *"Isn't* it?"

"It's got eel in it."

"Ain't either. *Isn't.* That's whitefish."

"Eel."

"You don't know whitefish from eel, you got no taste, lander."

"Then Jep's done something odd with the white-fish." Mondragon broke off a bit of the black bread, dipped it daintily in the soup and ate the edge of it. Turned it, dipped again. Altair chewed away at her own mouthful and regarded the elegant procedure with fascination.

He don't look like no canaler nor no riverman, either, does he now?

Lord, what kind of trouble?

"Isn't no uptown lady, is it?"

"I swear."

'Ummmmmnnnn." She mopped up the last of her stew and drank a mouthful of whiskey that made her eyes water. "Well, that makes me feel better. Y'know, if ever you want somebody uptown, you don't have to sneak around, all you got to do is say."

"It's not a woman!"

That almost passed whisper. She gazed full into his eyes across the table.

"That's real good, 'cause that way I won't embarrass you when I follow you out of here."

"Dammit, I *knew* you'd be like this."

"You knew damn well I'd be over to your place if you didn't show. Look at you! There ain't anybody here'd mistake you for a riverman. Look at you eat that bread. Look at you with them clean hands. You try to pass somewheres else but Moghi's, you can get a hook in you. Hear? You don't go wandering off canalside!"

He shoved the chair back and got up.

She did, and leaned on the table. "Hall?" she said. "Dammit, you walk on me I'll be at your heels."

"Hall," he said, and it was not Mondragon-the-fool that stared back at her with those burning eyes. It was Mondragon the Nev Hetteker, the foreigner, once an agent of the Sword of God. It might have made his enemies back up, that stare. She gave him his best back, that which made bridgeway bullies think twice about a gawky seventeen-year-old with a knife and a hook in her belt.

He gestured to the curtained doorway. She gestured with as grand a flourish. "After you."

He glared a moment more, then rounded the table, grabbed her by the arm and walked her through the curtain.

"Hoooo," came a soft voice at their backs, appreciating the theater.

She shook Mondragon's hand off, beyond the curtain and put her head back out the split of the curtain. "You mind your business, Gotter!"

Gotter lifted his glass to her. "Hey, that pretty man o' yours got something below the belt after all, don't 'e?"

Mondragon's hand closed on her arm and jerked her back through the curtain. Jerked her back, that was all, so fast it nearly took her cap off on the curtain. She snatched it off and whacked his arm with it. "Dammit—!"

"The man's drunk. Let be."

"You hear what he just said about you?"

"I don't need notice, Jones, for God's sake, don't. Stop it, hear?"

She caught her breath, stared at him with her mouth open. "You—"

"I don't need the notice."

"You don't want notice. You *got* notice, man." She spun about to put her head out the curtain again, and in the little view she had, Moghi was already advancing on Gotter's table—about the time Mondragon got her by both arms this time, dragged her inside and marched her over along the inside wall of the hallway, amongst the hanging towels and the staff's spare shirts and trousers and aprons, and along that hall to the upward stairs.

He marched her right up them, up the single flight to the Room, the door of which was open and lighted and waiting, the bed all turned down.

He pushed her toward it and let her go. She caught her balance, turned and dusted her cap against her leg, facing a face with nothing of compromise in it.

"You ain't thinking you're going to lay a hand on me! Dammit, Gotter wants his mouth fixed down there! What'm I going to get now? Gossip, that's what I'll get! All up and down the Grand, *hoooo, Jones, you want ter try me, Jones?* That's what you go off and leave me with? Thanks! Thanks a whole lot!"

Mondragon's face was flushed in the lamplight. Breath flared his nostrils. "This was a mistake. It was all a mistake." He walked over to the bedpost and took up the rapier which hung there in its belt and sheath, and headed for the door.

"F'God's sake, ye don't take *that* to 'im!"

He stopped. Turned. "Jones. He's not my business. I don't *care* about the man. I'm on other business. Does that get through? You started that down there. You made something out of a damn stupid drunk. It didn't need to happen, do you understand me?"

She blinked, dazed. "He yelled at me, dammit!"

"So he yelled. You've got a whiskey in you and a man yelled at you. You want me to kill him?"

"Damn drunk knew exactly what he was doing! He was trying *me*, dammit, trying *you*, and you hauled me back. Dammit, I may have to kill him now! I may have to kill somebody, all f' your doing!" Her breath failed her. She shook her head. "Oh, *damn*, Mondragon—ye don't understand. Ye don't understand. Ye go wandering out and ye say don't follow ye, and what d'ye leave me with but a damn drunk and likeliest all the trouble you got, too. It'll come to me. You don't think it will. You and your damn secrets, you think you keep me out of it, but it'll come hunting me. And me not knowing what it is, it'll slip up on me in some backwater in the dark, and they'll find me floating three days on. Is that what you want? You ain't never quit of me; I ain't never quit of you. You can go uptown and find yourself some uptown woman, all soft and perfumey, but it's Jones they'll hunt down when you get in trouble, it's Jones who runs the dark ways and who's so easy to take up and ask all them questions of—They'll get me 'fore they get you, I ain't got no doubt. And ye

won't even tell me who I got to watch out for—"
Breath ran out again. She made a futile gesture with
the hat. "Go on, get. I got to follow you, I follow
you, but, damn, I wisht ye thought I had sense."

He stared at her. It was no longer rage in his face.
It was a trapped look. "Jones."

"I pulled you out of that damned slaver's place!
That took sense!"

"Jones."

"*You* was in there; I wasn't."

"Jones, for God's sake."

"Kalugin knows who I am, you know."

"Jones, shut *up!*" He came and laid hands on her
arms, gently this time. Took her face between his
hands then. "Jones, there's someone on my track. I
don't know who. I took a hell of a chance coming
here, because I knew you were going to be a total
fool and come looking for me over at my apartments."

"Damn right I would."

"Listen to me. I walked over here. I don't plan to
go home till I can get the matter settled. If I make
noise, Jones, if I attract attention, my—patron—might
take offense at it. I suspect—I strongly suspect my
problem is one of his relatives."

"Tatiana Kalugin." Altair blinked, building a whole
sudden structure. Mondragon belonged to Anastasi
Kalugin—third in line behind the governor. First
was Mikhail the Clockmaker, feckless and harmless;
second was Tatiana, who was neither feckless nor
harmless. And if the governor's daughter had taken
some action to remove her brother Anastasi's agents—

"Or the governor himself," Mondragon said, "protecting Mikhail. You see my position. I have too
many embarrassing associations. If I become notorious, Anastasi will see I turn up dead. Or the governor will have me arrested, and it's the Justiciary, and
a long, long private session with the justiciar and his
little toys—*do* you understand me, Jones? I'm trying
to deal with this situation. Quietly. Downstairs didn't
help."

A shiver ran through her. "You want to listen to
me?"

"I'll listen. I don't say I'll agree and I don't say I'll have you along. I mean that."

"Two words: *hire Moghi*. He's got ways. He'll find out who it is."

"Listen to me now. Two more words: *Anastasi Kalugin*. If I bring in outside help, that means someone else knows about this affair. That means gossip. That means I've become a problem. Moghi's liable to find out more than Kalugin wants him to know. And there won't be a smoking stick left standing here."

"Then what're we going to do?"

"Jones—"

"You get hauled in by the College and the justiciar, just how long's it going to be before the black-legs come and arrest me, huh? I c'n move quiet. I c'n keep my mouth shut. And I got you out of that slaver's house. Didn't I?"

"That was noisy, Jones."

"Well, you're still here, ain't you? Did I handle that Kalugin right or didn't I?"

"You took a chance."

"Worked."

Mondragon shut his eyes a moment, opened them again. "Mercy."

FIRST NIGHT CRUISE

Leslie Fish

It was maybe half an hour to sundown, that first full day of Festival, when Jones came out of Moghi's and saw someone sitting on the pier near her skip. The woman saw her, nodded friendly-wise, stood up and pulled back her cloak, showing both hands empty. The big bag hanging from her shoulder might have concealed anything, but her hands weren't near it. She looked as if she might be a customer.

Jones sidled nearer, studying her: medium-tall height, lean-muscular build, long black hair held back by a red headband, pretty-good maroon pants and a fancy black shirt under the rusty-indigo cloak, plain black stockings and rope-soled canvas shoes. The face was vaguely familiar, seen somewhere canalside.

"You Jones?" The voice brought up memory: cafe-singer, heard at Hoh's, one half of a music duo—suspected insurrectionists, both. The other half was Rattail. This was Rif.

"Yey. What d'ye want?" Approach with caution: Rif was known to carry at least three visible knives, probably as many not visible. Also reputed to have a gun, though no one had ever seen it—at least, no one who'd lived to talk.

"Heard you're reliable for moving cargo."

"What cargo?" Jones asked, easing a step closer.

"Three barrels, two crates. Go up past Greve Fork

t' get 'em, bring 'em back south of here, lots of stops on the way. No questions, good pay."

Jones noticed that Rif was facing away from the water, pitching her voice so it carried just to its intended hearer and no further. So, sticky business. Careful. "What size barrels and crates? Got weight-limits."

"Standard fluid-weight barrels, small crates, maybe a hundred fifty kilos or a little over." Rif smiled briefly. "A skip c'n take it, I made sure."

Jones hitched her shoulders uneasily. Yes, her skip could take the cargo, but the weight would make it unwieldly and slow in the crowded traffic of first Festival night. She wasn't hurting for money, didn't need any new troubles. What was this trip worth? "Cost you four lunes." There. Enough to make casual trouble go look elsewhere. Maybe Rif would try to argue her down to something reasonable. If so, she'd stick to the stated price.

"Four pieces," Rif calmly topped her offer, "And be very cool." One hand did something quick and subtle, then opened for a moment to reveal the glint of four little gold pieces.

Jones blinked while the gold disappeared again. Hell, yes, that was worth some risks. How bad could it be? "What do I got to look out for?"

"Anyone trying to stop us, or take the cargo." Rif glanced upstream. Traffic was thick on the Grand Canal right now, but a lot of it was poleboats, many of them fancy with trims of ribbon, taxiing passengers around to early Festival amusements. That traffic might conceal attackers, but it could also provide witnesses and summonable help. "It'll be dark soon."

Yes, and a boat running dark would be hard to spot in the backwaters. Yes. "I'll take ye. Get in."

Rif sat back down on the pier's edge, eased one foot into the skip and slid her weight onto it in a single fluid motion. No fool landsman, her. Maybe she wouldn't do anything stupid on water. Jones got in, unracked the pole and yanked the ties loose.

Two quick jabs with the pole got them away from Ventani pier and well into the Grand. Jones peered at the Festival-dressed traffic and began picking her way through it, working toward the upstream lane.

From behind them, on Hanging Bridge, a woman's voice crackled loud and strong over the water. "No plague this Festival! May there be no plague this year, or any year, Jane willing. No plague, in the name of Jane!"

A Janist? Here? Jones turned to look, and saw a brown-robed woman turn and stride purposefully down the bridge toward the Bogar side. Right, best move quickly in a Revenantist town, in fact better have a quick hidey-hole somewhere, if the woman expected to get home unbothered after that act. There, she'd just disappeared in a doorway. Smart. But what was all that about?

Jones turned back to her steering, neatly side-stepped an oncoming poleboat, and got out to midstream. Then she noticed that Rif had pulled the hood of her dark cloak up over her head and was crouched down on the slats, glaring worriedly backward.

". . . ain't wasting any time," Rif muttered. Then, only a little louder: "Jones, it might be a good idea if you cut west soon's you can, and go up by the Lagoon."

"All right." Jones frowned. All this work to get out to midstream, only to go back west again. Why? Some connection with the shouting Janist? Or had Rif just spotted someone she didn't want to meet on the Grand Canal? Well, no matter. Cut over west.

Jones danced the skip portward under Fishmarket Bridge, waited for an opening, then cut fast around the northeast Ventani corner, under Little Ventani Bridge and into the Fisher Canal. A passing poleboatman cursed wearily as he jigged out of her way, but otherwise there was no traffic here at the moment. Jones poled in and shot the skip neatly down between Ventani and Calliste.

Empty water here. A dash of low sunlight licked briefly across the eyes, and from somewhere on the near rooftops a riverbird called: hoop-wawww, hoop-wawww. Almost a pretty evening, by Merovingen's standards. Now under Princeton Bridge and a cautious turn right, up the narrow passage between Yan and Calliste. Little traffic here: a poleboat unloading passengers at Yan's near wharf and the Brutkys easing their skip down toward Greely, too busy with a load of wrapped cloth-bales to give more than brief greeting. Now into the sun-patched intersection and on up the passage between Williams and Pardee.

They were right under the Williams-Pardee Bridge when Jones caught two sudden and odd sounds: the squawk of a frightened riverbird and an echoing rattle from the bridge.

"Midstream!" Rif snapped. "Quick!"

Jones was already jigging the skip fast to port. The prow came out from under the bridge a good two meters left of where the stern had gone in.

The falling mess of wood and tiles missed the skip by an arm's length, no more.

"Ware! Hof, you shit-for-brains!" Jones yelled over her shoulder, peering up at the bridge. She barely made out two running figures, dressed in nondescript dark pants and shirts, darting down the bridge toward the Pardee side. Maybe clumsy fools dropping a cargo, maybe crooks dumping evidence, maybe pranksters—or worse—trying to hole the skip. She hissed through her teeth and turned to glare accusingly at Rif. "Friends of yours?"

"Ney." Rif didn't take her eyes off the bridge as it receded behind them. There was a sharp ridge protruding under her cloak, the upper edge of something fairly long and bulky at the end of her hand. "How soon c'n you get to Port Canal?"

"Beyond next bridge," said Jones, swinging toward it. There was more traffic ahead, two skips and a crate-laden canal-boat heading toward the Grand, plus the usual cluster of poleboats. She recognized most of them. Good company to have around in case of more trouble, but going the wrong way.

"Word gets around fast," Rif grumbled, turning back to face the prow. "Just can't keep a secret in this damned city." The long lump under her cloak disappeared as if it had never been.

Then again, one might do worse than Rif in case of trouble.

Traffic was thick here, and working through it required some concentration, especially at the squeeze between Mars and Salazar. Beyond it lay the inter-section of the Port and West canals, anyone's guess where the crowds were worse. Jones paused to ask if Rif had any preference.

Rif glanced up at the rooftops, then behind them. During a moment's gap in the noise, the riverbird's call sounded again. It seemed to come from Mars Isle's roof. Rif smiled fleetingly. "West be fine," she said.

Jones duly poled into the West Canal, flicking glances at the rooftops whenever she could. At one point she caught a glimpse of a small figure, child-shaped, scampering among the drainpipes and tur-rets. Rif was looking that way too. Their eyes met. "More trouble?" Jones asked carefully.

"Ney. Friends, pacing us." Rif looked back again. "Go slow so they can keep up."

Jones shrugged and complied. This was a safer neighborhood, anyway.

The sun dropped behind the horizon of jagged roofs, steeping the canals in violet shadow, and the first Festival-lights came out, spilling gold on the water. Canal-noise dropped to an almost peaceful hush. Lamplight and echoes of street-musicians bloomed on the upper levels, and the day-birds took off for home in a rising clatter of wings. One last hoop-wawww sounded after the others.

"Clear road," said Rif. "Make time if you can."

Jones leaned on the pole and glided the skip smoothly down the darkening water, hoping for no more trouble. Figure another half hour to the Greve West Branch, maybe an hour up the fork of the Det. And then where? Back down the Grand in the dark? Another good hour, at least, not counting unnum-bered stops. Calculate being done somewhere along three hours after dark. Where could she tie-up for the night then? Back to Ventani's pier, most likely. Safe there, though not much quiet. Get a good dinner at Moghi's, anyway. Get the gold changed there, no questions asked.

As they pulled into the Greve West Branch and turned north the bird-call came again, but changed: Hoop-whee! Hoop-whee!

Rif sat up fast. "Shit," she muttered, and did some fast fumbling with her clothes.

Jones sighed and pulled the skip to a halt. "What kind of trouble?" she asked.

"No matter," said Rif, yanking her cloak aside and pulling open the big shoulder-bag. "Keep going and look innocent. It's blacklegs." There were flashes of simple jewelry at her throat now, and from the pouch came a flat-harp, tuning-wrench and finger-picks. She looked like a respectable musician on her way to entertain the rich.

Rif fussed with the harp while Jones eased the skip into motion. Bird-calls, rock-tossers, now blacklegs: no wonder Rif was paying well. It had damned well better be enough. Jones peered at the thinning traffic ahead, most of it with Festival-lights, and poled forward cautiously.

Rif put on the finger-picks, shouldered the flat-harp and stroked sweet chords out of it. "O sanctissima, O piisima . . ." she sang, a drowsy tune that sounded ancient.

As they came up to the bridge between Eick and Torrence, someone pitched a small stone into the water. It hit just ahead of the prow. A harmless pebble, no threat, just a signal. "Stop there," said a voice. A quiet, but carrying, tenor voice.

Jones stopped right there, and looked up. So did Rif. Only one blackleg in Merovingen sounded like that.

There he was on the bridge, catching the last of the sunset-glow in his cat-green eyes: a long, lean silhouette wearing an almost equally long pistol openly on one hip. He wore a plain black suit with very non-regulation black oiled-leather boots. It could only be Black Cal.

"Hello, Rif," he said, polite as anyone could ask.

It was unnerving to hear such a quiet, light voice

coming out of something that big. There were rumors that Black Cal was the tallest man in the city,
but nobody would dream of trying to measure him
and be sure. Nobody wanted to get that close. He
was the kind of legend best appreciated at a distance,
the sort everyone loved to see going after somebody
else. He was famous for treating rich and poor exactly the same and always getting whoever he set out
to get, much to the dismay of his fellow blacklegs,
officers and city officials.

He was said to be the only honest cop in Merovingen.
He couldn't be bought off, scared off, or stopped.
Nobody knew what to do with him, except avoid
him.

Jones grounded the pole, kept still, and tried very
hard to be just another piece of the scenery.

"Hello, Black Cal," Rif chirped up at the silhouette
on the bridge. "You taking a break, or is it just a slow
night?"

Jones shivered. One thing to act innocent with
Black Cal, another thing entirely to ask *him* questions.

Black Cal ignored that. "Where're you going, Rif?"
was all he said.

"Up Lagoonside, to sing for my supper." Rif ca-
ressed another chord out of the flat-harp.

One could barely see the wry smile on that long-
jawed face above. "Sure. And maybe try a break-in
or two?"

"What, with all the guards up and ready for Festival?" Rif snorted. "No way. I'll make better money
singing under the windows of the rich."

"Mhm. Where's your partner?"

"Working the same trade up in South Bank. Why?"

Jones flinched, hoped it wouldn't show. Those bird-
calls, and the glances back: she was sure that Rif's
partner was anywhere but South Bank tonight.

Black Cal was silent, thinking that over while the
whole hushed canal waited. The slightest of ironic
smiles flickered across his face and vanished. He
reached into a pocket. "Sing one for me," he said,
pulling his hand out. His fingers fanned, tossing a
silverbit over the bridge-rail.

Rif leaned over and snatched the twinkling pale coin before it could hit the deck, and dropped it neatly into her shirt-top. Carrying on with the same motion, her hand arched down to the flat-harp's strings and called up a heavy, marching, minor chord.

She's really going to do it. Jones shook her head in admiration at such nerves, such quick-thinking cool.

And Rif sang.

"See him stalking, day or night, the islands of
  the bay
Like some veteran tiger come to hunt his chosen
  prey.
He'll never lack for targets here,
  for scum will always rise—
And to the man who guards your streets,
  that comes as no surprise."

On the bridge, Black Cal smiled ever so faintly, and tapped his fingers in rhythm on the rail.

"And who will be the guardian, to take your
  dangers on?
Who will guard your streets at night
  when old Black Cal is gone?"

Passing feet rattled, paused, on the adjacent building walkways. Nearby voices muttered in admiring, hightown accents. An audience, growing. Black Cal ignored them, and listened. Rif ignored them and played on.

"For one in ten's a predator who treats the rest
  as prey,
So someone's always needed here to drive those
  wolves away.
We never left the jungle, we just brought it into
  town.
The leopards took on human form, and follow
  us around."

Jones wondered what a "wolf'" or "leopard" was.

Legendary animals, she'd heard said, but with no exact descriptions. How old was this song, really? How much had Rif tailored it for Black Cal, on the instant's notice? Fast-witted, Rif.

And Black Cal was smiling. Definitely smiling.

The song went on, verse after verse, while more feet shuffled and stopped overhead. How many, Jones wondered, were drawn by the music, and how many by the bizarre sight of a woman serenading Black Cal?

"Evolution never stopped; we always have to choose.
The thug who waits to mug you is collecting Darwin's dues.
And you can't drive hyenas off by kneeling down to pray,
So who will raise the weapon, then, to keep the beasts at bay?"

Black Cal visibly hitched his shoulders and sighed. Rif thrummed into the last chorus.

"Run like deer, or die like sheep, or take your dangers on,
For you must guard your streets yourselves when old Black Cal is gone."

A final ruffle of chords, and the flat-harp was still. Rif waited, looking up.

A rattle of applause wafted down from the walkways and balconies, and a thudding hail of coins fell. Jones snatched off her cap and snagged the ones within reach, made sure that none were wasted on the water. Rif never moved her head, kept watching the man on the bridge.

Black Cal sighed again, tossed them a wave that might have been a go-ahead sign or a salute, turned and walked away down the bridge. His thick boots made no sound, but the planks creaked under his weight. Shadows of the walkways swallowed him up.

Rif took off her finger-picks and put the flat-harp back in its bag. "Let's go," she said, calm as before.

The crowd above sighed and dispersed, now that the show was over.

Jones poled the skip under the bridge and onward, shivering a little. A long stroke sent them skimming into the Mansur intersection, and she paused to pick up the remaining coins scattered on the deck and drop them into her cap. "Here," she held out the prize to Rif. "Your singing-money."

"Keep it," Rif waved the cap aside. "Count it as hazard-pay." Her eyes were back on the rooftops, watching. Another bird-call sounded, off to the left. "Steer west around Bois. Can you duck out around Ortega?"

"Not this time of year," Jones shrugged, stuffing the coins into a pocket. "Too shallow. We'll hang up on mud-flats."

"Hmm. Between Ortega and Yucel, then." Rif glanced back once more. "But into the Lagoon as soon as you can."

Jones complied, dancing the skip around another lighted poleboat decked with flowers and stuffed with party-goers, the only other craft here but tricky to avoid in the narrow passage. It was a relief to get around Ortega's northeast corner, under the last bridge and out into the open space of the lagoon. The blossoming lights of Lagoonside buildings speckled the water heavily, then lightly, less, then gone. Last pale sun-streaks blazed low on the world's edge, most of the sky gone deep blue shading into violet. The smell of the air changed, thinned and freshened.

"Go further out," she said, "And let's make some speed."

Jones frowned, feeling for the bottom. "Too deep. Further out, I can't pole." *And damned if I'll use up my emergency fuel.*

But Rif didn't ask for the engine. She glanced back at the city-edge and sighed. "You got oars?"

"Only if you can row, too."

"Deal."

Jones shrugged, racking the pole and pulled out the oars, a luxury she had got after she took on a partner—and took to running his errands. She noted

Rif pulling heavy gloves out of her pack. Well, a musician had to take care of her hands, right enough. Also, she knew where to sit on the deck-rim and how to brace her feet and, yes, how to work an oar. Jones sat to the other oar, feathered it up and chanted quietly: "Pull . . . pull. . . ." The unladen skip moved smoother than seemed likely out into the depths of the lagooon.

"Far enough?" Jones finally asked, watching the city's lights dwindle behind them.

"All right," Rif breathed on the upstroke. She pulled hard while Jones backed, and the skip turned north. "Just keep out of sight, out of reach, and get us north of the Rock."

She looked back toward the city, frowning, and Jones realized that the bird-calls had stopped when they passed Ortega. There was a faint distant sound that might have been another set of oars, or maybe a pole bumping, back toward the city, but no way to be sure. Best to make distance, and speed. Jones leaned to the massive oar, saw Rif match her, and admitted to a grudging respect.

There was nothing else afloat on the lagoon, nothing they could see. The working boats were busy in-city, and the rich folks' pleasure-boats were tied up at the Lagoonside wharves for the night. They had this black stretch of water to themselves, save for the fish and night-bugs. The rising fog was cool, like a good wine after the day's soggy blanketing heat. Only curiosity itched and annoyed. Jones ignored it, and rowed.

The Rock loomed into sight and slipped past, dark and glittery against the fog-lighted sky. "Much further?" Jones asked, wiggling a beginning cramp out of one shoulder.

"Dunno." Rif sounded a little winded, not much. "Watch the west bank."

Jones watched, rowed, finally made out a faint glimmer of shuttered candlelight against a darker bulk some thirty meters off. "There. That it?"

Rif looked, paused, chewed her lip. "Not sure," she admitted. "Pull closer, but quiet."

The questions gnawed, sharp and demanding. *It's too damned dangerous, running blind.* Jones realized she was tired to death of too-well-kept secrets. "Look, who's after you? It's my boat and my neck. Who do I look out for?"

Rif shrugged uneasily. "Sword, sharrists, robbers, blacklegs—take your pick."

"That's a nice stew of enemies! Why'd you pick me to drag into this?" *Remember her gun. Watch her hands.*

Rif rattled her fingers on the oar, but left them there. "Word is, you got . . . protection, from high places."

Kalugin! Jones could have kicked herself for not thinking of it sooner. Of course. Everyone in Merovingen-under knew that.

"So, ain't likely trouble'd dare come after you in big, noticeable numbers—only a few sneaks here and there. Those we can handle."

"Oh, thanks much," Jones grumbled, not just at Rif. "Nothing we can't handle. Right." What did Rif think she could handle, anyway? How far had Kalugin's carefully placed rumors spread, and how much had they grown in the retelling? What kind of business had they brought her? Rif's story sounded too heavy for comfort, and that from a woman who could smile and chirp and sing for Black Cal Halloran. Still, there wasn't much to be done about it now, except to go on, and watch, and wait.

The dark shape resolved itself into a big riverboat tied up at the west bank of the Greve. Its sole light hung low by the waterline, off the port stern. Rif breathed a sigh of relief and steered toward it.

They were almost on top of the light before anyone onboard noticed. Then there were quick sounds of running feet, and unmistakable sounds of weapons drawn and readied. Rif pulled in her oar, fumbled the flat-harp out of the bag and fingered a whispery bright chord from it.

"No plague this Festival," she called up, softly.

"Right," a masculine voice answered. Ropes rattled down the sides and plashed into the water. "Tie up cargo-ready."

Rif grabbed the nearer line and tied on with respectable speed, an equally respectable jury-knot. Jones did the same with the line aft. No sooner were the knots on than a crane creaked overhead.

"Light," the man complained. "Give us some light down there."

Jones ducked into the hidey, feeling for the candle-glass, but Rif got to her bag-of-surprises first and came out with a sturdy dark-lantern and a match. Its light caught several scarf-hidden faces above and the descending bulk of a loaded cargo-net. She swung the lantern down, marking a clear space on the deck, and the net lowered. It touched almost gently, barely rocking the skip. In it was a standard-size barrel.

"C'mon, help," Rif said, then set the lantern on the half-deck and wrestled the barrel off the net. Jones helped her roll it, noting that the contents were heavy, and they sloshed.

The net whisked back up, disappeared, then came back a moment later with another barrel. Again, they rolled it off the net and secured it on deck while the crane pulled up. Rif took her fair share of the weight and rolled it with a nice economy of moves. Jones noted the muscles working in her arms, and doubted that she'd gotten those playing gitar. Curious.

A third barrel came, and then two small crates, just as Rif had promised. As the empty net went up, the ropes twitched.

"Cast off," the sailor whispered down. "Don't waste time."

Rif grunted disdain and yanked off the forward tie. Jones freed the aft one, and the ropes hissed back up the hull. An instant later, the lamp did likewise. Rif shuttered her dark-lantern.

"All right," she said, sitting down at the oarlock, "Let's get out of here."

"Which way?" Jones grunted as they pulled off from the darkened hull. The skip was sluggish with weight; rowing it back to town even downcurrent would be a monster's bitch.

"Mouth of the Grand," Rif panted. "How soon can we get poling?"

"Right past the Rock," Jones grinned in relief, glancing over her shoulder at the distant lights. Not too far, not too long to row.

"Just don't be seen," Rif muttered, bending over the oar.

Behind them, the riverboat was firing up. Sparks flared above her stacks. She was pulling out fast, back north, wasting no time. *Hot, hot cargo*, Jones guessed, eyeing the barrels. *Take no chances.*

Her arms were sore by the time they passed the tip of the Rock and moved into the eastward channel. It was a real relief to stow the oars, unship the pole, stand up and push for a change.

Rif rubbed her arms, worked carefully between the tied-fast barrels and crates, and took up watch at the prow. Hard to tell if she was looking for friends or enemies in the dark ahead. Probably both.

Jones dutifully hugged the east shore, keeping out of the growing lights of the Rock's residencies, watching for signs of anyone else on the water. There were none. She poled quietly into the mouth of the Grand Canal, almost under the windows of Tremaine House.

"Stop here," Rif whispered, casting her eyes around at the clustered lights ahead.

"Here? . . . Sure." Jones poled to a smooth stop, wondering what in all the hells of Merovin was so important about this particular spot. There were no craft near, no wharves, nothing but empty water flowing smooth and steady into the Grand.

Rif got up, reached into her trick-bag and came up with a heavy mallet. She padded to the nearest barrel, spread a corner of her cape on the lid directly over the king-piece, and quietly hammered it in.

Jones leaned on her pole and stared.

Rif tucked the mallet back in her bag and pulled her cape away. She tugged the slats of the barrel-lid into the gap left by the broken king-piece, pulled their ends out of the catch-groove under the barrel's rim, hauled the freed lid away and dropped it on the deck. The barrel was filled with thin fluid that gave

off a sharp and bitter smell. Rif freed the barrel
from its ties and heaved mightily, trying to tip it over
the side. It was too heavy to lift.

"Come on," she panted at Jones. "Help me dump
this."

"Sure." Jones reached for the short-anchor, tossed
it overside and racked the pole. "All this trouble to
get that barrel, and now you want to dump it in the
canal. Right."

Nonetheless, she went to the other side of the
barrel and got a solid grip on it. "Where do you want
it dumped?" It was a good, new barrel, well made,
fine wood.

"Just overside. And quietly." Rif strained at its
sloshing weight.

"I got a better idea." Jones thought fast, adding
coins in her head. "Just tilt it." She rolled the barrel
backwards a foot-length or so, then heaved. The
barrel tipped over against the gunwale, pouring a
good quarter of its contents overside. "You can't sink
'er; she's too well made. She'll float like a buoy. Don't
want that, do you?"

"Uh . . . No." Rif gave her a respectful look. Good
to see that. "You got a better idea, you say?"

"Yey. Just empty it." Jones muscled the bottom of
the barrel a little further back on the deck, letting
more of the dark fluid spill out. "Afterwards, turn
'er over and put 'er back, tied fast and all. Nobody'll
know from looking that she ain't still full."

"True," Rif considered. "Cover . . ."

"Let me have the empties when you're done." She
could sell them later, with only one question asked.

"Deal," Rif laughed. "They're yours, after."

"Just one thing . . ." How to phrase this politely?
"I ain't asking what's in 'em, just where the whatever-
it-is stands on the Barrel List."

"List?" Rif puzzled, tilting the barrel further.

Jones snorted, strode fast to the hidey and pulled
out an ancient piece of paper, flipped the cover on
the dark-lantern and displayed the scrap under Rif's
nose. "C'n ye read that?"

The Barrel List was one regulation that Mero-

vingians usually obeyed, if only for practicality's sake.
It simply listed cargoes commonly carried in barrels,
starting with flour at the top, ranging through food-
stuffs and packed crockery down to tar at the bottom. Rif studied the list, then turned mystified eyes
to Jones.

"She's real simple." Jones couldn't help a tiny grin
of triumph, catching Rif at something she didn't
know. "Pack a barrel with anything on there, and
afterwards you c'n use it for anything the same or
below it on the list—but nothing above. See?"

Rif studied the list again. "Why?"

"Aw, think! Would you put wine in a barrel that's
just carried arsenic salts?"

Rif laughed. "Yey, I see it." She paused a moment,
then jabbed a finger at a point halfway down the list.
"Here. It's right about here."

Jones looked. Rif was pointing at "industrial
chemicals."

Shit. No wine or beer in these barrels, ever. Who'd
buy them now? Still, they were too good to throw
away, chop up or burn. Maybe sell 'em to Foundry.
"Well, I'll still take 'em."

Jones took the list, shoved it back in the hidey
and shuttered the light again. Behind her, Rif heaved
the barrel onto the gunwale to drain out the last of
the mysterious fluid. Jones came back and helped
her turn it bottom-up and retie it in place. "Same
with the rest?"

Don't ask why Rif should be dumping "industrial
chemicals" into the Grand Canal, under cover of
darkness, with trouble hunting her. Damn, nothing
worse than what went into the water every day, that
was sure. Nothing could hurt Det-water. Damn lunatic.
Crazies. It was a set-up, had to be.

"Not here. Further downstream. Butt of the Spur."

Sure! Jones jabbed the pole almost viciously into
the canal-bottom. *Right under the eyes, ears and noses of
the blacklegs*! Maybe this trip wasn't worth the money
after all. Maybe she could catch Rif with a fast pole-
swipe, knock her in the canal, and be sure she couldn't
come up with that long hard shape under her cloak.

Maybe toss the cargo after her, and hurry away safe. Maybe, but the odds weren't good at all. Wait, wait and watch.

The bird-calls had picked up again.

Jones paused under Tremaine-Kristna Bridge to light the lamp, just to look proper. Lots of poleboat traffic here, ferrying the rich about, distracting the eye with lights, and no doubt lots of blacklegs watching from the upper levels and bridges. Be cool, look harmless, keep to the canal-sides like a proper skip-freighter carrying perfectly harmless cargo and a passenger for hire. Don't attract attention. Just stay humble and keep going.

Except that by the time they passed the end of Carswell, she was sure there was another boat following them. Hard to tell, among the press of poleboats, but she could swear there was another skip back there keeping the same route and a fixed distance back. Rif didn't seem worried, or—less likely—hadn't noticed. Her friends? Never mind. Keep calm, keep going.

The bird-whistles faded out at Carswell, which wasn't surprising. None of Rif's friends would want to go onto the Justiciary, or the Signeury, let alone the Spur. Leave that for the tracking skip. Friends in high places, and low.

At least hereabouts they didn't have to worry about attacks from the bridges.

Unless maybe Black Cal was up there, and feeling ill-tempered.

As the skip cruised into the wide stretch of water between the Justiciary and the Spur, Jones felt a thousand imagined eyes at her back. The thick traffic ahead was almost as bad. It was crowded here on the north fork: skips, poleboats, canal-haulers, even the foamy wake of a rich man's fancyboat rocking the water. And noise, and tossing lamps, and festoons and fancy Festival-trim everywhere. Noisy and jolly as only the second-biggest intersection of uptown could be, thick with rich folks' guards and blacklegs and Lord-knew-what else.

And here I am carrying an insurrectionist and hot cargo,

right through it. Jones clenched her teeth to keep them from rattling as she poled her way through the mob.

"Get under the bridge between the Spur and Spellbridge," said Rif, utterly calm. "Tie up at Spellbridge-side, if you can."

Jones nodded, and breathed a little easier. But only a little. Spellbridge was where the blacklegs went for fun, odd tool-repairs, boat-storage, and to meet their informants. On first night of Festival, they'd likely be on the upper levels or else out on the town. With luck, there'd be nothing at the under-bridge tie-up but a few empty boats. Maybe.

Rif studied the bridge as they passed under its edge. "Now," she said quietly. "Nobody watching."

After that they said nothing, for the dark cavern under the big bridge echoed every sound. Jones turned the skip and poled quietly for the tie-up, seeing nothing but a few police boats chained at the rings. She steered between them, softly, softly, and the skip's prow bumped the wall with no more sound than a child's footfall. Rif was ready with the line, and had it jury-tied before Jones finished racking the pole.

But opening the barrel made noise. The first muf-fled mallet-blow echoed in the thick shadows, made Rif glance around nervously. How much noise be-fore the king-piece snapped? Swearing silently, Jones went to the barrel, pushed Rif away and studied the lid. Damn, as tight and well-made as the rest of it. Think, think. Muffling. . . .

"Give me that cape."

Rif raised an eyebrow, but complied. Jones darted back to the freeboard near the hidey, groping in the thick shadows. She could swear she'd seen it here just a few hours ago. . . . There. A long thick dowel, too good for burning, kept in case she needed a new short gaff or hatchet-handle: perfect. She wrapped the cape around the dowel, padding double-fold at the ends, then held the dowel upright on the barrel-lid, just over the king-piece. Rif handed her the mallet without comment. Jones hit the padded dowel hard, once, twice.

The king-piece broke soundlessly, dropping most of the dowel and a good bit of the cape into the reeking fluid below.

Rif sighed as she pulled the cape back out, unfolded it, made a half-hearted try at wringing it out. She shrugged and put it back on.

Jones pulled off the lid, stuck it and the dowel safely off under the freeboard, and untied the barrel. The two of them tilted it quietly, quietly over the side. It seemed to take hours to drain.

Every sound of foot-traffic overhead, every bump of the tied boats nearby, made them flinch and glance around. Damn, what was that patch of shadow over there, just beyond the bridge? A big rat? A crouched watcher, waiting only to see how much news he had to sell? An ambush planned? Damn! Hurry.

The barrel finally emptied. They overturned it and lashed it tight, fast as they could without making noise. Rif pulled the tie loose, and Jones poled them back out toward mid-channel. Turn, now. Quickly. Noise approaching from behind, a boat-pole: maybe harmless traffic and maybe not. They'd been lucky to have no passing witnesses this long, though doubtless Rif had some story ready if anyone asked. Move out fast. The skip glided into the open water between North and Spellbridge.

More traffic here, and more bridges ahead. All busy with passengers, nobody looking, at least not that Jones could see. Edge of the wealthy neighborhood, nobody looking twice at a "trade" boat, nobody pausing on the bridges. A few familiar faces, though no real friends, working poleboats and a few skips, mostly carrying passengers. Enough neutral eyes, enough light on the water, that maybe there'd be no trouble here. Jones guided the skip, riding easier now, down toward the Novgorod crossing as fast as she could without looking hurried.

Rif came picking her way back between the remaining barrel and the crates, just to say quietly:

"Mars next, under DiNero Bridge." Then she returned to her perch at the bow.

Jones nodded agreement, and some relief. Down among the Residencies and into West End, canals good and wide, traffic steady but light on a night like this: too many eyes about for a direct ambush, too few boats for a jam-up where mysterious damage could so-accidentally happen. Good.

Except that the whistles were back, and there was definitely another skip following them. All right, Rif's friends, but still nervous-making.

And the stink of that nameless "industrial chemical" (dye? soap?) was all around them, off the barrels, maybe off Rif's cloak, and maybe from the water, and sooner or later somebody had to notice. They'd been lucky, staying unbothered all this way, but luck wouldn't hold.

Still, it did until they reached Mars island. They tied up at the corner under DiNero Bridge, Jones not quite believing they'd made it this far, and Rif whistling some damned cheerful tune into the shadows.

A darkness moved there, and Jones nearly jumped out of her skin. Rif spotted it, waved one casual hand—the other was under her cloak—and called in that quiet/aimed voice: "So, what's good tonight?"

A man stepped closer to the lantern Rif held up; dressed in dark pants and shirt, bare feet, dark canaler's hat, he could have been anybody. "Cheap fuel," he said, just as quietly.

Rif nodded, turned to one of the crates and pried it open. Jones glimpsed several wrapped packets inside. Rif pulled out one of them and held it out to the nondescript man. He took it, and handed back a small purse-bag that jingled. "Note inside," he whispered, barely audible. "Best read it before you go on."

Then he shoved the packet under his shirt and hurried off into the dark. A moment later a door shut somewhere near, then silence.

Rif pulled the purse open, took out a small folded piece of paper, scanned it, frowned fiercely and tossed it into the water. "Port Canal, east," she snapped to

Jones, stuffing the small purse into a pocket. "Get to Foundry, fast as you can—and stick to crowds."

"What trouble?" Jones asked baldly, poling the skip out. Curiosity be damned, she was sick of running blind through dangers nobody would warn her about. "Damn, what *is* this business?"

"Some rich bastards, this time," Rif growled, hitching her shoulders forward. "Don't want anyone rocking their fat fancyboats. Move it, can't you?" She kept her eyes on the bridges ahead.

Jones ground her teeth and pushed for the Port Canal.

A few long strokes brought them to the big intersection of Port and West, and the traffic here was thick and noisy. Bobbing party-lights on half the boats danced with their reflections in the pole-churned dark water. Smells of flowers, perfumes, sweat, food, drink and odd cargoes fought with the growing stench of the water. Nobody here would notice the faint bitter smell of Rif's soaked cape and empty barrels. Cackles of laughter, fragments of conversations, shouts of warnings, steering-calls, curses and arguments racketed off the water in a steady din that filled the thickening air. An odd sight would be noticed here, but yells for help could be missed.

At least there were some known and friendly faces here. Jones exchanged passing nods and hails with half a dozen canalers before she got past Salazar bridge. Expect plenty more ahead, too. That was something.

Rif tucked her gloves in her belt, pulled out the flat-harp and finger-picks again, strummed loudly and started up a cheery song about a blacksmith. She even stuck out a basket on the blunt bow, as if to collect tossed coins. It added just the right touch of cheerful Festival lunacy.

"Bide, lady, bide! There's nowhere you can hide.
The lusty smith shall be your love, for all of your mighty pride."

One corner of her cloak was folded over a long, narrow lump right within fast reach.

The bird-calls couldn't be heard in this racket, and there was no way to tell if the following skip was still following in this crowd, but Jones guessed that Rif's friends were still pacing them. Bless crowds. She leaned to the pole, trying to keep the skip out toward central water and watch for suspicious neighbors. Let Rif sing and watch the bridges.

The entry to the Grand Canal was a mob-scene. Half the city's boats seemed to be there, trying to cut across, turn in or pull out, all at the same time. Already there was a small jam-up at the Ventura corner, curses and poles flying thick and fast. Avoid *that*, certainly. Jones darted between two poleboats and shot out toward the center of the water, right in the wake of a big canaler's barge. The walls of Foundry lay dead ahead, less than a hundred meters away.

There was a different shout to port. "There!" A snap of satisfaction, excitement, and hunting hunger. Jones glanced that way and saw a big poleboat peel away from Ventura-side and come darting obliquely across traffic. Straight toward her. No accident.

The craft was stuffed with passengers, maybe five plus the boatman: really too much for a poleboat in this traffic. They were all dark-clad and heavy-set, and didn't look as if they were going to a party. They were bent unusually low, as if hiding something in their hands below the gunwales. Oh shit, shit, shit!

"Ware port!" she snapped to Rif as she leaned harder into the pole. Hook and sheath-knife were ready at her belt, come to that, but best hope now was the pole.

Rif shook back her hair—taking a fast sidelong glance as she did—then neatly pulled off her fingerpicks and set her harp down. Her freed hand slid under the fold of her cape. Under pretext of combing back her hair with her fingers, Rif kept her eyes on the pursuing poleboat as she leaned back casually among the barrels in the well and made less of a target.

Fine for you. What about me? Jones gnawed her lip and looked around for something to duck behind. Damn, but that poler was coming on fast! And, Lord, one of those big bastards had a hand under his shirt. At this distance he wouldn't be reaching for a knife. Would he dare haul out and shoot in a crowd this thick?

Ah, there ahead: a big canal-hauler turning, and an empty poleboat trying to swing around him. Go!

Jones darted to portside of the skip, jabbed the pole in and leaned hard in a half-turn, aimed sharp across the bow of the oncoming canaler. No time to shout warning, or the pursuers might hear it. Another jab on the pole, hard and fast.

The two boatmen on the canal-hauler yelled in shock and scrambled to shove away. The blunt bows crossed, less than a meter apart. Rif, fast as always, lunged to the rim, stuck her hand out, and shoved bodily at the canaler's hull.

The boats missed scraping by less than an arm's length. "Sorry!" Jones yelled at the boatmen's gaping faces. "Ware port! Port!" She waved back toward the loaded poleboat, perforce looking toward it.

At that moment the empty poleboat at the outside of the turn was scrambling to get away from the canal-hauler's sudden change of course. He just missed hitting the bigger craft, but shot right across the loaded poleboat's bow.

The thugs had been too intent on their prey to watch for other boats, and their combined weight made the craft unwieldy, hard to stop. Their bow hit the empty poleboat.

The booming impact could be heard across the canal, along with the screeched curses of the boatman. The empty craft rebounded sideways, tilting high while the boatman threw himself across the gunwale, and banged helplessly into the turning canal-hauler. The canaler's crew all screamed and swore together, flailed poles and tried to shove clear.

The thug-laden poleboat, stopped at last, wallowed and shimmied while its boatman tried to pull back and turn. His passengers, cut off from their target, snarled and cursed and tried to push off from the tangle of hulls. Those in front shoved with their hands; the ones further back pulled up the assorted gaffs they'd been hiding, and tried to push off with those. More often than not, they got in each other's way. A man in front, frustrated beyond his meager patience, took a spiteful swipe at the poler's boatman. He missed, but just barely.

"Bastard!" the boatman shrieked. "Assassins!" He got enough footing to make a good swing with his pole, and one of the thugs went overside.

The gang's commander lost his head, yanked his pistol out from under his shirt and took a quick shot at the poleboat. It went wide and high, and thwacked into the canal-hauler behind.

"Ware hey!" the canaler's crew yelled together. They stopped trying to finish the turn, and jabbed their poles across the empty poleboat at the loaded craft. Their aim was better than the shooter's. Another thug hit the water, and another slumped in the bilges with a cracked skull.

"Ware! Ware!" familiar voices took up from astern. Other skips: friends, or neutrals at least. They'd seen most of the squabble, if not all of it, and considered the pistol-shot a dirty blow in a pole-fight.

Besides, the overloaded poleboat was blocking traffic.

Two skips and another poleboat converged on the belabored gang, and added their poles to the general melee. The pistol-man was next to go into the water.

Jones glanced back at the fight as she skimmed under the Pardee-Foundry bridge, and grinned from ear to ear. No more trouble from that quarter, at least not tonight. Rif was laughing like an idiot.

"Which way?" Jones remembered to ask. "Lots of tie-ups here."

"Nayab Bridge, under,'" Rif barely made out through giggles. "Tie to port. . . . Ah, that was gorgeous!"

They laughed all the way to the bridge tie-up.

*   *   *

Here a woman was waiting for them, face hidden under a hat-brim's shadow. The exchange was fast and silent this time, though the purse seemed smaller. The woman hurried off with her packet while Rif got the tie loose, and Jones poled them back out into working water.

"Where now?" Back to business.

Rif scratched her chin for a moment before deciding. "Hmm, down the Grand. Cut into the Tidewater just at Fife's Corner and tie up. We'll wait there."

Fife, no less. All around the city and back again. Jones sighed as she leaned into the pole. Her arms were tiring, and the job wasn't over yet. "You keep me working all night, the price goes up," she grumbled.

"Maybe, maybe." Rif reached into the top crate and pulled out one of the packets. "For you," she said, tossing it neatly into the hidey. "Extra hazard pay. Look it over when you've got time."

Jones glanced at the packet, curiosity rising to a near-unbearable itch. She'd just seen two of those little prizes change hands for small bags full of coin; at rough estimate, whatever was in them was worth a hard night's work.

The bird-whistles paced them along the Grand. Traffic thinned, and there was no further trouble. Still, Rif put her harp away and watched the bridges as they passed.

They turned down the reeking channel of the Old Grand and around Fife Corner to the Tidewater, seeing no one ahead or behind. Rif set up the dark-lantern as they tied up under the Southdike Bridge, but kept it shuttered. Jones racked the pole, sat down on the halfdeck and rubbed incipient cramps out of her legs and shoulders. But for the scurrying rats and the stench of the Tidewater, this rest in the dark was almost a pleasure. Rif was silent, and Jones thought it best to imitate her, leaving no sound but the distant roar of the upper city and the faint slap of the oily water against the hull.

No, wait. There was another sound: the thump and plash of a skip's pole, a woman's voice singing, both coming closer.

"I will the wind shall never cease,
    Nor flashes in the flood,
'Til my three sons return again
    In earthly flesh and blood. . . ."

Jones knew where she'd heard that voice before: Hoh's.

Rif's lantern opened, low overside, casting a small circle of light on the water. "Here, Rat," she called quietly.

Damned if a fat rat on the piling didn't sit up and take notice.

"Hey, hey, Rif!" echoed under the bridge. A dim shape floated near, shadowy without running-lights, then caught in the raised beam of Rif's lamp.

Jones gasped as she recognized the craft. It was Mintaka's skip, and there was old Min herself, riding like a passenger, while a tall woman with short dark hair poled the boat for her. That was Rattail, Rif's singing partner. Tonight, partner in this lunatic smuggling too: their water-escort, all this time. She pulled alongside and tossed over bow and aft lines. Rif grabbed one, Jones the other, and they jury-tied the hulls together.

"So you're still in one piece?" Rat studied her partner in the light of the lantern. "I saw that cute splash-up on the Grand, but wasn't close enough to help. Who were they?"

"Can't be sure," said Rif, unlashing the crates. "Got enemies enough on this trip. It's getting pretty fierce. Best split the cargo."

Jones snorted at that, remembering that there was still the third barrel waiting, leaving her the heavy work.

Mintaka rolled rheumy eyes at Jones, unseeing but expressive. "Fancy company you keep, Altair," she cackled. "Moving up in the world, you are."

"I don't do this every day," Jones shrugged, quietly vowing that she wouldn't be doing it again, either.

Rif hauled the top crate to the gunwales and handed it to her partner. "You take these," she said, reaching for the second crate, "And I'll finish with the barrel."

"Sure that's safe for you?" Rattail asked, stowing the crates.

"I've got your little roof-rat for warning, haven't I?"

"He can't help you in the harbor."

Jones sucked her teeth. The harbor? Was that where they were going next?

"I'll move fast and trust my hand-iron," Rif promised. "Now get out of here."

Rattail untied and obliged, poling off silently in the reeking dark. Rif watched her go, then turned the lantern-light inboard and checked the barrel-ties.

In the passing light Jones noticed something dark on the slats, something like coarse glossy powder, framing the space where the lower crate's corner had been and dribbled thinly over to the gunwale. She reached down and picked up a pinch of the stuff. Hard, smooth, discrete grains. Not powder, no. . . .

Rif loosed the bow tie-line and pulled it in. "Now for the last of it," she said. "Out to Dead Harbor, by Wharf Gate. . . . Jones?"

Jones had unracked the pole, but didn't pull lose the aft tie. "I'll risk my boat and my neck for money," she fumed, "But damned if I can see doing it for a bunch of seeds!"

Rif laughed softly in the dark. "Okay, answer-time," she said. "They're a special kind of weed. Now let's go empty the last barrel."

Jones pulled the tie loose with a savage yank. "For what?" she insisted, knowing she was pushing dangerously. "Some new kind of get-you-high weed? Is that why the blacklegs're after us? I ain't asking for a cut, and I can keep my mouth shut, but I'd like to know what I might get killed for tonight!"

Rif sighed. "Something a little more important than funny-weed," she said. "Water-weed. Water-cleaner, in fact."

"Water-*cleaner*?" Jones almost missed her stroke on the pole.

,"A kind of special-bred water-weed. Roots on the bottom, floats on the surface—and feeds on water-garbage. A kind of living water-purifier, hey? Grow all over town."

"Lord and Ancestors," Jones muttered, thinking about that. Imagine the water clean. Imagine the Tidewater not stinking, the canals safe to swim in, good fishing up and down the city, food free and abundant everywhere. Imagine— "Then why in all hell is somebody tryin' t' kill ye?"

"Because it'll make change." Rif's voice was grim with years' worth of cynical knowledge. "In a town like this, there's people who profit—in money and politics—from the way things are. Even from dirty water and disease and lots of poor folk dying. Damn priests in the college they don't want to see that change. Besides. . . ." A passing bar of window-light showed a wry smile on Rif's face. "The people who bred that weed mean to take the credit, and their competition wouldn't like that."

"Shit," Jones whispered, spearing her pole into the water as if the scummy fluid were a living enemy. What kind of world was this, what kind of city, where people had to hide and sneak and fight just to do a little bit of good? What damned kind of world? "Dammit to hell! Ahh, this *is* hell. What did I do to get born here?"

"Prob'ly nothing at all. Life ain't fair unless you make it." Rif automatically checked the bridge ahead. "So, here's to some changes in hell."

Jones rubbed her eyes and steered on, just as grateful that at this hour the water here was mostly empty. Smooth and steady now under the looming shadow of Southdike, around the west corner toward the Wharf Gate.

Oh, hell, the gate was closed and locked! How had that happened? Nobody ever locked Wharf Gate, especially not during Festival. "Now what?" Jones asked, poling to a smooth stop in front of the ancient gate-grill.

"Shit, we'll just have to empty it here." Rif reached for her bag and felt inside it for the mallet.

A gunshot boomed, loud as a cannon, erupting a small geyser just off the bow.

"Deck!" Jones yelped, dropping flat. The pole clattered down beside her, almost bouncing away. Lord, another ambush, and no help anywhere near; the ears on Southdike and Amparo might hear, but nobody would so much as lean out for a good look, not down here. What in hell to do?

"What the fuck?" Rif squeaked, tumbling back among the barrels, pawing at her bag and trying to see where the shot had come from.

"This isn't your lucky day," snarled a voice from the top of the eastward gate-pier.

A quiet tenor voice.

Even before she looked up at the tall silhouette on the pier, Jones knew who it was.

"Black Cal, you gone crazy?" Rif gasped, poking her head out from between the barrels. "What're you shooting at us for?"

Black Cal leaned out over the edge of the gate, one hand keeping a good grip on the gatehouse ladder, the other holding his gun steady. It looked as big as a cannon, too. "Suppose you tell me what's in that barrel," he said, nothing soft about that quiet voice now. "And what was in the barrel you emptied under the Spur?"

Rif took fast glances over both shoulders. No help, no back-up, no percentage in lying to Black Cal when he was in a shooting mood—and anyone's guess how many listening ears to catch the news. Couldn't be worse. "It— it's plague-prevention," she confessed. "It kills the bugs that cause the plague. Nothing else, I swear."

"Sure. Tell me another."

"It's true! It's true! There's enough in those barrels to kill the bugs in the water, all over the city! That's why I had to throw it in where the current would carry it best, like under the Spur. Carry the stuff downstream, kill plague in the water all over town." Rif pulled her hair out of her eyes and gave him a brief glare of defiance. "Goddammit, man,

I've got to live here too, y'know. Think I want to die of fever-season?"

"Mhm." Black Cal didn't sound entirely convinced. "So you saved up your little copperbits and bought enough disinfectant to clean up Merovingen, out of the goodness of your heart. Sure."

"No, dammit, I'm being paid." Rif squirmed audibly on the deck-slats.

"Who? And why?"

Jones raised her head, wanting to hear this herself.

"The Janes, goddammit!" Rif had never sounded so desperate. "The Janes! They want a foothold in this town, and they figure to get it by healing, stopping the plague—and then taking the credit."

Jones remembered the brown-robed priestess prophesying from Hanging Bridge. Prophesying the minute Rif took off to get the cargo. Not wasting any time.

"And now, thanks to you," Rif added, "everybody who hates the Janes will know where we are, and what we're up to."

Janes' cargo, Jones thought. Plague-killing disinfectant, also the so-named water-purifying seeds that Black Cal still didn't know about. Janes: a healing-and-fertility cult, started in farming country clear over to the Liger. They'd bred those plants, made that stinking disinfectant-stuff. And somebody wanted to stop them. They hadn't figured on Black Cal, but then, nobody could. He wasn't stupid, but not all-wise, either.

Black Cal paused a long time, probably thinking along much the same lines. "So where's the last barrel going?" he asked.

"Into Dead Harbor, clean up the water there."

Right. Jones remembered the way the currents ran: Grand Canal, west-flows, everything ending in Dead Harbor. Dead Harbor, with all its accumulated city garbage: fever-season's surest breeding-ground. Now the whole crazy path of this trip made sense, with just one thing left over.

Black Cal holstered his gun and stepped back to

the gatehouse. A moment later the gate creaked, the locking-arm slid back, and the grill squeaked open.

Scarcely daring to breathe, Jones picked herself and the pole up from the deck, cautiously stuck the end in the water and shoved the skip forward. Rif crawled out from between the barrels, looking pale and glancing around to see who else had overheard.

"Best place to dump it," that quiet tenor voice echoed over the water, "would be off the end of Dead Wharf."

"Oh, right. Yes. . . ." Jones bit off further words, sure she'd start gibbering otherwise, and steered through the open gate. Once through it, she dared to look back. There was no sign of Black Cal, not anywhere.

"Damn that man," Rif muttered, quietly, quietly. "Nothing that big should make so little noise. Moves like a goddam shadow. And how'd he get here ahead of us, anyway? Like he wasn't entirely real, or at least not entirely human. Maybe he's a sharrh in disguise, or maybe not even in disguise. Ever think of that?"

Jones decided she didn't want to think of that. Think of something else. Like barrels and seeds. "Why didn't you throw them seeds in the water, too?"

"Huh? Oh. Wrong time of the year for them. They go in autumn." Rif sat up, brushed her hair back, and hunted in the bag for her mallet. "In a month or so, me and Rattail'l spend a couple days cruising all over the city, singing for pennies under every window, scattering seeds in every canal and backwater. Want to take the ferrying job?"

"No thanks. This here's enough." Jones peered at the mass of deeper darkness in the gray mists ahead. "There's the end of Dead Wharf."

"Ah, right. Stop a dozen meters off it, where the stink's the worst."

Stink was an understatement. The water was greasy and lump-strewn with all Merovingen's garbage, the last dumping ground of refuse that a cityful of hereditary scavengers couldn't use. The stench was like a smothering blanket, rising in visible curls of oily fog. Caught in the stagnant eddy of Dead Harbor's crooked currents, the sargasso of garbage floated here until it rotted enough to sink, scatter or blow away. Ghost Fleet, scavengers, fish and all stayed on the far side of the harbor. Not even dung-flies came here.

Rif muttered something about 'the heart of darkness' as she tied a bandanna around her nose and mouth. Jones tugged a mostly clean rag out of the hidey and did the same, then tossed out the tied-stone anchor—the cheap one, that she could afford to cut loose and throw away afterwards. Rif got up and went to the barrel with her mallet.

The first blow on the lid boomed across the reeking water, waking odd echoes in the fog. Rif hitched her shoulders uncomfortably, and struck again. The king-piece broke with a crack like a light gunshot. Jones winced at the noise.

The echoes were wrong. Too many, lasting too long, and not quite like breaking wood.

Something out there, hard to tell where. To starboard? Ancestors, toward the Ghost Fleet? Jones froze, glanced at Rif, saw that her eyes were wide.

"Shit," Rif muttered, yanking at the barrel-lid. "Jones, dump this thing!" She scrambled back toward the bow and crouched among the empty barrels, pulling something else out of her bag.

Jones swore, hurried to the barrel and dragged the lid free, then the ties. Now roll it—heavy, hard to manage alone—two steps back, and tilt. Damn, heavy. She glanced again at Rif.

The cloaked singer was crouched at the bow, peering into the streamers of fog, her hands clear of her cape and something filling them. Jones looked closer and saw why it was that nobody had ever seen Rif use her gun. The thing was big enough to fill two hands, dead-dull black all over: hard to see, and certain to kill whatever it hit. Waiting now, waiting for something that required it.

The odd sounds were closer, and definitely to port. Steady splashing. Poles in the water. A boat, skip-size or bigger. Another minute and Jones could see it: definitely the squared shape of a skip, loaded with crowding figures. From the way they held their hands, they had guns, too. Oh, damn, *damn*.

Jones dropped to the well beside the barrel, wondering how long the thing would take to drain, whether the oncoming crowd would see them or not, whether they'd pass by in the mist on other business.

The first gunshot cracked over her head, slugging into the top of the barrel.

Jones tried to spread herself flatter on the deckslats, and heaved at the barrel's bottom rim. It moved a little, the contents draining faster, but not by much.

Rif's gun roared, flashing an instant's orange light. Someone in the attacking boat yelled and went splashing into the water. Whether it was the poleman gone or caution, the craft stopped and erupted a hail of gunfire. Muzzle-flashes flickered like fire above the water. Most of the shots went wide in the uncertain mist, but a few of them thudded into the skip.

Jones winced, wondering if any shots had breached the hull, and if so, how bad the holes were. She scrabbled crabwise toward the hidey and her own gun. How many bullets did she have, anyway? How many of them reliable?

Rif, arms braced on the foredeck, fired again. She'd taken time to aim, and a screech of pain followed the shot.

Whoever was left in that skip decided not to sit back and continue being picked off. Someone aboard grabbed a pole and shoved the craft forward, straight on, the rest of the crew firing in a steady, covering barrage.

Jones felt a splash of water on her leg just as she got her hand on the pistol. A glance back showed nothing but shadows, no telling how big the hole was. She felt for it with her foot, touched a small rough-edged gap at the waterline. She crammed her heel into it, and the flow stopped. Small hole: she could patch it fast, given the chance.

Make the chance. She squirmed around to face the oncoming skip, reared up and fired at the top of the dark mass in the fog.

Rif fired at almost the same instant.

If either shot hit, there was no sign of it. The attackers were crouched under the gunwales, still coming on, still firing. Lord and Ancestors, barely a pole-length off.

Pole! Jones grabbed for it with her unencumbered hand, stuffed the pistol in her belt and wondered, fast, where to swing. Straight shove, probably. At least keep those bastards from board-and-storm.

Again Rif fired, this time angled down toward the water. The approaching boat thudded hollowly at the impact, maybe holed but still moving, and too close.

Jones poked the end of her pole overside, purely guessing from sound where the attacker would be, and shoved hard.

Contact! The attacker echoed like a dull drum, and both skips jittered away from each other. The unseen assault-team scrambled and swore.

They'll be ready when I try again, Jones realized. *Maybe stand up and shoot down at me. . . .* That would also give Rif a clear target, if she knew what was coming. "Rif, ware! Hin!" she yelled, stabbing out with the pole. "Port!"

The pole jabbed hard on the attacker's hull. A half-second later, Rif fired.

That one hit. Someone yelped, something fell heavily on the other skip's deck, somebody else swore. More gunfire answered, a barrage that didn't let up.

More bullets thwacked the hull. A few of them had to be getting through. Rif cursed and fired until her gun clicked empty.

Buy her time to reload! Jones pulled out her own pistol and fired a blind shot overside. No sign that it hit, and the other skip was so damned close, they'd collide in a minute. Then it'd be board-and-storm for sure, anyone's guess how many of them against only herself and Rif, and that would be the finish. She fired again, heard the bullet hit wood.

A booming like a small cannon thundered out over the water.

Someone gave a choked gulp and went overside.

Another roar—too big, too distant to be anyone on

these boats—and the sound of another body hitting deckboards. Whose shots? For an instant Jones had visions of the Harbor Angel coming to life.

Rif reared up on her knees, reloaded gun clicking shut, and fired three times fast into the enemy skip. A howl showed that at least one shot had hit. Rif dropped again and crawled back toward Jones, between the barrels.

Another booming roar, another thud, and whoever was on the other skip stopped firing.

Silence fell, shockingly fast and total. Jones could hear herself panting, and Rif as well. They looked toward each other, wide eyes meeting. "Who the hell. . . ?" Rif whispered.

Jones only shook her head. She could feel water pressing at the hole under her heel. No matter what else, she had to patch that thing fast. Nothing handy but her cap. Cursing the loss, she squirmed about on the boards, found the hole with her fingers and jammed her wadded-up cap into it.

"Shit," Rif murmured almost reverently, up on her knees now, staring at the other boat. Nobody shot at her. The reeking water was quiet.

Jones risked sitting up, then standing, to look at the other skip.

It was filled with corpses. Dark-cloaked, faces shrouded—some with no faces left at all. A few had small, still-bleeding holes in them—others had pieces blown off. Holes in the hull gurgled heavily, letting in enough steadily-rising water that the bottom was awash. Bits of bodies began to float on the blood-thickened deepening bilge.

Even Rif's gun couldn't have done damage like that. Neither had Jones' few shots, let alone pole-jabbings. Who had a weapon that could do that?

From somewhere near the end of Dead Wharf, someone whistled part of a tune: the chorus from Rif's song for Black Cal.

Who else?

Barely visible in the sky-glow and mist, a tall lean silhouette stood on the end of Dead Wharf, still holding a very large, long revolver in one hand.

"Nice shooting, Black Cal." Rif somehow managed to sound cheerful. "Very good, in the dark and all."

"Went by sound, mostly," replied that unnerving quiet voice. "Finish your business and go home."

"Right." Rif went to the barrel and tugged at it. Jones shoved the pole out of the way, got up and helped her. The barrel was almost half-empty, and the draining went fast.

The other skip floated sluggishly away to die elsewhere.

Just once, Jones glanced up toward the end of Dead Wharf, but saw nobody there. No doubt Black Cal was walking away, back toward the wharf's end at Southdike. No doubt. . . .

Rif upended the barrel and shoved it back against the hull, not bothering to tie it. Jones picked up her pole, cut away the stone anchor, and turned back toward Wharf Gate.

"Holes in the damned barrels," she griped as she poled, trying to keep from thinking about how tired her arms were, how close she'd come to dying, or Black Cal in general. "Can't sell 'em now."

"The wood's still good," Rif reminded her, running slow fingers over the skip's hull, checking for more damage. "Use it to patch your boat."

"Got to dry-dock her, any case," Jones sighed. "Get that rotten water out, and those damn seeds."

"Remember to throw 'em in the canal. Hmm, the gate's still open."

So it was. There was no sign of Black Cal, but he had to be around somewhere. Neither of them wanted to talk about him.

"Just drop me off at Fife Corner," Rif yawned. "Goddess, I could do with a hot meal and a hotter bath, and a fast dive into bed."

Goddess. . . ? Jones remembered a few details she'd wondered at earlier. Safe to ask now, after all this. "So, plague-killer and water-cleaning weed, and what else've we done tonight?"

"Hm?"

Jones nudged the packet in the hidey with her

foot. "That pickup back at Mars said "cheap fuel," not "clean water." What'd you give him? And me?"

Rif chuckled. "That's maybe the biggest changer of all. It's yeast-starter and instructions for making fuel-alcohol. Burns in every kind of engine. Make-it-yourself fuel. See?"

Jones glanced at her silent motor, and thought about that.

"Hell. Cheap fuel?"

"Damned right. And the yeast grows when you feed it. We'll be selling those packets all over the lower city. People'll use 'em, grow more yeast, sell it, spread it around. Soon everybody'll have it."

"You mean, *anybody* can make it?"

"Right here on the skip, if you wanted. Teeny-tiny brew tanks and stills could make enough to keep you in good money. Nobody could tell it from cook-pots. Hah! Not even the sharrh!"

Jones felt her jaw drop as the implications hit. "Damn, it could make us all rich!"

"Right." Rif reached about on the deck, shoving odd items back into her pack. The mallet twanged faintly against the flat-harp's strings. "Except the petroleum-sellers wouldn't like the competition. The rich and powerful don't want any change they can't control. The anti-tech types in the College don't want any change on general principles. Hell, it's safer to be a crook than to openly try and improve the world! In fact, safest and surest way to do it is to *be* a crook. Heh!"

Layers and layers, Jones realized. Rif worked as a musician to push her insurrectionist songs, used the rebel pose to cover her thieving and smuggling, and used the crooked work to cover her real business. She really was a revolutionary—maybe the kind that succeeded, the kind that nobody would suspect. Except maybe Black Cal. . . . But he'd *helped*.

"Tell me this. Why in hell are the Janes, of all people, doing this?"

Rif laughed again, not cynically this time. "The Janes want what everybody really wants—a way off Merovin. They also hate poverty and disease. The

only way to get what they want is through tech—
smart tech that won't attract the notice of the sharrh,
and can't be bottled up by the rich and powerful.
That means, it's got to be something that they can
spread far and wide among the poor, something
even the poorest can get and understand and use."

Jones thought about that as she pulled up at Fife
corner. The Janes, secretly producing a hideable tech-
for-everybody: plague-prevention, water-purifying,
even cheap fuel. The sharrh, the College—hell, not
even the high town of Merovingen would see it before it had spread too far and wide to stop. And if it
worked, if the Janes' plot could keep on like this. . . .

Hell, it was scary. It was real scary. Anything hopeful was.

Rif climbed stiffly out of the skip, turned and
pulled some money out of her pocket. "Here: five
pieces."

"We agreed on four."

"The extra's for damages and repairs."

"All right." Jones took the coins—damn, it was
half a dece, gold. "Hey, when you want to take those
seeds around, call for me at Moghi's."

"Sure thing," Rif promised, a quick smile flashing
her teeth in the shadows. "Serenade you all over the
city, and pay for it, too."

She turned and walked off, feet padding light on
the walkway, trailing a short song-chorus after her.

> "How do you make an underground
> In a town that's under water?
> Make your peace with the deep canals,
> And kiss the boatman's daughter.

Jones smiled, and poled off toward Ventani.

FESTIVAL MOON
(REPRISED)

C.J. Cherryh

It was the low side by Moghi's and the dark by
Fishmarket Stair, where a skip in trouble could haul
up; and a damned great mess, engine-heavy as she
was and with the fuel all to be drained before she
could be hoisted on the tackle Moghi's lads rigged
under the stair amongst the pilings, and a draggled
and a sweating Jones and a sodden and a much
be-cursed Daoud (the new boy) to work the sling
under the wounded skip.

Then it was out with the holed board and a damned
great hole into her credit with Moghi, who had roused
out old man Gilley, got him sober, and got him to
work in the back-entry shed back in the alley, where
near-dawn sawing and planing and hammering produced the precise few hull-planks to fit.

"We paint 'er?" Gilley had asked.

"Damn fool question," Jones had muttered with ill
grace. *"It's the damn night, Gilley!"*

Meaning no one who had to hoist and patch in the
small hours under Fishmarket at Moghi's prices was
going to wait on dry paint. It was patch now and fix
it right later, and Gilley was one of the best when he
was sober.

Right now she sat in the dark with her rump on
cold damp stone and her toes cold (but toes were
always cold in Merovingen-below) and her aching

arms pressed between her knees, hard, hands about her ankles, and watched Gilley waist-deep in the water tapping the patch in.

Damm, she wanted sleep. Damn, her back hurt enough to bring tears to her eyes. Damn, damn, and damn, she hurt from her worn feet to her aching head, and she had got holes in her skip and a stinking mess in her well that Moghi had already been asking about.

"What's that?" Moghi had asked.

And she: "Oh, I dunno, Moghi, damn, bad cargo, had to dump 'er."

"The hell. It smells like rotten eggs. It smells like the damn water, Jones—"

A shadow drifted up out of the black, one of Moghi's lads, she thought: here in Moghi's own armpit and tired as she was, she had her guard down.

When the feet turned out to be booted, the sound muffled in all Gilley's damned pounding, she scrambled and grabbed for her knife; but it was pale, fine hands on the man who dropped down by her in the dark, hands she knew before she even looked to the face.

"Damn ye, sneak up on me, why don't ye? We going to kill each other?"

"Sorry." He had a scarf about his head, dark clothes, that was why he was all face and hands in the night. "What in *hell* happened out there? What in *hell* were you doing?"

She sat down again, legs flat. "Ain't nothing. Just a damn fare."

"*Ain't nothing.* Jones—" There was the sound of a long breath. "Jones, just lie low. Stay out of sight. For God's sake."

"Hey, I figure whoever's after you is after me, right? So I confuse 'em. Make this little smuggle-run, throw this damn stuff out—"

"Good *God,* Jones!"

She ducked her head and winced. "Well, so, I didn't figure it. But, hey, ain't it? They get so busy to watching me, you c'n maybe kind of slip by 'em."

"So now the blacklegs are swarming like spawn in

a corpse, the governor and the College are going to be asking questions—damn it all—you stink like the whole damned town!"

"Thanks."

"Like rotten eggs. You're all over with it. My God, the reek off your boat—"

"Moghi's got some bad beer he give me. Going to sluice 'er down when we get 'er back in. She'll smell different." She gave a sniff at her sleeve and wiped her nose. "Maybe I spill it on me too, huh?"

"*Do* that. Lie low."

"I ain't going to lie low."

"That was noisy, Jones."

"So we found out something, huh?" Hopefully.

"Noisy. Listen. You get those patches painted. You lie low. Hear me—"

"Hey, lots of boats got a new plank 'r two. Ye stave a side now and again down by the Gut, that current's real fierce—"

"Explain it to the blacklegs. Damn it, Jones, *paint* it! And lie low."

She dropped her head into her hands and tucked her knees up.

"Hey," he said quietly, gently, and rubbed the back of her neck. "Come on, up to the Room. I'll get you a bath, put you to bed."

She shook her head.

"Jones."

"Ye don't buy me off, Mondragon, an' ye don't put me off."

"Let's go talk about it." Both shoulders now. "Come on."

Third shake of the head. "I ain't out of it."

"Talk."

She gave a great and weary sigh.

So did Mondragon. He squeezed the shoulders, leaned his head against hers. "Come on, Jones. All right, we've got some figuring to do."

There was a low spot in the bed and Jones rolled over trusting the warm body that ought to be there.

And kept going a fraction as there was no body in

that spot. She moved her hand on the one side, wondering where she had gotten to in the bed, wondering where Mondragon had gotten to, and felt after him with her leg.

Then she opened her eyes on total dark and felt with a wide sweep of her arm.

"Mondragon?"

Panic set in. She threw herself out of bed and fumbled after the night-light that had gone out in the windowless Room in Moghi's upstairs, then gave that up and grabbed after her clothes in the pitch black, pulled on her breeches and her sweater in a desperate hurry and felt her way toward the door knob. She shot the bolt back and cracked the door.

One breakfast was on the tray on the floor outside. One half slice of toast.

She hit the stairs running, bare feet spatting down the boards, down to the hall where Gilley was curled up among the rags, a bottle in his arms.

She made the main room in more calm, walked up to the bar where Jep was dicing fish, turned her shoulder to the few patrons that (O God! it was that late!) had meandered in. She leaned right over the scarred wood counter and caught the wrist of Jep's knifehand with a hard and nasty grip.

"Where'd he go, Jep?"

Jep had a resentful and nervous look. "Hey, I dunno." He jerked the arm back. "He left out, I dunno, boy said he'd took out the back—"

"*When?*"

"Hell, I dunno, well 'fore light."

"*How 'well', dammit?*" She was too loud. She choked it down. "Where?"

"I dunno, you got to ask Daoud."

"Well, *get* him!"

"He's to market, be back, oh, half hour—"

"Damn! I want my skip launched, Jep, get the boys, I want my skip."

"Boys is sleeping, Jones. You want ter wake 'em, I got ter wake Moghi, an' you know how Moghi don't like that."

"Jep." She drew a careful, a quiet breath. "I want

my skip down. I don't care if you got to wake the governor, ye get my skip down an' ye get me a fuel can and ye get me runnin'."

"I got ter wake Moghi." Jep scowled distressedly and wiped fish-tail off the counter with a stained rag. "We roust a crew 'fore breakfast, broad daylight, ye got talk up an' down. Just give 'er a bit, Jones, we get ye in, all easy like . . . 'less ye got real reason t' be out of here faster."

She leaned her elbows on the counter and slumped against it.

Damn, no knowing where he had got to, no damn reason to go off panicked and making a commotion.

Noisy, Mondragon would say.

Hang around the canalside, he had said. Listen for what you can hear.

Mama, ain't that what you said? Man wants his own damn way. Holes in my boat, town gone crazy, man sneaks out on me and Ancestors know where he's at.

Damn! he done it to me, all sweet in bed and give me the damn whiskey and out with the light and all.

Mama, your daughter's a fool.

TWO GENTLEMEN
OF THE TRADE

Robert Lynn Asprin

House Gregori and House Hannon were not particularly noteworthy in Merovingian hierarchy. There was old money behind each to be sure, but not enough to rate them as exceptionally rich. They had not specialized in commerce as so many other houses had, and therefore were not a controlling or even influential force in any given commodity or market. They were not old enough or large enough to impact the convoluted politics of either the town or the local religions. In fact, it is doubtful they would have been any better known than a fashionable shop or tavern, were it not for one thing: The Feud.

No one in town knew for sure how the feud between House Gregori and House Hannon began. Questions brought widely varying answers, not only from the two houses, but from different members of the same house as well. Some said it had something to do with a broken marriage contract, others that it was somehow related to a blatant criminal act involving either a business deal or a gaming wager. There were even those who maintained that the feud pre-existed the settlement of the town and had merely been renewed. In short, almost every reason for a feud to exist had at one time or another been touted as the truth, but in reality no one in Merovingen really knew or cared. What mattered was that the feud existed.

Violence was common enough in Merovingen-above. While differences were not always settled by physical confrontation or reprisal, the option was always there and never overlooked in either planning or defense. Feuds were also fairly commonplace, but they were generally short lived and nearly always limited in their scope by unspoken gentlemen's agreements. In direct contrast, the Gregori-Hannon Feud was carried on at levels of viciousness that made even the most hardened citizen uneasy. There were no safe-zones, no truces. Women, even infants were as fair targets as the menfolk. It was said that both houses retained assassins to stalk the other, as well as offering open contracts for the death of any rival house member. Whether it was true or not, it made each member of either house a walking target for any local bravo who believed the rumors.

If anything, the feud doubtlessly saved many lives in the overall scheme of things—by example alone. Many a dispute in Merovingen cooled at the last moment with the simple advisement of "Let's not make a Gregori-Hannon thing out of this." And while the more sane edged away from the Gregoris and the Hannons, the feud raged as the two houses mechanically acted out their obsessive hatred.

Festival time was usually Gregori-Hannon open season, each house stalking the other through the celebrations, each never pausing to think that they themselves were the bait that lured the other side out. This year, however, House Gregori remained barricaded in its holding. The elder Gregori was ill, perhaps dying. So for the moment, at least, natural death took precedence.

"It's the Hannons! It has to be!"

The doctor paused in his ministerings and scowled up at the pacing man.

"Pietor Gregori!" he intoned in a stern voice. "Again I must ask you to keep still! Your father needs his rest, and I cannot concentrate with your constant prattle."

"Sorry, Terrosi." Pietor said, dropping heavily onto a chair. "It just doesn't make any sense. You've said yourself that Father's never been sick a day in his life. The only time he's spent abed is recovering from wounds. He was fine when you gave him his yearly check-up last week. It has to be poison . . . and the Hannons must be behind it. The question is how did they do it?"

"Of course it's the Hannons." The elder Gregori was struggling to rise on one elbow, waving aside the hovering doctor. "You know it, and I know it, Pietor. Never mind what this doddering fool says. It's poison. I can feel it eating at my insides. Now quit fretting at what we already know. The question isn't how they did it, it's what you're going to do about it! You're the eldest since your uncle was killed. The house will look to you for leadership. I want you out hunting Hannon blood, not sitting around here trying to hold my hand."

Pietor looked around the room uneasily, as if looking for allies in the furniture, then, as was his habit, ran a hand nervously through his unruly hair.

"Father . . . I don't want to argue with you. You know I fear for what this feud is doing to our house. We can't afford to lose you, much less anyone else if the Hannons see them first in the crowds. As for me, I've never killed anyone, and. . . ."

"Then it's time you did!" the elder Gregori broke in. "I've pampered you in the past, Pietor, but it's time you woke up to the facts of life. Get it through your head that this feud will only end when either the Hannons or we Gregoris are all dead. You owe it to the House to be sure it's them and not us who face extinction. Kill them, Pietor. Kill them all, or they will certainly kill you as they have killed me!"

Exhausted by the effort, he sank back in his pillows as Terrosi leapt to his side.

"That's enough . . . both of you!" the doctor snapped. "Now listen to me. I don't want to have to say this again . . . though I'll probably have to. It isn't poison. Believe me, in this town I know the symptoms. More likely one of the marketfolk sold you some overaged fish. You'll be up and around in a few days, *if* you get your rest and *if* certain parties can refrain from airing old arguments and getting *you* so upset my medicines get negated. Am I speaking clearly?"

Pietor shrank before the physician's glare.

"Terrosi's right," he said, rising. "I should be going."

Reaching the door, he hesitated with one hand on the knob.

"You're sure it's not poison?"

"OUT!" the doctor ordered, not looking up from his work.

Terrosi was genuinely annoyed by the time Pietor had closed the door behind him. It was obvious that the son loved his father, but his concerns didn't make the physician's work any easier. Most annoying of all was the reluctance on everyone's part to believe the diagnosis.

The doctor had served the Gregoris his entire career. In fact, the Gregoris had financed his training and education to insure his loyalty to their house. His retainer was sufficient to guarantee him a comfortable life without seeking other patients. Everything possible had been done to see to his needs, and the Gregoris' strategy was successful. His loyalty was total and unquestioned. Terrosi would never dream of accepting commission from anyone outside the house, whether or not it was potentially harmful to the Gregoris. His skills (and they were considerable) were solely at the disposal of the house. Over the years his treatments were accurate and effective, so that now it was unthinkable to have his diagnosis challenged. Unthinkable and annoying, for Terrosi knew that the elder Gregori had *indeed* been poisoned. Terrosi knew this for a fact, as he had been the one who had done it.

It had been easy enough to effect during the old man's check-up; just a drop or two of poison on the tongue depressor was all that was necessary. The only tricky part had been to keep the dosage low enough to cause illness, but not death, for immediate death would have cast suspicion on him. The fatal dosage would be reached through his continued treatment of the elder Gregori's "illness."

Of course, Terrosi did not see this as a betrayal of the Gregoris' trust in him. After all, it had been a Gregori who had paid him to do the murder, and while he was sworn to help no one outside the house, he felt that this was merely an extension of the services he offered to his retainers. What surprised him was that it was not Pietor who had made the request, but one of his younger brothers. Had the commission come from the eldest, Terrosi would have understood it as a bid for the inheritance and control of the house. As it was. . . .

The doctor sighed and turned once more to his task of administering yet another dose of poison to his patient. His job was to see to the "how," not the "why." It would have been easier if Pietor had been a party to the plot. It was hard enough to work under the watchful eyes of the elder Gregori without having his eldest son fluttering about as well. Still, Terrosi was a professional and used to doing his job under adverse conditions.

With a reassuring smile, he held out the spoonful of death.

Torches blazing on a score of boats lit the assemblage and served as a beacon for latecomers as the boat people of Merovingen pranced and capered in one of their rare parties. It was late, well after most of the Festival activity had finally staggered to a halt, but flushed with the energy of the day's frenzy and buoyed by the lavish earnings and tips from drunken Uptown revelers, the canalers were disinclined to rest, even realizing the chaos would start anew on the morrow.

A dozen boats had lashed themselves together in the middle of the canal, and planks had been scavenged and laid across the gunwales to form a large, if unstable, platform, as the crowd beat on anything

wooden with hands or sticks to provide a steady
rhythm for those who eased or fed their tensions by
dancing. Wine and occasional bottles of liquor, usually closely hoarded, passed around freely in acknowl-
edgement of friendship or generosity. It was Festival
time, and purses were too fat for the canalers to be
miserly.

The man known only as Chud perched on a low
cabin roof, beating time against the wall with his
heels as he leisurely drank in the spectacle with his
eyes. He thoroughly enjoyed the canalers with their
earthy speech and robust zest for life. Clapping his
hands and whistling at a particularly outrageous bit
of capering, he reflectively smiled at the contrast
between this emotional outpouring and the more
restrained, formal gatherings that were the pattern
Uptown. There one had to watch every word, every
gesture for fear of inadvertently offending the powerful, as well as tracking everything that transpired
within hearing in hopes of gleaning a clue of the
shifting favors and trends. While his work often required it, it was not a particularly relaxing pastime.

That was why he had chosen to establish himself
with the canalers, buying his own boat and donning
the worn garb of the working class to labor among
them for days at a time. Acceptance had been slow,
but eventually he learned enough to be acknowledged as a fellow, if poorly skilled, boatman. He
never asserted himself in competing for the small
hauling contracts, meekly taking whatever fell his
way by chance. His few acquaintances were annoyed
by this, and harangued him to stand up to the boat bullies who crowded him out of fares in mid-negotiation,
but he just smiled and shook his head until they gave
up in disgust, vowing never again to give advice to
someone not man enough to fight for himself.

In truth, Chud did not need the money and enjoyed the luxury of being gracious. His normal work
was profitable enough to make his venture into boat-
ing more of a vacation than a vocation, and much of
what made it relaxing was that he could accept sec-

ond place without losing more than an unearned handful of small coins.

Someone lurched up to him offering a wineskin, but Chud refused with a smile and a wave of his hand. This, too, was part of his character on the canal: the quiet one who never drank or chased women. Combined with his tendency to disappear for long periods of time, this habit led people to believe that there was another part of his life which kept him from becoming truly one of them. There was idle speculation as to his reasons ranging from an ailing parent to a demanding mistress, but no one was interested enough to follow him or even ask directly to confirm or deny suspicions. The canalers were inclined to respect each other's personal privacy, and whatever it was that had unmanned Chud and kept him from being more open and assertive was generally deemed to be nobody's business but his own.

As caught up as he was with the celebration, Chud was never completely unwary, and he suddenly sensed a new presence in the crowd. There was nothing which specifically alerted him to it, yet he knew it with the same instinctive certainty that lets a bug know when it's going to rain.

Without changing expression or breaking the rhythm of his heel drumming, he casually scanned the growing crowd for the source of his subconscious alarm. Despite the fact that he was already alerted it took three passes with his eyes before he identified what he was looking for.

She was standing well back toward the edge of the raft having just stepped aboard but yet unwilling to push her way forward as did the other new arrivals. What finally drew Chud's eyes to her was this lack of forward motion, that and her tendency, like his own, to watch the crowd around her rather than the dancers. Dark of hair and slight of build, she was wrapped in an old blanket which both protected her from the night chill and hid her garments at the same time. Though unremarkable in appearance, once Chud's attention was focused on her she seemed to stand out in the crowd like a pure-bred in a pack of mongrels.

Of course, his knowledge of who she was sharpened his perceptions.

For the barest moment he thought of ignoring her. She was no threat to him, and this was his chosen retreat from her world. Then the reality of the situation rose to dominate his mind; a chance meeting like this was a rarity, unlikely to be repeated. It was not wise to ignore what fate had so conveniently dropped in his lap.

Once resolved, he had to fight back an impulse to rush to her side before someone else noticed her or she retreated. Instead, he made his way across the raft in leisurely stages, zigzagging his way through the crowd as he paused to exchange greetings with acquaintances or to listen to a heated conversation. Watching her obliquely all the while, his heart leaped each time someone glanced her way or brushed past her, but maintained his pace.

Finally he reached her, or rather the position he had targeted; squatting a few feet away, facing away from the dancers, staring out over the water.

"You shouldn't be here, m'sera," he said loud enough for her to hear. "It's dangerous."

The girl started and looked at him as if he were a venomous snake.

"What did you say?"

He shook his head without shifting his gaze.

"Don't stare at me. It'll draw attention." he instructed. "I said it's dangerous for you here."

"Why do you say that? And who are you? You don't talk like a canaler."

"Neither do you," he said pointedly. "I'm just doing a little slumming, myself. These folks will usually leave a man alone if he's fit and seems to have his wits about him. There are people on this raft, though, who would love nothing better than to have an Uptown lady for a plaything ... when they spot what you are."

Chud felt her relax as he spoke and congratulated himself on his word choice. He had been rehearsing his approach as he made his way across the raft, and it seemed he had been correct. His expressed concern was for "what" she was, not "who" she was, and this confirmation of her anonymity eased her fears.

"I thought if I dressed. . . ."

"The first time you open your mouth, it won't matter what you're wearing, they'll know. What are you doing here, anyway? Does your family know you're here?"

"I . . . I slipped out of the house after they were asleep," she said. "I've heard . . . I'm looking for a woman named Zilfi. The boatman said I would find her here."

"Old Gran Zilfi?" Chud frowned. "The boatman cheated you, or was too lazy to pole with his pockets full. She's not here. Her tie-up place is up in the Spur Loop."

"It is? Then how. . . ."

"Don't worry. I'll take you there myself. Come on."

He rose and started to move away, then realized she wasn't following him. Had his eagerness betrayed him?

"How do I know you aren't as crooked as the last boatman? Maybe you're lying to me to make a few extra coins yourself."

Chud smiled at her, though his expression was prompted as much out of relief as for reassurance.

"It's Festival time, m'sera. A few coins one way or the other doesn't make much difference. I was more thinking to help you out of a bad spot."

She nodded, but still hesitated.

"Tell you what," he said, "I'll take you where you want to go. On the way, you mark the buildings and docks to be sure I'm not poling in circles. When we get there, you pay me what you think the trip's worth. Fair enough?"

A rare smile escaped her then as she nodded again, more firmly this time.

"Fair enough. Forgive me for being suspicious. I was raised . . . I haven't had much experience dealing with people. I hope my clumsiness doesn't offend you."

He made the proper reassuring noises, but guided her to his skip as he did. Now that she had agreed to accompany him, his major concern was that they get underway without drawing too much attention. There seemed little chance of that, though. The canalers were too preoccupied with the festivities at the center of the raft to pay much mind to anything happening at the edges.

After seating her securely, Chud cast off, then moved to the stern of the craft with his pole to back them out of the tangle of gathered boats.

"Ware, hey!"

The call came out of the darkness behind them, and he desperately dug in with his pole as he echoed the warning.

"Hey, ware!"

The regular boatmen were far more adept at handling their vessels, and he usually found the safest course in potential collision situations was to hold steady while they maneuvered around him.

"That you, Chud?"

A weathered skip eased into the torchlight with a white-haired crone wielding the pole as she peered at the craft blocking her path. Chud groaned inside.

" 'S me, Mintaka. Got a fare."

"This late? Good, good. You young 'uns kin keep the canal open 'round the clock. Good fer the town."

He felt her eyes studying them as the boats passed.

Damn! That arthritic old lady was one of the biggest gossips on the canal. It was unthinkable that she'd be able to resist spreading the news that Quiet Chud had left the party with a young girl. Anyone who didn't hear it tonight would know before noon tomorrow.

"You handle the boat very well."

The girl's words dragged Chud's thoughts back to the task at hand. If any of the other canalers had heard her, they would have laughed aloud. While he was not the poorest boatman on the canal, his skills had a ways to go before they would even be considered mediocre.

"Thank you, m'sera. It's really easier than it looks once you get the hang of it."

They were picking up a bit of speed now as Chud got the rhythm of the poling going, the sounds and lights of the party slipping away behind them.

"You said you were slumming. How is it that someone who can, and apparently does, move freely Uptown choose to spend time with the canalers—even to the point of having his own boat and learning to pole it?"

"One tires of intrigues and politics," he said in a rare display of honesty. "However frugal their existence, the canalers control their own lives. In their company, I can at least enjoy the temporary illusion that I'm in control of my own life instead of dancing to the tune of factions and houses."

The girl was silent for a while, watching the piers and bridges slide by in the darkness, and Chud wondered if he had offended her with his candidness, or if she were simply bored with the conversation.

"I envy you," she said suddenly, proving her thoughts were still with him. "I, too, tire of being controlled by the politics and feuds of this town's hierarchy, but I am never offered the chance you have to escape . . . even temporarily."

"Never?"

He smiled, confident that the dark would hide his expression.

"Well, rarely. So rarely that my one venture into independence only served to show me the extent to which my life is normally controlled by rules and traditions of my family. Even worse, it made me admit to myself that I was not strong enough to stand alone against them."

"Is that why you decided not to have the baby?"

His words hung in the night air as if they were sketched in fiery paint.

The girl was still for a moment, then he saw her turn, staring at him in the dark.

"What did you say?"

"Come now, m'sera. It is not so hard too deduce. Your sneaking out alone tonight is in itself evidence of a degree of desperation. And looking for Gran Zilfi . . . there are only two medicines she offers that can't be had easier and cheaper Uptown. One renews the potency of elderly men, and I somehow doubt you require that; the other rids a woman of an unwanted pregnancy. Do you see my logic?"

He thought she might argue or at least deny his assertion, but instead she simply shrugged half-heartedly.

"It's true. As I said, there are some things I'm not strong enough to face alone."

"Alone? What of the father?"

"The father? He's part of the problem . . . most of it, really. My house would never accept him, nor his me. He says he'll find a way to take care of things, but it's been more than a week since I told him and he hasn't been in touch. Whether or not he has abandoned me becomes inconsequential. I know now that I'll have to deal with this problem myself."

"Perhaps the matter will be resolved for you."

"What do you. . . ."

His pole caught her on the side of the head, sending her over the side into the inky waters.

She floundered weakly, too stunned to even cry for help, and Chud debated for a moment whether she stood a chance for survival, weighted down as she was with clothes and blanket.

Better safe than sorry, he decided finally. Reaching out again with his pole, he anchored it between her shoulder blades and pushed with all his strength until he felt her pinned against the bottom, then held her there until the water was smooth.

Several of the menfolk were present as the assassin was ushered into the elder Gregori's presence. This had been the custom ever since they had lost a member to a killer supposedly seeking a private pay-off.

Pietor Gregori was uncomfortable with the interview, but as the next in line to head the House it was his duty to be present, both as part of his training and to ease the strain on his ailing father.

"This man claims to have killed one of the Hannons last night, Father," he said, "but he has no evidence. . . ."

"It was Teryl Hannon, the youngest daughter," the assassin interrupted, clearly annoyed. "I drowned her in the canal, and her body should be discovered shortly if it didn't get hung up in the silt at the bottom. I'll wager nobody else even knows she's dead, much less the method. There's a possibility that witnesses may associate me with her disappearance, so I'll have to lay low for a while and would just as soon not have to wait around for my payment."

The elder Gregori waved aside the hovering family physician.

"This man has killed Hannons for us before, Pietor. Do you have any reason to suspect he's lying to us now?"

"Even if he's telling the truth about the girl's death, it may have just been an accident that he's trying to claim credit for."

"An accident?" the killer hissed. "I may have ruined one of my favorite identities for that death, and if you think. . . ."

"Pay him." the elder Gregori ordered. "Even if it was an accident, there's one less Hannon, and that's worth something to us. If you want to be sure of how they die, Pietor, you'll have to kill them yourself instead of waiting for assassins to do your work for you. It's good to see that *someone* is hunting Hannons this Festival."

Pietor flushed at the reminder of his negligence, but fumbled in his purse for the required sum.

"Thank you, sir." the assassin said stiffly, still irritated at the haggling. "You're lucky I don't charge you for two deaths."

"How's that?"

The elder Gregori was alert now.

"The girl, Teryl, was with child. That's what got her out from behind the Hannons' defenses so that I could get a crack at her. By rights that's another Hannon that won't be around, even though the death was a little premature. I should probably try to find the lover who abandoned her and get payment from him. He's the one who's interests I really served."

"Pay him half again for the child, Pietor." the old man cackled, sinking back into his pillows. "He's served us well, and if he's going into hiding, he won't be able to scour the town for some rake."

"Father, you shouldn't excite yourself."

"Pay him! This kind of excitement is the best medicine for me."

Despite his patient's agitated state, Terrosi was covertly studying the reactions of Demitri, Pietor's middle brother.

The lad had gone pale, his eyes almost sightless with his apparent shock.

It was becoming clearer why Demitri had commissioned his father's death. With the elder Gregori out of the way, Pietor would be in charge of the house, and that son's sentiments on the feud were well known. Yes. If little brother Demitri *had* wanted to bring a Hannon bastard into the house, Pietor would be far easier for Demitri to deal with as Househead than his father would have been. If anything, Pietor might have seized on the idea of legitimizing the Demetri-Teryl Hannon pairing as his chance to try to make peace between the houses. It was thoroughly logical on Demitri's part, but all for naught now, of course.

Terrosi wondered if Demitri would try to cancel his commission now. If he did, would he still be willing to pay the full fee, or would he try to haggle for half? There was only one way to be sure. The final dosage would have to be administered today, before Demitri had a chance to speak with him alone.

Fumbling in his bag, the physician happened to glance up, and met the eyes of the assassin. The man was watching Terrosi with the same calculating gaze that the doctor had directed at the killer when he first entered the room. Bottle in hand, the doctor gave a small nod of recognition which was mirrored by his colleague. Then the assassin excused himself as Terrosi turned to his ministerings . . . two killers returning to their work.

FESTIVAL MOON
(REPRISED)

C.J. Cherryh

It was up and down the canals on foot by day, listen
to gossip; carry a little cargo by late afternoon, park
and listen. It was maddening how a man that tall and
blond and conspicuous could sink out of sight, but
there was no talk at all to tell her where he had gone,
it was all the business of the water and the rotten egg
smell and the rumor about the Janes and how the
blacklegs were stirring every which way hunting the
Jane from the bridge. Some said it was a Nev Hettek
plot to poison Merovingen. Some enterprising lander
had taken to selling pills he claimed for an antidote.
The Astronomer had gotten up on a podium up by
Golden Bridge, pronounced it a hoax, reeled off tide
statistics, and said the smell was only the seasonal
bloom worse than usual.

A priest from the College decried the shooting as
Adventist assassins and the stink as a diversion.

And thank the Lord and the Ancestors, Black Cal
and whoever else knew about those barrels had kept
mouths shut, for whatever reason.

So Jones prowled about glad enough it was a fine
coat of brown paint covering those new boards and
glad enough to have the skip smelling like bad beer
and spoiled grain.

But in all that stir, little rumors were hard come by,
and Mondragon was, she reckoned more and more,

gone to Boregy: that was the likeliest place a tall blond Falkenaer (folk supposed) who happened to be (rumor said) an unacknowledged Boregy—could hide himself with no one remarking on it.

She even poled past Boregy, just to see if it raised anything, but it did nothing, and there was no Mondragon, and no news.

She poled past the Signeury too, and even past the Justiciary, that hulking mass that bulked so grim by Archangel, and past the College, fretting and worrying and thinking of those terrible things the Justiciary had inside, and what happened to folk who went in there and did not come out again, except sometimes they floated up, when the Governor wanted to have the rumor out, and make an example.

She picked at dinner at Tesh's on Foundry—sometimes he came there.

But she figured finally that it had to be the Room. The Room was where he had left from, the Room was where he would come to, quietly, when he needed to find her.

Or when he knew he had damn well pushed her far enough and scared her enough and she would have his guts on a hook.

She slept once, maybe, in that expensive bed upstairs, on sheets sweat-soaked in a too-hot room, listening for every little sound, every creak of boards that might be a door about to open downstairs and him about to come in.

Then she would kill him.

But when the night-candle had burned down and she dressed, all bleary-eyed, and walked down to sip Jep's too-strong tea and eat Jep's eggs and toast:

"Hoooooo!" a voice said from the doorway. "They be floating this morning! Got four bodies from that shootup hung up down by Ramseyhead, got a skip dragging up some damn hightowner up by the Spur—"

Her heart stopped. She turned from the bar. She looked at the man, Teely, his name was, another skip-freighter. "Long dead?"

"Ney, pole hit the body. Damn fool hooked it

up—it's that damn Mergeser, prob'ly hunting a ring or two, ain't that him?—but some lander seen 'im, an' raised hell, don't know him, sure, but there was canalers by, ain't no doubt who it was."

"Man or woman?"

"Didn't say."

"Where?"

"Over by Mansur, hell, you know, where they always drift."

She shoved the plate away. She felt her heart like to burst her ribs. She walked quietly out the front door.

"Something ridin' Jones?" she heard at her back.

She kept going. She untied the skip, ran out the pole, and shoved off, hard, hard out into the Grand and up the long haul for Port, by the West branch at Mars. Her arms ached. Her blistered feet hurt worse. But the unladed skip moved; moved right along in the stagnant water, as far as Gallandry and Gallandry Cut, where there was a safe tie.

Then she left that dark hole for Gallandry Stair, bare feet pounding the boards.

Bolado Isle; Ciro; Novgorod, Yesudian, North— her heart was aching now. She saw the crowds that attended disaster to the rich. She saw the sleek police boats, the balconies and upper bridges of Mansur all full of onlookers.

"Who is it?" she asked someone, and had a shrug for answer.

"Who drowned?" she asked another one. She saw the body, draped in white, on the foredeck of the police boat below. But that was another shrug. She forced her way further, started down the steps and down onto the next level, and down again, canalside, the dangerous place, the place aswarm with blacklegs.

A hand grasped her shoulder. She spun around in fright, and stared right into Mondragon's pale face. "You—".

He jerked her into the stair-underpinnings, in amongst the pilings and supports, and shook her and stared at her. "Dammit, Jones!—"

"Where you been?" She hit his arm with her fist and broke free. "Where in *hell* you been?"

"What are you doing down here?"

"What are *you* doin' down here? Where you *been*, dammit, scare a body half to death—"

"They said a woman drowned. Said she had dark hair."

"They said it was a hightowner."

There was fright left in Mondragon's face. Pure panic, gone to relief. He gripped her arms, she gripped his. Maybe her face looked like his. She thought so.

Then: "You damn fool," he said. "Where did you tie-up?"

"Gallandry." She mostly had her breath now. The blacklegs were still swarming about. He was in his uptown clothes, fine coat, fine breeches. "Come on. I fetch ye home, dammit."

"Can't, like this. Sense, Jones, for God's sake, *sense*. Go on back, get back to Moghi's—I'll pick up my clothes, I'll be there."

"Like you was in *bed*, you sneak?"

"Were."

"I ain't going!"

"Get back to Moghi's!" he hissed. "Damn it, Jones, don't balk on me. I'll get the clothes, pick up some other stuff, and I'll be there—I have to talk to you. This time I need your help."

"*We* get the clothes," she said. "Hell, I'm a shipper, carry yer packages wherever ye like, ser—just gimme a silver, hey?—Or I follow you, damn your cheating hide, I follow you one end of this town to the next, how's that, hey?"

CAT'S TALE

Nancy Asire

The crowd inside Hilda's Tavern was loud and likely to get louder as the day wore on. The first few days before 24 Harvest were always this way: those whose natures were more subdued abandoned themselves to riotous living; those who lived in that state as a matter of course became wilder still.

From his seat at his usual table, one hand hooked in the handle of his beer mug, the other stroking the large, gold cat that lay curled up and purring in his lap, Justice Lee looked across his empty lunch plate at the revelers. On the opposite side of the room, Hilda Meier stood behind the bar, her heavy arms crossed, watching her customers with a wary eye. A fight had broken out a few hours ago and, from the expression on Hilda's face, she was not likely to stand for another one.

Justice grinned slightly: Hilda ruled her tavern and adjoining rooming house with an iron hand, and there were few foolhardy enough to take her on. He had been living in that rooming house on the backside of Kass now for two years, and had never seen Hilda slowed down by much of anything.

There were other students in the tavern, dressed in Festival best: dark blue, gray or brown shirts, a few sporting a yellow sash emblazoned with the seal of the College. This, and their comparative youth, set them apart from the other customers.

Several fellows of indeterminate origin, probably small shop owners, sat at the table to Justice's right. Revenantists all, they were discussing an earlier public ceremony they had attended. Justice frowned and looked away; he had attended the selfsame ceremony, going through the motions like all the rest, though his Adventist soul rebelled at the notion. But the one condition (save receiving high marks) his patron, Father Rhajmurti, set on his entry to the College had been that he convert.

Justice had considered that step for days, had discussed it with the Adventist aunt and uncle who were his legal guardians, and had finally agreed, knowing that conversion and were patronage was the key to hightown society where an artist could make a living.

"Justus!"

He looked to his left: a stocky young man was threading his way across the crowded tavern, a mug of beer in hand. Hightowner, this one, dressed in student garb. The slim sword at the fellow's left hip, the set of his shoulders and head, his very way of walking, screamed money and position. Justice lifted his mug in greeting as the other hooked a chair out from under the table with his toe and sat down.

"Where you off to, Krishna?" Justice asked.

Krishna's face darkened and his brown eyes took on a sorrowful expression. "Me? Nowhere. I haven't got a libby that I can spare. And where I'd *like* to go isn't free."

"Huhn. You paid off your dueling damages, eh?"

"Oh, yes. Took the last of my ready cash to do it, too. Papa refused to help me out again."

Justice leaned back in his chair, sipped at his beer and stroked the sleeping cat. Krishna Malenkov, youngest son of The Malenkovs of Martushev of Rimmon Isle, once more (seemingly) at odds with his father. Karma had seen to it that Krishna had been born to money and power, but Krishna's father was making sure his youngest learned the responsibility of his position.

"How am I supposed to enjoy the Festival with no money?" Krishna complained, staring down into his mug with a morose expression on his face. "*Everything* costs more these few days."

"Oh, well. There are still a few things you can do for free." Justice finished his beer and set the mug to one side. The large, gold cat stirred, tucked his head under one outflung front leg and sighed. "Surely you can find something that doesn't cost you money."

"I'd like to know what!" Krishna studied the cat a moment, then took another drink. "Now Sunny there," he said, gesturing toward the cat with his free hand. "I'll bet any number of people would pay plenty for a truly domesticated cat! Plenty, don't you think?"

Justice shrugged. "I suppose so. But Hilda's got this one."

"Oh, yes, doesn't she. Fairly dotes on him, along with all the other half-wild cats she feeds." Krishna rubbed the end of his nose and peered down into his nearly empty mug. "And here I sit, Festival upon me, without the money to go where I want to, or do what I want to do. You'd think Papa could at least spare a demi."

"Huhn." Justice tried to look sympathetic. He and Krishna had rooms across the hall from each other in Hilda's rooming house, which made them acquaintances. Krishna complaining about his lack of funds was beginning to be a bore. It was always the same story: Krishna spent what allowance his father sent him nearly as fast as it came into his hands.

"Hey, I thought I'd find you here, Krishna!"

A thin, dark-headed student leaned on their table, nodded briefly in Justice's direction, and turned back to Krishna.

"I'm going to the Grand to watch the boat parade. Are you interested? We could stop in a few of the bars uptown after."

Pavel Suhakai was another of the moneyed students at the College; he and Krishna had grown up together (both their parents living on Rimmon Isle),

and often went to the places only those with capital
and connections could go.

"I have no money!" Krishna muttered. "I spent
the last of my ready cash paying off that damned
bar."

"Ah, the duel." Pavel took a chair. "Cost you a
bundle, eh?"

Justice took the opportunity for what it was worth
and shoved his chair back from the table. "Sorry to
run. I've got to get some fresh air. Will I be seeing
you later?"

Krishna shrugged. "I'll probably be sitting here
when you get back, unless a shower of gold falls on
me from the ceiling."

Justice smiled, lifted the limp, relaxed cat from his
lap and stood. "You'll figure out something, Krishna.
You always do." He set Sunny down in his empty
chair, scratched the cat behind the ears, and started
toward the door.

And nearly ran into a group of blacklegs who
filled it.

A pall of silence settled over the tavern. Justice
stepped back from the door and stood leaning up
against the wall, keeping his stance as relaxed as
possible. He saw Hilda stiffen behind the bar; Guy
the bartender moved uncertainly a few steps toward
Hilda, his thin face going through a raft of expres-
sions, finally settling on one of interested innocence.

The blacklegs, on the other hand, seemed to be
satisfied with a brief look at the occupants of the
tavern—two of them exchanged a few hushed words,
then they all turned and hurried off.

A murmur of conversation flowed into the void
they left. Justice straightened, drew a deep breath
and glanced across the room at Krishna and Pavel.
The two of them sat close together at the table now,
their heads nearly touching, whispering to one another like nearly all of Hilda's customers.

The blacklegs had been stirred up lately, a fact
everyone in Merovingen was aware of. What no one
seemed able to agree on was *why*, never mind the
hightowner drowned by Mansur. Festival might ac-

count for some of it: there was always trouble of one sort or another at this time of year, but the high profile the law maintained was unusual, even for Festival time.

Justice shook his head, turned and walked out of the door to Hilda's Tavern, and stood for a moment on the wooden balcony-walkway. He leaned up against the railing and looked off across the canal to the large mass to the southwest.

The Pile, everyone called it. A rock used as a connection point for bridges leading from it to Kass, Spellbridge and Bent. A three-tiered stairway, honey-combed with tiny shops, benches for sitting, and platforms where people could meet and talk. And standing on the second tier at the moment was a large group of blacklegs.

He shook his head again and set off toward Borg Bridge. It was axiomatic: in Merovingen, death of a most painful and gruesome sort often followed sticking one's nose into others' business.

Borg Bridge stood at the far end of Kass, three-tiered like many of the bridges in Merovingen. Justice took his time, walking slowly among the crowds on the Kass second-level walkway. Here was a true meeting of all three worlds: the under-city of canals, docks, wharfs and less savory places; the middle-city of small but prosperous residences and businesses; and the upper-city, that rarified world of those with money enough to afford a place that actually saw the sky.

Justice walked along, mingling with denizens of all three levels, though those of the upper city were rarer. He paused as he reached the edge of Borg Bridge and sought a place to sit down out of the line of traffic.

Out on the walkways, the sights and sounds and odors of Merovingen were overwhelming. And at Festival time, the ribbons and banners that decked the buildings and bridges added to the riot of color humanity provided. People called to one another, hucksters shouted their wares, and the steady beat of footsteps on wooden planks ran an *ostinato* beneath. Warm weather and a slight breeze wafted the ripe smells of the canals below to shops and residences above. Right before the bridge began, a fried-fish seller had set up his stand; a sweetseller stood across the way. People stopped periodically and bought themselves a treat and wandered off again, in search of excitement. Justice smiled at the frenetic scene, for it was home to him and loved.

His pocket sketchbook was always handy, along with drawing implements, in a small pouch at his side. Selecting a seat right up against the bridgehead, partially hidden from passersby, Justice took out sketchbook and pencil, chose another resting citizen at random, and began to draw.

Then, a familiar voice intruded on his concentration. Lowering his pencil, he glanced up from his brief sketch. There, not more than a few paces away, walking past him toward the Grand Canal, was Krishna Malenkov, accompanied by his friend, Pavel— Krishna with a large heavy cloth bag in his arms.

And, looking out of that bag, feline face bearing an expression of bewildered contempt, was Hilda's cat.

"Sunny!" Justice closed his sketchbook, shoved it and his pencil into his belt-pouch, and stood. Sunny's plaintive meows drifted over the noise of the bridge. What the hell was Krishna doing with Sunny?

Krishna and Pavel disappeared down the Borg Bridge and, hesitating only a moment, Justice started off after them.

The bridge was crowded, most of the traffic headed toward Borg; once across Borg, one came to the Grand Canal. As the first cross-over to the Grand from the upper-class neighborhood on the north end of the lagoon, the bridge leading from Kass to Borg was heavily traveled—at Festival time, always jammed, and today was no exception. Justice hurried along, trying to keep Krishna and Pavel in view, weaving in and out of other walkers, of standing groups of talking revelers, and staggering drunks.

He lost sight of his fellow students, but spotted them again over the heads of the crowd.

A wide walkway led through the heart of Borg and, like the bridge, it was crowded. Justice nearly lost sight of Krishna and Pavel again. He kept his pace set to theirs, hanging back from them in the seething mass of people, not willing yet to be seen. He chewed on his lower lip and clenched his hands. The entire thing *could* be legitimate.

The hell it was.

Justice tagged along behind Krishna and Pavel, trying to look like any other person out for Festival. No one seemed to be paying any attention to him. In front of a furniture maker's shop, a knot of people had gathered around a thin wisp of a man who was addressing anyone who stopped to listen. The crowd appeared composed of drunks and other aimless folk; the speaker must have had some entertainment value, for no one had run him off yet. Justice frowned and quickened his pace. An Adventist trying to stir up the crowd? Huhn. Best to keep moving.

Krishna and Pavel reached the druggist's shop at the far end of Borg and continued on. Justice cursed and stopped for a moment, his heart lurching, and a smallish fellow, well into his cups, bumped into him.

" 'Scuse me, ser," the man said.

Justice nodded, stepped aside, but the fellow moved in exactly the same direction.

"Damn!" Justice fended the drunken man off—the fellow seemed determined to step into the way again. Abandoning manners, he shoved the shorter man aside, and glanced frantically around for Krishna.

Lord and my Ancestors! If I lose them now, I'll never find them!

No. There they were—crossing Junction Bridge that ran from Borg across to White, on canalside and mid-level. Justice dodged traffic and quickened his pace.

Where was Krishna going? He was certainly not heading home, for even if he had been inclined to walk, he would have turned right to go over to

Bucher. The image of Sunny's puzzled face flashed in Justice's mind, and he increased his pace again.

Junction Bridge was even more crowded than Borg, though the throng that jammed it was mostly stationary, come for the late afternoon boat parade, Grandside. The steady din of footsteps on the wooden planking had faded to the sound of his own bootheels and those of the few others who walked back and forth across the bridge.

Krishna and Pavel stopped a moment, conferred hastily, and then went off the bridge onto White. Justice followed, slouching a bit. Most of Merovingen's people were of medium build, but his English ancestry made him taller than many he met. Thank the Ancestors he at least had black hair.

He was on White now, an upper-class isle. Krishna and Pavel turned left and, committed now to seeing what was to become of Sunny, Justice had no choice but to follow. His heart started beating heavily: whatever Krishna had up his sleeve did not bode well for Hilda's cat.

Oh, damn! Now what do I do? Krishna's got a temper and that sword he's wearing's not there for show. And Pavel doesn't like me anyway. What's one more accident at Festival?

He licked his lips, squared his shoulders and walked on.

Escape, Sunny! he whispered inwardly. *Get the hell out of that bag and run for it!*

Krishna and Pavel had stopped now; Justice kept on a few more steps and then came to a halt. His two fellow students were talking to a gatewarden who stood before a closed doorway leading to White's upper-level stairs. The gatewarden smiled, nodded a few times, then opened the gate and waved Krishna and Pavel through.

Justice stared, his heart sinking down to his boots. For where Krishna and Pavel had just gone, a student like himself would find it hard to follow.

Justice faced the stairway and the gate that had not slowed down Krishna or his companion in the least. He shrugged, straightened his shirt, and walked purposefully over to the gate.

"Excuse me, ser," he said in his best hightown accent. "Have two students been through here recently?"

The gatewarden, a burly fellow who sported a drooping mustache, eyed Justice for a moment. "Why would you be wanting to know?"

"I'm trying to catch up to them." Justice smiled in what he trusted was a disarming fashion. "We're all getting together for a party before the boat parade. I was late setting off, and they told me to follow."

"Oh?" The gatewarden leaned against the wall of the fabric shop against which the gate and stairs had been built. "And who might these two gentlemen be you say you're to meet up there?" The last words with a significant lift of the heavy-jowled chin.

Justice sighed, keeping his expression utterly polite. "Look, I know you're only doing your duty, but I *am* in a hurry. It was Krishna Malenkov of Martushev Isle and Pavel Suhakai of Takezawa. Now have they been through here, or did I get the wrong directions?"

The gatewarden blinked a few times, obviously set back by Justice's ability to name names, and by his refined manner and upper-level speech. "And your name, ser?" he asked, obviously convinced now he was talking with someone who had a right to ascend that stairway.

Justice flinched inwardly: there was no hope for it now. The gatewarden could call in the law if he felt the situation warranted. "Justice Lee of Lindsey," he said, not bothering to mention that it was second-level Lindsey, not upper.

"Huhn." The gatewarden thought it over. "All right, m'ser. Pass through. Them two students you're hunting for can't be more than a few minutes ahead."

"My thanks," Justice said, relief weakening his knees. He bowed slightly as the gatewarden opened the doorway to the stairs. "Good karma to you!"

The gatewarden blinked at the Revenantist blessing. "With a name like yours, m'ser," he grinned, revealing a gap-toothed jaw, "I'd've thought you was Adventist."

Justice smiled. "J-U-S-T-U-S," he said. "Happy Festival."

And with that, keeping his steps firm and deliberate, Justice began climbing the stairs. Behind him, he heard the gate close, a heavy sound, bleak in its finality.

Halfway up the stairs and out of sight of the gatewarden, he stopped for a moment and leaned against the wall. Now what the hell was he to do? Here he was, headed toward the upper-level neighborhood of an isle he had never visited, in pursuit of two denizens of Merovingen-above who more than belonged there. He took a deep breath, straightened his shirt once more, and headed on up.

And stood blinking in the sunlight.

Sunlight everywhere, even this late in the afternoon. And sky. He threw back his head and looked up at the vast blue vault above him. Even though he inhabited the second level, and not the lower hell of canalside, open sky was something he rarely ever saw. He glanced down at the residences around him, at the broad walkway that ran between them. There were few people out here, and those went dressed in hightown best, velvets and silks, in colors those with less funds could never afford.

The entire spectacle, quiet and refined though it was, dazzled him, though he dare not let that show. He stopped gawking and looked down the walkway. There! He caught sight of Krishna and Pavel not all that far in front of him and, trying to appear nonchalant, followed after them.

A tall man, near his own height, passed him going off toward Boregy Bridge. Justice could not help staring. The fellow was conspicuous, being fair of skin and dressed in clothing befitting a minor aristocrat. The very blondness of the man's hair would have made him hard to forget. Not more than two steps behind went a dark-skinned girl of about sixteen or seventeen, her arms loaded down with packages, canaler's cap thrust back on her head. Her bare feet padded near soundlessly on the wooden walk-way as she shifted her load on the run.

Justice looked quickly away, afraid of missing Krishna and Pavel, but they had stopped before one of the houses of White's upper level. Justice stood for a moment undecided and chewed on a trouble-some hangnail. He had two choices: he could con-front Krishna, demanding to know what he was doing with Hilda's cat, or he could stay far enough away that he could at least tell what was going on. He glanced around—there were fewer people out now than when he had left the stairs, and confronting Krishna on a level where he and Pavel belonged could be a bad idea.

To say nothing of deadly.

With a shrug, Justice sat down on a bench at the far end of the building where Krishna and Pavel stood. Neither of them had noticed him, a bit of luck if nothing else. With so few places to hide, now that he was away from the shadows below, Justice could only hope that luck held.

It was quiet here, so much quieter than the levels below. Justice closed his eyes briefly and listened. Ancestors! What a peaceful place to live! He opened his eyes again as he heard the door to the large house open and Krishna answering the questions of the doorman.

Then Krishna lifted the bag that held Sunny, turn-ing it from one side to the other. The cat's meows were more strident now, pitiful in pitch. Justice half-rose from his position on the bench, a flush of anger warming his face.

And what can you do about it, Justice Lee? Rush right up and call Krishna a thieving liar? Here? On White? Where he obviously knows the household? He laughed bitterly. *Damn, fellow! They'd throw you off the edge into the Grand quicker than quick!*

The doorman gestured, stepped back and Krishna, Pavel and the howling Sunny disappeared inside the house.

The door slammed shut and Justice was left alone in the afternoon sunlight.

* * *

For a long while Justice stared at the closed door, knowing that events had just passed his ability to alter them. There was nothing, save pounding on that doorway and accusing Krishna of being a thief, that he could do except leave. He thought of poor Sunny in that rich house. Not that Sunny's life would be an unhappy one. He would be fed the choicest foods, sleep on a bed finer than many humans in Merovingen could boast, and be coddled near to death. Tamed cats were a rarity uptown folk would spend good money to own.

Justice sighed, took several long breaths, and turned back toward the stairs leading down to the second level of White. His bootheels hollow on the wooden steps, he slowly descended the stairs. The gatewarden turned at the noise of footsteps, got up from his stool and opened the gate.

"Missed 'em, did ye?" he asked, stepping back as Justice came through the gate. "Didn't think they was all *that* far ahead."

Justice thought frantically. "They were in a hurry, I guess," he said, pausing by the gatewarden's side when every instinct screamed *run!* "They probably crossed over to Boregy or Eber. They never told me which isle they were going to, only that I should follow." He shrugged. "I suppose I don't have a choice. I'll meet them later at the boat parade."

"Now that's always a sight," the gatewarden said, closing the gate and locking it. He straightened. "Hope you find your friends and have a good time, m'ser."

"Thanks."

Now that he was on the second level again, back in the shadowed walkways, Justice could understand why hightowners thought Merovingen-below oppressive. He walked over to the edge of Junction Bridge, found an unoccupied spot, and leaned back against the railing. Looking down at his feet, he sighed quietly.

And now what are you going to do? Short of stealing Sunny, there's not much chance of getting him back. He rubbed the end of his nose. Without Sunny around, Hilda's Tavern would seem empty.

"Hey, you! Student!"

The rough voice jerked Justice out of his thoughts, and he looked up from his feet to find himself surrounded by blacklegs.

"What are you doing?" one of them demanded, fingering the hilt of his stick.

An angry retort on the tip of his tongue, Justice looked from that man to his companions and back, setting his face to an expression of puzzled indignation.

"Waiting for the boat parade to begin, sir," he replied, keeping his voice carefully neutral. "Should I be standing here?"

"Thought he was drunk," muttered a woman who stood at the rear of the group of blacklegs. "Drugged, even."

"No." The leader glanced around as he spoke, seeming preoccupied and not really all that interested in what he was doing. "All right, boy. Thought you were someone else."

Thought I was someone else? Hah! Likely story! Damned eels! What are you really after?

"No damage done," Justice said, using his best hightown speech. The blackleg flinched slightly, hearing the accents of the privileged. "Have a good Festival."

The blackleg mumbled something, gestured curtly at his men, and turned away, heading off down the second level of White. Justice stared after, his heart beating loudly in his ears. Something was going on, something with a capital S. He could not remember having seen the law this stirred up in a long time.

Now there was a thought. He could always tell Hilda. Turn Krishna in to the blacklegs for the thief he was. No. Whose story would they believe? Krishna's or his? Besides, if a hint of any trouble reached White, the family who lived in that lordly house, being more than likely adverse to involvement with the law, could always insist the cat had been theirs for years.

Justice sighed again and, no longer interested in the boat parade, turned back toward Kass, walking down the Borg esplanade and hardly seeing those he passed. Sunny was gone. The only thing he *could* do now was to tell Hilda what had happened to her cat, leaving Krishna's punishment in her hands. After all, it was *her* cat, not his.

And then what? Krishna would not let this pass unnoticed and Justice had seen first hand how proficient the young Malenkov was with the rapier he wore. *Dammit! You're no duellist! He'd skewer you like a fish on a spear.*

And yet—

Justice, he chided himself. *You love that cat near as much as she does, and you know it. You don't have a choice. You've got to tell her!*

But what could Hilda do? Go to the law? Justice snorted a laugh. He was right back where he had started from. She could always throw Krishna out of the rooming house, explaining to his father why she had taken such an action. Now that was the best idea of all. Yuri Malenkov was known all over Merovingen as being one of the most honest merchants trading on the Det and overseas. To know that his son was not only a liar, but a thief—

Justice drew up sharply, nearly running down the fried-fish seller who had moved down into Borg; the afternoon nearly over, the fellow had packed up his stand and was headed for home.

"Sorry," Justice muttered, stepping around the little man and continuing on his way toward Borg Bridge and home.

"Damn drunken students!" the fellow growled after. "Think they own the place, they do!"

Bootheels echoing on the crowded bridge, Justice started across to Kass, a thousand ideas of vengeance flitting through his mind. Things he would like to do to Krishna. To all those individuals whose money and connections made them think themselves above others.

Control your temper, idiot! A fine line of thinking for a convert!

Yet where, by the Lord and everyone's fool Ancestors, did a cat and the selling of that cat, fit on the ever balancing scales of Revenantist karma?

*   *   *

The lights inside Hilda's Tavern had already been
lit, for on the backside of the second level of Kass,
blocked from the west by Spellbridge, evening fell
sooner than elsewhere. Justice paused at the doorway, hearing the familiar rumble of conversation
and laughter, and studied the crowd inside. None of
the revelers of midday were present; it was a new
group, one even noisier, who had been in their cups
longer, and who cared less.

And there, sitting at Justice's usual table, was Father
Rhajmurti, his saffron shirt bright in the lamplight.

Justice waved to Hilda who was occupied with
explaining something quite serious to Anna the cook,
and walked over to the table, secretly glad he did
not have to tell Hilda about Sunny yet. Father
Rhajmurti pulled back a chair, gestured Justice to it,
and signaled Guy for another mug of beer.

"So, how is your holiday going?" Rhajmurti asked
once Justice had seated himself. "Are you glad to be
away from the books for a while?"

"Holidays are always welcome," Justice murmured,
waiting for Guy to give the mug to Jason, who brought
it to the table. Nodding thanks to the waiter, Justice
took a long swallow, only now realizing how thirsty
he had been.

"All right, Justice." Rhajmurti's black eyes glinted
in the lamplight. "What's the matter?"

Justice blinked. "What's the matter, what?"

"Something's bothering you. After all these years,
don't think you can hide it from me."

"I should've known better," Justice said, rubbing
the tip of one finger around the rim of his mug. "I
got a problem, Father, and I suppose you can at least
listen to me, if nothing else."

Rhajmurti cocked his head, his bright eyes taking
on an expression of extreme curiosity. "A problem
regarding what? Your schooling? Karma? Your social life?"

"Huhn. What social life students are allowed." Justice tried to laugh, but it came out wrong. "It's

Krishna, Father. He's stolen Hilda's cat and sold him to one of the families on White."

"Sold Sunny?" Rhajmurti's eyebrows rose. "How do you know?"

"I saw it all, Father. All of it! He—"

"Wait a moment. Before you get launched, let's have dinner, eh? I'll buy."

Justice nodded, thankful for the time to get his events in proper order. Rhajmurti called Jason over to the table and ordered two meals of Hilda's best fish. As Jason left, the priest gestured to Justice to continue the story.

And so, sparing no detail, Justice related the entire sequence of events, from Krishna's complaining about being moneyless at Festival time, to seeing Krishna and Pavel Suhakai enter the house on White's upper level, Sunny howling in the bag Krishna carried.

"This," said Rhajmurti, "is serious, not only for the karma Krishna's taken on his soul—but because the law could eventually be drawn into it."

"Frankly, I wish they would be, Father. I'd love nothing more than to see that—"

"Now, now. He'll end up paying in his own way without the law to help him along." Rhajmurti's eyes focused behind Justice's right shoulder. "Ah, Hilda. We were just talking about you."

Justice's heart did a flip in his chest and he looked up into Hilda Meier's broad, ruddy face.

"Oh? All good, I'm sure."

"Naturally. Justus has something he wants to tell you, I think."

Hilda wiped her hands on her apron front, pulled out another chair and sat down with a sigh. "Been one blasted long day," she said. "Be glad to see it over." She turned her blue-eyed gaze on Justice. "Yes . . . what'd ye want to tell me?"

Justice swallowed heavily. "It's Sunny, ma'am. Krishna stole him and sold him on White."

For a long moment Hilda was silent, then the ghost of a smile touched her mouth. "This afternoon? I'd wondered where Sunny'd got to."

Justice stared. Of all the reactions Hilda could

have evidenced, this was the last one he expected. Hilda, to put things mildly, was short of temper, and her rages were notorious. Now, faced with the theft and sale of her cat, she accepted the fact with little more than a shrug.

"But, ma'am . . . Sunny's been *sold!* We may never get him back!"

Hilda's smile was genuine this time, a smile that softened the harsh lines of her face. "Krishna'll end up paying for this 'un in the long run, Justus. Dishonesty like that carries a lot of karma. Don't worry. Everything'll work out all right." She straightened in her chair and stood. "Well, time's flying. I got to get back to work. And the two of ye got yer dinners coming."

Hilda was right, for Jason came across the room, two plates and two mugs on a tray he balanced with ease above his head. As Hilda set off back toward the bar, Jason laid out the meal, set the mugs alongside the plates, and returned to his station by the kitchen door.

"Eat up, son," Rhajmurti said, lifting his fork and cutting off several large bites of the excellently prepared razorfin. "You're thin enough as it is."

Justice looked back to his plate from staring after Hilda's retreating figure. Revenantists! He would much rather *help* karma along in Krishna's case. He shrugged, and started his dinner.

Rhajmurti seemed to want silence as he ate, so Justice obliged, washing down the bites of fish with what proved to be some of Hilda's best beer. Thank the Lord Rhajmurti was picking up the tab; this was one meal he would have thought more than twice about buying.

Justice was nearly finished when a familiar voice drifted over the conversations around him. He stiffened in his chair and looked off across the room.

Krishna!

Back from selling Sunny, seeming unaware what he had done had been witnessed, Krishna was in high good humor. He and Pavel had taken a table close to the bar and Krishna was busy telling his friend what the two of them could do for entertainment. He had bought himself and Pavel the best wine in the house and was loudly ordering one of the most expensive dinners Hilda served. Justice's jaw clenched and he looked down at his plate, trying to curb his anger.

It was no use. The more he thought about what Krishna had done, the angrier he got, and he could stand it no longer. Slamming his fork down beside his plate, he shoved his chair back and stood.

"Justice," Rhajmurti said quietly, catching at his sleeve. "Don't do anything you'll regret later."

Both Krishna and Pavel had taken off their swords to eat dinner. Justice glanced down at Rhajmurti. "Stay out of this, please, Father. This is between Krishna and me!"

Justice left the table, threaded his way between the two other drinkers and diners, and came up at Krishna's side.

"Well, Justus," Krishna said, looking up from his drink. "I didn't see you over there. Will you join us?"

"Later, perhaps. Will you do me a favor?"

"What?"

"Come out front and I'll tell you."

"Oh. All right." Krishna turned to Pavel and waved at the table. "Hold things down for me here, will you? I'll be right back."

Justice turned away and walked across the room and out the front door, hearing Krishna come along behind. Once outdoors:

"What can I do for you, Justus?" Krishna asked, still in good humor. "Do you need a loan?"

"Where did *you* come up with the cash?"

"Oh—" Krishna's gaze wandered "—I have ways."

"I'll bet you have lots of them," Justice said. "But in this case, I think your benefactor was a cat."

Krishna stared, his face going a bit pale in the lamplight. "Whatever are you talking about?"

"Sunny. And you damned well know what I'm talking about, you lying sneak! How the hell could you sell Sunny like that? You're no better than the scum down at Megary!"

"Now you just wait a moment," Krishna said, drawing himself up to his full height. It did him no good, for Justice overtopped him by at least a hand. "Who do you think you're talking to? Nobody calls a Malenkov a lying sneak!"

"All right," Justice said equably. "You're a lying thief!"

Krishna's right hook came so suddenly that Justice barely had time to dodge. *O Lord and my Ancestors! Not a fight! That's the last thing I need!* He struck back, catching the younger man square on the chin, feeling the force of his blow all the way up to his shoulder.

Krishna staggered back and grabbed for his sword, but he had left it inside at the table. He snarled something best unheard, leapt at Justice, shoved him off his feet and landed right on top of him. The wind knocked out of him, Justice struggled against Krishna's surprising strength, trying to get some kind of hold on his opponent.

"Fight! Fight! Hilda! You got a fight on your hands!"

Justice thought he recognized the voice but was too busy warding off Krishna's wild punches and connecting with his own to bother guessing who it was.

"A silverbit on the tall 'un!" someone called out.

"Done! And I'll raise ye a half!"

Damned fools! Justice narrowly avoided a knee to his groin, finally got one leg hooked between Krishna's and slowly began turning him over onto his back.

To see in front of him, not more than three steps away, the black-stockinged legs of the law.

Justice stood somewhat unsteadily on his feet and wiped at the blood oozing from the corner of his mouth. Krishna was in worse shape, his jaw swollen and a black eye beginning to form. But it was small comfort to have beaten Krishna, for now they both stood backed up against the wall outside Hilda's Tavern, five blacklegs facing them, riot sticks in their hands.

"Ma'am?"

The voice came from Justice's right. He risked a

sidelong look: Father Rhajmurti had pushed his way forward through the gathered crowd and stood facing the sergeant, a tall, dark woman who looked set on no further foolishness from anyone. Motioning for her men to keep Justice and Krishna in line, she turned toward the priest, nodding in respect.

"Yes, ser?"

"I'll speak for both lads. They're students of mine. If you'll recognize the authority of the College, I'll take them into my custody."

Justice's heart leapt. He glanced at Rhajmurti, then back at the sergeant.

She considered the priest's offer for a moment. "Yer name, Father, so I c'n list it on my report?"

"Rhajmurti, Alfonso Rhajmurti. Initiated at Third Level; instructor of fine arts."

"Huhn." The hint of a smile tugged at her mouth. "More likely instructor in martial arts t'judge by these two." She took a small notebook and pencil from her pocket, and wrote down Rhajmurti's name. "All right, Father. I'll release them to yer custody. But I got to take their names."

"Justice Lee and Krishna Malenkov. J-U-S-T-U-S."

The sergeant's right eyebrow rose slightly as she jotted down the names, but she refrained from any comment. Flipping the notebook closed, she turned to Justice and Krishna. "Ye heard the man, gentlemen. Ye're damned lucky he came along, or it would've been a trip to the Signeury for both of ye. Ye're free now, in his custody. And I don't want to see neither of ye in trouble again this Festival, or even the father here won't keep ye out of the Signeury. Hear?"

"Yes, ma'am," Justice mumbled, wiping at his mouth again. He glanced sidelong at Krishna and elbowed him.

"I hear you, ma'am," Krishna said.

"Good. Don't forget it." She shoved the notebook in her pocket, motioned for her men to follow her, and started off down the walkway toward Borg.

Now the interested crowd began to disperse, those who had been passing by headed off about their business, and Hilda's customers headed back inside to theirs. Justice kept his eyes on his feet, not willing to look Rhajmurti in the face.

"All right," Rhajmurti said quietly. "We have a problem here and that problem's a missing cat."

Krishna glared. "Damn you, Justus!"

"I didn't tell your father, did I?"

"Quiet!" Rhajmurti snapped. "We'll never get this solved if the two of you start fighting again. Krishna, do you think you can buy Sunny back?"

Krishna swallowed heavily. "I don't know," he mumbled.

"You'd best hope you can,'" Rhajmurti said. "You've already collected quite a bit of karma today, young man, and will likely collect more in school after the holidays. You understand what I'm saying, don't you?"

"Oh, yes. Quite."

"How much did you sell Sunny for?"

"A demi, sir."

Justice groaned inwardly. A demi was a lot of money; to Krishna, it was the price of an evening of high entertainment. But Sunny was worth far more and, had Krishna appeared in all ways to be the cat's legitimate owner, he could have probably gotten a sol out of the deal.

"I see. Well, let's get going. I want us back here before nightfall."

"Where?" Krishna asked.

Rhajmurti looked him in the face. Krishna ducked his head, and led the way down toward Borg Bridge.

Justice followed after, rubbing his knuckles, still itching to pitch Kirshna into the canal. "If they won't sell Sunny back— "

"Things could get messy everywhere," Rhajmurti said, "very messy indeed."

"Buy the cat back?" The doorman at the hightown house on White appeared quite surprised to be facing two students, one of whom he had met earlier in the afternoon, along with a priest of the College. "Why, m'ser, I don't think that's possible."

Krishna looked stricken and glanced at Rhajmurti.

"But it was a mistake," he said to the doorman, spreading his hands in appeal. "I've got to right it."

"Well, I'm afraid you'll have to right it somewhere else. The Mistress is very happy with the cat."

"But if I can't buy the cat back, I'll—"

"I *said*," the doorman glowered, "the Mistress is *very* happy with the cat. Now, if you'll be good enough to leave, I—"

"Precious!" a woman shrieked. A golden blur rushed through the doorman's legs and headed down the walkway.

"Get that cat!" the doorman bellowed. "Hurry! He'll be hell to find again!"

Justice reacted without thinking and ran. Behind him, he heard the doorman yelling and Krishna exhorting him on. A few aristocratic passersby paused in open-mouthed wonder. Justice dodged a woman, called back an apology, and kept up the chase.

Sunny, meanwhile, headed directly for the second level stairs, gaining ground as he went. Justice stumbled once, his breath rasping in his throat. "Dammit, Sunny! Come back here! It's me, Justice! I'm trying to take you home!"

But the last thing on Sunny's mind was listening— even if the voice was Justice's: he tore down the stairs in a flash of a gold tail. Panting, Justice hooked a hand on the railing, swung around the corner and pelted down after, just in time to see Sunny disappear through the bars on the gateway to the walkway beyond.

His heel caught on a step, and grabbing the railing, Justice caught himself before he tumbled to the bottom.

"What's going on here?"

Justice looked up, rubbing his ankle; the gatewarden was staring at him, his expression halfway between amusement and anger.

"Lost a cat," Justice panted. "It belonged to one of Krishna's friends on White."

"Huhn." The gatewarden turned to stare off down the walkway. "Well, m'ser, you c'n kiss that cat goodbye. He's gone, for sure."

Gone. But where? Justice cringed. Merovingen was not the most hospitable place for a loose cat. Sunny might fall into the hands of someone far less friendly than the rich lady of White.

He shook his head and turned back up the stairway, nursing his twisted ankle as he climbed. It took him a while to walk back to the Uptown house, and by the time he reached Rhajmurti and Krishna, the student and the doorman were involved in a violent, escalating argument.

"I refuse!" Krishna exploded. "*Refuse!* I'll give you a demi back for him. Not a libby more."

"M'ser," the doorman said stiffly, "this entire thing could be turned over to the law, you know. Since my Mistress no longer has her cat and the chances of finding him again are next to none, I repeat my demand for an additional gram to cover her pain and suffering."

"*Her* pain and suffering!" Krishna yelled. "What about mine! I haven't *got* it!"

"As I said, there's always the law."

Krishna cast an agonized look at Father Rhajmurti but the priest remained inscrutable.

Justice stood close by, his knees still shaking from the run, and his ankle beginning to throb. Suddenly— an idea . . . a true inspiration. *Damn! You've got him, man . . . got that rich bastard right where you want him.*

"How much of that demi did you spend, Krishna?" he asked.

"Uhh . . . two grams. Dinner and drinks at Hilda's."

Three grams, counting the additional punitive gram the doorman demanded. Justice calculated swiftly. He had always lived frugally and saved quite a bit from his monthly allowance. Three grams would hardly give Krishna pause under normal circumstances. But these circumstances were far from normal.

"I'll lend you the money," Justice said.

Krishna stared. "You? Me borrow money from you?"

"There's always the law," the doorman repeated.

Justice smiled smugly. There were only two choices

Krishna could make: he could send to his father for the money, having to explain *why* he needed it; or he could take the money Justice offered, and the karma.

"I'll take it."

"Such gratitude," Justice said, digging inside the deep inner pocket of his shirt. He came up with one gram, then two more. The silver caught the fading sunlight as he extended the money to Krishna.

Krishna meanwhile had found what remained of the demi he had received for Sunny. He reached for Justice's three grams, combined the two sums, then extended the total to the doorman.

The doorman counted the coins, nodded briefly and turned to Rhajmurti. "I'm not even going to ask what happened here," he said, "but as a priest of the College I hope you'll note that both parties are satisfied. My Mistress has her money back and m'ser has no cat to resell."

Rhajmurti nodded and the doorman bowed slightly to Krishna, turned and shut the door behind him.

"I'll pay you back, Justus," Krishna growled. His brown eyes glinted in the dimming light. "A Malenkov always pays his debts."

He stalked off then, leaving Justice and Rhajmurti to follow slowly.

It was chill and fully dark when Justice and Rhajmurti returned to Hilda's Tavern. Beneath the sadness he felt over the loss of Sunny, Justice admitted he was rather pleased at having Krishna in karmic debt.

The warmth indoors was welcome, even after the brisk walk. Justice stopped and stood blinking in the bright light, Rhajmurti at his side. Then, he stared in disbelief.

There, sitting in an empty chair at Justice's usual table, was Hilda's large gold cat. Justice glanced at Rhajmurti, then looked back again. But Sunny seemed totally unconcerned by the afternoon's events and, lifting his front paw, set about taking a leisurely bath.

Hilda came from behind the bar, a wide grin on her ruddy face.

"There now . . . ye see? I told ye."

Justice looked back at Sunny.

Hilda laughed and patted Justice on the cheek. "Sweet lad to have worriet so— But do ye honestly think this is the first time one of my roomers has tried to sell ol' Sunny?" She smiled fondly and looked over at her cat, who was now busy with a rear leg. "That there's the cat that always comes back."

FESTIVAL MOON
(REPRISED)

C.J. Cherryh

The lamps and lanterns were out again, gliding along the black water below Boregy's tall windows, and that was an unaccustomed view for a canal-rat to have from the inside of those windows outward.

Unaccustomed too, the feel of the tight long trousers and the silk on her shoulders and the way Mondragon's hands smoothed down it. It was a scary kind of thing, like coming in here in the first place, up to the big bedroom with the huge bed and the fancy bathroom with its brass toilet—even his hands felt scary, like they wanted something more than she had, reminding her of lessons and lessons and lessons and she could never remember when it was isn't and when it was aren't and how to walk with one foot in front of the other like hightowners walked and not fall out of the damned slippers.

Them she had kicked off. They hurt.

And she felt a damn fool.

"You going to talk to me?" she asked, ignoring the hands. "You going to answer me?"

Where he had been was not the question. It was Boregy, proper enough, with her skip clear across town in Gallandry Cut, with everything she owned in all the world.

But Mondragon called this safer.

"They have their excuse now," he said. "There'll

be blacklegs from one end of town to the other. They'll harass every Adventist house in town—Gallandry, Mantovan—right down to the little ones."

"You saying that's my fault."

"No. I'm not." He turned her around and the damned slick blouse slid half open in front, but he had her hands and he was looking in her eyes, not there. "I'm saying it's an excuse and they'd have made one. Festival time and all that goes on out there—they could well have made one. Maybe they did."

"Well, what're ye doing *here*, f'God's sake?" She freed her arms and buttoned up to the collar. "What're we going to come here for, why we going to talk to *him*, when ye don't know it ain't damn Anastasi himself come hunting you?"

"I thought of it. Believe me. But there's nowhere to hide, then, is there?"

"Ye got the canals, ye got—"

"I had no choice . . . but to come here. To be loyal to one side." He touched her chin softly and rolled his eyes up and about, sending a little chill down her back. She straightened her collar, thinking of watchers and listeners. And being a damn fool again, talking out.

"Yey, well—"

"Put your shoes on."

It was down the hallway full of electrics that spent a canaler's week's take every little while they burned; it was into a little room full of books, true books; and a table, and Anastasi Kalugin himself sitting at it, him with his pale, pale skin and his black hair and enough jewelry at his collar to buy half the lives in Merovingen-below.

And guards, three men with guns, the sight of which made Jones near turn an ankle on the carpet-edge. Mondragon's arm was there, steadying her. She felt her face go red; and her heart was hammering.

Every weapon she had brought was back in the room. Mondragon's idea.

No choice, he said. Now they had none.

"M'ser," Kalugin said, and with a look up and down that sent the blood hotter still in Jones' face: "m'sera Jones. Amazing. Sit down."

Mondragon steered her to a chair. She let herself into it, never taking her eyes off Anastasi Kalugin, glowering the while.

Damn arrogant sherk, him with the white teeth, look at him smile.

Mama, I listened to this man of mine. Ye told me.

But we're easy to drop in the canal. He wants something.

It was something, Mondragon had said, which brought Anastasi in from Nikolaev; something which had brought him into Boregy, to associations he did not make public.

"You have problems," Anastasi said, leaning back in his chair, themselves sitting across the table from him. "How are they, Thomas?"

Mondragon shrugged.

"Do you want help?"

A second shrug. "If you found it convenient. Yes. I could use a little help. I don't think it's going to go away with Festival."

"I might build some nuisance to distract her. My sister can be very difficult. I warned you, didn't I, Thomas? And where she interests herself, my dear father follows. I did warn you. You're very close to being an inconvenience. Do you follow me?"

"Yes, m'ser." Short and clipped.

"Why should I do this?"

"Because I ask you to, m'ser. Because I am useful."

"Ah. Because you've held things back from me?"

"No, m'ser. I trust you have your reason."

Kalugin's face acquired harsher lines, and eased again. "So readily you understand me, Thomas. M'sera Jones—I do trust you have scrubbed more than your face . . . like the well of your skip, m'sera."

The breath she had sucked in on the first half of that came out again, and her wits went with it for a moment.

He knows. Damn.

How does he know?

Then: "I keep her clean, ser," she said. "Real clean. You got a cargo in mind?"

"Just Thomas, here."

"And your help, ser?" Mondragon asked.

"It does require you expose yourself," Kalugin said, "to certain agencies."

Long silence, then.

"What's he mean?" she asked.

"That we stir the waters," Kalugin said, "and you deal with—shall we say—whatever comes of it. That's all. Not a public exposure, no, no, never fear that—as long as you're discreet. I'll try to handle your other problem. And yours, m'sera. You know that I do watch over you. Thomas knows. Thomas knows the price of things. Do stay out of trouble."

She clenched her hands. "Yes m'ser."

Like Mondragon. Like Mondragon had no choice but say, like this snake put them both to.

And someday, someday they could turn up like that poor woman off by Mansur. There was no forgetting that.

DEATHANGEL

Mercedes R. Lackey

It was a deathangel. The only catch of the day, and it *had* to be a godforsaken *deathangel!*

Rigel Takahashi—called "Raj," since Adventist names weren't terribly healthy for anyone in Merovingen to own up to, and most particularly not for him—stared at the fishtrap (the best and newest one he owned) and the contents (flopping around and getting the long poisoned spines nicely wedged) and cursed a curse long, literate, and alliterative. The words did not match with the speaker; a painfully thin, ragged sixteen year old, dressed only in tattered breeches, balanced on his haunches on a scrap of raft cobbled together from waterlogged flotsam. A swampy—the townfolk and canalers said "crazy". His dark hair was nearly waist-length, indifferently clean, and held back in a tail with a twist of marsh-grass; his lean, tanned face smudged with mud above the almond eyes and along the cheekbones. This was not the sort of creature from which one expected anything intelligible, much less intelligent.

Raj was flat out of patience, with the day (which was hot and stank), with his luck (which smelled almost as bad as the day), with the world (which smelled worse than his luck). For anyone else on this mudball of a planet, for anyone else in this wreck of a city, a deathangel would mean cause for rejoicing—

all you needed were gloves to keep the spines from getting you and a good sharp knife. Then you had a kilo of pure intoxication worth plenty to an Uptowner, plus the poisonous by-product, which any number of people would be willing to take off your hands . . .

But Raj hadn't even *seen* a glove in five years, and his "knife" was a shard of glass with one end dipped in tar and wrapped with string. All he could do was stare at the three-times-damned-and-burned thing wedging itself more and more tightly in the depths of his fish-trap and try not to cry. The only catch of the whole day, useless, and he hadn't eaten since yesterday morning. Damn the Ancestors, damn the trap—his only hope of recovering anything was the chance that the fish might relax when it died, enough to let him slide it out. Or if he could find a mark.

He poled the raft toward the Dead Wharf in hopes of one; there was just the barest possibility there would be someone with a bit of coin or something edible to trade out there—he'd willingly swap fish, trap and all for a little bread. He hadn't had any real bread in months.

Real bread—the smell of bread baking—used to drive him nearly out of his head. Mama would laugh at him—tell him he'd never be a fighter, he wasn't carnivore enough.

Mama *had* been; but bigger carnivores got her.

He almost missed the shadow under the Dead Wharf pilings that moved wrong. Almost. But living with the swampies gave you paranoia if nothing else, and when it lunged down from its perch on a cross-beam he already had in his hand the only thing on the raft that could count in a fight.

The trap full of deathangel.

The trap wasn't much more substantial than a swampy's promise; it shattered as it hit the man (all dressed in dark colors he was; real clothes and not rags, and his face covered) and he got a spine in one eye and the rest in the hands that came up to fend it off. He was dead when he hit the raft; which promptly capsized, but Raj had been ready for that. He dove with the push of the raft behind him, took deep water and shoved off the mucky bottom, and came up with a rush that got him halfway back onto it before his attacker finished his death agony. The man floated, a dark bundle that twitched and rolled, being slowly pulled back under the Wharf by the current. No more danger from *him*, for very sure.

Raj got himself back onto his raft—and started to shake.

Man—waiting there, like he knew it was part of Raj's regular circuit. Man dressed all dark, with his face covered. Man that came down on him like he *knew* exactly what he was doing, who he was going for. Assassin. Had to be. *They* were after him—after five years, *They* were after him; now They'd found him and They'd get him like They'd got Mama. Oh, God.

He poled back to the swamp in a fog of panic, hunger forgotten, casting glances back at the Wharf to see if anyone had found the body; if there were any more of Them after him. But all he could see were the rafts of the other swampies out bobbing in the Dead Harbor—most of them too busy fishing or dozing in the sun to take notice of anything, the rest not wanting to notice trouble lest it fall on them, too.

Got to hide; that was what he knew, his pulse pounding in his ears and his knees getting wobbly with weariness. He pushed the scrap of raft into the swamp, in where the high, yellow reeds made a maze you could get lost in, easy. He brought it in up against a particular reed-islet—which only he and May and Raver knew wasn't an islet at all. He looked around again; then crouched and listened—nothing out of the ordinary. Sea-birds mewling, reeds whispering the stories the Dead told them, nothing else. He jumped off the raft—water was just a bit more than waist-deep here, though the bottom sucked at his feet—and picked up an edge of the islet. It was a kind of basket made to look like a hummock with reeds sticking out of it, resting on a much larger (relatively speaking) raft. Raj heaved his little raft atop the big one, climbed onto them, and lowered the basket down to cover himself and his "home" again.

There was maybe enough room under the "roof" to sit hunched over, with your chin on your knees—but it was safer than anywhere else in the swamp, especially with Them out after him. Only he and old May and Raver had these hideys that he knew of. Raver taught the two of them how to make them, swearing they were called "blinds" where he came from, and you used 'em to shoot birds from. Raj's hidey was the reason he was still alive; he'd waited out many a crazy-hunt in his, and no few searches by Old Ralf.

But would it hold against Them?

Whoever They were. Mama had had plenty of safeguards, but none of them had helped *her*—

Ends of reeds tickled his back and arms as he pushed the thought of discovery resolutely away. No. He wouldn't think about it, he needed to think of something else. But songs weren't any good—the only ones he could remember right now were all grim. *Think. Get calm. Keep your mind occupied, or you'll panic.*

He began breathing deeply and quietly, willing his pulse to slow, making himself a bit calmer, telling himself he had nothing to worry about. The raft bobbed a little; if anyone came by he'd know it by the disturbance of the water. No way anyone could get near him without him knowing. Now—if you started with a load of salt fish; say forty barrels, say two hundred thirty seven fish to a barrel, and you started up the Det, with your costs going up but the worth of those fish going up the farther you went. . . .

The heat under the basket, the bobbing of the raft, the close air and exhaustion all conspired to put him to sleep.

It began again.

Deneb tugged at his elbow. "Yo?" Rigel responded absently; he was doing Mama's accounts, and there'd been a lot of business today.

"Mama said I could stay with Fedor overnight— Raj, can he be on the ship? Please?"

Rigel smiled at his nine-year-old brother (just barely nine—which was the reason for the special treat of overnighting with a friend). The starship was their special, secret game—*Victory* it was called, and Rigel had been making up stories about it for Deneb since Denny was old enough to understand him. Forbidden to mention starships, forbidden even to think about them—but weren't they Adventist? Wasn't Mama Sword? It was their duty, almost, to remember that they belonged in the stars. So Denny was First Officer now, in the game, and as proud as if it had been a real starship they were talking about.

Rigel made himself look serious—Captains are always serious. "Well, First, we have a real problem on our hands."

"Aye, Captain," Deneb responded, waiting enlightenment.

"The Engineer is hurt bad—we've just—uh—had an accident. We've gotta find a replacement or we're not gonna be able to take *Victory* out! Any ideas who to recruit on this station?"

"Aye, Captain," Deneb replied eagerly. "A real good man—uh—uh—"

"Wouldn't be Fedor off the *Harmony*, would it? Now that *Harmony's* been scrapped—"

"Aye, Captain!"

"Then see to it, First. And have a good time."

Deneb hugged his brother with artless enthusiasm—he'd been an affectionate child from his very birth, always responding to cuddling. "Raj—you're the best!"

"Sure, kid. Just so you remember it's you an' me—"

"—against the world—" Deneb made the response.

"—all the way!" they finished together, raising clasped hands.

Rigel turned back to the accounts, smiling.

Now, as it always did, the nightmare skipped ahead—past when Mama came running up the stairs, fear on her face, a paper in her hand. Past when she pushed him out the back bolt-hole window that led to the fire ladder in the air shaft, telling him to guard that paper with his life. Past when he hid under the eaves of the building until dark. Past when

he came back to the shop and apartment, to find
both wrecked, and Mama gone. And blood—lots of
it. Even in nightmare he didn't want to face that—

He made a sack of the remains of a curtain, fear
drying his mouth as he searched the wrack for anything useful that an eleven-year-old boy could carry.
The place had already been pretty thoroughly looted;
there wasn't much. He daren't stay too long, and
daren't go to Denny—They might be watching, waiting, and he would put Denny in danger if he did.
No, he had to find some place to hide, and quick.
Mama had entrusted that paper to him, and it was
his duty to see it stayed safe until he could put it in
the hands of a Sword of God agent. And hope the
Swords would get Mama out of Their hands—whoever
They were. But surely they would—

He slipped out of the splintered door and padded
barefoot along the walkway, around the corner to
Hanging Bridge. He was about halfway across when
he saw three men, cloaked and hooded, following
him and making no pretense about it.

Panic then—and a race across town, hiding under
bridges, losing them, then finding them back on his
trail—all of it in dark or half-dark, all of it clouded
by blackest terror. He thought about trying to make
Gallandry—he knew, even if Mama didn't, that
Gallandrys were supposed to be keeping an eye on
them. Otherwise why send a bargeman down once
or twice a month, just for things they could have
gotten a lot easier on their home island—and why
the casual questions about how the family was doing?
Rigel smelled Granther Takahashi's hand in that—he
might have sent Mama away and told her never to
come back to Nev Hettek again, but he really didn't
mean it when he'd told her he didn't care if she lived
or died. He cared. Cared enough to have Gallandry
set them up quietly in Merovingen; cared enough to
want to know they were still all right.

But Gallandry weren't Sword, though they were
Adventists. They weren't necessarily safe territory.
Only one place he could think of, one place no one
would ever follow: the Marsh.

Dream-skip again; stumbling 'round in water and mud up to his waist, lost in the dark and crying—that was how the swampies found him.

And beat him up, and robbed him of everything but his britches and the paper he kept clenched in one hand. He lay in shallow mud and water; freezing, dazed, hurting, and crying. . . .

And woke crying—but silently, silently, he'd learned never to make noise since then. He wiped the tears from his face with the tail of his hair, and listened. Nothing. And getting on sunset, by the red that filtered through the basket, and the go-to-bed sounds the marshbirds were making.

O God—tonight was the night he was supposed to meet Denny. He had to warn him that They were on the hunt again—Denny could be in as much danger as Raj. But first he had to find May and Raver.

They were out on their usual squat—the bit of dry sand beach along the end of the Seawall that had formed during the last really big storm. Old May and Raver—as unlikely a couple as ever decorated the face of the Dead Harbor—May about forty and looking four hundred, Raver ten years older and looking thirty. She who'd been a canaler until a barge ran down her skip and took her man and kids and everything she owned down to the bottom—he who claimed to be everything from a stranded spacer (ha!) to the Prince of Kasparl. She who was the closest thing to a medic the Harbor boasted, and so was inviolate from most of the mayhem that raged among the swampies—he who proclaimed himself to be the One True Prophet of Althea Jane Morgoth, herself. They'd found Raj, all pain and half delirious—and for some reason known only to themselves picked him up and carted him back to May's diggings, and nursed him back to a semblance of health. They taught him how to survive, during that vague six-month period during which shock had kept him pliant enough to adapt. He'd paid them back for their care, though—sharing the scoungings Denny got to him; writing down Raver's "prophecies"—for Raver induced "visions" by drinking swamp-water and obviously was then in no condition to record his prophecies himself. Why he wasn't dead twenty times over—well. It was a mystery, like where Raver got the paper was a mystery, and what he did with it after Raj filled it with the "holy words" in his careful, clear hand. Raver kept him safe, too—Raver wasn't big, but he was all wire and muscle, and even the Razorfins were afraid to tangle with him. And only Althea Jane knew why he did that—for he'd put himself into a bit of risk by protecting Raj. The Razorfins wanted Raj as their slavey; Big Ralf wanted him for—other things. All of them were crazies, and no telling what they'd do to someone between them and what they wanted. But Raver stood by him until he was big enough to fight back and canny enough to hide from what he couldn't fight.

Raver and May had lit a small fire of driftwood and were grilling fish spitted on reeds over it. They looked like images out of Hell; red-lit, weather-and-age-twisted faces avidly watching what cooked over the flames.

Raj didn't make much noise, but they heard him anyway. "Tha' you, boy?" Raver called into the dark.

"Yo—" Raj replied, "Raver, I got trouble."

"Boy, the *world* got trouble. Neveryoumind. What's the trouble this time? Big Ralf? Them Razorfins?"

"Wish it was—Raver, somebody jumped me out to Dead Wharf—a man dressed all in dark clothes, with his face covered, and waiting like he knew I was coming. I think They found me."

"Damn! That be trouble, and more'n ye need!" May coughed. "Ye got any notion who They be?"

"No more than I ever did. Could be anybody; sharrists, blacklegs, even—"

"Sword," Raver growled.

"Damn it all, *no*! Not Sword, *never* Sword. Sword would be trying to help me, not kill me!'

"I'll believe that when I believe—" May hushed Raver before he could say any more.

"Fine, Raj said, "But whose Mama was Sword,

huh? Who saw Sword coming and going? So who should know?" It was an old argument.

"And whose Mama was probably killed by the Sword she served, hm? Ah, leave it, boy; got less polites than you—I notice ye may ha' thought "Jane" but ye didn't say it. You off to give Denny a warning?"

"Got to. He's in danger too."

"Boy—" May laid a hand on his arm, a gnarly brown thing like a root, and to Raj, beautiful. "Lissen—if Denny's got a way t'hide ye, take it. Don' come back here."

"But—" This was another old argument.

"No buts. Ye're young; this ain't no life fer th' young. Hell, ye've never even touched a girl, and all of sixteen! We'll be all right."

"She's got the right of it, boy." There was a suspicion of mist in Raver's slightly-crazed eyes. "The Words are complete now, thanks to you. You go—"

Raver claimed the Words were complete about once a month.

"Look, I'll be back, same as always. Denny won't have any place safe for me, and I won't put danger on those as is keeping him."

For the first time in this weekly litany Raver looked unaccountably solemn. "Somehow—I doesn't think so—not this time. Well, time's wasting, boy, be off—or They might find Denny afore ye."

May's face twisted comically then, as she glanced between Raj and their dinner; she plainly felt obliged to offer him some, and just as plainly didn't really want to have to share the little they had.

"You et?" she asked reluctantly.

Raj's stomach churned; the adrenaline high he had going made the very thought of food revolting.

"S'okay; I'm fine."

She smiled, relieved. "Off wi' ye, then. Ye'd best hurry.'

Raj went, finding his way back to his raft, and poling it out into the black, open water of Dead Harbor.

Lots of lights in the town tonight—lots of noise. Raj blessed it all, for it covered his approach. Then remembered—and shame on himself for not remembering before this!—that it was Festival; Festival of the Scouring. What night of Festival it was, he couldn't remember; his only calendars were moon and Dogs these days, and seasons. By the noise, probably well into it. But that meant Denny would be delayed by the crowds on the bridges and walkways. That might prove a blessing; it gave him a chance to check all around their meeting place under Dead Wharf for more of Them.

He poled all beneath the Dead Wharf, between the maze of pilings, keeping all senses alert for anything out of the norm. There wasn't anyone lying in ambush that he could find, not by eye nor ear nor scent, so he made the raft fast and climbed up into their meeting place among the crossbeams out near the end of the Wharf.

First time they'd met here—after Raj had slipped into the town with his heart pounding like an overworked motor and passed Fedor a note to give to Denny—they hadn't said much. Denny had just wrapped his arms around his brother like he'd never let go, and cried his eyes sore and his voice hoarse. Raj had wanted to cry too—but hadn't dared; Denny would have shattered. That was the way the first few meetings went.

But small boys are resilient creatures; before too long, Denny was begging for his stories again, and the tears only came at parting—and then not at all. But now the stories included another set—how they would find more members of the Sword; get Mama's message to them. The original paper was long gone, but the contents resided intact in Raj's head—and what Raj memorized was there for good and all. That was why Mama had taken him everywhere with her—when she'd ask him later, he'd recite what had been said and done like a recorder of the Ancestors. And just as a precaution, Raj had made plenty of copies over three years, making a new one as soon as the previous copy began deteriorating, and keeping it with him at all times, mostly hidden on his raft. Well, they'd get that message back to the Sword—

and the Sword would rescue them, take them home
to Nev Hettek, and train them to be heroes. And
both of them would earn their way to the stars.
Denny hadn't liked that story as much as the starship
tales, but it had comforted Raj.

When had Denny started scrounging for him? Raj
wrinkled his brow in thought, and picked at the
splintery beams under him, staring at the stars reflected on the wavelets in Dead Harbor. Must have
been that winter—that was it; when he'd shown up
as usual in nothing but his trousers, shivering, and
pretending he wasn't cold. Denny had looked at him
sharp, then cuddled up real close, and not just for
his own comfort; he'd put his little body between Raj
and the wind. Next meeting, Denny'd brought a
sweater; one that Fedor's father wasn't likely to miss—
old, faded, snagged, and out at both elbows. After
that he'd never come to a meeting empty-handed,
though Raj refused to ask him for anything.

Lord knew he needed those meetings himself;
needed the comfort, needed to hold someone, to talk
to somebody sane. Raver and May were only sane
sometimes. He'd needed that more than the material
comforts Denny brought, and he needed those desperately. Lately though, the meetings had left him a
little troubled. Denny was evasive when Raj asked
about Fedor and the family; and had become a bit
distant. Raj guessed he was trying to act "grown
up"—by pulling away, avoiding physical contact. Raj
understood—but it was making him feel mighty lonely.
He missed the cuddly child he'd been more than half
parent to.

Pad of bare feet overhead—then tiny sounds that
marked someone who knew what he was doing and
where he was going climbing down among the
crossbeams.

"Yo, brother?" Denny's whisper.

"Right here."

"Be right with you." A bit of scratching, rasp of
wood on cloth and skin, and someone slipped in
beside him; with a quick hug, and then pulling away.
"Riot out there tonight."

"Denny—I got to go under again. One of Them nearly got me today. Assassin. He was waiting for me, Denny. He knew who I was and where I was going. Has to be Them."

Swift intake of breath. "God—no! Not after all this time! How'd you get away?"

"I just—outran him." *Don't let him know what really happened. He'll think he has to share the danger,* Raj had been careful never to let his brother even guess that he'd had to kill—and more than once.

"All right." The voice in the dark took on a new firmness. "That's it. You're not gonna run any more, brother. Running don't cut it. You need a protector, somebody with weight."

"Get serious!" Raj answered bitterly. "Where am I going to find somebody willing to stand for me?"

Denny chuckled. "Been thinking about that. New man in town—got contacts, got weight—canalers, Uptown, everywhere, seems like. Been watching him."

"Big fat deal—what reason is he going to have to help me?"

"Name's Mondragon. Tom Mondragon. Familiar?"

Raj sucked in his breath. "Lord and Ancestors—"

"Thought I 'membered it," Denny replied with satisfaction.

Raj did indeed remember that name—it went all the way back before their exile to Merovingen, an exile Granther Takahashi thought would take them out of reach of Mama's Sword of God contacts and her Sword lover. Tom Mondragon had been Sword— friend of Mama's lover, Mahmud Lee. Lee was (presumably) Denny's father—and that was probably why the name "Mondragon" had stuck so fortuitously in Denny's memory.

"You never forget anything, brother. What's the Mondragon you saw look like?"

Raj closed his eyes and rocked back and forth a little, letting his mind drift back—Lord and Ancestors, he'd been seven, maybe, eight—

"Blond. *Pretty* feller. Moved like a cat, or a dancer. Green eyes—tall, dressed real well."

"Dunno 'bout the eyes, but the rest is him. Same man. 'Pears to me he'd have reason to help. 'Pears to me you'd want to get Mama's message to 'im, ne?"

"Lord—" Raj said, not quite believing this turn of events, "It's—"

"Like that story y' used t' tell me? Yeah, well, maybe. I'm more interested in seeing you safe, an' I think this Mondragon c'n do that. Right then, we go find him. Now. Tonight."

Raj started to scramble up, but Denny forestalled him. "No *way* you're gonna pass in the town, brother. Not dressed like that."

"Oh. Yeah."

"You wait here—I won't be long."

Denny thought he'd managed that rather cleverly; he'd thought he'd remembered Mondragon's name when he'd first heard it, and he'd just been biding his time for the opportunity to get Raj to take the bait he was going to offer. That swamp was no place for Raj—sooner or later someone or something would get him. Town was safer, far. Besides, since he'd drifted away from Fedor's family, he'd been getting lonelier and lonelier. He had friends—but he wanted his big brother back.

Well, now—first things first; a set of clothing that wouldn't stand out in the Festival crowds. Denny took to the rooftops on Southdike and thought while he climbed. Nearest secondhand clothing store was Fife, where he hung out—no go. That was off limits. He could hear Rattail now, cracking him over the ear for even thinking about it. "Never soil your own nest, boy. Rule one."

The air up here was fresher, carrying away a lot of the stink. Denny slipped around chimneypots and skylights and over rooftrees as easily as if he'd been on a level walkway. Okay, the next closest was Greely. Old man Mikles was a stingy son, too cheap to see to good locks on his windows. And wouldn't miss the loss. Greely it was.

He crossed the bridges on the support beams below, keeping a sharp eye out for watchers, finally getting himself up on the supports of the third-level bridge that linked Greely with Ravi. Mikles had a second-story window just below and to one side of it. Denny unwound the light rope and grapnel from his waist, spied a sturdy cornice, and made his cast.

Solid. He pulled three times ("*Always* three times, no matter how rushed ye are," came Rif's voice from memory) and swung himself over, in the shadows all the way.

Within a few minutes Mikles' shop was lighter by a pair of britches, a shirt and a sweater, all sized for someone thin and not over-tall. And Denny was most of the way back to the Dead Wharf, dancing across the rooftrees and bridge-beams like a half-grown cat.

"Huh-*uh*," Denny said, keeping his grip tight on the bundle he carried and handing something small that shone white in the starlight to Raj instead. "Down, brother; in the harbor. Get clean first, or they'll know y' by the smell for a crazy."

Raj flushed with embarrassment—living in the swamp was changing him, and in ways he didn't like. He used to be so fastidious—

He grabbed the proffered soap and dropped straight down into the water next to the Wharf—trying not to remember the twitching thing that had so lately floated there. He was so used to being chilled that the cold water wasn't much shock to his system. He soaped and rinsed and scrubbed until he thought his skin would peel off, then washed his hair three times for good measure. Denny had shinnied down to his raft and handed him back up onto it with a sniff that held approval. "Better. Y' smell better than a lot of canalers now. Here—" a piece of sacking to use for a towel, and a comb. Getting the tangles out of all that hair was a job—Raj had to be content to just get most of the major knots out, and smooth down the rest, tying it back with the piece of ribbon (Lord—*ribbon!*) Denny handed him. Then into the clothing—oh, heaven, clean, and warm and not ripped in a dozen places—and even the right size. The precious Message went into his shirt pocket.

Raj stood up straight with one hand steadying himself on the piling, and felt like a human being again for the first time in years.

Denny grinned at him, teeth flashing white in his shadowed face. "Know what, brother? You clean up real pretty. I c'n think of a couple girls just might like to share a blanket with you."

Raj blushed hotly, and was glad the dark hid it.

"Thought I'd warn you—'cause that's who we're gonna go see first."

They took to the rooftops, much to Raj's bewilderment; oh, he still remembered how to climb, he was fast and agile enough to keep up—but why not take the walkways openly? And—where had Denny gotten this kind of expertise in roof-scrambling?

It was even more of a maze in Merovingen-above than it was in Merovingen-below. If there was a level space up here on the roofs that was more than three feet square, it was a rarity. "Up here" was a patchwork of towers, cupolas, skylights and spires. Denny danced along the spines of peaked roofs and jumped from structure to structure as if he were half cat. Raj followed as best he could. He was just lucky that "above" also sported rain-gutters and collection-pipes on every surface, for without these aids he'd never have been able to emulate Denny. From time to time Denny would half-start toward something Raj *knew* was unclimbable—then glance back as if suddenly remembering his brother's presence and choose some easier path. Raj couldn't help but wonder what he'd have done if Raj hadn't been along.

Denny paused on the roof-edge overlooking the bridge to Fife from Southdike, balancing carefully and scrutinizing the bridge and attendant walkways. "Looks good—" he said finally, in a whisper. "If anybody followed us, they've lost us. C'mon." And he shinnied down a drainpipe to the walk below them. Raj followed suit. Shielded torches on the bridge danced and smoked, placed so far apart they did more harm than good. There seemed to be no one about in this area, and their bare feet made no sound on the bridge, which contributed to the gloomy atmosphere.

"From here we go to Salvatore, then Delaree—just in case we get separated," Denny said in an undertone, walking uncomfortably fast for one not used to walking, but to poling a raft. "The ladies I want to talk to should be in a tavern on Delaree—it's down on the water, it's called Hoh's. There'll be a lot of canalers tied-up at it. Got that?"

Raj nodded, saving his breath.

"Good, 'cause once we get to Salvatore, we'll be goin' up again."

They didn't get separated, but Raj was weary and aching by the time they stood in the tavern door. And confused, and lost. Only rarely had they crossed bridges by the normal paths—more often they'd scrambled underneath on the cross-beams, or worse, inched along the support-cables overhead. It made good sense in a way—for surely no one would ever have been able to follow them—but Raj was thoroughly exhausted by the time they reached their goal.

They descended to the walkway, cold and wet under bare feet, and walked decorously enough to the wooden porch that marked Hoh's front entrance. There were boats tied-up here, and lanterns everywhere; light and noise and confusion that dazzled Raj's eyes and made him more than a little nervous. The water of the canal looked very black and cold compared with all that light and warmth, and Raj found himself hoping they weren't likely to find out just how cold it was.

There was food-smell; fish frying and bread and beer. There was smoke, little wisps of it, from the lanterns. There was sound—people laughing, talking, arguing, and singing. Most of all, singing. Just as they got to the wooden porch a great roar of a chorus bounced out the open door and off the brick of the wall opposite.

"Hoo—they're rabble-rousing t'night, fer sure!" Denny grinned. "They best hope there ain't no blacklegs 'round!" Somewhat to Raj's surprise, he was talking just like the canalers, chameleon-like acquiring the coloration of his surroundings.

Raj began to make out some of the words, and Denny had the right of it. Skirting just the high side of treason—but, oddly enough, he couldn't identify what cult or faction the song was in favor of.

"Who is that?" he hissed into Denny's ear. "Whose side are they on?"

"Rattail and Rif, an' they ain't on anybody's side." Denny elbowed his way in the front door with Raj trailing warily behind. "They just like t' rile people up, I guess."

The tavern room was hot and redolent; crammed full, every table and chair occupied and people jammed in against the walls. The objects of their attention were perched on the bar, grinning insolently and singing for all they were worth. Their voices were amazingly strong and clear; Raj could hear them long before he could see them.

Denny finally wormed a place for them in behind the bar, and Raj managed to get a good view under someone's elbow. They were something to stare at, were Rattail and Rif, though which was which he couldn't guess. One was playing a gitar, her hands moving on the strings so fast he could hardly credit his eyes. She seemed to be the older of the two by ten, maybe fifteen years. The other was setting up a complicated pattern on a couple of hand-drums, but Raj could see another gitar leaning up against the bar next to her. Both had dark, nearly black, straight hair, tied around with red scarves. The older one wore hers long past her shoulders, the younger shorter than Denny's. Both had sharp features and ironic grins. Both were wearing black trousers, and dark sweaters, the tightest Raj had ever seen, like they'd been molded on. Both had pale, pale skin as if they didn't see the sun much.

And both of them were wearing at least three knives that Raj could see.

"Hope they get the crowd calmed down 'fore they

finish up," Denny muttered, "or with this lot, half-drunk as they are, no tellin' what they might do."

To Raj's relief they did just that, finishing up at last with something melancholy enough that one or two of the more sodden customers began sniffling into their beer. Then, ignoring demands for more, they picked up their instruments and hopped off the bar. Denny waved at them—the older one spotted him and motioned him over. Seeing that he'd been summoned by one of their darlings, the crowd parted politely so that the two boys could make their way to the singers' tiny table, crowded into a cramped nook to one side of the bar itself. There was barely room for both women, the boys, and the instruments.

The older one reached over the table and tweaked Denny's nose. "Where've y' been, kid? Y' haven't been here since Festival started—we was beginnin' t' think y' didn't love us no more."

"Out an' about. You tryin' t' get yourselves invited down to the Signeury? What'f they'd been blacklegs around?"

"Huh, blacklegs are all dead drunk by now. 'Sides, that was classical—preScouring litra-choor, I'll have y'know. Kipling."

"With additions by you, Rif, I got no doubt," Denny snorted. "One of these days y're gonna find y'rself taking High Trade, an' not because of what y' do outside walls."

"Listen to the kitten, tellin' the old cats how to prowl!" the younger crowed. "Who taught you, hm? Ins and outs, ups and downs—"

Denny cleared his throat with a sideways glance toward Raj—and only then did the women seem to see him.

"Well! Who's *this*? Can't be related to you, kid—he's too pretty."

Raj felt his ears burning.

"This's m' brother Raj. *You* know."

"Oh-ho. Brought him out of hiding, hm? And y' need something, I don't doubt. Make him someone's cousin?" Rif—the older woman—caught Raj's chin in one long, sharp-nailed hand, and turned his face from side to side, examining it closely. "Just feeding him'd do for you, I'd think—a little flesh on 'im, and no one'd know 'im."

Denny shook his head. "No go. He needs more; needs protection, needs somebody with weight backing 'im. So I'm askin'—you seen that pretty blond that ain't canal 'round lately?"

Rif shook her head, letting go of Raj's chin. "Not me. Rat-love?"

She, too, shook her head. "Ney, ney. Know who might, though—that canal-rat that used t' be Moghi's. Tommy."

"*Oh*, no—" it was Denny's turn to shake his head. "Ain't messin' that one. That Jones keeps an eye on 'im; push him, she'll know—I damn sure don't want her knowin' I'm trying' to touch her man. She's got a nasty way with folks as bothers 'im."

"Point," Rat agreed. "All right—best I can say is try that runner-fluff of yours, Lady-o. She's been doin' runs down along where he mostly seems t' hang out— 'specially lately."

A fistfight broke out across the room, interrupting them. For a few seconds it remained confined to the original two combatants—but a foot in the wrong place tripped one up and sent him into a table and its occupants—and things began to spread from there.

Rat and Rif exchanged glances filled with unholy glee.

"Shall we?"

"Let's shall—"

With reverent care, they handed their instruments to the bartender, who placed them safely behind the wooden bulwark. They divested themselves of knives— this was a fistfight, after all—then charged into the fray with joyful and total abandon.

"Women," Denny said, shaking his head ruefully, "Well, at least they'll come out 'f that with full pockets. Back way, brother." Raj followed him outside with no regret.

Denny led the way again, back over rooftops, climbing towers and balconies, inching along drainpipes

and across the support beams of bridges until Raj
was well and truly lost. Fatigue was beginning to
haze everything, and he hadn't the least notion where
in Merovingen he could be—except that by the general run of the buildings, they were still in the lower-
class section of town. When Denny finally stopped
and peered over a roofedge, Raj just sat, closing his
eyes and breathing slowly, trying to get back his
wind, with a gutter biting into his bony haunches.

"Yo!" he heard Denny call softly, "Ladyo!"

Sound of feet padding over to stand beneath where
Denny hung over the edge. "Denny?" answered a
young female voice. "You in trouble?"

"Ney. Just need to find someone."

By now Raj had recovered, enough to join Denny
in peering over the roofedge. On the walkway just
below him was a child—certainly younger than
Denny, pretty in the way an alleykitten is pretty.

"I'm waiting," she said, and "Oh!" when she saw
Raj.

Denny shook his head at the question in her glance.
"Not now. Later, promise. Gotta find that blond
you're always droolin' after."

She looked incensed. "I *ain't* droolin' after him! I
just think he's—nice."

"Yeah, and Rif just sings cute little ballads. You
know where he is?"

She sniffed. "I shouldn't tell you—"

"Oh c'mon! Look—I promise I give you that blue
scarf of mine—just tell."

"Well, all right. He's in Tesh's on Foundry. I just
run a message over there and I saw him. I think he's
gonna be there awhile."

"Hot damn!" Denny jumped to his feet, and skipped
a little along the edge of the roof while Raj held his
breath, expecting him to fall. "Brighteyes, you just
made my day!"

Denny had traded on the fact that he was a known
runner to get into Tesh's. It wasn't a place Raj would
have walked into by choice. The few faces he could
see all looked full of secrets, and unfriendly. They

approached the table Mondragon had taken, off in
the darkest corner of the room, Denny with all the
aplomb of someone who had every right to be there.
Raj just trailed along behind, invisible for all the
attention anyone paid him. This place was as dark as
Hoh's had been well-lit; talk was murmurous, and
there was no one entertaining. Raj was not at all sure
he wanted to be here.

"M'ser—" Denny had reached Mondragon's table,
and the man looked up when he spoke. Raj had no
difficulty in recognizing the Mondragon from Nev
Hettek. Older, harder—but the same man. "M'ser, I
got a message for you—but—it ain't public."

Mondragon looked at him; startled at first, then
appraisingly. He signaled a waiter, spoke softly into
the man's ear; the man murmured something in
reply, picked up the dishes that had been on Mondragon's table, and motioned for them to follow.

The waiter led them all to a tiny room, with barely
more than a table and a few chairs in it—but it
had a door, and the door shut softly behind them.
Mondragon seated himself at the table, and picked
up his tea-mug. The way he positioned himself, the
boys had to stand with him seated between them and
the door. The lantern that lit the room was on the
wall behind Mondragon's head, and made a sun-
blaze out of his light hair.

"I'm waiting," was all he said.

"M'ser—my brother's got information that you
might could use—it might be you an' him know the
same people. We wanta sell it."

He poked Raj with his elbow, who shook himself
into awareness.

"Information?" Mondragon did not look amused.
"What on earth could you two have that would be of
any use to me?"

"M'ser, somebody thinks it's important. He's been
havin' to hide out in the swamp because somebody
thought it was important. Our Mama was killed because somebody thought it was important, but she
passed it to Rigel, here. See, we know who you are.
We know where you're from. We reckoned you would

be the right man to know what he's got. And we figured you'd be the best man to pay our price—an' that's t' keep him safe after he's told you."

He began to look angry. "If this is some kind of a scam—"

"Brother," Raj said clearly and distinctly, "the Sword is drawn."

Mondragon, who had just taken a mouthful of tea, coughed and practically choked.

Raj took the most recent of his precious copies of The Message from his shirt pocket and handed it to him.

Hazed with fatigue, Raj was blind to Mondragon's reactions—but Denny wasn't.

Within a few moments, Denny had figured that Mondragon was not pleased with their recognition of him as Sword. Moments after that, he knew by the worried look that Mondragon wasn't Sword anymore.

This required recalculation.

Then Mondragon's mouth began to twitch as he read the paper Raj had given him.

"Where did you come by this?"

"Told you," Denny said, stalling for time. "Our Mama was something with the Sword—passed 'em messages an' whatall. 'Cept somebody figured that out an' came for 'er, an' Raj ran for the Marsh t' hide out with the last thing she got. Figured things was fine until he got jumped out there today, and 'tweren't no crazy, was an assassin. Takahashi's who we are; ye might know the name—ye might know people here Mama knew—Gallandrys. You gonna help us out?"

"Nothing here for me," Mondragon said, his mouth amused, though his eyes were hard. "What you've got is an out-of-date infiltration schedule. Useless. And worthless."

Raj's mind went blank. All the hope—the plans— all in ruins; and the man Mondragon didn't seem the least bit interested in helping, much less being the shining rescuer Raj had prayed for. "But—*somebody* must think I know something—" he replied desper-

ately,"—or why try to kill me? And why send a
trained assassin? They could have hired one of the
swamp-gangs, easy." Now all he wanted was to be
able to think of something useful to Mondragon;
something worth the cost of protecting both himself
and Denny. It was far too late now to go back to the
swamp. "Maybe—maybe I know something someone
doesn't want out—like a name, or a face—can't you
use that?"

"Affirmative—Raj never forgets anything," Denny
chimed in. "That's why Mama took him everywhere
with her. He knows all kind of things—things maybe
still worth knowing."

"Like—I remember you, m'ser. You were with
Mama's man, Mahmud Lee—it was—around the be-
ginning of Harvest, I think, about nine years ago.
You were wearing brown velvet, and you and Mahmud
talked about the bribes your father'd been paying—"
Raj trailed off at the grim set to Mondragon's mouth.

"Sides—damn Sword's out after us along with you,"
Denny interrupted, stepping hard on Raj's foot.
"Mama would have sold us to slavers if they'd told
her to. Sword never got us anything but trouble, an'
I betcha it's them sent the assassin. You need something to keep them off, I bet Raj knows it. And you
need us for more than that. You got to hide real
bad—Raj can tell you, nobody goes into the swamp—
but he knows it, how to live there. You need something, well, I can get it, or I know who can; I can get
things done, too—get people disappeared—get you
disappeared too, only less permanent. We've got connections you can't get from the families or the canalers.
You *need* us, m'ser—'bout as much as we need you."

"Interesting," Mondragon said, then said nothing
more, obviously thinking hard. Raj turned on Denny.

"What the hell—"

"Truth, damn it!" Denny whispered harshly. "It's
all true and you know it! Mama *used* you—why
d'y'think she never paid me any attention? Fedor's
folks knew what was going on; told me, too. Told me
it was probably Sword that got Mama."

"Uh—"

"That's why they turned me out, couple years ago. They were afraid, an' I don't blame 'em. Lucky I ran into Rif an' Rat."

"They're thieves! I know cant when I hear it!"

" 'Course they're thieves! How d'ye think I scrounged all that stuff for you? Where'd ye think it came from? The Moon? I've been livin' in a bloody airshaft on Fife f'r two years now! Look, brother—I mostly gave up thievin'—the odds aren't in it. I'm a runner now. But I couldn't get stuff to you and feed me on what I make runnin', and I wouldn't leave you without. So I stole. An' I still steal. An' I'd keep doin' it. Cause you're worth it—like Mama wasn't. Tell ye what else, this Mondragon may a' been Sword before, but he damn sure ain't now! Or didn't ye notice him have a fit when ye hit 'im with the password? Our best bet is t'figure somethin' he needs bad."

The fog began to clear from Raj's head; as Denny's words and memory started to come together, certain things were coming a lot clearer than they'd ever been before.

Item: Raver and May had been trying to tell him—in gentler terms—exactly what Denny was telling him now. If three so very different people—one of them his own flesh and blood—were saying the same things about the Sword of God and Mama's involvement with it, well, it followed that he had probably been dead wrong and dreaming all these years.

Item: stripped of the fairy-tale glamour Mama had decked them with, the members of the Sword of God were not in the least attractive. Take the holy cause away, and they became little more than highly trained, professional killers.

Item: they were now alone with this unhappy professional assassin. Who probably was thinking no one would miss them.

Raj looked over Denny's shoulder at Mondragon, who was contemplating them with a face of stone. Raj's blood ran colder than the Det at midwinter.

Item: they were a liability. And Mondragon was

looking at them like someone who couldn't afford
liabilities.

Denny suddenly broke off, seeing Raj's face turn
pale and still. "Brother—you all right?" he whispered,
unable to fathom why Raj should suddenly look as if
he were watching the Angel draw His Sword and
begin Retribution. He knew some of what he'd told
Raj was bound to come as a shock, but he hadn't
thought any of it was enough to turn him white to
the ears!

He shook Raj's arm a little, beginning to feel worried. The way Raj was staring at Mondragon, sort of
glassy-eyed—it wasn't like him. Raj was always the
quick one, the alert one—except—

Denny went cold all over. Except when Raj had
been sick—

Raj was watching Mondragon's eyes, the only things
in his face that were showing any change. They were
growing harder; and Raj's blood acquired ice crystals.

Item: they were quite likely to be very dead very
soon. Denny, with the panache of a thirteen-year-old
unable to believe in his own mortality, had led them
into dangerous and unfriendly hands—and with no
way to escape. Mondragon was between them and
the door, in a room barely big enough for all of
them and the table.

Looking at those calculating eyes, Raj *knew* exactly
what their fate was going to be. They had, at most, a
few more minutes.

He forced himself to smile at his brother; he
couldn't protect him from what was coming, but at
least he could keep him from knowing it was coming. "Nothing—just—you're right. About all of it.
I've been plain stupid—"

Denny shrugged, "No big deal. Hey, everybody
makes mistakes, an' hell, I prob'ly wouldn't believe
anything bad anybody said about you, either."

"And I never told you how much I missed you,
First." The old nickname made Denny grin. "That

was even stupider. We're the team, right? So, from now on it's gonna be you an' me—yo? All the way."

Denny dropped his pretense of adulthood and threw both arms around his brother in an affection-starved hug. Raj tightened his own arms around Denny's shoulders and stared at Mondragon, trying to beg with his eyes, and figuring that it was a lost cause before he started.

Mondragon nursed his tea and pondered the problem of the kids as dispassionately as he could. Realistically speaking, the canal was the safest option. It was bad enough that there was *anyone* beyond Jones and Kalugin who knew who and what he was—and these kids were likely to tip the whole town off. He knew what Jones would say about it—she'd be right there with a piece of rope and two rocks.

The whispering stopped, and he focused his attention back on them. The older one was staring at him with an expression utterly unlike the lost-pup befuddlement he'd shown before—as if he'd just now begun to realize what they'd walked into. He said something to his brother that made the kid drop about five years and fling himself into his older brother's arms with joyful enthusiasm. The older boy tightened his arms around the younger's shoulders and stared at Mondragon, his expression so easy to read he might as well have been speaking his thoughts aloud.

I know you now, it said, *I know what you are. I know you're likely gonna kill us. But—you're the only hope we've got left; we've got nowhere to go with Them on our heels. . . .*

He knew that expression from the inside. Hadn't been so long ago he'd worn it himself.

As he set his face like stone, the hope visibly drained from the older boy. His eyes went tired and sick; bleak, and somewhere past fear. He whispered something else in his brother's ear, ruffled his hair, and pushed his head against his own shoulder—a casual, caring gesture that "accidentally" left his hand so positioned that the boy could no longer see Mondragon without shoving his brother aside. Then he raised

his chin with pathetic bravery, and he locked his
eyes with Mondragon's—a look as sad and wise as
Mondragon had ever seen—and far, far older than
his few years.

All right then, it said, *Do it. But get it over with quick,
and do it while he can't see.* The mouth tightened, he
shivered and the eyes closed. *And don't let me see it
coming, either.*

And he waited quietly for Mondragon to take them.

Mondragon knew that expression, too; in the dark
watches of the night a too-vivid imagination had
painted that same hopeless, despairing courage over
other faces—

His gut twisted and he cursed himself for a soft-
hearted fool even while he made his decisions.

He cleared his throat; a little sound, but the older
boy started as violently as if a gun had gone off in
his ear; and his eyes jerked open to show nothing
but dazed pupil.

"You say your mother had connections with
Gallandry?"

Raj stared, unable to get his mouth to work. It was
too much to comprehend—he'd expected the touch
of a knife, and he'd only hoped Mondragon was
good enough to make it fast and relatively painless.
And then—this—

His ears roared, and little black specks danced in
the air between his eyes and Mondragon's face.

"Gallandry?" he heard himself say stupidly, as his
knees suddenly liquified on him.

Denny felt Raj start to collapse, and held him up
by main force. *Oh, God, please—no—*

The last time Raj had done this, he'd missed the
meetings for the next month; and when he finally
showed up, it was pounds thinner, with eyes gone all
hollow, and a rasping cough that lasted weeks. *Please.
God—* he begged, struggling to keep Raj on his feet
long enough to pull a chair under him, *don't let it be
fever, he might not make it this time—and we're almost
home free—*

* * *

"M'ser, just let me get him sat—m'ser, he's all right!" Raj heard Denny over the roaring in his ears, over the scrape of a chair on the floor "You don't— m'ser, you don't need—"

Something shoved up against the back of his legs; hands were under his armpits letting him down easy, the same hands then pushing his head down between his legs.

"Stay that way for a bit—" Mondragon's voice. And the roaring went away, his eyes cleared. When his head stopped spinning he looked up. Mondragon sat on his heels beside him, Denny looking frantic, trying to get between them without touching Mondragon. "Better?"

"I—" Raj managed. "I—"

Mondragon took his chin in one hand, tilted his eyes into the light, scrutinized them closely.

"I'm sorry, m'ser, I'm all right," Raj whispered, thinking—*Daren't, daren't show weakness in front of this man!* Honest, I'm all right."

"You're not—but you will be."

Ignoring Denny's worried protests (*Great*, thought Raj dizzily, NOW *he realizes we could be in trouble*), Mondragon went to the table, poured his own mug full of tea, and spooned sugar into it recklessly. He brought it to Raj, who took it with hands that shook so hard the tea slopped. Poison? No—not likely. Not when he'd had the chance to kill them easily, and hadn't.

"Get yourself on the outside of that."

Raj sipped—the tea almost like syrup, the warmth going from his stomach to the rest of him. His hands stopped shaking, slowly.

"When did you last eat?"

"Eat?" Raj was taken totally by surprise by the question and the funny half-smile on Mondragon's face. "Uh—I don't remember—"

"Then it's been too long. Small wonder you're falling at my feet. That's reserved for women, you know."

As Raj tried to adjust to the fact that he'd just made a joke, Mondragon busied himself at the table again, and turned around with fish stuffed into a roll. Raj stared at it as though it was alive, not taking it.

"Go on, eat—" Mondragon pried one of Raj's hands off the mug, pressed the roll into it. "Rigel—"

Raj looked up to meet his eyes squarely. And the eyes were warm, like the sea on a sunny day, and the little, amused smile was reflected in them.

Lord and Ancestors, they were saved. Raj's head spun—this time with relief.

"About the Gallandrys—"

Raj took a tiny bite of bread, swallowed around a lump in his throat, and began.

"You've got a bloody lot of gall, Mondragon—"

When Raj had finished telling Mondragon all he knew and most he guessed, and when his knees could hold him upright again, Mondragon had chivied them across to Gallandry (Denny, for once, looking appropriately apprehensive) and brought them into Gallandry proper. Though those that had let them in hadn't been at all pleased with his being there.

They'd been brought in through a water-door, down long, unlit halls of wood and stone, and finally into a room piled with ledgers and lit so brightly Raj was blinking tears back.

Now they fronted a man Mondragon called by name, and that man was coldly angry.

"Granted. However, I'm not the only one standing here with an unpaid debt and a broken promise. These boys are Takahashi. Rigel and Deneb Takahashi."

Raj had rarely seen words act so powerfully on someone. The man's anger faded into guilt, visible even to him.

"I've brought them here," Mondragon continued deliberately, "—so that we can all even some scales. You made a promise to Elder Takahashi, and didn't keep it. I—lost you some personnel. Both these kids are useful—"

Now the man looked skeptical, as if he doubted Mondragon's ability to judge much of anything.

"M'ser," Denny piped up, "—ye've used me, I know.

Ask yer front-office people. I'm a runner—a good one. Don't take bribes, I'm fast—"

"You could take him on as staff runner, and train him for bargework as he grows into it. And the older boy clerks," Mondragon continued.

"You don't expect me to take that on faith—"

Raj took a deep breath and interrupted. "Set me a problem, m'ser. Nothing easy. You'll see."

The man sniffed derisively, then rattled off something fast; a complicated calculation involving glass bottles—cost, expected breakage, transportation and storage, all ending with the question of how much to ask for each in order to achieve a twenty-percent profit margin.

Raj closed his eyes, went into his calculating-trance, and presented him with the answer quickly enough to leave him with a look of surprise on his face.

"Well!" said the man. "For once—I don't suppose he can write, too?"

Mondragon had that funny little smile again. "Give him something to write with." He seemed to be enjoying the man's discomfiture.

Raj was presented with a pencil and an old bill of lading—he appropriated a ledger to write on, and promptly recopied the front onto the back, and in a much neater hand.

"You win," the man said with resignation. "Why don't you tell me exactly what's been going on—and how you managed to resurrect these two?"

Mondragon just smiled.

The man took Mondragon off somewhere, returning after a bit with a troubled look and a bundle which he handed to Denny.

"You, boy—I want you here at opening time sharp, and in this uniform. And you're not Takahashi anymore, you're—Diaz; you're close enough to the look. Got that?"

Denny took the bundle soberly. "Yes, m'ser."

"As for you—" Raj tried not to sway with fatigue, but the man saw it anyway, "—you're out on your feet—no good to anyone until you get some rest.

Besides, two new kids in one day—hard to explain. You get fed—and clean, real clean. We have a reputation to maintain. And get that hair taken care of. I want you here in two days. With those eyes—you're no Diaz. Make it—uh—Tai. I don't suppose you'd rather be sent back to your family? They'd be glad to have you."

"No m'ser," Raj replied adamantly. "I won't put danger on them. Bad enough it's on me."

The man shook his head. "Lord and Ancestors— you're a fool, boy, but a brave one. Right enough— now get out of here. Before I remember, I'm *not* a fool."

Mondragon escorted them to the door, stopping them just inside it.

"This wasn't free—" he told Raj quietly.

"M'ser, I know that, m'ser."

"Just so we both know. I'm going to be calling in this debt—calling in all those things you promised me. I may call it in so often you wish you'd never thought of coming to me."

"M'ser Mondragon," Raj replied, looking him full in the eyes, "I *owe* you. And I can't ever pay it all."

Because you had us in your hand, said his look, *And you didn't kill us—when you had every right and reason to—and then you went over the line to help us. I know it, and you know it. I don't know why you did it, but I owe you.*

"Well. . . ." Mondragon seemed slightly embarrassed by the intensity of that stare. "They say the one who wins is the one left standing, so by all counts you came out of this a winner. Be grateful—and remember to keep your mouth shut."

Raj figured that was the best advice he'd had in a long time.

Denny hauled Raj back to Rif and Rat before taking him "home." The Raj that came from their hands was much shorter of hair by a foot or two; and a bit darker of complexion—not to mention a lot cleaner and with a good hot breakfast in his stomach. It wasn't quite dawn when he and his brother descended to the bottom of the dry air-shaft on Fife that Denny had made his home. Denny gave him a pair of blankets to roll up in, and he was sleeping the sleep of the exhausted before Denny had gotten into his store clothes. Denny smiled to himself, a smile warm and content with the world, and set to one last task before heading back to Gallandry.

He pried up a particular board in the bottom of the shaft, felt around until he located the little bag he had hung there, and pulled it out. Jones was bound to hear of this—and he reckoned he'd better have a peace-offering. And there was that scarf he'd taken off that duelist to prove to Rif he was able.

After the Gallandrys let him go for the day, he waited under Fishmarket Bridge, knowing she'd be by. When he spotted her, he swung down to hang from the support by his knees.

He whistled. She looked up.

"Yo—Jones—" he called. "Peace, huh? Truce? Okay? Here's something for sorrys." He'd knotted a pebble into one corner of the scarf—and it was a nice one; silk, bright red. He dropped it neatly at her feet, and scrambled back up before she could get over her surprise. With Jones it was a good idea to get out of line-of-sight and find out about reactions later.

Besides—he warmed to the thought—he had to get back home. His family was waiting.

FESTIVAL MOON
(REPRISED)

C.J. Cherryh

Jones carefully tucked the skip up in the midnight
shadow of Princeton Low Bridge, on the backside of
Ventani. Meritt warehouse was to shore on the one
hand; and a papermill on the right, not an interesting neighborhood for Festival celebrants or foot traffic on the low bridges. Boats with lanterns glided
past on the canals to either end. This was dark, inky
dark, where she snagged a bridge timber with the
boathook, and drew close.

There was a low odd whistle. A shadow unfolded
itself out of the bridge supports and a weight dropped
lightly onto the well-slats.

"That you?"

Thump.

"Damn," Mondragon said softly, and tackle went
rattling off across the slats. "What's this junk?"

"Hey, this here ain't no fancyboat." She squatted
down on the halfdeck, holding them steady with the
boathook locked in knees and arms, toes flexing as
the skip bobbed against the hook-hold and the motion of old Det shoving at them. "Turn up anything?"

"Nothing I was looking for." The boat rocked to a
new motion as he worked aft and came up closer, to
stand bracing them against a bridge timber. "Fish
won't take the bait. I think they know."

"Good! Maybe they suddenly got sense."

"Take me home."

"You gone crazy?"

"Home."

"Now, why don't I just run ye out to Megary, go knock on the door and *ask* 'em take you in?"

"I can walk."

"Ye can damn well use sense! If you ain't heard nothing, it's because they heard your Friend is into it. You got Her and Him stalking each other round and round now, is what, and what they're looking for ain't stirring, no way they move in on that."

"Move the damn boat, Jones. We're up against shore."

Noise, the man meant. She unhooked and pushed, ran the hook-pole butt out end down and stood up, poling out from under the bridge-shadow as her passenger sat down, a blackness up against the hidey entry, his arm on the halfdeck under her feet.

Around Ventani and into Margrave East, under Coffin Bridge and out onto the Grand, where Festival lights spilled gold and red and green onto the inky waters, and the Angel watched with sword half-drawn.

Fools, Angel, fools, two of us, right here in this skip, enough to set the Retribution back a hundred years.

"Home," he said.

"You just been kidnapped," she said. "I got you, you ain't going nowhere till you got better sense. You ain't going nowhere near Petrescu—'less you drink Det water doing it."

"Jones, don't be an ass."

"I ain't. I ain't taking you where they can get you."

"And where do we hide? Kalugin pays my rent, dammit, and it's Tatiana's bullylads he's scared off us. Where do we hide from *him*, when the money runs out? You think he'd drop me? You think he'd let me slip?"

"He ain't asking ye to commit suicide! Ye go out in public, ye sit in the bars where we got friends, ye wait for Lord knows what—that's one thing. But it ain't your fault if there ain't nothing going to try, if it's a fish going to spit out the bait—ye don't got t'go swimming with the sherks!"

"And when *do* I go home, now?" he asked softly. "When *do* I go—now, when we have Anastasi's attention—or later, when Festival dies down? When I have to live there and wait? No, Jones. Anastasi didn't just happen into this. He knows something he isn't saying. He's onto something. He wants me for bait—we're not alone out here. Take me home. Let's do what he says—stir the water, and see what surfaces. The word is out—in some places. I know that much. Justiciary may not know. But it's out. And if they're going to move, I want it face-on. Hear me? Not at my back, three months from now."

Her gut hurt. She missed a stroke with the pole. "He don't want to lose you."

"No. He doesn't. But coin's for spending, isn't it?"

"I dunno."

"You want help poling?"

"Yey."

SWORD PLAY

Janet & Chris Morris

The sword is drawn, slow clearing its scabbard, but drawn nonetheless, riverboat captain Michael Chamoun thought as his pilot steered the great boat toward its New Harbor slip at Rimmon Bridge past the statue of the lesser angel standing guard over the harbor, toward the trellised town beyond. Coming into Merovingen in sunset, two nights before 24th Harvest, everything seemed fraught with meaning to Chamoun.

Especially the angel, whom the Revenantists called Michael. His angel, his namesake. They shared the name, if not the stock the Revenantists put in it. Ain't nothin, ain't squat, Michael Chamoun told himself, spread-legged on the poop above his captain's quarters in the gilt-edged dusk, letting the pungent wind buffet him.

They'd come past Rimmon Isle, home of the Nikolaevs, who had their fingers in the Revenantist College and the Signeury, both. Deep waters, there. That passage had brought him out onto the deck and kept him there, it had, chasing his ghosts and his hopes, fending off notice and questions from his pilot's boy. He'd outright stared up at the Rimmon Isle houses, ignoring the bustle on the main deck of his crowded boat, the *Detfish*, as if none of it existed. Because it didn't, not when he passed Rimmon, where the Nikolaev family lived; where the Nikolaev girl,

Revenantist and forbidden, lived: Rita Nikolaev, Revenantist, devout, off-limits and out of bounds.

"Michael? Like the Angel back home in Merovingen", Rita had said to him delightedly, that day five-odd years ago, in Nev Hettek at the inauguration ceremony for the present governor, Karl Fon. Then she'd smiled like salvation, this girl-woman, adding gravely, *"Touch my hand, Michael, for luck. My karma's improving. . . ."* When he'd done that she'd fled, giggling, into the crowd of uptowners and foreigners. A Revenantist, a ghost, a forbidden nymph who was by now probably prematurely aged with child-bearing, fat and ugly like some contented cow.

Wherever she was now, then she'd been above his station—a hightowner from a political Merovingian house, and a Revenantist to boot, who worried about her personal Karma—entanglements to her future lives.

But he'd taken this trip because he might see her at the end of it, no matter the dangers, no matter the difficulties.

And if he saw her, so what? The Revenantists think the Angel is named Michael. I'm Michael Chamoun, a Nev Hetteker Adventist, he reminded himself. If I weren't what else I am, it would still be impossible. *Her family's patroned by Anastasi Kalugin same as Boregy, and you'll not be popular with Kalugins of any degree if you screw around with both, Michael boy,* Romanov had told him.

Not popular by a long shot, if he took too heavy a hand, or missed his cues; not when Anastasi Kalugin, youngest and most militant of the governor's three children, had certain families in his pocket; not when Anastasi was about to be confirmed as "advocate militiar"—chief justice for Merovingen's entire military justice system, including the blackleg militia. Not when the chief militiar's commission was all but in Anastasi's hands as well, making his sister, Tatiana, understandably nervous that something might happen to Papa Kalugin before she could move against her little brother.

And most especially not when Anastasi Kalugin

wanted nothing so much as war with Nev Hettek, and the Nev Hetteker governor, Karl Fon, had ideas of his own along those lines.

Fon wanted a war, all right, but one that would gain him the whole Det Valley, and perhaps Merovingen as well—a war on Nev Hetteker terms, a war he couldn't lose. And Nev Hetteker terms were quite different from Kalugin's Merovingian ones. They had nothing to do with fielding forces to fight the blackleg militia that was the law in Merovingen in peacetime, its army in wartime.

Nev Hetteker war was already under way. It was war in the shadows, war in the streets, war by intimidation, by assassination, by terror. Karl Fon had become governor of Nev Hettek under the bloody auspices of the Sword of God, shadow movers, empire shakers, revolution makers. Karl Fon was secretly Sword of God, publicly orthodox Adventist, and cramped in Nev Hettek.

Sword of God: Adventist crazies, militants, assassins, so far as Merovingians were concerned. The Sword trained its people in martial arts and taught that a second Scouring was coming, a Scouring that would bring Retribution on earth. Toward that day, everything was channeled: the alien sharrh and sharrist influence must be obliterated so that technology could come again; temporal power must be increased, no matter the personal cost; self-sacrifice in the cause brought rewards in God's good time—when the sharrh were obliterated back to their homeworld. Meanwhile, you readied for war with the alien sharrh and you knew damn well that Revenantists and sharrists and Janes and the rest were all alien sympathizers. Or, at least, you ought to know it.

There was only one group capable of steeling this world for what was to come, and that was the Sword. Based in secret cells in Nev Hettek, where tech was more than a remembered dream, it was growing stronger. Needed to grow. Didn't care what it took.

Bases had to be expanded, power coordinated. For up there, beyond the placid sky, there might be sharrh right now. Sharrh in orbit, sharrh with planet-singeing tech, sharrh ready to fry you to cinders. You couldn't know, not for certain—the tech level it would take to find out, to build the devices from the books the Sword had, would draw sharrh fire if you dared to power it up. Emissions were deadly.

So you made your weapons out of men, and you spread the strength. It was Karl Fon's doctrine of revolution and it was digging into Merovingen at a bedrock level, reaching right up where it counted, into high-town—into Merovingen-above.

Yo, angel, Michael Chamoun called out silently as his boat passed beneath the harbor statue, *say hello to Rita for me.*

He'd plotted a course past Rimmon to a farside slip on the excuse of picking up some contraband from Megary, all by the charts and the notes and the contacts that the previous captain had left for him. It was as close as Michael Chamoun was going to get to the Revenantist girl he'd only seen once, unless she was at the Merovingian governor's 24th Eve Festival Ball.

Chamoun fervently hoped she wasn't going to be. He had a cargo more illegal than slaves and more deadly than pathati gas weapons: his riverboat, the *Detfish,* had Sword of God aboard.

The *Detfish* was bringing five Sword of God men (two hidden among her crew and three hiding in plain sight, bold as brass, flaunting their diplomatic invitations via Boregy) to Anastasi Kalugin's party.

" 'Ware! 'Ware aft!" came a call from behind, and Chamoun looked back. He saw a small craft, a woman at its helm, a woman with a cap down over her eyes and no business crossing his wake and bitching about it, nearly invisible in the afterdusk swathing the Harbor.

" 'Ware my ass, where's your running lights?" Chamoun called back, and realized he'd made an error. It was too poor a boat for running lights, a flimsy thing with an ancient outboard.

And there were others, as they nosed their way toward the slips, where the Sword wanted to go—

boats of all descriptions, but small. Not like the craft he's seen headed toward Rimmon Isle, a long black yacht belonging to the Nikolaev. Now Chamoun was entering unknown territory: Merovingen was all stories and second-hand knowledge; he'd never brought any boat this far south before, let alone a riverboat.

It was getting too dark to see anything but the shapes, at any rate. His pilot knew the Harbor, but Chamoun worried anyway. You couldn't trust 'em, not a one: not the uptowners, not the Merovingian Adventists, not his contacts ashore or, most especially, not the Sword members he had on board.

They would be wondering where he was. They wouldn't understand, nor give a damn that they should. His itinerary was planned, this trip arranged by cooler heads and colder hearts. What Michael Chamoun wanted didn't count for eels to those who'd gotten him this boat, this trip, this . . . chance to see her again, yeah. Rita was why he'd taken it. Rita was why he'd agreed.

Tie up at the seawall, walk Grand Detside till you find a pole-boat with a white flag on the bow. Take it to Boregy. Opposite the Signeury, that is. Their own bridge across to it, their own ways into it. . . . It'll do fine there, just do what you know to do. All told to Michael Chamoun through a carved screen in an Adventist meeting hall back in Nev Hettek, under dim electrics, by he-didn't-know-who.

He didn't care to know. He was coming in as a possible suitor to some rich Revenantist Boregy woman, with enough surreptitious Sword of God flanking him to make sure he did it right. He'd have agreed to marry old Iosef Kalugin himself if it would have got him here, out of Nev Hettek, where he could see Rita again.

Didn't matter who you were married to. . . . Merovingian women slept where they wanted, whelped brats by different fathers, did much as they pleased. Didn't matter, unless you were an Adventist and the woman was devout Revenantist and scared of fouling up her life and lives.

Hopeless. Helpless. Bringing the Revenantists to

their knees had seemed like a close second to courting a Revenantist woman who wouldn't have him, when
the right Nev Hetteker did the asking. Chamoun's
family were river-boaters now; were *shippers* and new
society; *Detfish* was theirs to keep if Chamoun did his
job and lived to captain it home.

He took the steps from the poop with care: there
was a slick of mist everywhere; then he pulled open
the hatch to his cabin and descended.

The Boregys were hiding an ex-Sword in and
among their hightown holdings. Somewhere up in
Merovingen-above, where the occasional light twin-
kled like a whole new spiral of stars, was secreted a
liability and a troublemaker called Mondragon.

One final look at the city-upon-city-upon-city stacked
like a house of cards up toward heaven, and Chamoun
let the hatch close, finding his way in deeper dark
with a familiar hand, trailing it along the paneling:
this riverboat was in camouflage—more than it
seemed, more than his family could refuse.

Like Mondragon, Michael Chamoun had dim
prospects—if this gambit failed. He felt a kinship with
the man whom the Sword was hunting. Mondragon
was the last of his line left alive (after he'd fallen
afoul of his one-time friend, Karl Fon, and Fon had
decreed Sword vengeance), if proof were needed.
Chamoun didn't want to become the last of his.

There were three men in Chamoun's cabin.

The man who sprawled, under a closely shielded
electric, on the captain's bed as if it were his own,
was Dimitri Romanov. "Well, Det-man, have you seen
what you wanted to see?" he asked Chamoun. Fine
diction, fine manners, fine control of what Sword
was aboard the *Detfish*, and of more back in Nev
Hettek.

"Ain't nothin' t' see," Michael Chamoun replied,
sinking into one of two unoccupied chairs at the tiny
table catty-corner to the bed. "C'mon, Mita," he added,
river-talking to a man who despised such talk, because he had to gain control of something, and Romanov had all the authority aboard the *Detfish*, no
matter who was captain. "Charts say a boat big as

this, she can't clear the Rimmon bridges." Defensive. Too much so. Chamoun shrugged at Romanov: *don't push me.*

Dimitri Romanov didn't like being called "Mita" so familiarly by Chamoun. He looked from Chamoun to the two other men in the small cabin, and smiled sourly.

Romanov was pale, blond, covered with a layer of good-life fat that belied his Sword training. The other two Swords were dark like Chamoun, hard and lean like Chamoun, and nearly ten years younger: Rack and Ruin al-Banna, brothers of the revolution, youngsters who took ears from their kills and strung them on necklaces they wore at Sword parties. Monsters of the revolution, Romanov's trained and lethal pets.

Chamoun lowered his green eyes and looked at the dark hair feathering his wrist, at the dark skin tanned olive under it. He wasn't fish or fowl; he was mixed blood and mixed up. If his family were richer or poorer, life would have been clearer, right and wrong better defined.

Chamoun trusted only tech, and lusted for it like it was the Revenantist woman. His father had been government until the revolution, a tech supervisor; his mother had been a teacher. Now they had a fledgling shipping business, thanks to Karl Fon, who always paid his debts. And Chamoun's tail was firmly caught in the door that swung between his parents and Nev Hettek's governor.

He flushed under Romanov's scrutiny, wishing he hadn't come down here. The al-Banna brothers eyed him suspiciously, too. You could have cut the tension with the fish knife on Chamoun's hip, probably because the Sword pilot, up on deck, had questions about the berth Chamoun had chosen.

The pilot abovedecks was as tall as Michael Chamoun, taller than average, fairer and more solidly built. Up in the pilothouse, he ought to have been calling down by now.

The silence down in the little cabin grew until Chamoun's ears began to thump with his pulse.

"Cool feet, m'ser," said one of the al-Banna broth-

ers, rising to his feet, "don't matter now. Too late's
the time, ain't no doubt."

Chamoun looked up at the hook-nosed Sword and
said, "I didn't say nothin'. I wouldn't. I know what
I'm into."

It was the pale aristocrat who nodded, "Good boy."

They called you that, these Uptowner Swords, even
if you were of an age with them. Michael Chamoun
had five years of manhood on the curly-haired Sword
youths who watched him with restive violence in
their velvet eyes. A matter of power, matter of money,
matter of class.

"Once you've cleaned up, Chamoun," continued
Romanov, "and gotten into these,"—he gestured to a
pile beside him on Chamoun's bed: velvet, lace, wool,
polished leather and a scabbarded dress sword—
"we'll deal with the fine points. All your papers are
in order. Vega Boregy is expecting you. I imagine
he'll present his daughter, Cassiopeia, at the first
opportunity." When Chamoun didn't answer in the
pause Romanov provided, the Sword aristocrat rose
up, dusted his white-clad knees, and motioned to the
al-Bannas: "Come, boys, let's let the suitor dress in
peace. He must appear at his most fetching."

"Damn," said Chamoun, running a spread hand
up into his dark brown hair, finding a knot, jerking
irritably. His fingers came away with a few strands of
hair, some graying prematurely, curled around them.

He felt like a paid woman must feel, he imagined.
Or a trapped cat about to be let out in someone's
attic full of rats.

He just looked at his worn shoes and listened as
the other men made their way toward the door. Too
late, got to do it now, or die of not doing it. He knew
the Sword. They didn't take no for an answer. If he
found Mondragon somewhere there in Boregy, he'd
be finding what was left of somebody who'd tried
saying no.

The door hadn't closed yet; Chamoun didn't raise
his eyes. "Be a good boy, Michael. So much depends
on you. We're all hopeful of your success. I know
Magruder is."

At last, an outright threat. The pilot, Chance Magruder, was Sword with a capital S. "Mita," said Chamoun to Dimitri Romanov, "go. . . ." Mustn't tell Romanov where to go. ". . . Check procedure, or something. Else we'll be congratulating each other in the Justiciary's torture chambers."

The door closed and Chamoun slumped as if someone had cut strings holding him upright. Romanov was tactical Sword, one of Fon's best; the al-Banna brothers were the worst kind of Sword assassins, all muscle, no brains; Magruder, up in the pilothouse, was more frightening than all the others rolled together. Magruder was a twenty-year man, a man who'd been doing Sword business so long that you had to look straight into his granite eyes to realize he didn't believe in any of it, not the cause, not Retribution. He didn't have to. Chance Magruder *was* Retribution, the will of Karl Fon incarnate.

And that made four smuggled members of the Sword of God, brought into Merovingen to wreak havoc and deal death. Brought by Michael Chamoun, if anybody took the blame, because you couldn't hit back from here to Nev Hettek. That was what tech and the Sword itself were worth: protection for Fon and his kind in Nev Hettek.

If smuggling the Swords ashore were the extent of Michael Chamoun's involvement, he'd have been nerved up, but not nearly paralyzed. Damn girl, damn Rita. Doesn't even know I got drunk and took this one because of her. Doesn't know or care. Probably doesn't remember me. If only the Sword wanted a Nikolaev girl instead of Cassiopeia Boregy. . . .

But they didn't. And of all the candidates Fon thought likely to succeed in making a marriage with the Boregy family, Michael Chamoun had been chosen.

Because women liked him; because he was the right age and the right build and of the right mercantile profile to interest the Boregys, thanks to the Sword.

And, most of all, because Michael Chamoun was the fifth man aboard the *Detfish* with orders from

Nev Hettek that must be obeyed: Michael Chamoun
was Sword of God.

Chance Magruder had changed into sable velvet
and cream silk by the time Chamoun came on deck.
Only the revolver tucked against his spine, the sword
on his hip, and the pathati-ampules nestled among
throwing stars in his belt-slung purse were familiar.
The rest of this, by his reckoning, was as bad an idea
as had ever come out of one of Karl Fon's drunken
stupors.

The younger man, who stopped half-way through
the hatch to stare at Magruder, wasn't right for this
gambit. The gray in Chamoun's hair was as sporadic
as his nerves and as non-indicative of his perfor-
mance as his record.

But you worked with what you had. Magruder
had an invitation to the Merovingian Governor's 24th
Eve bash, and a bash it was going to be, if the Sword
had anything to say about it. This Chamoun was just
a pry-bar. With him, Magruder was going to open
whatever barrel contained Thomas Mondragon. From
there on, events tended to depend on discretion—
Magruder's. Bring Mondragon back, kill him, compromise him . . . whatever worked.

One thing was certain in Magruder's mind: the
Sword needed to make it clear to all and sundry that
there was no such thing as *ex*-Sword. Especially
to fellows like Chamoun, who tended to stare at
Magruder as if Chamoun were a cornered rat and
Magruder the feral cat.

Which wasn't a bad analogy. You didn't quit the
Sword. Mondragon had tried and Mondragon's life
or death from that day on had to be an example of
what happened to traitors. Mondragon's death wasn't
the best choice, unless it was particularly and spec-
tacularly terrifying. To Magruder's mind, the fate of
Mondragon was history in the making—the future
of the Sword lay in how the traitor fared.

And Mike Chamoun was a poor chisel for sculpt-
ing history, in Magruder's estimation. Better than no
tool at all, though. So Magruder had kept Chamoun

primarily in the dark—he knew only what he needed to know.

It could be that Chamoun didn't even know that, Magruder thought as he said in a flat voice, "I'm going with you. Hurry up."

"I know the way, don't need no—"

"Cut the river-talk, Det-man. Your Nev Hettek accent's all that makes you any better than a pole-rat dressed up in a dead man's clothes. You don't know squat. Now I'm telling you what you need to know. You know I'm from the Nev Hettek Bureau of Trade and Tariffs—Customs man. You know I've got an invite to Kalugin's party. And you know you oughtn't to cross me, or you won't be shipping anything, anywhere. Now, let's go. I got to get you there to get any use out of you, and it's Festival. If I want you gutted, floating along the Grand, I'll do it myself. There're too many crazy people with the Melancholy out there for one man, m'ser."

That softened it: acknowledge Chamoun as a man, give him a m'ser, tell him he's worth a bodyguard. And make sure he understands the briefing he's just gotten. There was, Magruder knew because it was his job to judge the edge on a sword or a man, a chance that Chamoun would balk. He didn't need another Tom Mondragon; nobody did.

So it was down onto the Harborside, and walk with shoulders brushing, commanding the dockside walkways two abreast, until a certain pole-boat was found.

Then it was show a piece of silver and try to understand the gutter talk of Merovingen-below. The pole-boater was a woman, and Magruder's silver spoke loudly enough. She'd have poled them to the Scouring and back for a handful of silver skimmers.

"Hey-hin, m'sers," the female pole-boater said. "Hey-hin and yoss right up to Boregy, I will."

It was gibberish until you thought about it. Then it was as close to a welcome aboard and assurance of competence as these Det-trash could get.

She poled and hollered at other polers, and Magruder watched the bridges to make sure she was taking him, by the fastest route, where he and Chamoun were bound.

Someone called, "Jones! Ware starb'd; a starb'd!" and two boats almost collided—theirs and another.

Nearly, he took the pole from the woman in the loose sweater. Probably drunk. Possibly hostile. But Magruder slid his hand from the knife he'd grabbed reflexively and watched carefully, dividing his attention between landmarks, the woman, and Chamoun, whose instincts seemed good in this circumstance.

At least, Chamoun's "fish" knife had come into his hand. You trained them and trained them, but you had to see them in a situation like this to know if they were really Sword, or just talked a good game.

The name Jones had lodged in Magruder's mind, but he doubted luck: if this was *that* Jones, then Magruder could slit Chamoun's throat, push him into the canal, and go to Plan B. But it wasn't clear which female of the two who'd exchanged shouts was Jones. And it wasn't clear how many Joneses there might be poling these canals. And it wasn't clear yet that Magruder ought to grab Mondragon's girl, Jones.

There were other ways.

The best of those began at Boregy House. When the pole-boater brought them to it, he let her go with an extra skimmer for her tip once she'd poled them in through the water gate, where a demon's face had lit when a watchman answered the bell she'd pulled.

The iron gate, closed after sundown, that had opened to admit them once Magruder identified himself as Nev Hettek Trade and Tariff, gaped wide again for the pole-boater, and she glided away.

Iron screeched as the gate closed and there was a shock of finality as it shut, like a prison door slamming. Magruder could feel Chamoun, beside him, shiver. Good instincts, once again. They were in this place, locked up tight, under the watchful eye of the gatekeep. There would be more and more of his kind, armed retainers of the house, up those stairs.

Prison. Magruder had been there more than once. He took a last look out toward the canaled city and

freedom, and glimpsed the Signeury, out beyond
Signeury Cross where no boats moored.

The Boregys had their own damned bridge, private, to the signeury, beyond which was another bridge,
to the Justiciary, which had interrogation and holding
facilities in its depths, down in the solid bedrock into
which the government center was set—special facilities for special, politically sensitive prisoners, the kind
you wouldn't want to execute publicly on Hanging
Bridge. The kind of facilities you wanted for a Chance
Magruder, if you got your hands on him.

Mike Chamoun they'd probably just hang, if things
went awry. His type didn't know enough to be worth
protracted interrogation. But Magruder was. And
Tom Mondragon was.

"C'mon, m'sers, if ye please," said an impatient
voice and Magruder turned to see a white-stockinged
houseman come down from upstairs to get them.
The man had shiny buckles on his shoes and a defi-
nite air of impatience. Didn't come down here much.
Didn't have to. The kind he usually greeted walked
the hightown bridges from place to place, never
came in the water gate. The water gate was for
family. And for shady dealings. The fellow wrinkled
his paunchy face into the time-honored put-upon
demeanor of class-conscious servants everywhere, and
held his lamp high.

Turning, the servant preceded them up dimly lit
stairs. From niches and narrow corridors off the
gardeporte, Magruder heard shuffling feet: go with
this one, or get a heavier escort.

He elbowed Chamoun and they followed, up and
around and up again, Magruder watching everything, memorizing turns and twists, where the scattered electrics burned, in case he might have to run
for it.

Prison feel here, and a real prison over that connecting bridge, one from which the Sword probably
couldn't extract him. Magruder was sweating in his
Merovingian foppery. Chamoun, beside him, didn't
have sense enough to sweat. He just gawked.

Take a good look, boy. Engrave every window on the

water-side in your memory; count the doorways, the corri-
dors. Might come back this way in Retribution's own hurry.

Prison two bridges away across the canal, and
Mondragon wasn't in it. Tom Mondragon should
have been, that was the root of Fon's distress. A
renegade Sword who had tried for Karl Fon's guts, and
he slipped prison and was living high in Merovingen
on Boregy sufferance and borrowed money. Something reeked. Reeked like deals with the Merovingian
government. If Mondragon wasn't dead and wasn't
locked up in the Justiciary's underfloors, babbling
answers to questions before they were asked, there
had to be a reason why. Karl Fon and Tom Mondragon had been the best of friends, once. Now Fon
figured Mondragon for the worst of enemies. Fon
couldn't rest easy while Mondragon was sucking up
to Merovingen's governing family, which was the
best reading of what was going on here.

Not the preferred reading, just the most likely.
Magruder shot a look at Chamoun on a stair landing, up where the electrics were more frequent and
the servant leading them was beginning to wheeze. A
long run down them, or a long dive into the canal.
Detwater funerals beat long conversations, to Magruder's way of thinking.

Chamoun didn't seem to be thinking at all. He
wasn't pale or flushed, he was just putting one foot
in front of the other. Good boy, so far.

Either the Det-man hadn't heard the stealthy foot-
falls behind—at least a landing's turning behind,
always, but never out of earshot if you knew what to
listen for—or he wasn't worrying about it.

Why the hell not, Magruder didn't spend energy
wondering. Chamoun was the choice because he wasn't
looking too deeply into things. Naïvête wasn't the
most unlikely thing to keep you alive in a situation
like this.

Finally the climbing stopped and the retainer's
buckled shoes clopped on a floor of polished red
stone until a columned door was reached. There the
pasty man displayed the flourish which was probably
his only real skill, opening the door and bowing low

and announcing, "The Nev Hettekkers m'ser Michael Chamoun, captain of the *Detfish*, and his excellency Chance Magruder, Minister of the Nev Hettek Bureau of Trade and Tariffs."

Still bent low, the servant gestured them forward.

Magruder could see Chamoun draw a deep breath as they entered the Boregy reception hall, or study or whatever it was. More red stone, white-veined; black and white marble as well, statues and mantle and columns, all setting off a huge gilt table desk up yet more stairs.

Like a damned courtroom, or a governor's palace.

Airs to beat the band, these Boregys had—and trade balances to back 'em up.

Desk lamps and wall lamps, electrics shaded by eggshell-thin stone and cloth, and even a chandelier . . . and under that, a black-haired man with a fierce, down-turned mustache and coal eyes to match, dressed like a wedding present in brocade and velvet pantaloons: Vega Boregy, Chamoun's future father-in-law, if all went well.

"Gentlemen," said Boregy, coming around the desk with long strides. "I've been expecting you. Your office, Minister Magruder, was at pains to make sure I was." Boregy came to the head of the stairs.

But not down the stairs. They climbed the dais to take his outstretched hand, Magruder finally thankful for the lace shirt and cuffs and the velvet and the silk he was wearing.

He'd played high-toned games before. He took Vega Boregy's jeweled fingers in his and met a forceful squeeze with one more forceful, then let go before test became threat.

Mondragon hooked up with this house? Magruder said to Boregy, "Then my office also sent the credentials and official exploratory on the matter of your marriageable daughter?" His eyes slid to Chamoun, who was in his turn taking Boregy's proffered hand.

"Indeed," Boregy said and inclined his head toward Chamoun, who seemed to have lost the power of speech.

Say something, boy! Any damn thing.

And that was what Chamoun said: "Glad to meet you, ser. It's been a long voyage up here, the *Detfish's* first. She's our new flagship, you know. Maybe you'll come see her?"

Diction, passable. *Don't slip.* Magruder was as near to praying as he could manage. *No river-talk, Det-man. We need to prove you're classy enough for this bunch.* It wasn't going to be easy.

Vega Boregy called for chairs and wine, "refreshments," without answering either question directly.

Servants trained to near-invisibility turned up, soundlessly gliding over the floors with gold and silver service.

They all sat, Vega behind his desk, backlit. Just a bit too much light shining in the visitors' eyes. *Nice touch, power-broker.* Magruder leaned back in his velvet-stuffed chair and put his hands on its gilt arms, carved like whales. The chair's back pushed the revolver he carried against his spine. The pressure was comforting.

Vega told the servants to leave the wine and go and that wasn't, apparently, normal procedure.

Then he picked up his glass and Magruder followed suit, Chamoun one beat behind.

"A toast," offered Vega Boregy, "to a possible merger—and marriage—of unlimited potential."

Slick bastard, he hadn't said squat: "possible; potential." *Just show me Tom Mondragon, and I'm out of here,* Magruder proposed silently. But he couldn't say that. This wasn't that kind of situation, or that kind of man. All innuendo and oblique fencing, on the other side of that table.

What can I get out of you, Customs man? Vega Boregy wanted to know. Magruder was prepared for that. He reached slowly, with his left hand, into his breast pocket and came out with a fold of documents bearing Nev Hettek's Trade and Tariffs seal. Leaning forward, he said, "This contains the Bureau's proposed easements, projected tax rates, what we feel is a fair arrangement to all concerned. Considering that this would be the first official merger across state lines since the Fon administration took power, we've left sufficient room for your own people to emend or amend specifics." *In other words, buddy, your kid marries ours, and you're a dual citizen, or at least your trading ventures are treated like you are—better than your uncle was before Fon kicked the Boregy office out for consorting with Mondragons. You get special privileges up the ass, is what you get, more perks than any of your canal-rat buddies. And we get a permanent ear to the door of everything worth knowing that's talked about in Merovingen-above's privy councils, because we expect Chamoun to be treated like one of your own sons—maybe better.*

Vega Boregy reached very slowly for the document, his coal-black eyes resting first on Magruder, then on Chamoun. Magruder could almost hear the hiss as heat met cold when that gaze came back to his and Boregy finally took the document.

"Cheese, gentlemen? Fruit? It will take me a few moments to look this over."

There was eagerness there, Magruder thought.

Whatever Chamoun thought, the young Sword slid down in his chair, drinking fine wine like beer in a tavern, slugging it down.

Magruder fixed on the mirror over the mantle, in which their tableau was reflected. He could see only the back of Vega Boregy's long black-haired head, the white neck, the shoulders rounded from too many of these meetings under burning electrics too late into the night. As on similar occasions, ignoring all else with a skill that made it inoffensive, Vega Boregy sat still and read.

Mike Chamoun's reflection was no less troubling: the premature gray in his hair was the most distinguishing feature Chamoun had, something to recommend him besides youth, size, and health. Under thirty, free of physical defect, with a dark Det-man's tan and green eyes to lend breeding to a mongrel face of uncertain provenance. Attractive, perhaps, if that meant anything to this endeavor. An honest face, square forehead and flaring jaws; nose a trifle long, lips as thin on a mouth too wide; folds and hollows from tension and weathered all over from the wind—no aristocrat's face, by any stretch. But a body fine enough, long limbs and delicate hands that startled because everywhere else, muscle fleshed him out: stamp of honest work, not a good thing here. But heir to a shipping house: that was.

Next to Magruder, Chamoun was slight for his height, spindly, somehow inconsequential and brief. But Magruder had been through a revolution and survived with everything his people had had before, intact. Magruder was a creature of balance, coming into middle age without concern for its marks on him. Privation might be read by the Boregys as dissipation, something they understood. The lines around his narrow, colorless eyes didn't need to be explained; the eyes themselves had faded in harsh sunlight to a no-color gray; punctuation marks framed his tight mouth and the sardonic twist at its corners could be controlled—when he had to. If he'd been what he pretended, the weight he carried would be fat, unless he was vain beyond measure. His big hands were scarred from fire (it looked enough like freckles); his neck was broad from years of weighty helmets; his hairline was receding, the hair above once reddish, now straw and dirty blond and white.

It struck him, studying the mirror's reflection, that Chamoun could have been his son, if he'd bedded a fine-boned, dark-skinned river-girl when he'd been in his early teens.

But Magruder was married to the Sword, and that would show if he ever had to take his clothes off, here. Maps on him, a white line here, a patch of keloid there—his souvenirs. More than the hardness in his face, excusable because rich men and powerful men, as well as violent men, needed that, his body under all this silk and velvet might play him false.

But only if the Boregys could see beyond the profit in the offer he was making. Gold had a way of blinding men. And a lot of sweat in Nev Hettek had gone into making sure that the offer was dazzling enough to do the job, without being suspicious.

Chamoun ate cheese and crackers and brushed crumbs from his fancy pants. Disciplined enough—he didn't look to Magruder for help or reassurance directly, only let a tentative smile cross his reflection in the mirror.

Finally, Boregy looked up and asked, "Have you seen my daughter, then, Captain Chamoun? Or is this generous offer based only on mercantile considerations?"

Magruder wanted to intervene, interrupt the boy before the Sword lost everything.

But Michael Chamoun said, "I'm looking at her father, aren't I? We were told she was your daughter, as well as your wife's."

Magruder's hand slid toward his spine, every inch of him ready for all hell to break loose there and then. A shout, guards, being thrown ignominiously out the water gate. . . .

Three breaths of silence, and then Vega Boregy laughed a hearty, cultured laugh. And said, "I like you, Chamoun. It's not imperative, but it's a help. Cassie's my blood daughter, yes. You'll know that when you meet her—she's a mind of her own, I'm afraid."

"And half of Merovingen paying her court," Magruder eased in, deflecting Boregy's attention. "But the dowry's substantial, we think. And the merger historic. The first step toward better relations between our governments must be at the mercantile level. Surely your daughter's a patriot."

Boregy didn't quite grimace. "I'll not force the issue with my daughter—a three year marriage is no small thing—and an Adventist—but I'll tell you both—this is most tempting. Captain Chamoun," Vega Boregy leaned forward, turning his wine glass absently, "I must ask a personal question."

Magruder's hand was still in his belt.

Chamoun leaned forward also, as if he and Boregy were courting one another instead of trying to get Vega's daughter contracted. "Ask, m'ser."

"Would you be willing to convert—to make your home here, with us in this house? Otherwise, communications and coordination would be so cumbersome as to drain profit from the venture tie. A tie of convenience is out of the question."

"Convert?" Chamoun frowned. "Live in Merovingen?"

"In Boregy House. Bring your ships, base your activities here—become devout—it's the only way I'll be able to gain concessions from the Kalugins to match those you've gotten from Karl Fon. They'll be nervous. There is some current tension, you must be aware."

"Must be aware," Retribution's heart! But Boregy had taken the bait and Magruder didn't dare let the boy jerk the line too hard and lose this spiny, canny fish. "We expected some such proposal, and Customs—" The slip was purposeful, letting Boregy know that Minister Magruder could deliver all he promised. "—that is, uh, Tariffs and Taxes is prepared to smooth the way for such an unprecedented move."

A Nev Hettekker base in Merovingen is what it will be, old fool with diamonds in your eyes. A Sword base. A tech funnel is what you want, I know it and you know it. To get it, make the marriage, set up the Chamoun Company Main Office, and we'll give you all the electrics you can eat.

But you won't be eating 'em long. And you're going to give me Tom Mondragon first, and then Mikhail, Tatiana, or Anastasi Kalugin, whoever succeeds to the governorship.

"Fine. Propitious, in fact," said Boregy with enough caution there that Magruder knew the man was weighing the dangers against the gains. "As I say, it's up to Captain Chamoun and Cassie. Perhaps, though you already have invitations to the Festival Ball, you'll stay at Boregy House tonight and tomorrow night as well?"

"We've got to leave the morning after the Governor's Ball," Magruder said.

At the same time, Chamoun said, "We'd be honored."

Before Magruder could drive home his point, Vega Boregy, stroking his moustache, asked Chamoun, "Captain, do you believe in love at first sight? If you do, and my daughter does, we might announce the wedding—and your conversion—at Kalugin's party, give the right people something more pleasant to think about than Anastasi's assumption of the advocate militiar's post."

And he winked, having just come one step toward treason, to prove that he was a reasonable man, to prove that his heart was in the right place (his pocketbook) and to let both Nev Hettekkers know that he, Vega Boregy, was a man of the world who was willing to hear—and voice—valid criticism of his governing family as long as the patois was mannered and the company safe.

Magruder raised his wine: "A toast, then, to a Festival Eve such as Merovingen has never seen."

The governor's bash was going to be that, with or without the announcement of Cassiopeia Boregy's betrothal to Captain Michael Chamoun, young lion of Nev Hettek shipping.

Dinner was really going to be weird, Cassie thought as she hunted through her jewelbox for a triple-strand choker of pearls to go with her crepe de chine blouse.

Daddy was smug as a ratter with a bellyful, off on an unscheduled trip to the Signeury with some Nev Hettekker named Magruder to "see about setting up a Nev Hettek trading mission here in Merovingen. You'll entertain our other Nev Hettekker guest, my dear, in the Blue Room—a private supper."

"Oh, Daddy!" She'd had plans to go out; there was a party. At the party there was to be avante garde music, poetry; all her friends were going. "I have plans!"

"Surely you can include our young guest in them. He's not more than five or six years older than you, and a stranger, here for the Ball. If you get on, perhaps it will be the start of something . . . possibly he'd suit as an escort tomorrow night."

"Daddy!" she'd said again, aghast at the implications. Cassie was one of the most sought after young women in Merovingen-above; the Ball was a place to dance with every boy trying to make a score. Though none of them had a chance to get their sweaty hands into her blouse, or their pimply cheeks against hers.

Then Vega said gravely, "Sit down, dear. We must talk." She'd flopped on her bed and her father had pulled her dressing table's chair close, turning it round and straddling it.

Cold had gripped her. Cassie knew her father. He'd found out about the herbs she'd been smoking with her friends, or about her secret comings and goings in the dead of night, or about. . . .

"Cassie, this young man from Nev Hettek is a riverboat captain. A ship owner, heir to a rising company."

"Oh, you don't have to tell me to beware, Daddy. I'm not loose like—" Don't tell him what he may not know; her friend Kika was pregnant against her family's wishes and even she couldn't figure out by whom. When she started to show, Kika would be forbidden to see her uptown friends, or to give parties, unless Kika got it fixed. And Kika's parties, like the one tonight, were the most sophisticated in Merovingen-above. Then she thought about what her father had said: a riverboat captain—a man, not a boy. A "young man," as her father had said—young by Daddy's standards. But a *man*, not a boy—six years older. No pimples then, no sweaty palms and glassy eyes after one kiss. An *Adventist*. But a moneyed riverboat captain sounded so romantic, so . . . grown up. Kika would be green with envy. Cassie resolved on the spot to bring Daddy's exotic houseguest to Kika's party if she had to let him put his hand in her blouse to get him there.

"Yes, Daddy, go on. I'm listening," she finished smoothly.

"This man, Captain Michael Chamoun is his name, will be staying with us until after the 24th Eve Ball."

"I know; you told me already."

"Don't be impatient, dear. He's come down the Det with a business proposition that could be very lucrative, very good for the Boregys—and our contacts."

Boring, boring. Business was boring. She tried to concentrate on the image of a dashing, dark-tanned riverboat captain, a Det-man who'd fought pirates and had the deep-running Det's mysterious currents in his eyes. "I've agreed to be nice to him, polite, a perfect lady. I'll take him to the party," she told her father.

"Good, because the business proposition concerns you, in a way—Captain Chamoun is here to sue for your hand in a three-year marriage, and his offer is too rich to ignore."

"I—" Fingers twisting in her lap, she'd panicked. Unable to speak, she just gazed at her father. What did he want her to say? Half the high-town families had already come sniffing around her, looking for an alliance. "He's *Adventist!*"

"He's willing to convert so that's not important." Vega leaned his chin on the back of her delicate, lacquered chair so that his mustache drooped. "What's important is that, if you fancy one another, we move to solidify the arrangement."

"The arrangement? Don't you think I should have some say in—"

"Cassie, I asked you to listen. Possibly, this will be the most important two days of your life. A merger with a growing Nev Hettek shipping house is not simply profitable. There is power to be gained. Information to be gained. But you must want the young man. Captain Chamoun is no child. He will know if you act out of duty. You must not. Any marriage is serious business. You must decide. If you do, we'll announce it at the Ball. If you choose to decline, the house will survive it. If you were not my own daughter, I would not be so fair, with so much at stake. But you are . . ."

On and on it had gone. Daddy had explained the boring politics of it all, promised that she'd not have to leave Merovingen, that Captain Chamoun would move into Boregy and live here with her. Any issue would be Boregy, under the Boregy name. And proper Revenantist. Her uncle in the College would put College approval on it.

She clung to that promise, buffeted by conflicting emotions. How her mother would hate it if Cassie made such a powerful marriage. Mother had other children by other men; it had been Mother's money,

Mother's status, Mother's connections which had mattered in the early days of her parents' association. She knew because Mother reminded her whenever possible. And Mother favored her sons.

Cassie loved her father. She understood what he was asking, what was at stake for him. She was her father's blood daughter. Her father would be able to tell her Yakunin mother where to get off, if Captain Chamoun was what Daddy said he was.

If the Chamoun family could do for the Boregys what the Nev Hettekker from Customs said that they could.

So dinner was terrifying: would she like him, would he like her, was he as mysterious and romantic as Daddy had said?

He was a Det-man, her father had warned. The Chamouns had made their money in one generation, these last years after Karl Fon's takeover in Nev Hettek. His parents might have been revolutionaries, though Daddy had said nothing of that.

She went down to dinner in her creme silk and her finest choker of pearls. If she liked him, she'd change to tight pants for the party and they'd go together. Unless he was too sophisticated for Kika and her silly friends. Six years, maybe seven—a grown man, and she was just eighteen and holding out for M'ser Right, whoever and wherever he was.

Girls her age had children and alliances; married girls her age had their own stipends, their own families.

Down two flights of stairs she tiptoed, terrified she'd run into him in the halls, wanting him to see her at her best, over aperitifs in the saloon adjoining the Blue Room.

She should have known when Daddy said the Blue Room—Daddy and Mother dined alone there, when they were on good terms. Children never ate there.

But tonight, Cassie was not a child.

Servants clustered around the door to the salon, whispering, tittering behind sheltering hands.

The butler murmured, when she asked, her back ramrod straight and her hands on her creme silk

breeches, that "Captain Chamoun awaits in the saloon, m'sera. And when should dinner be served?"

Woman of the house tonight, with everyone off
somewhere—Mother with her friends, scheming; her
brothers and sisters out carousing or in the main
dining hall or in their beds—she demanded the menu,
pronounced it good, named a time and swept by
them, through the carved door the butler opened.

In a loud voice, the butler announced her: "M'sera
Cassiopeia Boregy," as if she was entering some state
reception ball.

Captain Chamoun was standing by the false mantle, one elbow on the white marble, smoking one of
Daddy's blends in a briar pipe—she recognized the
smell of her father's tobacs. He put the pipe on the
mantle and took a step toward her, then another and
another.

He was *beautiful!* Tanned, dark, tall, weathered
and with adventures in his eyes. And so, so, grown
up—he even had gray in his longish, Nev Hettek-
cut hair. Nev Hettekker. Tech. Civilization. Won-
ders. She blurted, "This is so awkward, with no one
to introduce us. My father assures me you will not
take offense that I'm the only one to greet you. I'll
try to keep you amused—" Rapid-fire, it came out of
her, a girl's chatter, stopping only when he reached
her, took her hand and brought it to his lips.

"Awkward?" He straightened up. "You? Never,
m'sera Cassiopeia. I only hope my arrival hasn't disturbed your schedule."

He was still holding her hand and her palm tin-
gled. His hand had horny callus ridging its heel;
from that callus to her blood, electrics streamed, so
that the tingle ran up her arm and into her throat.

His eyes were wise, green as the Det in winter,
and hiding kindly amusement—or hiding something.
She felt even more awkward, and mumbled, "Cassie,
m'ser—Captain. It's permissible that I call you
'Captain?' "

"If you like."

His voice was husky; his body under his good,
modest silk and velvet, was honed on the Det. He

was the kind of man you dreamed would sneak in your window some dark night and carry you off to sea. "I like."

Only when he raised an eyebrow did she realize how silly her last comment must have sounded. Only when she took an embarrassed step backward did she realize he was still holding her hand.

Her body, and now her face, was on fire. She said, "Dinner is waiting," in what she hoped was a sophisticated tone. Perhaps Kika Nikolaev's party would be too juvenile for him, too boring, but God and Retribution, she wanted to show him off to her friends.

He led her into the dining room, taking her elbow with studied decorum, not saying a word.

Once her panic receded, Cassie realized that the silence he offered wasn't awkward. It was, in fact, companionable.

By the time he'd pulled back her chair and seated himself opposite her at her parents' private dining table, Cassiopeia Boregy was making small talk just to hear the timbre of his voice when he answered, hardly listening to the words.

For the first time in her life, Cassie was in love.

Magruder was sitting on the edge of the Grand, watching the Festival lights sparkle on the black water and the night traffic come and go, waiting for Mondragon to come out of his hidey-hole in Petrescu where the Sword's agent, Romanov, swore they'd found him.

Down at canalside, with level after black level of Merovingen above his head so that he couldn't see the stars, he was perspiring despite the salt-laced breeze. Magruder didn't like being hemmed in; he didn't like Merovingen-below one bit.

Maybe he should have argued with Dimitri Romanov and gone to Mondragon's apartment on dilapidated Petrescu's second tier, back there behind the Foundry somewhere. But Romanov had Rack and Ruin al-Banna behind him, and Romanov had been abroad in Merovingen-below, using what connections the Sword had here, while Magruder had been "hob-nobbing with society."

Mita Romanov hadn't been pleased about that—wasn't pleased now, sitting in the fancyboat's stern by the motor, glowering up at Magruder with a hand-kerchief to his nose. The canalside stank, so what?

Behind Magruder, lounging against the wall like they'd grown there from bad seeds, were Rack and Ruin al-Banna. Magruder wasn't entirely sure they were waiting for Mondragon—the Sword had its fac-tions; Romanov was a heavyweight in one of them, Magruder in another.

If Romanov's informants were wrong—and they could be, considering the botch his boys had made of cornering Mondragon on their last outing—Magruder was going to use the excuse to confine Romanov to the *Detfish.*

He could do it. Would have done it now, except for the al-Bannas at his back and all those spindly wood bridges and heavier timbers of multi-leveled Merovingen-above towering over his head.

He shivered and hugged himself. *Come on, Mon-dragon, show!* The Boregy play had gone well because of Mondragon, in a way: Romanov's Sword boys had gotten into Boregy House a while back and assassi-nated the Boregy in charge, making trouble for Mondragon, whose family had been friends of the eldest, senile, presently comatose, Boregy. The Boregy who'd stepped in and taken control, Vega, was an Anastasi partisan.

So, according to Romanov, Mondragon had been stashed out at Petrescu, a seedy safe house, now that the Boregy who might have sheltered him was out of the picture. But that chalked up no points for Roma-nov's marauders: they'd been sure that murder in the Boregy household would mean the death of Mondragon. They'd been wrong.

They'd just pushed the traitor deeper into Mero-vingen.

God, Magruder wished he'd gone up to Petrescu's second level and broken down Mondragon's door. Mondragon could recognize him; they'd both been around Karl Fon too much for Mondragon not to remember him.

Magruder had to make sure, before tomorrow night's 24th Eve Ball, that Mondragon didn't piss his pants or point his finger when they ran into one another, which they were almost sure to do. Otherwise, all the work and all the trouble they'd gone to, bringing in Chamoun as a riverboat captain and Magruder as Minister of T&T would be for nothing.

A boat glided by, hardly visible in the low-lying miasma of cook fires and canal fog; farther away, revelers shouted and sang: Revenantists on holiday, drinking and screwing themselves into Karmic debt. A little more hellraising wouldn't be remarked in Merovingen tonight.

Another body on its way to the Det wouldn't mean squat. The al-Bannas, behind his back, knew it as well as Magruder did.

Magruder wished he had a drink. He could have gotten one in the tavern nearby, but he never drank when he was working. And he wasn't fool enough to dull his edge, with the al-Bannas there breathing down his neck, pretending to dice on a convenient barrelhead because a group of waiting men would scare Mondragon off, if the ex-Sword remembered any of his training.

But the weight of Merovingen-above was getting to Magruder, and the waiting was getting to him. Easy, Sword. First Mondragon, then Romanov, then Romanov's rats. He wasn't half so claustrophobic here and now as he'd been in the Signeury with Vega Boregy.

What a damned stroke, Boregy taking him by the hand like that: " 'Come with me, friend Magruder, and we'll grease the wheels a little.' " Grease them Vega had, but at what cost, Magruder still wasn't certain.

Strolling over the Boregy's private bridge right into the Signeury, making mental maps of everything he saw ... easy going until the weight of Merovingen's government buildings closed over him and he could hardly breathe, thinking of the prisons across the canal and wondering whether Boregy hadn't seen through him all along.

Deliver me right into a nice padded interrogation cell and then they haul out their toys . . . rock all around him; the damned Signeury was solid rock with windowslits too narrow for a man to squeeze through. Take the place with pubescent boys, maybe, if you had enough of them, half-starved kids recruited from Merovingen-below. . . .

Trying not to sweat himself into a lather that would betray him, he'd listened to Boregy explaining how they were going to "facilitate the re-establishment of Nev Hettek's trade mission" by talking to so-and-so and bribing this one and promising that one he could rake off a percentage of the take.

The two of them had walked right into Tatiana Kalugin on the way to the office of the Seal, in a windowless corridor that had Magruder's skin crawling.

Bam! Vega Boregy stopped in his tracks when the tall woman, coming down the hall from the other direction in a close-fitting gray velvet jacket and pants, had called his name.

Magruder hadn't the foggiest *who* she was, at first: dark hair with red highlights, pulled back severely; strong face with wide green eyes; folio under her arm. But the command in her voice made him hold his breath. And the calculating look in her eyes made him wish the stone ceiling with its frescoes would go ahead and fall—if it didn't kill him, it would hide him.

She'd said, "Vega, what a surprise. And so late in the evening? You ought to be out celebrating, no? May I be of assistance?"

"Tatiana . . ."

First time Magruder'd seen Vega Boregy at a loss for words; first time he'd seen blood drain from a Boregy face. See a lot more of that, however things went. The Boregys were allied with this woman's rival and brother, Anastasi.

"Yes?" she'd prompted, more like a sovereign than governor's daughter.

"M'sera Tatiana," Vega Boregy began again, recovering, "I'm on my way to the Seal Office—I'm sure you'll have the harbormaster's record—"

"So? And this is?"

"This" meant him, Magruder. He was wondering whether it would be worth it to haul out his revolver, blow away the two of them, and run amok in the Signeury ... if Vega Boregy's miscalculation had just derailed the Sword's play, he could salvage something. ... He flicked a glance at Boregy, obviously deferring to someone who ought to know what the hell to say in a situation like this.

Meanwhile, Tatiana Kalugin's jade-green eyes were boring into him with more force than he'd thought possible. He met her gaze and felt a physical shock, as if he'd tongued a battery pole or stuck his finger in a live socket.

Vega Boregy had regained full composure. "M'sera Secretary, Tatiana Kalugin, may I present Minister Chance Magruder, of the Nev Hettek Bureau of Trade and Tariffs."

"Indeed," said the governor's daughter, one of the heaviest power players in Merovingen—and one of the most dangerous, if Sword reports could be believed. "I'm sure I do have the report. And lodged in Boregy. How kind of Boregy to remember its old trading ties ... in the name of peace."

Flaming Retribution, Tatiana Kalugin! I should have known! But he hadn't known; he'd been too shocked by the waves her proximity produced. "I'm honored, m'sera Kalugin." He shot an acceptably desperate look at Vega Boregy, who was stone-faced.

"Yes, but *why* are you honored?"

Hostility crackled between the two Merovingians, now. Magruder drew a deep breath, the first he could remember since Tatiana had started staring at him like some specimen under glass.

"Minister Magruder comes from Nev Hettek with a ... trade proposal ... for my family. And as a goodwill ambassador."

Her free hand balled on her hip. "In unofficial capacity, of course."

"Yes, m'sera Kalugin," Magruder dived in: he couldn't botch this worse than Boregy already had. "Customs—T&T, actually," he stumbled, making the same purposeful mistake so that she'd back off and listen: when Nev Hettek Customs talked, anybody who wanted in and out of Nev Hettek, or who wanted any tech out of Nev Hettek, listened. "Unofficial, if personal visit, under Boregys' auspices. The Ball . . . the Secretary knows with no embassy staff here—"

He didn't remember what else he'd said. He'd spouted his rote-memorized line, steering clear of the marriage part—that was supposed to be spontaneous, between Chamoun and the girl—hoping to hell that he was judging the waters correctly.

When he'd finished, there was a pause in which he studied Tatiana's face and couldn't decide what he saw there because her eyes kept trying to suck him up whole.

Then she'd nodded and said, "Interesting. There will be an official approach to follow—to reinstate the embassy? You'll be staying, if Nev Hettek's request is approved? As Trade Minister?"

Lord, I'm dead or dreaming. "If it pleases the Secretary to request. . . ."

"It might," Tatiana said and smiled like a predator. "You'll be at our little party tomorrow night, Minister? Do make sure to save a dance for me." And she'd turned on her heel and gone back the way she'd come.

Leaving Vega Boregy enough privacy that he dared slump against the wall momentarily, and wipe his fishbelly brow before he blew out a noisy breath, shaking his head at Magruder: "Minister, I'm not sure what we did here just now, but we did something, have no doubt. Now, on to the Seal office. Without the proper endorsement, we won't have you around for Tatiana to toy with."

Easy, man. Don't they have spies here? Or don't you care? Or are you saying what you want them to hear?

It was too damn deep for Magruder, deep as the Det down here where it was like a different river.

Deep as the Grand and the hole he was in, a man-made hole that hemmed him on every side.

When you don't know the rules of the game, you change the game. If Boregy was telling him that Tatiana Kalugin, the governor's only daughter, wanted to get into Magruder's pants, he could handle that. If he meant something more sinister, then that was easier—Magruder liked rough games. If he had to stay here, well then, that was what the Sword wanted. Though no one had thought it would happen so soon.

Magruder had lots to learn, lots more to see than what Boregy showed him next: the ornate office of the Keeper of the Seal, an unctuous staff fawning over Vega Boregy, and an inlaid sanctum door through which Magruder wasn't invited.

When Boregy had come out of that office, he carried a sheaf of papers as thick and finely-printed as what Magruder had brought from Nev Hettek: letters of intent to negotiate; conditions of leasing and lists of suitable sites; a statement from certain officials of qualified support, headed for Governor Iosef Alexandr Kalugin's upstairs office.

Nothing more could be done until Chamoun either succeeded or failed. It all hung on two kids now, whether they'd marry. Without the marriage and Chamoun Shipping, the trade delegation had no reason to come to Merovingen; creating a mission without reason was asking permission to open a Sword office. A Sword presence in Merovingen, officially tied to Nev Hettek, would give Anastasi Kalugin an excuse to start the sort of war Kalugin wanted. And Fon didn't want that. Perhaps . . . neither did Boregy.

So it was find Mondragon and shut his mouth, whatever that took. Find him fast.

Magruder's butt was going numb, he'd been sitting so long. He got to his feet to stretch his legs and the al-Bannas moved restlessly in the shadows. Loitering without a permit, was that a crime here? Talking to Romanov in the boat below was a no-no, for sure.

Magruder sauntered toward a floating chips stand, feeling in his pockets as if for change. Weapons check; everything where it ought to be. Over to the boat and buy something, any damn thing. Whatever kind of fish came fried and wrapped in seaweed, and thin beer to go with it. He needed something to hold in his hands.

When he'd finished making unfamiliar change and turned back, the al-Bannas were out beyond the shadows and their barrel. There was enough background noise from the tavern at the corner and the canal that Magruder hadn't heard a warning, if one was given.

Stopped by the al-Bannas blocking his path was a man in natty evening clothes.

Magruder saw a flash of steel as the man drew a weapon.

He dropped his beer and chips and sprinted, wishing he dared yell.

By the time he got there, the man was backed against the wall between two barrels, the al-Bannas on his left and right.

The sword the man carried was rapier-like, no match for the two guns pointed at him, but this man wasn't thinking about the odds. His stance was that of a duellist. The blade hummed twice, slicing the air, keeping the al-Bannas at bay.

Behind Magruder, as he reached the threesome, he heard a woman's voice and Romanov's, some argument in low tones on the water. He didn't have time to worry about Romanov. If the fool got into an argument with a canaler that he couldn't win, that was one less problem.

Magruder bore down, inserting himself between the two al-Bannas and heard the quarry saying, ". . . ain't nothin' worth robbin' me of, y'see. M'life, tha's 'nother thing."

For a moment Magruder thought the al-Bannas had made a mistake, gotten the wrong man. Then he looked closer, among the shadows and the play of reflected light from the canal.

The face before him was pale, handsome, tired, and there were dark circles under hunted eyes. The man's blond hair was beginning to darken with nervous perspiration that beaded on a furrowed forehead.

"Whatcha gonna do, Mondragon?" asked Magruder aping the feigned patois he'd heard. "Throw tha' thing? That'll account f'r one a' us, then you're fish food." And waited, to see what the ex-Sword did, whether the use of his name would jog memories.

Mondragon squinted as if into the sun, though the rapier's tip never wavered. "Lord, I know you!" Low, urgent voice, "You're—"

"Easy, boy." And, to the al-Bannas: "Back. Back off, I say."

They did, three paces, muttering together. Magruder's divided attention could still pick up the argument going on between Romanov and someone female, out of line-of-sight at canal-level where their borrowed Boregy fancyboat was tied.

"Thanks." Mondragon's nod was caustic with cynicism. "I just go on my way now, right?" The accent had thinned. The trapped traitor's eyes were nearly devoid of pupil, despite the bad light.

Man's ready to jump, any way will do: one surprise too many, tonight. "*Not* right, you're smart enough to know that—aren't you, Tommy?"

Eyes closed for an instant, not long enough for even Magruder to step in and disarm him. Then Mondragon said warily, "Your boys? Your play? To what do I owe the pleasure?"

He'd heard that tone elsewhere, this night. Magruder showed empty hands, raising them slowly: "No weapons, see? But we can't have you running through the streets yelling 'The Sword is come' now, can we?"

"That's it?" Now the rapier did waver, lowering until it was pointing at Magruder's belly.

This man before him had plenty of hell in his face, his entire family's eradication on his soul. And a girlfriend running cargo on the Grand. The question was, kill him or play him? Mondragon ought to know that. The rapier's angle said he probably did. Magruder laid it out: "That's not 'it.' *'It'* is return to active duty, m'ser. Because we're moving in here for a long stay."

"You're dreamin'," again in the gutter style, a small defiance. "You can't push me any harder than I'm pushed already, Chance. I won't say who you are, no matter what you do here, if you leave me alone."

"Can't do that, Tommy. We hear you're privy to Anastasi Kalugin and his buddies, especially the Boregys. We want reports. Bi-weekly. It'll keep your girl, Jones, from finding out how long it can take to die. You got your parents killed; they weren't Sword— your whole damned family, because of you. You don't want another noncombatant hurt on your account, especially not your m'sera Jones." Card played, offer made. *Take it, fool; you'll do no better, anywhere. By rights and for Fon's sake, I ought to kill you. But you don't deserve an easy out.*

Both Mondragon and Magruder heard the scrape of the al-Bannas' feet as the Sword muscle edged in closer. Magruder raised one empty hand higher: Halt.

The shuffling stopped.

Mondragon's face was expressionless, but his gaze darted from one opponent to the next.

Magruder had the distinct impression he was considering breaking for it. Magruder's midsection was directly in the rapier's way. "Talk to me, Tommy, while you still can."

"What's the use?" Mondragon's weapon retreated with the rest of him as he took two steps backward and leaned against the wall. He lay his head back against the timber, as if for support. His lips seemed stiff when he said: "You can't do her any more harm than Anastasi Kalugin can, and he's threatening me with her, the same as you. So she's dead, isn't she? From one of you or the other? Which does me a favor, in a way."

No, no. I'm not making it that easy for you. "Don't think you can pull some stunt and I'll let these boys kill you quick. And don't tell me you're more afraid of what Anastasi Kalugin will do to her—and to you—than what I'll do. Because you're not that stupid. And neither am I. Say 'Yes, m'ser, I'll hand over every shred of news, report every question that

Kalugin asks, and every answer I give.' Say, 'And when I don't know what the Sword wants me to say, I'll keep my mouth shut until I find out.' "

"I—Yes. All right?" Mondragon's eyes sparkled. "Whatever you want, Chance. Just call off your crazies and leave Jones out of it."

Boy's tired. "Minister Magruder, Nev Hettek T&T, to you. After we're introduced. Until then, you don't know squat. On your way, then."

He motioned the al-Bannas and they retreated, obedient to learned signals if not to him personally. "Go on, Tommy, go. We'll find you again when we need to set up reporting schedules."

Mondragon eased forward, rapier carefully angled away from Magruder's gut; then sideways, inching around a barrel, eyes on the al-Bannas who turned with him as if on the same axis.

Magruder watched the ex-Sword as the duellist walked quickly, with jerky steps, toward the chips boat. Then the Nev Hettekker gathered his al-Bannas. "Put those revolvers away. The boat, let's go. Move."

They moved, but by the time the three of them got to the boat there was no sign of whatever argument had been under way there.

There was no sign of Dimitri Romanov, either, which could mean a number of things, the best of which was that he was belly-up in the harbor by now, riding on the currents out to sea.

Magruder didn't care to speculate. He didn't care to search or to wait around for trouble to find him, if trouble had found Romanov. If he saw Mita Romanov again, he was going to kill him anyway. There was no other way to assure a smooth-running operation, or to get the al-Bannas under control.

In the fancyboat, he took the tiller, putting the al-Bannas in front where he could see them. They didn't say anything about leaving Romanov high and dry, if that was what the Sword was doing. And they wouldn't say anything about what they'd witnessed here tonight.

The engine caught on his second try and he headed the fancyboat up the Grand. There wasn't much night left, and he had to ditch the al-Bannas and get back to the Boregys' with his borrowed fancyboat before morning.

If he was going to make sure Michael Chamoun got married and the Kalugins allowed Minister Magruder to establish a trade mission here with a re-opened embassy, he had lots to do before the governor's party.

The Sword of God had lots to do here, one way or the other.

The pants Cassie Boregy changed into for the party she was taking him to were so tight that Chamoun had trouble taking his eyes off them.

And off what was under them, as she climbed down into the Boregy launch waiting at the water-gate to take her and her friends to the party. It was an elegant launch, steered by a retainer; elegant friends, four of whom had come knocking at the Boregy's front door when aperitifs were being served in the drawing room.

Chamoun tried not to stare at the rich folk's kids in outrageous clothes, once Cassie, giggling, had dragged him by the hand to greet them at the door.

Michael Chamoun's head was spinning, and not just from the wines, as he followed Cassie down into the boat with the others and the steersman cast off.

The other two couples, in riotous, layered Festival garb, fondled each other openly, sprawling on velvet cushions as if the servants were blind and deaf. Cassie went forward, seating herself in the bow, and Chamoun followed, ignoring all else as if the ritual of the water gate were something he saw every day.

It wasn't, by a long shot. Chamoun hadn't expected Cassie Boregy to be attractive, flirtatious, or charming. It hadn't mattered. It still didn't matter, he told himself. Don't be too sure of yourself, Detman. You've got a long way to go. Interloper, that was what he was here.

Out in the Harvest night, he cast surreptitious looks back at the other two couples. They seemed so young. So carefree. One of the boys waved at him.

These were all children, but children who'd accepted him at face value.

And that face value had stunned Chamoun nearly senseless more surely than a well-placed blow to the head during Sword training.

When Cassie had dragged him to the door to greet her friends, she'd introduced him as, "Captain Michael Chamoun, everybody, heir to Chamoun Shipping of Nev Hettek. Captain Chamoun's a riverboat captain. And a convert."

A chorus of approving "ahhs," had come from the throats of the Boregy girl's two young women friends. From their escorts, he'd sensed a certain bristling, the distrust of young men feigning sophistication faced with their vision of it.

Then Cassie had added, sparkling eyes mischievous as she took his arm and laid her cheek against his shoulder, "Captain Chamoun's come all the way from Nev Hettek to be my escort at the Governor's Ball. And we may have a surprise for you there. . . ."

And left it hanging, so that her girlfriends squealed and begged to know what, what surprise.

No one was as surprised as Chamoun, and he'd been in a daze ever since. Did she mean what she'd said? Did she *know* what she'd said? The implications? The innuendo? Or had he misunderstood, what with all the fancy wine, smooth as silk and so cultured he'd misread its potency, drunk more than he ought.

Lord and Retribution, what was he into? A fast crowd, hers. Fast the way only the very rich or very poor could afford to be. Boys' hands under girls' blouses, back there, and a tangle of hands between velveted thighs.

Cassie was looking at him with those huge brown eyes expectantly. He lay back on his elbows, not quite sprawled on the cushions in the bow, and watched the bridges pass overhead.

Fast times, fast crowd. What was he supposed to do, with so much at stake? What *had* she meant, in the house with her friends? He was supposed to be courting her for marriage. Did she expect him to paw her? Was that good manners here? Would she be insulted if he did, or insulted if he didn't?

She lay back too, in a perfect mirror-image of his posture. Good sign, his training told him: mating-ritual mimicry, he'd been taught. He put one hand behind his head to see if she would; she did.

He'd never been so uncomfortable. He watched the bridges, asking about the first one: "Is that Golden Bridge, then?" so she'd have small talk to make.

When they came to Hanging Bridge, he didn't need her running commentary to recognize it, or the Angel there, sword partly drawn, to remind him how much hung in the balance.

Months of preparation—years, for all he knew. Money and time and all he could see was Chance Magruder's unreadable face, and Romanov's perpetual sneer, and the al-Banna brothers hovering over him in his mind's eye.

Better do it right, Chamoun, whatever right turned out to be. It was a sobering thought, sobering like the Angel sliding back into the distance and the past.

". . . tell me, Captain Chamoun, about Minister Magruder. Daddy was quite taken with him," Cassie proposed, sliding across the cushions until her hips were near his head and her hand trailed on the launch's prow.

"Tell you what?" He sat bolt upright, looking for treachery in her face, startling her. Easy, son. Don't scare her. "Chance Magruder's the best . . . and the worst . . . man I know," he said. God, where did that come from? "Look," desperate, rushing on, "call me Michael, at least in private, or I can't call you Cassie and feel right about it."

"Michael," she said tentatively, as if tasting it. She licked her lips. "Michael, if you find Kika's party boring, we can just leave. My friends will stay all night; I'm not responsible to provide their transportation home. But we'll need a secret signal." Again, the mischief.

They devised one, heads together. Her loose, dark hair tickled his cheek. He reached up to brush it away, got his hand tangled; her fingers closed around his.

Their eyes met and he had to ask her, or kiss her. . . .

"Cassie, do you understand what you said back there? I mean, did your father . . . what did Vega tell you about me?"

They were so close he could feel the warm puffs of her breath on his face. Remember, it's Sword business. You can't care what she's like, just if she'll agree. If she'd been a fat, hairy-faced cow, it would be the same. But she wasn't. She was firm with youth and round with health and she had her father's coal-fire eyes. . . . Suddenly, superimposed, he saw Rita Nikolaev's face. Rita wouldn't have let him slide his hands up her thigh. But Rita wasn't Sword business. . . .

Her hand reached out and touched the fish knife in its dress sheath, then ran along his belt. "Captain . . . Michael, my father told me you came to sue for my hand in marriage. And about your offer to stay here, in Merovingen, bringing Chamoun Shipping with you." Carefully phrased, words chosen slowly, she took a deep breath and continued. "It's good for my family, for my father. I love my father. Boregy power is very important to me. I meant what I said back there."

"God, girl, I haven't even kissed you yet."

"We can remedy that." She closed her eyes and leaned forward.

Her breasts touched him at the same time her lips did, and then he was at pains to show her he was as sophisticated as she thought he was.

When they sat back, he said, "Are you always this impetuous?"

Her chest was heaving. "Never." She smiled tentatively. "Again?"

He realized then that she was trying to impress him, afraid she'd do something wrong.

That makes two of us, girl. Whatever you think you've got at stake here ain't nothin', compared to what's really going on.

He let his arms slide around her and his body press against her, faking passion until he could find some, because this had nothing to do with the malleable girl in his arms, or free choice, or whether she was as soft as she seemed or as charming. *Rita, I've never done this with you . . . ain't my fault.*

Her healthy young body did its work and everything he was afraid of not being able to feel came rushing over him.

By the time they got to the house where the party was being held, he was worked up into a near frenzy, like the teenagers in the stern.

He took his hands off her and said, "Ain't no reason we can't leave early," on short, sharp breaths, forgetting his grammar. "If your boat'll oblige, I'll take you over to the *Detfish* and show you what you're getting. Got a present for you, too—" He swallowed. "A betrothal gift, if you'll have it . . . and me."

She closed her eyes and bent her head, laying her cheek on his shoulder. "Oh, yes, I'll have it . . . and you."

And that was that, unless he screwed it up some way. Elation flooded him as the launch started to dock.

And then, for the first time, he paid attention to where he was, and where the launch was docking.

"Rimmon! Angel's flames, you didn't tell me . . ." Panic. Rimmon Isle! Rita! Maybe, he told himself quickly, not Rita. On Rimmon, the mercantile elite made their homes: Yakunin, Khan, Raza, Balaci, and more. Seven families in all, he remembered from his briefing.

The kids astern were laughing, coming forward, silver flasks in the boys' hands.

Cassiopeia Boregy looked at him quizzically. "A problem, Captain Chamoun?"

Call him "Captain," where her friends could hear. Rub it in how exotic he was, what a catch she had in hand. Her cheeks were aflame, though. "No, no problem, I guess. It's just that I came in this way, and saw a Rimmon boat, a black yacht—serious trading money, up here."

"That was a Nikolaev yacht, silly, our hosts. Don't fret, dear Captain, we'll probably have as fine a pleasure boat, if you want one—Daddy will give us anything we want for a wedding present." Whispered, this last. Then, louder: "The Captain wants to see Kika's father's pleasure yacht close at hand. Let's not forget to ask if we can."

Everyone chorused that that was a fine idea, and one of the boys said knowingly that if Kika was in a bad mood, then Cassie would deny *him* nothing, and all the youngsters tittered.

Chamoun followed Cassiopeia Boregy woodenly, off the boat and onto the property of their hosts, the Nikolaev family.

He was a pretender, a thief and a cheat. It was all he could think of, once they reached the Nikolaev stairs and started climbing. He was almost home free; he couldn't give himself away. Cassie had said they'd leave if he wanted, and he wanted—already.

He focused on the luxury here, contrasting it with the misery perpetrated on Merovingen-below by Revenantists such as the Nikolaevs. The price of one of the paintings hung on this landing, in carved frames covered with gold, would have fed a canaler family for a year, maybe two.

Soft life, if you were born lucky. Hellhole here in Merovingen, if you weren't.

The Revenantists explained their good fortune and their oppression of the less fortunate by the construct of karma.

It was going to be Rita Nikolaev's karma to be nice to him, polite to him, whatever her feelings. If she had any. If she even remembered the man she'd met at Karl Fon's inauguration where she'd been because she was going into the family business.

"But aren't the Nikolaevs rivals of yours?" he asked when they'd reached a dazzling hall alive with crystal and flowers—flowers!—and music and pampered children. The smoke hurt his eyes and they were smarting by then. One arm around Cassie, he leaned down to hear her murmured reply.

"Don't be silly, Michael—not yet, we aren't. At least, not until you came. Everyone's friendly, as friendly as the Rock can be with Rimmon Isle." Her voice lowered even further: "Kika's pregnant, but don't say anything. Her parents don't know yet, so maybe she won't have it."

Cassie explained it all: Kika didn't have any idea who the father of her child was; *probably* the Nikolaev poleboat-man—to the scandal of her well-bred, ambitious and Revenantist house. But maybe Kika would get it fixed. . . .

In the marble-floored drawing room there were too many youngsters, dancing to a loud band of horns, drums, gitars, and sithers. And the smoke was making him light-headed.

It made him more than light-headed when a pipe was passed to him by Cassie and he tried some.

Then things became completely disjointed. His only salvation, the only thing he recognized, was Cassie's hand clamped on his, dragging him from group to group, introducing him always as "Captain Michael Chamoun from Nev Hettek, my escort to the 24th Eve Ball."

There was food and he was hungry. Unrecognizable food in little bits on silver trays. "Here, Michael," said Cassie, her face swimming into view, "try some deathangel, it'll wake you up."

He didn't know how much he'd eaten before her words percolated to his reasoning mind. Then he stopped eating. Deathangel: a stimulant, a euphoric. It could kill you. He wasn't used to it. Deathangel poison was another thing; he was used to dealing with that.

She'd left him, gone somewhere. He was alone with his senses reeling in a room full of strange children, some of whom were rolling on the floor in couples, wearing less than they must have worn to get here.

Then there she was, another blurry face saying things he couldn't quite hear in an accent suddenly

hard to decipher. The face came closer and it wasn't
Cassiopeia Boregy's face.

Rita!

"I'm here with Cassie," he mumbled, intoxicated
beyond measure. "And I've lost her somewhere . . ."

"It *is* you, Michael, yes? Michael the angel from
Nev Hettek?" She held out her hand and he took it.

Then he just stood there, remembering he mustn't
do anything wrong, but not remembering what
"wrong" might consist of.

Rita Nikolaev was cool and collected, older than
most of her guests, an ice sculpture with a blazing
heart he could feel across the distance. Her hair had
golden highlights, her smile was perfect, dazzling.
She said, "Again, you bring my karma with you, is
this so? Cassie told me to come and find you, and I
never thought I'd find such an omen. Come . . ."

He went, helpless, but fighting for control. The
deathangel was winning out over the smoke, and his
heart was beginning to pound. He had a headache,
suddenly. He let his hand fall from hers and followed the woman in the black tights with a sheer,
hot-colored acre of silk wrapped about her rump.

Revenantists feared entanglements. Cassie had told
her—what? That they were getting married? That
he was Boregy property? She remembered him, damn
and all, did Rita Nikolaev.

In and out of three rooms, and into a fourth,
some personal sitting room of the family where the
velvets were dark and flocked and the blue walls
gaudy with gilded moldings. Another damned palace; all that was wrong with Revenantist-controlled
Merovingen, sported without humility in this palatial
lair.

Easy, Det-man. That's what you're here for. You
bet, the Sword's ploy wouldn't have worked with
Rita's family. But a few nights here and there with
Rita Nikolaev, later, consorting with the enemy for
information—that was good Sword tactics.

Suddenly he was afraid that those few nights might
begin on this night—until he saw Cassie sitting grace-

fully on a dark lounge, her feet up and arms curled around her.

"Ah, success, then, Rita! You've got him. Isn't he wonderful?"

"Wonderful," agreed the older woman. *His age. His type. God, you're in over your damned head, Chamoun!* "But I knew that," Rita finished.

"Rita told me, Michael"—proprietary—"that you'd met briefly in Nev Hettek. I shall go to Nev Hettek, once we're married, and be presented to Karl Fon, too."

"You want, no sweat," he said before he got control of his tongue. "On our honeymoon, of course. When you come to meet my family." *Did that suffice?*

It must have. Cassie uncurled, rose and stretched, showing him everything, promising him a better look at what lay under those tight pants. "Rita's arranged for us to board the yacht you wanted to see. Then we'll leave, before these children drug you into a stupor."

And you're not a child, oh, no you're not. He almost sat down; he wanted to sit down very badly.

But Rita Nikolaev was talking to him: ". . . any time, the hospitality of our house is extended to you, Captain Chamoun. Anastasi's partisans must stick together. Perhaps a business venture or two, to get your shipping company off to a good start? Your Nev Hettekker connections, our . . . other assets."

Oh yeah, Rita. Just let me out of here, please God, before I step in it. *Anything, anywhere, as long as I'm married first.* "Vega and my fiancée are my guides in all matters Merovingian, m'sera Nikolaev, but I'll transmit your kind offer—"

"Oh Michael, don't be so stuffy." Cassie came over to rescue him. "Rita's just Rita, when we're alone. And of course we'll do something with the Nikolaevs. Now come on. Let's look at that ship you liked. Rita has promised to put us in touch with the builder, if Daddy agrees." She tugged on his arm and he followed, getting just a glimpse of the pensive frown on Rita Nikolaev's angelic face.

Once he'd toured the Nikolaev yacht, he was no longer in a hurry to show off the *Detfish.*

"It's not this fancy, it's a working riverboat . . . I hope you won't be disappointed."

Cassie looked at him probingly, up on deck with the wind in her hair. The sky, out beyond Rimmon Isle where the wild water was, showed his over-stimulated Det-man's eyes traces of night's end.

If he was taking her to the *Detfish,* he'd have to hurry. "It's getting late. Your father might take offense if I keep you out until dawn. . . ."

"Captain Chamoun, you promised to show me your riverboat, and to give me my betrothal gift. Unless, of course, you're no longer interested?" Arch and combative.

He reached for her, intent on proving that he was still interested.

When they'd broken the clinch and walked hand in hand to the waiting Boregy launch, she said, "You mustn't trouble yourself about Revenantist displays of wealth, or about what I will think of a working riverboat. What's attractive is just that: you're a self-made man, a ship's captain, new blood and new strength for us."

If only she knew. But she didn't know, couldn't know, who and what had made him. He cuddled her with what was the best mix of control and affection, of drug-stimulated passion and gentlemanly consideration, that he could manage, letting the retainer plot their course to the *Detfish.*

It was a wonder, still—a wonder because it was his. More of a wonder than any of what he'd seen tonight, for exactly the reasons Cassiopeia Boregy claimed to understand: because he *was* its captain and he'd never dreamed to reach even that high; because it and he had a reason to be here; because, without it and him, the Sword would be back at Square One, sending out al-Bannas and counting on Romanovs and their blackleg militia connections to disrupt Revenantist Merovingen as best it could.

He took her aboard and thought he saw common sense, understanding, satisfaction and excitement in her mercantilist's eyes. It would be hers too, and all it represented: freedom, her own say. Power, as she'd said—hers, not her family's.

He took her down into his cabin and agonized over what to do next. He knew what he wanted to do: if he made love to her, would it help or hurt his cause? Things were not as simple as they seemed.

So while she asked nervous questions he opened his seachest and rummaged in it, coming up with a black box. In it was the betrothal gift he'd promised her—not pearls or emeralds or gold such as he'd seen on women here, but something only a Nev Hetteker could give.

And he might get in trouble with Chance Magruder for offering it, but the Sword had slipped up and brought him in here empty-handed, in the personal sense. They'd neglected to suggest what token he might give to his intended bride.

He held the box out, standing at arm's length. "Here's my gift, to seal it."

"It?" She feigned ignorance. "You'd best be more specific, Captain Chamoun." A teasing smile, to let him know she wasn't rejecting him. And, when he stood dumbly, holding the box out to her, she prompted: "Go on, Det-man, propose to me."

"Ah . . . will you marry me, Cassiopeia Boregy? Really marry me, not like these marriages of convenience?" And he couldn't help that. He wasn't the sort of man to look the other way while his wife caroused, the way the Nikolaev women obviously did. The way Rita obviously did. Or re-negotiate after three years. It shouldn't bother him, but it did. Obviously.

She took the box, finally. Before she opened it, she said, "I'll talk to Daddy. Maybe. I might. But you must say you love me, if that's what you mean."

He said it but he didn't mean it.

She repeated it and it sounded like she thought she meant it. A child was what she was. Then she said gravely, "After I open this, you must prove your love." And her eyes flickered to the captain's bed, narrow and rumpled from Romanov sprawling on it, giving Chamoun his orders.

"Fine. Open it." He knew what to do now, at any rate; what was expected of him.

She lifted the box's hinged lid and gasped, then shook her head: "It's tech, I know. And I'm thrilled, truly I am. But . . . what does it do? Is it illegal?" Her voice was breathless with excitement.

He chuckled, then choked it off when he saw the hurt in her face. "Not illegal, just uncommon. Valuable. It's a flashlight, a . . . personal . . . light. So you won't trip in the dark. Here, let me show you."

And that brought them close together, so that he could feel the way her flesh seared his through their clothes. The flashlight was battery powered. The batteries were experimental, the acid in them citric, the rest copper and pottery. He explained that there was no cord necessary and promised he'd refurbish the batteries when, as must happen, their power ran low.

Her brows knitted as he explained and when he showed her how to turn it on, she gasped and hugged it to her. Then she looked up at him with tears in her eyes. "This is the most wonderful present anyone's ever given me, Michael Chamoun, my . . . love."

He reached for her, and eventually he had to take the flashlight from her unresisting fingers and turn it off. No use wasting the light.

And they didn't want light for what they were doing—she was shy. He'd thought she was profligate, perhaps more experienced than he, and when he realized that he'd been wrong he stopped halfway into what he was doing to her.

"Lord, Cassie, you've never been touched. Why didn't you tell me?" His breath was short now and his soul was aching for her. But the Sword's needs hung over his head.

She turned her face away on his pillow and said, "Michael, go on, don't stop. Please. We're almost married. It's all right."

From then on, it was Retribution on wings of flame. Only when he lay beside her, feeling her sweat dry and her limbs tremble and explaining that she shouldn't be frightened if she found a bit of blood—only then did he hear footsteps coming down the stairwell.

"Up, quick." He moved like he was trained to move, grabbing her clothes, shoving them at her.

"What?" She was a huddled gray statue in the predawn dimness.

"Somebody's coming. Get dressed. Fast." He was pulling on his own pants, buckling his belt and the fish knife in place. Who was it? Coming down his private hatchway, it wasn't crew. The nightwatch had seen him come aboard, they wouldn't dare disturb him, unless there was trouble—

He was almost certain there must be trouble when the door opened without a knock and he saw a specter there, dim and backlit.

Cassiopeia Boregy aimed her flashlight at the doorway and turned it on.

In the spotlight stood Dimitri Romanov, bedraggled and wet, his face a puff of bruises. He threw a hand up to fend off the light.

Whether he'd seen the Boregy woman, Chamoun wasn't certain. He knew damned well Romanov couldn't see her—or him—now. Cassie had the makings of a revolutionary. He could have made love to her all over again.

But there was no time. He and Romanov spoke simultaneously: "What is it, Mita? Your timing is terrible."

"Chamoun, is that you? You bastard, you'd better watch yourself. And give Magruder this message—the blacklegs here are still mine. Tell him to watch his back. One false move, and he's past tense."

"Lord, Romanov, I've got company here—"

But the door was already slamming, and Cassie was swallowing gasps of terror on his bed, and wanting to know "who that man was and what did he mean?"

"Nothing, love, nothing. Just a drunken riverboater, that's all. Don't worry your sweet self about that—

worry about what your Daddy's going to say if I don't get you home by sunrise."

She was dressing with awkward movements by the flashlight's glow. He flipped on the electrics. "Turn that off. Save the juice. I'll help you. I'm sorry . . ."

She came into his arms and he was almost certain that she was rattled enough and exhausted enough to forget the intrusion—after all, she'd had her first night with a man—when she said, "Michael, he mentioned blacklegs. The militia. Are you sure we shouldn't tell someone? Minister Magruder? Someone?"

"Right, I'll tell Magruder." He seized on that, the only safe thing he could tell her. "Tell 'im first thing after I get you back. Cassie, honey. . . ." He took her elbows, held her hands from the buttons she was struggling to fasten. "We don't want to know, either of us, what that was about. Chance has enemies by the score. He's trying to do a difficult thing, setting up that trade mission. Plenty of people don't want better relations between Nev Hettek and Merovingen. So we give Chance the message and then we forget the whole thing, hear? Even your father oughtn't to know what happened here. Understand?"

"Yes." A very small voice.

"Promise?"

"I said, yes." She broke away from him to cradle her flashlight against her throat. "I still . . . love you, Michael. I won't tell anyone. But if you're in trouble, Daddy can help—if you ever want me to ask."

That was a relief. All he needed was her running secretly to Poppa about this to protect him from some imagined bad guys. "I told you, it's Chance's trouble, and he's always got some. For the sake of everybody, we forget this, both of us, by the time we walk up on deck."

She understood politics; she must have heard something similar from her father or mother, one time or another, for she squared her shoulders and raised her chin high: "You don't have to worry about me, Michael. I understand. All that matters now is us . . . our family, our new life. We'll tell Daddy only that

we've pledged to marry and that he can announce it
tomorrow night. If you agree?"

"Oh, love . . ." He hugged her against him, genuinely grateful for her good sense and the way her
father had raised her. He'd hate like hell to have to
murder his wife because she knew too much on their
honeymoon, before he even got to know her.

It wasn't that Magruder hated parties particularly,
he just hated crowds. And this bunch, at Governor
Kalugin's 24th of Harvest Eve Festival Ball, was a
crowd easy to hate: Revenantist bigwigs, a few Adventist compromisers, all the money and power in
town.

You needed a diagram to tell who was in whose
pocket. Magruder made the practical assumption that
everyone was in everyone else's, here, and walked his
mental tightrope from one clique to the next, listening and making his presence felt where it might do
some good.

It did some good with Mike Chamoun, who was
spooked beyond Magruder's ability to affect in the
time he could allot to the young Sword. "Yes'ser,"
Chamoun had come to him this morning saying, "it's
all set—the marriage. They're going to announce it
at the Ball, her father says. A *five* year contract."

Good boy, real good, Magruder had thought, until
he heard the rest, about how Chamoun had decided
to lay the Boregy girl on the *Detfish* and run into
Dimitri Romanov there.

Couldn't be helped. Romanov was more and more
of a problem, though, and when, as the band took a
break, Magruder sighted the pale head of the Sword's
Merovingen tactical officer, he headed straight for
Mita's brocaded back.

I'd take him out right here and now on some
pretext, if it wouldn't get me a reputation as a duellist.
But it would, and Romanov was flying his own flag,
tonight—some Sword disruption was on the agenda.

During, or after, buddy; that's a promise.

Romanov made Magruder a promise of his own,
once they'd taken their drinks off into a corner,

hiding behind a clutch of women chattering about their fashions. "Magruder, you ever leave me adrift like that again, you're dead meat. Understand?"

You're not going to live that long—not long enough for any 'ever again's,' Mita. "The way I heard it, Dimitri," use his whole name, drawl it slow, let him know what's coming; "you about blew everything, spouting off in front of Michael Chamoun's intended."

"What?"

Romanov hadn't known the girl was there, hadn't realized. Reason enough, in a sensitive venture like this, to retire him—the Sword couldn't afford sloppy, and Romanov was real sloppy on that riverboat. "Don't 'what' me, fool. Spouting off about blacklegs. Whatcha' think the pawn made of that? You want me, you come get me. Otherwise, stay on your side of this gambit and I'll stay on mine." Now, louder, loud enough for a few of the ladies to turn their heads: "Anytime you wish combat, in memory of your personal honor such as it's shown itself to be, m'ser Romanov, I am at your disposal."

Turn on your heel and stalk away, push right past those scandalized ladies with their gloves and see how long it takes for word to get around.

Now to Anastasi, who's pretending he didn't see; Boregy right there with him, looking like a couple of mannequins in their fancy dress. "My apologies, Your Honor—" Probably not the right title for the baby son, but flattering and boy, he'd like to be just that: top boss and rat-trainer of this show. "I have a short fuse with meddlers. Some people, it seems, don't favor a trading mission from Nev Hettek being established here."

"One of your own citizens, I believe, Minister Magruder. One has to expect a certain amount of resistance, after all." Anastasi Kalugin was black-haired, fairer even than Romanov, like a marble come to life. He knew the strength of his impression and used it like a sculptor's chisel. "Change doesn't come without disruption, even change for the better."

Kalugin, you're going to bullshit yourself into an early grave. Change for the better, that's the official line.

Behind Anastasi, Magruder caught sight of Tatiana, with her brother Mikhail and her father Iosef, all three with damned red ribbons draped crosswise over their torsos like royalty, ribbons just like Anastasi's. The oldest kid, Mikhail, was into locksmithing or something harmless; a dimwit, a dullard here, where tech wasn't accessible; would that the other two were as harmless.

"Change for the better," Magruder answered after a long, assessive pause, "won't come until my people and yours are ready to put away these outmoded prejudices. And Romanov's not the only one—isn't that one of your militia commanders he's with now?"

Set the hook, and maybe Kalugin'll take Romanov out for me. If Kalugin was as smart as his sister, the natural assumption that Magruder was Sword had to be stifled. Giving Romanov up as Sword would do the trick, if Romanov was dead by the time suspicion solidified.

Kalugin puffed out his chest as he looked past Magruder, toward Mita Romanov: "As of this evening, Minister Magruder, I'm Chief Advocate Militiar, as you know. I'll look into your Nev Hetteker friend's connection with my blacklegs, and let you know. In the meantime, try to avoid a duel if possible. We of the government must attempt to set civilized standards for our constituents."

Point taken, and you bet I won't say "Sword" if you don't. "I'll do my best, but you must realize that, between two Nev Hettekkers, Nev Hettek codes apply, especially if Your Honor grants us the mission, which will be Nev Hettek territory, however small." *In other words, I won't kill him on your turf, promise. So if he gets it elsewhere, don't look at me.*

Vega Boregy, silent and a discreet few paces off, edged into the conversation: "I'm about to announce the contract of your Captain Chamoun to my Cassiopeia, Minister Magruder. Care to share the honor?"

"I'd be delighted, Lord Boregy." And off we go, thick as thieves, to seal the doom of all of these. *Up to the podium, or whatever you call it here, and get the band to give you a drum roll, Vega.*

"Ladies and Gentlemen," Vega Boregy began when the crowd had come to attention, "I'm pleased to announce, this evening, with the kind permission and blessing of Governor Kalugin and his family, one more reason to celebrate."

While Boregy droned on, making sure that no one, especially the Kalugins, thought Vega was trying to steal their thunder by announcing his daughter's wedding as if it were as important as Anastasi's promotion, Magruder surveilled the room, looking for Romanov.

Romanov was nowhere in sight, which made Magruder want to check his weapons. Probably the only weapons in the room except on other government types—thank the Lord for his diplomatic status—since he was assuredly going to need them when the Sword went into action. Which it would.

He saw the Chamoun boy and the Boregy girl edging toward the podium in front of the band, and watched them climb it, distracted the entire time because he'd noticed Tatiana Kalugin staring at him again. Got to do something about that woman.

But first he had to say his little piece about better relations between Nev Hettek and Merovingen being the first step toward a better, richer Merovin for all, and commend the youngsters on their bravery. As emissary from Nev Hettek, it was part of his new job.

Then he slid into the background and off the podium, stage left, hoping to reconnoiter until he found Romanov, and found Tatiana Kalugin instead.

"Ah, our new foreigner-in-residence," she breathed over her wine glass.

A smile like the biggest fish in the Det. *Ready to swallow me whole.* "You don't entirely approve of me, is that it, m'sera Secretary?" Bold as brass, but that was her nature, too.

"Oh, I wouldn't say that, Minister Magruder."

"Call me Chance. What would you say, m'sera Kalugin?"

"I would say, Chance Magruder, that the jury is still out on you."

"Then maybe I'll have time to compromise the

jury's foreman—curry favor. It's my intention to try." *You read me, lady? You want friendly, I'll give you friendly. You want adversarial, I'll give you that. You want either or both in bed, you got it. In spades.* "There are too many Nev Hettekker hopes riding on how I fare here for me to give it—and you—less than my best."

"I imagine that's so," said Tatiana Kalugin with languid, grudging, surprise.

She liked the game, so far. Good. He liked it, too. Maybe Mike Chamoun wasn't the only one who'd be unsheathing his Sword tonight, for the good of the cause. Tatiana Kalugin was nearly as tall as he, lean and well along in her thirties, with a woman's softness right where it ought to be. Get her out of the sequins and the damned official ribbon and she might be just the kind of hellcat she was telegraphing to him she was. And the danger of the mind behind that perfectly aristocratic and marble-cool face added spice to it.

C'mon, lady, touch my arm, move on in, show me how it's going to be.

She did just that, a professional's move—her fingers light to direct his attention to the door, through which a retainer in the livery of the Nikolaev family was hurrying, his face pale and his gait jerky with control.

"Let's see what the trouble is, shall we, before that fellow disturbs my brother. After all, this *is* Anastasi's big night."

He held out his crooked arm and she slipped a hand through it. Together, decorous as all hell, they intercepted the Nikolaev retainer before he could reach the new Advocate Militiar or anybody else.

"Yes?" said Tatiana in a whiplike voice that had started concise reports out of any number of men like this.

"The House—it's been attacked! Nikolaev House. Two casualties, m'sera Secretary, besides one house-girl. But the other . . ."

"Go on," Chance Magruder said, because this was man's business, death and violence, and he wanted Tatiana to know he was chivalrous.

She cast him a haughty, sidelong glance as the retainer said, "m'sera Kika's been killed. The Sword of God, we think . . . assassins in the night; black-clad men. Pathati-gas and poisoned stars."

"That's enough. You may go find a captain of the guard and report all this. Don't bother my brother. We will inform m'ser Nikolaev for you. And don't spread this around among the help. It will ruin our party."

"But m'sera . . . m'sera Rita's been wounded, as well. It's an affront and their mother demands more blacklegs."

"The lady said," Magruder said in a clipped, impatient voice, "Get lost, keep your mouth shut, do your job.' Now do that, or we'll find somebody to replace you that knows how to take a direct order."

Pushin' it, Magruder. But the man scuttled off and Tatiana Kalugin raised an eyebrow at him: "Nicely done, Chance Magruder. If your stint as a Nev Hettek representative comes to a close, perhaps I'll make you a Merovingen citizen. We could use a few more intelligent men who know when and how to speak plainly."

"Whatever pleases you, m'sera Kalugin."

Now, at last, she said, "Tatiana will do, though not in public, of course. Perhaps, considering the violence abroad tonight, you will be my escort when I leave for home?"

Home wasn't here, then, in the Signeury; home was on The Rock, where only the very oldest and best Houses flourished.

"My honor and pleasure to do so," he said, wishing he could get away from her to see where the retainer had gone.

"Certainly one, if not the other," she said, and disengaged her hand from his arm.

Has her own agenda tonight, he thought as she eased away.

He wanted to find Chamoun before the news did. Chamoun didn't know they knew, maybe, but the Sword was aware of his interest in Rita Nikolaev.

Probably the reason she'd been hit, if Magruder knew
Romanov like he thought he did.

"Mike," Magruder said when he reached the boy
and his fiancée, letting the form of address cue the
boy to the urgency here, "I need to see you for a
moment."

Chamoun's face drained of color and emotion. He
muttered to his betrothed and went Magruder's way,
out onto one of the balconies.

"What is it, Magruder? What have I done wrong?"

"Nothing. The Nikolaev House has been hit; Kika
Nikolaev's been killed; Rita Nikolaev's been injured.
And you're *not* to go to her, not to *ask* about her—no
more than's natural for a Boregy-in-the-making like
you are. It's probably Romanov's doing. Trust me,
I'll take care of it. That's a promise."

Chamoun blinked like a startled animal. His face
worked.

*That's right, Michael boy, you heard me: I'm fighting
your battles for you, from now on in.* "Did you hear me,
man?" Softly, because Chamoun was hurting, thinking the bloodshed at Nikolaev House was his fault—
and not mistaken.

"I . . . I heard you, ser. I'll be fine. I'll do my job.
I'm *doing* my job, damn it, best as anybody can."

Pain and defiance, par for the course. "You want
me to reassure you that it's worth it? It is." That was
all Magruder dared say, here and now. It would be
enough; Chamoun could add and subtract. Lots of
people paid for their mistakes the hard way; one
thing Chamoun knew for certain was bound to be
that he didn't want to end up like the Nikolaevs, or
like Romanov—with Magruder on his track.

He left the boy on the balcony and smiled at
Cassiopeia Boregy, who looked at him with huge
eyes. Somebody'd told her, then.

"M'sera Boregy, why don't you go out there and
help Michael through this? We don't have these sorts
of incidents in Nev Hettek. He's going to have you
on the *Detfish* by morning, headed home to his family where he can protect you, if you don't convince
him otherwise."

Utter fabrication, but the sort to appeal to a romantic young girl. And the sort to take her mind off the death of one friend and mauling of another. Damn Romanov, Magruder was thinking when all hell broke loose in the Signeury function hall.

Black-clad men were dropping from windows on ropes; pathati-gas all over so that Chance ripped the front of his shirt off and bound it around his mouth and nose even before he went for his gun.

Tables and chairs upended, people running, people falling flat to the floor.

You'd think it was a damned army come in here, instead of half a dozen Swords with the al-Bannas coordinating—easy to spot if you knew what to look for.

He got off one good shot before the gas made his eyes smart—one less al-Banna to worry about: the black figure slid limply down the rope in which it had tangled in death.

Yelling and surging, the crowd of elite was a real problem. He knew what he ought to do, and he did it: pushing past bodies, shoving people down out of the line of star and bullet fire, he headed toward where he'd last seen the Kalugins.

And found them, when he got there, surrounded by blacklegs: some militia had been in plainclothes, which was a handy datum. Magruder filed faces and realized Tatiana wasn't among the brocaded pile of dignitaries on which the militia were fairly sitting while they fired back, and kept searching.

He grabbed a bottle of sparkling wine as he passed a table, and then saw a leg sticking out under it. Getting off one more shot through tearing eyes, ignoring the coughs that racked him and made him miss, he dived under the table.

Tatiana Kalugin was heaving her guts out. He knocked the neck off the bottle and tore a strip from her blouse, wet the strip, tied the whole mess around her resisting head and face: she couldn't see him through her streaming eyes. She thought he was the enemy.

Well, he was, just not acting like it right now. The

carbonation in the sparkling liquid, and the liquid itself, poured on cloth, provided a filter for the poisonous effects of the gas.

He couldn't tell her—she couldn't hear him over all the screaming, anyhow. He just pinioned her arms to her side and got on top of her, holding her until she realized that she could breathe, that she wasn't being abducted, that she could even see through the wet cloth.

Then he rolled off her and doused his own, dry mask from the bottle before he wriggled out from under the tablecloth to start shooting.

Wouldn't do to be caught with any ammo unexpended when it was time to analyze what had happened here. He ran through the four shots left in his revolver and the twelve additional bullets in the back of his belt in short order, then started dispersing his stars and pathati-ampules, looking back once to make sure Tatiana didn't see him with weapons attributable to the "enemy"—to the Sword.

Having added to the carnage, he went back to her. She was huddled but still fighting bravely to recoup, trying to breathe, to clear her eyes, to get the vomit out of her nose and throat.

He put both arms around her, yelling into her ear, "I've got to get you out of here," and went about doing that, dragging her out from under the table and toward one of the inner doors.

The militia had killed one more Sword, the others had gotten out okay, and all that was left in the reception hall was confusion: gas residues, spilled blood and food and drink, wounded and terrified guests, and militiamen scurrying around, hoping like hell they hadn't injured any civilians in the fray.

He dragged Tatiana Kalugin through a door he'd never seen before, one arm inarguably around her waist, and half-threw her onto a handy couch in the dimly-lit anteroom.

"Water?" he yelled at her, realized he didn't need to yell in here, and modulated downward: "Water, you need to clean up and so do I."

She's not sure she's alive yet, Magruder; easy.

She was still hacking; with a valorous effort he could appreciate, she straightened up and pointed, croaking something unintelligible.

He found the water on a sideboard and brought it; ripping his own blouse further, he poured the water on a sleeve and started cleaning her up.

She didn't object too much, and then not at all.

Eventually, when they were both free of vomit and most of their clothes, she reached for him.

"Thank you," she said hoarsely. "Chance . . . you saved my life."

"Possibly," he said as he reached for her in return.

From here on in, for better or worse, it was history in the making. He'd get Romanov eventually; if Mondragon had come to the Ball, Magruder hadn't seen him, which meant Mondragon had sensed which way the wind was blowing; young Chamoun was well on his way to becoming everything the Sword wanted him to be, and this evening's little demonstration had not only made multiple impacts on those whom it was intended to impact, it had gone down without a hitch.

With his credibility now established as best could be—a man who'd fought with the Kalugins against a Sword attack wouldn't be suspected as Sword without proof—it was time for Magruder to deal himself the best hand he knew how. And, for better or worse, Tatiana Kalugin was the first card he'd drawn—a Queen.

FESTIVAL MOON
(REPRISED)

C.J. Cherryh

It was quiet again on the Grand, after so much of
fire and smoke going up; quiet, except the hundreds
of boats that lined the Grand and Archangel and
every canal around—folk wondering was the governor still alive; was Anastasi, was Tatiana or feckless
Mikhail.

And Mondragon.

O God, Mondragon.

Stay put, he had told her, on no uncertain terms.
Jones, if I come out of there in a hurry I don't want
to have to find you—just *be* here.

So she stuck it out, standing on her halfdeck, as
most everyone on the canals were standing, black
figures against the glare of fire, huddled together in
speculation what might have happened to Merovingen
in there, or to their lives, or their livelihoods.

There was a Nev Hettek riverboat in the harbor.
There was fire and gunfire in the Signeury and
trouble down by Nikolaev, and the hooks were out
and the poles were ready in Merovingen-below, for
any trouble that came, be it inside or outside. The
big bells were tolling alarm and disaster and still the
issue of it was in doubt.

A shout went up near the Signeury walls, where
no one was supposed to tie up. Something was happening; and Jones clung to her pole and tried not to

let her supper come up in sheer fright. There was lantern-light, the brighter glare of electrics; the crowd nearest started yelling as if there was someone to yell at—Lord, the answers were all over there, and she was here, and she was dying inside.

O Angel, keep 'im out of it, bring 'im back, get us out of here—

If he's hurt I'll gut the governor himself, I will, him first and all the rest.

O God.

Engine-sound then, big one. The murmur grew over the crowd-noise, and the monstrous sleek shadow of a Rimmon yacht nosed out from Archangel Cut and cornered to the peril of boats all along that side. Canalers swore and scrambled to their poles as that dreadful engine got itself underway and headed at them.

That's Anastasi. Anastasi's away.

As the towering prow came closer and the engine-noise thundered off the walls of the Signeury. It blotted out the lights. It had none of its own. It was just there, like the barges in the night. No more Festival lanterns. It was black and it was deadly and it owned the canals by sheer force.

Wood splintered. There were cries of rage and panic. Some poor sod had not been fast enough.

"Ware, hey," went up. And: "Hey, hey, *bo-hinnn-nnnnn!*" that was the direst cry on the canals. "*Haneys underrrrr!*"

Haneys had kids. One a five-year-old. The monster passed, leaving its wake churned white, leaving flotsam, leaving a wake that hove like a wall in the confines of Archangel, and Jones leapt to the well and shoved hard at the wall as the wave hit and near capsized the skip. There were screams. Curses and the grating of wood as boat ground against boat, and the wave and its backlash battered at would-be rescuers.

Haneys is under. God help 'em. I can't. I can't, I got to be here—

Damn 'im, damn 'im to bloody hell.

Footsteps raced down the Archangel walk, people

running past, some in hightown clothes, some glittering with jewels.

And one of them leaped for her well and landed wide-legged on her deck slats with a thump of uptown boots. "Jones. Come on."

"We got a boat down, damn Kalugin rode the Haneys down, I got to help, dammit! Lend a hand!"

"Move it!" Mondragon yelled at her, heedless of witnesses, and ran and jerked the bow-tie loose. She jumped up on the halfdeck, squatted to clear the other and shoved off, the skip still rocking like a cork in the churn of the yacht's boil-up. But Mondragon came up by her and caught her arm. "Out of here. Go."

"I got to—"

"Now!" He grabbed the pole from the rack and shoved with it, all in ball finery as he was, all uptowner, and his blond hair shining plain in the firelight as the glitter on his collar and his cuffs.

"Dammit, they're Trade!"

"There's boats to see to it. Come on, Jones."

"Ye live on the water! You want help of the Trade, ye damn well don't stand off when a boat's rode below—help me, dammit, we got a family boat down out there." She grabbed his arm. "Where d'you live, hey? What are you?"

His face was stark and pale in the fire-glow from the Signeury, in the swing of lights out over the heaving water as boats set out to probe the bottom. He had a wild, a desperate look.

Then he turned and pushed with the pole, shoving the skip out where he wanted it, out into the chop and the chaos of boats; and she shoved from her side, steering hard. The firelight broke up in glitter. There was a knot in her throat and a bad taste in her mouth. They were Trade, all around her; and Mondragon stopped the skip with a push of the pole, out in the middle of the chop with the rest of them. There was a cry went up. One Haney was up on shore. Somebody had another.

There were bits and pieces all about. A doll floated in the light, eyes wide.

"Who's that?" a voice yelled when a skip bumped them in the search. "Who *is* that?"

Meaning the blond man in the evening shirt, wielding a pole and hunting the dark and the currents of Archangel to see what Old Det might give back, like all the rest of them.

"That's Jones," someone yelled, "that's *her* feller—"

It was all they could do. Someone called down they had found the Haney eldest, a broken arm and all, but holding the baby when they got him up.

"They got 'im, they got 'im, Ol' Det don't get 'em, damn that boat t' hell—"

Jones let the pole ride then. She was shaking as she sat down on the halfdeck.

Mondragon shipped his pole and sat down too, head in his hands.

He was still like that when she got up and pushed again, taking them out, out from among the boats, out onto the Grand.

"Boregy," he said then, out of the dark and the bridge-shadow.

"Yey," she said. There seemed nothing in her. It was all drained. "They get ol' Iosef?"

"Not him, not Tatiana, not Anastasi."

No one ever counted Mikhail.

"Damn shame," she said. "Damn shame." With a hollow hurt at her gut. "He got the warning, huh? Ought to be real grateful. Him and that black boat."

"It's not over."

"Get out of it, dammit, Mondragon, let the high-towners cut each other up for stew, they ain't nothing here—say you was knocked silly. Say you spent the night in the Det. You give him enough a'ready, he ain't going to ask more."

"You got a wave coming, Jones, which way do you face?"

"To it," she said. There was a copper taste in her mouth. "Yeah, I hear ye. Hey-hin! *Yoss!*"

As she swung the bow and hit the Grand current.

FIRST-BATH

Lynn Abbey

Meanwhile . . .

The house of Kamat was quiet. The whirlwind festivities preceding the 24 Harvest holiday had passed it by. Properly solemn banners had been draped from its porches and balconies—Andromeda Kamat, dowager of the house, was too aware of the Kamat's *position* in Merovingen to overlook such a fundamental display of ostentation—but their annual entertainments had been canceled and the family had shunned all but the most restrained and intimate invitations.

Certainly their absence was scarcely noted, as every family, whatever its station, pursued both its interests and its amusements. Had they appeared, however, tongues would have wagged—for wasn't Kamat still in mourning? Had they not, this Greening past, sat in somber state as the longboat took Nikolay Kamat on his last journey down the Grand Canal? House Kalugin could scoff at tradition, or Boregy or Ito, but, among the ambitious, appearances were important and so the Kamat *behaved*.

Discretion suited Richard Kamat this year, at least. He was not yet comfortable with his sudden elevation to Househead. His father had been fifty-two that Greening evening when he died and healthy as the proverbial and storied horse. Richard—eldest son, only son—had expected another decade or two of seasoning before responsibility settled unalterably around his shoulders.

They had been celebrating Nikolay's birthday. The house was filled with guests enjoying the Househead's largess: cold, fragrant syllabub; lively music floating across the balconies; guest-gifts of silk dyed with rich, First-bath indigo. Nikolay had excused himself, probably to visit the same elegant library where his son now sat by candlelight, but had hesitated—spun around to look back into the room—just before the landing. Had someone called his name or known of the vagrant slice of tamarind waiting beneath his heel?

Richard shook his head. Philosophers at the university said a man could not remember a sound—reproduce it in the silent space between his ears—but merely recognize it at a later time. But Richard still heard the sound his father's head had made as it struck the lip of the first stair below the landing. His father had lingered a week, never speaking nor recognizing, only waiting for the new moon ebb tide to drain through the pilings far beneath his house.

It must have been an accident, the young man mused. No assassination could have been so perfectly, so absurdly contrived. Certainly it had answered no unspoken prayer of Richard's but had thrust him, unwilling and unprepared, into a position which remained ill-fitting these several months after the funeral.

A single chime, muffled by heavy drapes, rang through the study. Richard reached into his pocket and fingered the repeater knob of his watch. Patrik was right on time, as usual. Punctuality and devotion to Kamat affairs defined and completely described his father's lackluster younger brother; no one, certainly not Patrik himself, had ever considered him as Househead after Nikolay's death.

Reaching behind the drapery, Richard tugged a rope twice then, with Nikolay's spyglass tucked under his arm, headed up a narrow stairway to the roof. He gave passing notice to the revelry in the

canals, hoping only that the festival lanterns and
electrics would not obscure his view of the ocean
horizon. There was, after all, a second reason that
Kamat was quiet; that it would have been quiet this
night even if Nikolay rather than his son peered
through the wedding-cake jumble of spires, turrets
and bridges that created Merovingen's nighttime silhouette. Whatever phase the moon had been when
the Scouring had begun, it was dark tonight and
Kamat had work to do. Cursing the ambient lantern-
light, Richard waited for the flash of phosphorescence heralding the monthly flood-tide surge through
the Det estuary.

The new moon surge, which was about as reliable
as anything on this forsaken world of Merovin, would
drive the waterwheels deep in the Kamat basements.
More importantly, some peculiar aspect of that faintly
flickering green water would wash amid the wool,
the mordants and the indigo to create the midnight
blue which Hosni Kamat, patriarch and founder of
the clan, had simply named *First-bath*.

Hosni had never cared why the luminous Det-
surge fixed the blue dye so fast and firm into the
wool—so long as no one else knew either. Nikolay,
frantic in those months when the new moon surge
remained opaque and the wool was lifeless, had spent
years tinkering with flasks and retorts trying to un-
lock the secret. His son, Richard, took after Hosni—so
far: he had no time for curiosity, only results.

As soon as the horizon flashed green in the spyglass, Richard returned to the study and yanked
hard on the cord. Patrik would have the gates cranked
open by the time the young man had descended the
half-dozen or more levels of the artificial island. The
great bricks of indigo would be set beside the vats
along with the acrid sacks of chemical mordants for
although the polluted Det-water was the most secret
ingredient in the First-bath soup, it was far from the
only jealously guarded secret in the process.

Patrik knew how much of each substance to add to
each vat and in what sequence as did Richard himself. Richard's mother, Andromeda, knew the secret,

too, though she descended to the workrooms no more than once or twice a year. But no one else witnessed the actual making of First-bath. The precise formula, and the even more precise instructions for its proper recreation were written down; old Hosni believed in luck, both good and bad. Three vaults, only one of which rested inside Kamat's walls, held the master recipe; one of Richard's personal duties was assuring their sanctity each month.

Such contingencies were, however, for other moments. He lit a lantern as he extinguished the oil lamp on the table and headed for the private stairs to the workrooms. He had little need of the light as he plunged downward—the twists and irregularities of these passages had been locked in his mind before he learned to read—and no expectations of meeting anyone coming up.

He kept a firm grip on the lantern, though, when collision rocked him back against the bannister and he kept his balance—which was more than could be said for his opposite number who stumbled and sprawled at his feet. With the memory of Nikolay's death still powerful in his mind, Richard had the lantern on a hook and an arm around the body before his thoughts cleared enough to wonder who he had encountered on the private stairway.

"I'm all right," a woman assured him, wrapping her fingers around his wrist and using all his strength to rise, unsteadily, to her feet.

"Marina?" he murmured, nearly motionless with surprise as the light fell around her.

His sister kept silent, not that there was anything she could say which the wild-animal brilliance of her eyes hadn't already told him. Her sweater, a lacy affair glittering with metal threads and plunging dangerously low in front, was ripped—and hadn't ripped when she fell. Her hair was mussed; her cosmetics smeared and her perfume long-since replaced with gin. She wove a little under the silent pressure of his disapproval and let her fingers fall away from his arm.

"There was a party at Nikolaevs," she admitted. "Carrolly had an invitation."

"We're supposed to be in mourning." The words burst out of his mouth and hung between them, sounding patronizing even to his own ears.

"I didn't embarrass us. I'm wearing one of mother's designs—everyone noticed it."

"Ree, take a look at yourself. You're drunk."

"Not quite, Richard, and *that* didn't happen at Nikolaevs."

"We'll talk. Later—at breakfast."

She sighed, and a portion of her defiance ebbed away. As different as day and night, they were barely a year apart in age and until Greening they'd never had any secrets from each other.

"We'll talk it out, Ree," Richard said more gently, leaning forward to kiss her forehead. "There's First-bath tonight; come up to the study for breakfast."

The liquor smell was potent, almost as if she'd been drenched with the stuff. There were marks revealed by the torn sweater which he did not realize were dried blood until she'd pushed past him on the stairs. For a moment he considered that Marina might need him more than the wools, silks and cottons in the workrooms did. But, no—though she undoubtedly did need someone—he knew her pride well enough to let her stumble on up the stairs. She'd be in the study when the First-bath was rinsing and that would be soon enough.

The conglomeration of pilings, piers and ballast that separated Kamat's island from the Det shuddered as the tide-gate fell open. Richard quickened his pace down the stairs, arriving in the workrooms as the pungent sea-water sluiced through the vats. Patrik, distributing the bricks of dye and mordants from a maze of catwalks, acknowledged his nephew's presence with a brief nod. "The kilns are ready," the wisp-haired man shouted over the roar of the water. "One and two are filled."

Unlike the dyeworks depicted in pre-Scouring texts or, indeed, other such enterprises throughout Merovingen, Kamat heated their dye water with white-hot

ceramic bricks—which Richard released into the first
two baths with a rumble and hiss of steam—and
maneuvered their great webbed spindles of cotton,
wool and silk yard hydraulically.

It was a mare's nest of wooden gears and pulleys;
vaned, horizontal turbines and enough knotted rig-
ging to bring tears to a proper Revenantist's eyes:
the Det tidal surge, a modest enough fist of water as
ocean currents were measured, did all the work.
Twice a day (though the phosphorescence necessary
to the First-bath process coincided only with the new
moon in late summers) the water rushed through
the tide-gates here on Kamat and at similar, but
larger, works off the Nikolaev wharves. The ebbing
tide ran with strange odors and stranger colors from
time to time but, all in all, Merovingen's power looked
favorably upon Kamat's inventiveness—seeing it as a
bulwark against the less-benign technology coming
downriver from Nev Hettek.

When all the vats were filled with dark liquid and
the turbines had begun their tasks of churning the
yarn-filled spindles through the bath, Patrik joined
Richard by the kiln and congratulated him on yet
another month's production of First-bath fiber.

First-bath: midnight indigo, pride of the house of
Kamat. A richer color and a softer fiber than anything else yet produced on the forsaken world of
Merovingen. But Hosni Kamat considered First-bath
more than just a fortuitous dye bath; to the departed patriarch, First-bath meant the highest qual-
ity ingredients brought together under the most
disciplined and refined conditions—and it applied to
people, most especially his own family, as well as
fibers and dye.

"I'll get the workers to help with the unloading,"
the older man said: telling rather than asking. "You'll
be wanting to catch some sleep now."

Richard wiped the sweat from his face. "Later. It's
Festival; we'll be shorthanded and they like to see us
here, too, on First-bath night." That was true enough,
though he admitted nothing about his breakfast with

Marina or his concerns for her which would keep him awake under any circumstance.

"More important you be rested when company comes calling."

Richard shot a glance that was both questioning and commanding tow: d his uncle.

"Your mother got a letter after dinner . . . from her father and hand delivered by some Hetteker official."

"She didn't tell me—"

"She didn't *tell* me, either. I saw the messenger leave. You'd already gone to the study."

"Might not mean anything . . . certainly not company tomorrow," Richard pondered aloud.

Patrik shrugged—the "hands off" motion that penetrated to the core of his being and meant that within Kamat he'd always be number two, never number one. "Who knows? It's your decision."

Richard returned the gesture and headed for the double doors of the loading bay in silence. Workers, about a half-dozen of them, waited on the other side of the heavy, locked doors. The Househead greeted each of them by name; he'd started here on the loading dock back when he stood no higher than the bales he tried to move. There was no false camaraderie—no pretense that he was not Kamat nor they from the lower city—but there was understanding that they needed each other and as much genuine affection as their differing conditions would allow. "Good Festival to you," Richard added, shaking each hard-callused hand.

"And you, m'ser."

"The Angel watch you another year, Thom . . . Dana . . . Rhys." Formal and stuffy, perhaps, but his grip was dry and firm as the workers expected.

The doors swung shut and Richard was alone again with a handful of hours before dawn. There wasn't time for sleep and, in any event, he had enough to think about between his sister's behavior and his mother's unannounced message from Nev Hettek. Not that his imagination could draw a bridge from one to the other: Marina's misadventures could have no bearing on grandfather Nemesis Garin's sudden, after twenty-six years, re-emergence into his mother, Andromeda's life. No, mostly it was just that he, Richard, was Househead now and the problems of the house were his problems no matter how little he understood them.

With a sigh, Richard swung through the rafters and landed, light-footed, in the slip where the Kamat stored their private boats—where he stored the sleek punt whose care, before Nikolay's death, had absorbed most of his leisure time. Years might still pass before the Househead's study up along the eaves felt comfortable, but the burnished wood punt was Richard's final, private refuge.

Loosening the ropes, he eased the craft down to the black water. Its waxed and varnished keel cut the surface without ripple or sound. Richard notched the pole against the house pilings and pushed off for the grate that opened onto the Kamat-Foundry Canal.

"Be stayin' put if I was you," a voice called from the darkness beyond the grate.

Water riffled around the pole as Richard brought the punt to a halt. He recognized the voice of Celotta, who had House permission to tie-up against the grate in exchange for keeping her night-eyes open. Celotta had brought her boat deep into Kamat's shadow; Richard could hear her voice but he did not see her. Such caution on a Festival night was noteworthy and as Househead, Richard gave her his full attention.

"Has some boatman got the Melancholy?" he asked affably, heeling the punt around the pole so he and Celotta could speak yet remain well within the shadows of Kamat and her boat.

Celotta gave a coarse laugh. "Don't get the Melancholy here down below." Melancholy being that complex of behaviors which struck some around Festival inflicting them with a profound knowledge of the futility of life on Merovin—and, in truth, the Melancholy— if it actually existed—required a broader horizon than usually occurred canalside.

"Then what's the problem? Why're you tied up so tight, so early?"

"Strangers on the waters."

"Who?"

"Can't say—but they be lookin' higher than the canals. Wouldn't be out alone and lookin' so fine."

Can't say or won't say? Richard thought, knowing full well that Celotta knew more than she let on. Still, Merovingen had always been a brawly sort of town. Taking the sleek punt out after sundown entailed a certain amount of risk—and Celotta had never objected before.

"I've got my pole," he reminded her, fishing for more information.

"Won't help."

"What kind of strangers we got on the canals of Merovingen tonight? Have the sharrh, themselves, come back to Scour us off for good?"

He had inserted a believable amount of levity into his voice but Celotta's face reflected no amusement. "There's strangers on the water, m'ser Richard," she said, shaking a gnarled finger at him. "Strangers enough that *I* tied up in shadow. Don't need to see the face of trouble when you can smell it. Don't want to find you fetched up in the harbor someplace."

Celotta had been his mother's age once, a long time ago when she'd had a man beside her in the poleboat. Andromeda had changed, her cheek bones had risen and a fine network of lines crept out from the corners of her eyes and mouth, but Celotta had changed more. She'd swallowed more than Det water in the past twenty years: her eyes were red-ringed; her cheeks were crevassed and her grin nowadays showed more gaps than teeth.

If he hadn't known her since childhood, Richard knew he would have judged her mad and simply ordered her from his path. But knowing her, and knowing how she had become what she was and how canny she remained, he trusted her and let her tie-up be.

"You have wool?" he asked as the tide pushed the punt back into the Kamat under-house.

"First-bath?"

Celotta was one of more than a hundred boat-dwellers who helped make ends meet by converting Kamat wool into Kamat sweaters. Each week she delivered at least one well-wrought garment to the loading dock; every couple of weeks more, Richard guessed, she sold a similar sweater on the black market. Kamat didn't mind the private enterprise of its workers, but the First-bath fibers now drying in the workrooms wouldn't leave the House before they were finished into garments for the Uptown trade. "Not tonight, Celotta," the Househead laughed. "Not tonight."

"Can't blame a girl for tryin'."

Richard grunted an agreement as he shoved the pole into the mud and impelled the punt back to its slip. He took great pride, and not a few awards, for his boat handling in the races and regattas that proliferated through the highest and lowest strata of Merovingen. The punt barely touched the straw bumper at the end of the slip before coming to a smooth stop.

The grate was dark and quiet as he hoisted the punt out of the water. Celotta had battened her boat winter-tight. Whoever these strangers were, she feared them.

And Richard had no doubt, as he bypassed the door to the workrooms, that Celotta knew who the strangers were—if not by name then by affiliation. The canalers spoke in code, as did almost everyone else in Merovingen; they gave only what the conversation demanded. If Richard had asked the right questions, or known the right answers, Celotta would have shared more of the substance of her fears. As it was, she had given him, a hightowner, all that she dared.

There was no simple route from the loading dock to the third-level bridge gate that served as the main, civilized entrance to Kamat's private quarters. Richard was forced through a series of dark, narrow passages; decaying exterior stairways and semi-private thoroughfares as he circled and wove through Kamat Isle. As a child he had learned every twisted corner of his home. Now, after many years' absence, he was stymied by crawlways too small for his adult-sized body and gaping holes or new walls where Merovingen's constant reconstruction and the river's constant erosion had changed the facade of the island.

Kamat Isle was more stable than many in the city's archipelago. Good gray rock supported at least part of the cantilevered structure—or, at least, it had when Richard was younger and had led his sister and his cousins beneath the storerooms. They might simply have found an ancient ballast room designed to offset the tilt and skew of subsidence into the river, but Richard still believed he'd discovered a true island in Kamat's gut. He still had the rock he'd found that long ago afternoon and used it as a paperweight on his father's desk.

He emerged from the shadows by the gatehouse where the descendants of the Adami, whose fortunes had crumbled about the time Hosni Kamat was looking for a suitable residence, eked along in genteel poverty and obscurity as servants to their successors. The Festival banners still fluttered in the breeze, but the lanterns had long been extinguished and the bar lowered. Feeling more than a little foolish and uncharitable, Richard hauled on the knotted rope and roused Ferdmore Adami from his sleep.

"Didn't know you were out, m'ser," the servant, who was just about Richard's age, said as he struggled with the bar.

"I had a notion to find my childhood route from the loading dock to the gatehouse. The Island's changed, Ferdmore. I don't know it half as well as I once did." Richard strove to make light of the inconvenience he was causing.

"Wouldn't have gone to bed if I hadn't thought you weren't all inside," Ferdmore replied as if the whims of the successful were none of his concern.

The young man winced as a sliver jabbed into his palm; Richard resisted the urge to reach through the grating to steady the bar. It wouldn't gain the Househead anything to assist his servants—especially not the Adami who clung to the remnants of their pride with a desperate stubbornness—but that didn't make it easier to say goodnight when he could see dark liquid dropping down to the walkway.

"Good Festival, Ferdmore."

"And you, m'ser Kamat," Ferdmore mumbled, sucking his skin as he scurried back inside the gatehouse.

The lower hall was deserted with only a single night lamp to cut through the darkness. Richard took a candle from the box, lit it on the lamp flame and continued deeper into the house. Kamat had electrics—the Adami had ssen to that in their days of glory—but the family seldom used them. As Merovingen measured these things, Kamat was new to its wealth and remained inclined toward thriftiness.

Richard had his free hand on the newel post when the itch of curiosity snared him. Unlocking the butlery, he examined both the guest book and the House's stack of outgoing messages. It was Festival and a half-dozen callers had paid a formal visit to the vestibule. Richard recognized them all save one: an R. Baritz had signed his name shortly after dinner. Ser Baritz hadn't left a properly seasonal message in the creamy vellum beyond his signature, but Ferdmore had made a pencil notation that the gentleman had asked for m'sera Andromeda and stayed for only a short time.

R. Baritz—not a Merovingen family name nor even one of the Nev Hettek names his mother had let drop in her conversations over the years. But R. Baritz was undoubtedly the messenger Patrik had seen. Why else, in this Revenantist city, sign with just an initial, unless your given name were Retribution or some other Adventist brand?

Richard flipped through the outgoing messages. There were several smooth envelopes embellished with his mother's fine handwriting, and none of them the least bit suspicious. Surely after twenty-six years and two children, Kamat had no reason to suspect Andromeda, even if she was the youngest daughter of the Garin-Cassirer Conglomerate in Nev Hettek.

The death of Nikolay had struck his mother deeply, Richard mused as he headed up the stairs. Perhaps she had even taken a touch of the Melancholy. Perhaps she wished a reconciliation with the family which had expected her to lock Kamat in Nev Hettek's orbit rather than the other way around. Perhaps she wanted to go home—but even *that* should be no cause for alarm.

Still, the unexplained visit set uneasily with the young Househead. He ignored the landing which would have taken him to his bedroom and an hour or so of rest and continued upward to Nikolay's study where a touch of the Melancholy seemed to settle around him as well.

"Richard? Richard, it's me, Marina. . . ."

Richard jerked upright as his world flew back into focus. An hour's worth of sunlight slanted through the eastern windows. He'd fallen asleep hunched over an account book and felt lousy for his rest. Closing the book and reflexively shoving it under an untidy heap of papers, he welcomed Marina.

His sister, dressed in what was her usual fashion, could have passed for any one of hundreds of almost-pretty, anonymous women of the middle and lower strata of the city. Her shirt and trousers were a dark, muddy color—neither brown, nor blue, nor black and certainly not First-bath—that grated against Richard's eyes and sensibilities. She carried a servant's breakfast tray; Richard had to remind himself it was a sign of their enduring friendship and not another manifestation of her stubborn determination to be "like everyone else."

Andromeda said it was just a phase: a harmless form of rebellion, and cautioned her son, as she had cautioned her husband, against making an issue out of Marina's wardrobe or behavior. Still, his sister's rag-tag appearance blunted whatever relief he felt on seeing her well and smiling after her misadventures.

"Tea?" she asked, setting the tray down.

He nodded and, turning her back to him, she set about preparing the beverage exactly as he preferred it.

"I suppose you want to know what happened last night? That you're worried about me again, and the company I'm keeping. Well, it wasn't like that, really,

Richard. A disaster: yes, but not the way you think and not in a way I could have prevented."

Richard took the metal-wrapped glass and stirred it, needlessly. "You could have stayed home." It was said lightly, as in the old days before Nikolay's death, and Marina chuckled as she settled into the chair opposite his desk.

"That would have been out of character, and you know it. Carrolly had an invitation for two and no one to take her. Well, you've been complaining that I don't associate with the right people, how much *righter* do they have to be than Nikolaev, hmm? I didn't think you'd *really* mind. Chiro Ito, after all— wouldn't he be a great sire for the next Kamat heir?"

Sighing, Richard took a long sip of the tea—and scalded his tongue. "Marina, I don't want to go through this again—"

But they did, recovering well-argued territory. Not that Marina didn't have some valid discontents. So long as the house was the source of power and position in Merovingen, blood relationships were going to be important. So long as women did not have to marry, nor even disclose the names of their lovers, parentage was going to be problematic. A man, a househead, might never know who his children were (unless he took the extreme step of sequestering his wife, as Adromeda had sequestered herself for Nikolay) but, on the other hand, he could be certain that his *sister's* children shared at least a few of his genes.

Nikolay Kamat had two children: Richard, whom he trained as his successor, and Marina, who, in the usual course of things here in Merovingen, would provide Kamat with an heir. Most of the elite, nubile daughters found this state of affairs entirely to their satisfaction, but Marina found it insufferable.

"I am not a cow," she snapped as the discussion neared its oft-rehearsed conclusion. "If I don't find a man I love as much as Momma loved Poppa, I may just die a virgin!"

That was the trouble with a life-long contract. Unrealistic expectations.

The last of the tea was tepid and tasteless. Richard put the glass back on the tray then leaned back in his chair. "No one is rushing you, Ree," he explained with taut patience. "I'm not going to ask you to have children for love of me or Kamat or anything else. And if having an heir were all that important to me, believe me—I would buy a year out of the life of some poor woman who needed the money. So don't you ever use the House as an excuse to endanger yourself. You're more important to me than a dozen heirs. Now, why don't we go back to the beginning and you explain to me how you came to be charging up the stairs with your sweater shredded and your hair down. If you had a problem at Nikolaev's, I want to know."

Marina tucked her legs beneath her in the chair. "It wasn't at Nikolaev's," she said with a strangely conspiratorial grin. "Nikolaev's was utterly boring: everybody, and I mean *everybody*, was there and nothing was happening. Carrolly and I found Chiro and Ben Ventani and they were as bored as we were. Ben said he knew a little tavern, a smuggler's dive, that operated below Ventani . . ."

She has no idea of the risks involved, Richard thought as Marina spun out her tale with schoolgirl enthusiasm. Going canalside at Ventani was just another adventure—like going below Kamat had been when he led the way to the bedrock. He had been forced to see Merovingen's rough side—he did know how to use that boat-pole better than most of his friends knew how to use their fancy swords—but Marina had been sheltered. And infected with a dangerous dose of his mother's notions of romance.

"They wore masks but they talked like they were blacklegs and I think they'd been there before. They took one look at Ben and rousted him. He drew his sword and—"

Richard rocked forward in his chair. "Is Ben Ventani all right?" Blacklegs rousting junior members of elite houses put a different, even more dangerous, light on Marina's tale.

"Yes—now let me finish. *Everybody* started fight-

ing, Carrolly and me included. Lord, Richard—I
don't even remember anyone grabbing at me, but
they kept a hold of Ben and dragged him out of
there with the rest of us yelling and screaming at the
top of our lungs."

Marina saw Richard's jaw twitch with unspoken
questions; she stuck her tongue out at him and kept
him silent.

"Well, after that everything changed. The old man
behind the bar got friendly. He got us brandy and
said he'd get us all back home safely if—if we'd stick
around and talk to a friend of his: the man they'd
really been after when they rousted Ben. Carrolly
and I thought we should go straight to the authorities right then but Chiro said we'd wait 'cause he'd
realized that the barkeep wasn't half as friendly as he
was pretending to be.

"It was about high second watch when we heard
somebody moving around upstairs and we were taken
to a back room. Richard, you'd have to meet him. He
mumbled his name—Tom Mon-something-or-other—
but he oozed elegance . . . and power. You'd like
him."

She paused and Richard realized, with a horror
his sister did not perceive, that whoever or whatever
this Tom truly was, Marina had already fallen in love
with him.

"He said he'd get Ben out, and he did; there was a
message from him when I woke up. He—Tom, that
is—must have been in some real trouble but I know
he hasn't done anything wrong. I just know it, Richard. There must be something we can do to help
him."

Richard steepled his fingers and hid behind them.
"Yes: stay away from him. Whatever kind of trouble
he's got there's nothing we can do for him and
plenty he could do to us."

"Oh, Richard, you're no fun anymore. You're turning into a dull lump of a merchant." She shook her
fist at him in mock-anger; despite himself, Richard
felt a smile creep across his face.

"I'll make inquiries," he conceded. "Discreet inquiries—and until I learn something one way or the other, you keep out of it, you understand?"

"You're a love, big brother."

She came around the desk to give him a hug and he knew he'd keep his word. If they'd been at a smuggler's dive, the canalers would know the place and if there was an elegant, powerful stranger holding court in one of the upper rooms, they'd know that, too. It was only a matter of asking the right questions.

Richard didn't start to put the pieces together at that exact moment, but his suspicions exploded with nauseating clarity the moment his mother, Andromeda, walked through the door bearing another tea-tray upon which perched a folded calling card. For a moment his heart seemed to have forgotten how to beat and then, as his pulse started to race, he had lost the capacity for coherent speech.

Andromeda was blonde and pale with a prominent bone structure normally described as aristocratic or elegant but which lately, since the death of Nikolay, had given her an almost skeletal appearance. Her once crisp, efficient movements had refined and quickened to the verge of hysteria. There was no doubt that she was trying to recover her equilibrium after her husband's death—she had resumed all her social, domestic and business obligations—but the effort had pushed her to the brink of madness.

She presented Richard with an unrequested glass of tea. Her son stared at the russet liquid before starting to speak.

"Mother, do you remember a family in Nev Hettek: Mon-something-or-other?" He did not look up into those smiling and too-bright eyes.

Andromeda set the tea-pot back on the tray with a loud clatter. "Mondragon," she said with an exhaustive sigh. "Oh, thank god, Richard—you already know. I didn't know how I could ever explain it to you."

Richard took the calling card from her but did not read it. The details might still elude him, but his worst suspicions had just been confirmed.

"Tell me anyway, Mother. Start at the beginning."

*   *   *

The sun had circled to the other side of the house, coming through the open shutters, falling on Richard's face and awakening him from a restless nap. Most of what his mother had told him wasn't new but there had never before been a pattern to his knowledge of Nev Hettek; he had never needed one.

Merovingen was Revenantist; Kamat was Revenantist; he himself accepted a moderate Revenantist creed without hesitation. There were Adventists in the city—lord, his mother had never really *stopped* being Adventist—and there were places on this world where Revenantists like himself were in the minority. He had always believed it didn't make much difference one way or the other in anyone's walkaday life.

But it did. Revenantism caused the machinery in Kamat's dyeworks to be made from wood instead of metal; it caused Kamat to strive for the best—First-bath—rather than the most; it caused them to be craftsmen instead of neophyte industrialists and capitalists like the controlling families of Nev Hettek. Revenantist fatalism accepted all manner of quirks and oddities and shunned all things judged "progressive" —which could drive an Adventist to fanaticism.

Adventism bred individual fanatics who sliced through society on their appointed rounds of purification. Tom Mondragon, whom all Merovingen believed a Boregy cousin lately returned from the Falken Isles—so Andromeda said—had been such a fanatic in the rise of the Fon government of Nev Hettek and, more importantly, the militant Sword of God in that city. Adventism also bred a larger-scale fanaticism which festered in the ruling houses of Nev Hettek and led them to regard Merovingen with thoughts that were as much avaricious as purifying.

The city resisted Nev Hettek about the same way it resisted the Det river: with cunning, adaptability and outright stubbornness, but somehow the balance had shifted this past season. An individual fanatic, one Thomas Mondragon, trained and honed by the Sword of God, had slipped his leash and come running down to Merovingen. Probably the young man would be swallowed and lost in the spired city but that was not a chance Nev Hettek intended to take now he had sheltered in Boregy patronage. The power clusters of Fon's government were emitting a desperate sort of vengeance.

Most obviously, once suspicions were properly roused, there was Sword of God muscle moving through the canals—the strangers who had cowed Celotta into a winter-storm tie-up. But the more legitimate powers of Nev Hettek were active as well. Baritz was an Adventist minion, with impeccable credentials from the Fon governor and the upriver mercantile interests.

Baritz had appeared at the Kamat gate with a sheaf of messages. Officially Baritz offered himself as a factotum in the Kamat businesses, unofficially he reminded Kamat that they were dependent on Nev Hettek for the iron, tin and chromium salts that made colorfast dyes possible. Even more unofficially, he reminded Andromeda that her Nev Hettek family, the Garin, was modest, vulnerable and very, very eager that *this time* she behaved properly.

The risks, the note from her father had said, were enormous. Failure to give Baritz the latitude he requested would certainly result in the downfall of the Garin's small metallurgy operation. Blackmail, pure and simple—but also effective, even if Kamat had not been truly dependent on those barrels of salt mordants. . . .

Richard shook the downward spiral of thoughts from his mind and concentrated on the mirror before him. Dark-haired, round-faced and with a softness of feature that led many to suspect he was still a school-boy, Richard, like his sister, was Kamat from skin to bone. He had inherited none of his mother's natural elegance and therefore relied upon the precision of his wardrobe to make the Househead impression his face and gestures could not.

Ironically, he shunned the highly fashionable clothes Andromeda designed for the House atelier, preferring, instead, simple styles tailored to perfection. His velvet jacket—First-bath, of course—lay smooth around his shoulders and hugged his waist with just the right degree of snugness; his trousers hung without bulges or wrinkles and the foulard silk cravat which he stabilized with a pigeon's blood ruby finished his apparel in a way which diminished the pudginess of his features.

"Now or never," he whispered to his silver-backed counterpart as he whisked a brush one last time through his hair.

Richard retained a youthful tendency to rush from one place to the next—a habit, his father had always claimed, utterly incompatible with a man in control of his own actions, much less one controlling the actions of others. When he heard the gatehouse bell clattering it took all of his restraint to keep from bounding down the stairs to be in the main hall when Baritz arrived. As it was, Ferdmore was closing the front room doors when the Househead rounded the last landing.

"Has our guest arrived?" Richard asked, schooling himself to speak as calmly as he was descending.

Ferdmore gave a disparaging grimmace at the closed doors. "He's here. I've poured him some sherry—to loosen him a bit."

There were no secrets in the great residences of Merovingen. The servants knew everything and the best the families could hope for was loyalty and discretion.

"Mother? Patrik? My sister?"

"M'sera Marina's alone with him. The others are still dressing. He's *early*, you know."

And no class of citizens was more punctilious in its adherence to strict manners than those same servants. They judged the ruling families without charity or mercy. It was poor form that Marina was left alone with an unexamined guest, but it was far worse that the guest had crossed the threshold before the six o'clock bells mentioned in his invitation had pealed.

"You'll go below and tell them dinner is still planned for eight with dessert back in the drawing room at nine."

"Yes, m'ser."

When the hall was cleared, Richard allowed himself one last moment of apprehension, then pulled the double-doors open and faced the Nev Hettek unknown.

"Richard, this is Rod Baritz," Marina announced before the Househead had fully taken in the scene before him.

"Pleased to meet you," Richard responded, automatically stepping forward to pump his guest's hand firmly.

The Nev Hetteker was no more than five years his senior with wispy, nondescript hair slicked down around an equally nondescript, almost porcine, face. In fact Richard noticed little about Rod Baritz except his eyes—and almost dismissed those because they were a watery, red-rimmed gray, as if the man were allergic to something in Merovingen's air. But Rod was smart, a moment or two locked with those gray eyes convinced Richard that Nev Hettek hadn't sent its amateurs to Kamat.

Marina distracted him with a light touch to his elbow. "Sherry?" she inquired.

Angling his body away from the visitor, Richard whispered as he took the glass. "Be careful, Ree."

His sister flashed one of her rare, dazzling smiles. She, too, had paid careful attention to her appearance but where Richard had sought an aura of solid confidence, Marina had captured a worldly sophistication. The effect was both practiced and predatory; Richard regretted that his Househead duties had created an ever-widening gulf between them.

"I'm always careful, Richard."

Between sips of sherry, Richard tried, as he'd seen his father do many times, to draw information out of his guest. The Nev Hetteker, however, would reveal little about himself and nothing at all about his expectations in Merovingen or Kamat.

"Your mother will be joining us, won't she? I really would prefer to talk with m'sera Garin as well." Baritz allowed the merest hint of contempt to seep into his voice.

It was no secret—and certainly not unknown to

Rod Baritz—that Andromeda had renounced her
family name when her family disinherited her.

Richard felt the back of his neck grow warm with
anger. "My mother and uncle will be joining us shortly.
You are a bit *early*, you know," he replied, falling
back on servants' judgments.

His counter-insult was lost on Baritz who merely
nodded politely as he settled back in his chair, determined to ignore everything else until Kamat's elder
generation made its appearance. Richard retreated
to the tall windows to pursue the relaxation tech-
niques his father had taught him, but Marina continued the campaign to lure Baritz into revealing
conversation.

Her technique was artless—a barrage of unrelated
questions—all of which Baritz was able to answer
with non-committal grunts and shrugs as he stared
at the fireplace. As a brother, Richard wanted to
stop his sister's embarrassing display but as Househead
he let it continue. Kamat's glass was smooth and
reflected a good image of what was happening behind him. The Nev Hetteker's shoulders had tensed
and he had finished his sherry in two long swallows.

With proper politeness, Richard got the decanter
and refilled his guest's glass. Baritz ignored him as
he ignored Marina, and Richard began to believe
that Kamat would triumph over this latest Nev Hettek
intrigue.

"I'm sorry to have kept you waiting," Andromeda
announced as she swept into the room with a silent
Patrik in her wake.

Baritz was out of his chair and bowing awkwardly
from the waist. Andromeda dismissed the gesture
with a brittle laugh.

"Rise, Nev Hettek. Didn't anyone ever tell you not
to imitate customs which make you uncomfortable?"

In one sentence she had thrown Baritz farther
off-stride than her children had managed between
them. Their guest fumbled through his jacket, producing an envelope which he laid in Andromeda's
hand as if it were coated with poison.

"Another letter from your father, m'sera."

She broke the seal, glanced at the script then passed the paper to Richard. "What do you *really* want, m'ser?" she demanded.

Richard scanned the letter. If Nemesis Garin's first missive had been a request to his wayward, rejected daughter, this was clearly a demand. *Cooperate,* the old man had written several times. *The sword is long and you have nothing with which to bargain.*

"You are known to have connections throughout the lower city; you employ their aged and infirm to do your piece-work. Nev Hettek has a sizable under-class as well. I'm here to appraise your success in dealing with these people."

Marina, who now stood where Baritz could not see her face, wrinkled her nose in distaste but the rest of her family remained tensely polite.

"We are always glad to help our trading partners," Richard confirmed, extending his hand in friend-ship. "I'll take you around myself."

"That won't—"

"Richard!" Marina protested. "Don't give in to him! You know what he wants to do—"

But Andromeda had gotten to her outspoken daughter by then and dug her carefully manicured fingernails into the flesh inside the young woman's wrist. Marina's eyes widened more with outrage than with pain, but she kept quiet.

"We won't be giving away secrets," Richard assured her, trying to make light of the whole ex-change. "First-bath never leaves the House, anyway. You don't need to see the ateliers, do you, Rod?"

A sly, knowing grin bent the Nev Hetteker's face. "No," he averred, shaking his head slightly for emphasis.

The first round, then, might be considered a draw—as might all the others that followed through another glass of sherry and an excellent, if all but unnoticed, dinner. Tutored by Andromeda and led by Richard, Kamat defined its perimeters.

Nev Hettek ties were not without use, Richard resolved as the main course dishes were cleared from the table. Get Marina clear of this Mondragon. And the next time Kamat needed a favor upriver—well, whatever else was said about Nev Hettek, no one ever said their collective memory was bad.

Indeed, the affair seemed headed for a more favorable resolution than Richard would have believed possible only a few hours before. The Householder and those around him began to relax. Except for Marina.

His sister couldn't accept the wisdom of remaining within the family perimeter. It was enough to make Richard briefly curse his father's memory; the patriarch had spared nothing in his own education but he had smiled indulgently when Marina drifted away from the rigors of learning and management toward romance. Nikolay himself had begun to regret his lack of wisdom before his death; Richard found he had inherited Marina's recklessness along with every other Kamat responsibility.

"Why don't you get out of the house for a while," he suggested quietly to her as the small group began its migration toward the drawing room and dessert. "There's no point to staying here and aggravating yourself." He tried to ignore the hard, angry and disappointed set of her face.

"Who'll you sell up the river when I'm gone? Lord, Richard—don't you care? Is Kamat and First-bath so damned important?"

Her words pricked deep; his anger flared behind his defenses. "Now that you mention it: Yes, they are. Listen, Ree, I don't like this *m'ser Baritz* anymore than you do. He wouldn't know wool from linen and if he's official, he's sure not from the Nev Hettek board of trade. But let me tell you, your dear Mondragon was Nev Hettek and Sword of God to the bone before he quit them: his family was massacred and they say his hands aren't clean of it—"

Her mouth fell open. "It's lies, all lies. I looked at Mondragon and I know what I saw."

Richard bit back the retort that stuck to the tip of his tongue but his rage was not so easily resisted. "Find your friends, Marina. Get Carrolly or whomever and pay a call at Nikolaev—but stay out of

Merovingen Below and, until you see things a bit more clearly, stay the hell out of family business."

"With pleasure, big brother," she hissed back at him. There was a smile on her face that could have come direct from Baritz. It made Richard nervous but before he could reassure himself Ferdmore interrupted him.

"It's the armagnac, m'ser. The bottle we drew off this afternoon's gone cloudy and the rest're behind the grate and the lock's gone rusty—"

In other elite residences, Richard knew, the servants not only knew their place but kept the house running smoothly without constant intervention. At Kamat, however, where many of the servants were the grandchildren of the former masters, the natural order of things was apt to get turned around.

"You just be careful," Richard warned his sister before giving his complete attention to untangling the problems with the brandy. Marina smiled again and disappeared out the door.

Nothing could pursuade Ferdmore to find a mallet and break the winecellar lock himself. It was not his place, the youthful servant insisted, to go breaking the master's property. Quick mental arithmetic convinced Richard that he'd waste less time descending to the winecellar himself than in arguing with a recalcitrant butler. He took a certain satisfaction, though, in borrowing a meat-mallet from the Adami-descended cook and all but destroying it on the rusted lock.

"Now, decant it and take it to the drawing room," he ordered Ferdmore, "while I go upstairs and clean my jacket."

Richard bounded up the private stairs and brushed his jacket with all the vigor his frustration could muster; First-bath, the Angel be praised, was as tough as it was expensive. The cloth looked none the worse for its beating as he grabbed the newel-post and took the main stairs like an adolescent.

"Richard, where have you been? We've looked for you everywhere," Andromeda called from the entranceway still some distance beneath him.

Leaning over the bannister, he saw concern in his mother's face. "Why aren't you in the drawing room with our guest?" he demanded in return and watched as the concern became full-blown anxiety.

"There is no guest," his uncle interjected as he emerged from the shadows, surprising Richard more than his mother did. "Your sister's made off with him."

Kamat was no end of surprises today. As if blackmail-minded visitors from Nev Hettek weren't enough, Marina was sending up a storm of rebellion and his meek uncle was becoming not merely assertive but downright challenging.

"Is this true, mother?"

"It seems to be. That is, they're both gone and Ferdmore says they left together."

Bless his pointed little head, Richard thought as, gripping the bannister for balance, he arched his back and escaped from his elders' questioning stares. The Adami tongues were already clacking, no doubt. With his eyes closed he resolved that if he got through the ongoing crisis, he'd retire the Adami to another island and get Kamat some ordinary servants.

"Well, Richard," his uncle's somewhat nasal voice interrupted, "what are you going to do about it? It's bad enough we're giving dinners and having guests while we're still in mourning for my brother."

"You didn't have any objections this morning," the Househead reminded him as he descended the last flight of stairs.

"That was this morning."

Richard resisted an impulse to gape at Patrik's flushed and sweating face. His uncle simply wasn't used to getting angry. He glanced at Andromeda and saw that his mother's eyes were narrowed and her thoughts also momentarily distracted from the immediate problems. It was easy to overlook Nikolay's younger brother. Nikolay, himself, had done it most of his life; his wife and son were certainly guilty of the same blindness. Patrik had sired, and brought back to Kamat, three acknowledged, unlegitimatized children. The eldest was not yet twenty and had always seemed as stolid and unimaginative as his father—but ambition had taken root in less likely soils.

"Marina took it hard that we were going to cooperate with Baritz," Richard said to his mother, relegating Patrik's aberrance to the same category as Ferdmore's subtle insolence.

"But she's gone off *with* him. What can she possibly hope to accomplish?"

Richard felt his palms go cold and his legs go strange as if there were some unfathomable discontinuity between the floor and his gut. He knew himself to be nearly sober, steady on his feet and possessed of his reason—it was the rest of the world, or more specifically the pillars of his family, that seemed to have slipped a few gears.

He, at any rate, had no difficulty imagining why Marina would have taken off with Baritz, his only insurmountable problem was guessing where she had gone and what dangerous scheme she had concocted.

"I'm going after her," he announced.

The odd feeling in his legs receded, transferred, perhaps, to the two others beside who both began to look as if they'd seen a ghost—Nikolay's ghost, or Hosni's. Richard hesitated a moment, in case either found their voice, then retreated, two steps at a time, up the stairs.

It could hve been ghosts. He could almost imagine his grandfather smiling down on him—though he knew the old man only by family legends and a fierce portrait in the front room. Hosni, the stories said, had established Kamat's primacy with his fists as well as his brain. He'd approve of the patched canaler's sweater and cap and the soft-soled shoes Richard hauled out of his clothes chest. He'd have wrinkled his nose when his canal-costumed grandson lowered the sleek punt—but Richard wasn't Hosni-reborn.

The young man had hoped—expected, really—to find Celotta at her cautious tie-up but the canal-woman was nowhere to be seen. Richard hauled up the heavy grating himself, eased the punt under its teeth, then carefully lowered it again. With the punt riding steady beneath him, he braced the pole against the damp, black pilings and got a feel for the water beneath him.

Tide had turned, running toward high and just one night after flood—not the best time for an uptowner to be on the water without a motor, but he felt equal to the challenge. Indeed, all the tensions and frustrations of the entire day unwound from his shoulders as the pole locked and the punt skimmed against the current toward the Grand. He'd circle Ventani when he reached that bend but his best hope, he figured, lay harbor-side in Nikolaev among whose reckless offspring Marina was apt to find accomplices.

Revelers shouted and sang on the bridges above him. Some, mistaking the punt for a poleboat, shouted down to hire him. He affected not to hear and heard, instead, the streams of abuse his kind dealt out to the lower city. The punt bounced hard over the wavelets of the rising tide as Richard's inner turmoil took physical form.

Ventani, like every other isle, glittered and echoed from its banner-festooned residence to the lower levels where the tavern Marina had mentioned belched its own raucous entertainments onto the walkways. It didn't sound like a place to welcome strangers and, acting on an instinct that said Marina at her most impulsive would still balk at entering a lively working-class tavern, Richard continued down the Grand.

There was a tricky chop on the water here reminding him that he was out of practice these days. He hugged the wharfline along Ramseyhead, then drenched himself in sweat and spray weaving through the bridge pilings to Rimmon Isle. The salt stung his enthusiasm; he'd be hard pressed to bring his sister and the Nev Hetteker back to Kamat if he did find them.

Relations between Nikolaev and Kamat were longstanding but strictly commercial. The largest of the Kamat dyeworks extended from the Nikolaev buildings into the harbor where turbines were lowered into the water to take advantage of the greater strength of the tide here. Nikolaev demanded three gold sols a month for Kamat's privileges on its property. Richard had seen to the delivery himself when he was younger but, like his father before him, had never felt the urge to socialize with his landlord.

Marina had felt differently.

The Nikolaev slips were filled with at least a half-dozen fancyboats. Richard eased up to the outmost of the craft and called for a tie-rope. No one hailed back so he nosed the punt back to the harbor, headed around the shallow side of Rimmon for the dyeworks. The servants were probably in some lower hall having their own Festival celebration and, anyway, it would likely be easier to enter Nikolaev through the dyeworks gate than its main boatslip.

Richard poled through another tangle of pilings and made his tie-up at the dyeworks dock which, owing to the Festival, were deserted despite the incoming tide. He hauled hard on the bell rope and waited while the strains of a string quartet filtered down from the upper levels of nearby Bogar. The waiting did nothing for his temper; he passed the lengthening moments contemplating ever more extensive changes in the Kamat way of doing things. His family had always paid an honest wage and stood by its workers; it expected no less from them in return.

Finally he heard the dogs barking and the grilled guard-panel creaked open.

"Open the door. I'm Richard Kamat—owner of these works." He waved his left hand, the one on which he wore the Kamat signet, past the grille. In the darkness it did no good: a threatening gesture rather than a source of identification.

"Y'er a pie-eyed canaler," the watchman retorted.

What followed was no worse than Richard had expected. Merovingen was not a trusting city, especially after dark, and the least the watchman might lose if he let the wrong man past the door was his job. Still, Richard had another powerful persuader slung on a baldric beneath his sweater: the ornate steel key to the lock between them. When the young man proved he could, indeed, turn the metal bolt, the watchman did his part and raised the inside bar.

"Ye do have the look of the Kamat to you, after all," the workman said, holding the lantern while Richard shook water from his cap and hair.

"I am exactly who I said I am."

That continued to stretch the man's credulity but he and his lantern accompanied Richard upward to the bridge gate without further comment.

"I'll be back in a while with two people from Nikolaev. I'll ring the bell twice and I expect to be let in without interrogation—"

"Yes, m'ser."

Though he might have preferred more confidence and acceptance in the watchman's tone, Richard knew better than to expect miracles and walked quickly to the Nikolaev gate. Shadows moved behind the backlit guard-panels, convincing him that he had been observed leaving the dyeworks. He expected some difficulty getting inside the Nikolaev establishment but no more than he'd had getting into his own and rapped on the wood like a man with absolutely nothing to hide.

"I'll see the Householder, if you please. Tell him Richard Kamat's come to fetch his sister home," he informed the darkness now obscuring the guard-panel.

The demand was repeated and discussed within, then the door swung open—a sure confirmation, Richard judged, that Marina had, indeed, come here.

"M'ser Nikolaev's not home; the whole family's not home," the servant said—which meant only that no one was dressed for visitors. Kamat's guests had been getting much the same story this past week as well.

"My sister's here, though, isn't she? With a gentleman friend." Richard waved an open hand at the Nikolaev retainer, a hand that showed two things: a silver lune and the massive signet ring—a Householder's ring.

A noncommittal shrug. "M'seras—" the servant explained reluctantly, "—the young ladies—they do as they please now, don't they?"

"I'll look for her."

The servant took the coin, flipped it and was pleased by its weight. "Be quiet about it. Y'er not dressed for Festival visitin'."

Richard grunted and headed up the stairs. He knew the business rooms of the house from the days when Nikolay had sent him out with the rent money. Those were all here on the bridge level and were unlikely hiding places for Marina and the Nev Hetteker. In the usual order of things within the residence spires of Merovingen's various islands, the higher you went the more private the rooms got. He didn't begin to wander the corridors until the entry-way was three flights down.

Househead or not, he couldn't kick open the doors of every private room but knocked politely instead and wished to god he could remember the Nikolaev sisters' names. Most rooms were quiet, some were locked and no one came forth as he repeatedly identified himself and called his sister's name.

He was on the fourth level now. If Nikolaev were Kamat he'd be hammering on his mother's bedroom door and he was beginning to feel more than a bit conspicuous.

"I'm looking for Marina Kamat," he called from the head of the hallway, having just removed his ring and decided that he'd claim to be a lesser member of the family if his presence here was questioned.

"South spire," a woman's voice replied from behind one of the closed doors, he couldn't tell which.

He had descended halfway to the entry hall when the stair shaft echoed with a loud crash followed immediately by a woman's scream that ended sharply in mid-warble. He paused and heard the faint sound of running and what might be the moving of heavy furniture. An accident in the kitchen, perhaps—none of his business either way except that the lower hall was empty when he reached it and no one noted his movement through the business suites to another stairway.

Intermittent shouts and other sounds of disorder penetrated the hallways of this spire as well but not so loudly as the sounds of intimate partying and lovemaking behind the nearest doors. She'd be here, if she were anywhere, and, thinking now that commotion might add up to fire—the ultimate physical catastrophe in wooden Merovingen, Richard no longer bothered to knock or call his sister's name before opening the doors.

He surprised one of the sisters in bed with her current lover and a group of her friends in groping, drug-reeking orgy—but no Marina. He checked the quiet rooms next and found four of them empty and one locked with no one answering on the inside. There was another scream from deep in the house and he gave the door a flying shove from across the hall. The latch popped and stumbled into the room.

His nose flared with the smell of gas—potent enough that he didn't wait to search for a lamp but searched the place in the faint light from the corridor. The nauseating smell was stronger by the day-bed; strongest on the damp pillow where Marina slept—or had been left unconscious—alone.

Richard staggered backwards overwhelmed by the enormity of what he had discovered. He stayed frozen in his outrage until another scream echoed through the corridor. Something horrible was happening in Nikolaev; something that included Marina and Baritz—wherever the Nev Hetteker might have run off to—and yet went beyond them as well. Without understanding, or questioning, his instincts, the Kamat Househead silently shut the door and raised the window.

He dragged his sister from the bed—observing with unindulged relief that she was still breathing—and shoved her face into the harbor breeze. There was a walkway some ten feet below the window—part of the permanent scaffolding that adorned almost every residence. Richard tore the draperies loose and bundled them around Marina's shoulders. Limp and drugged as she was, she'd survive the drop to the walkway with nothing more than a few bruises.

Richard wasn't as lucky. He was no acrobat to be hanging from a windowsill and too keyed up to collapse as he touched the planks. The ache in his shoulders was dull and ignorable but the pain in his ankle brought him belatedly to his knees.

A quarter-way around the spire a window was thrown open and a man's head and shoulders thrust out into the night. Richard grabbed his sister and held her tight against the wall, her face against his sweater to muffle the cough-spasms that had overwhelmed her.

"It's all right," he whispered, stroking her malodorous hair. "It's going to be all right."

"Richard? Richard? O my god, is it really you, Richard?"

He held her closer—this wasn't the time for conversation or emotional reunions—and, in return, she hugged him with enough strength to say she wasn't permanently harmed by her ordeal.

"He was Sword, Richard. Baritz was—"

"I know," he whispered, though in truth he hadn't known, only suspected. "Not now, Ree; not until we get home."

The man had withdrawn, leaving the window open.

There was Sword in Merovingen; Sword, for some god-unknown reason, inside the spires of the Nikolaev residence. And Richard knew he wasn't as smart as the Sword of God—not when the games were played by their rules. He wondered if Nikolaev had caught their wrath as innocently as Marina had, then wondered if there were assassins swarming over Kamat as well.

"Come on, Ree," he urged her as he pushed himself, wincing, upright. "We've got to try to get home."

The young woman nodded and climbed gamely to her feet. The breeze had become a salty wind that slapped noisy waves against the house pilings even as it cleared the gas from Marina's head. Brother and sister passed steadiness and strength through their clasped hands as they crept along the scaffolding toward the bridge gate and the safety of the dyeworks beyond it.

Richard peered out over the last of the scaffolding at the deserted bridge unwilling to believe their good fortune. But, no—the Sword hadn't come to Nikolaev across its bridge to the harbor-works; they'd come in those poleboats moored in the family slip out north. He sat back with a shudder and the realization of what he had almost tied-up with.

"What's out there?" Marina asked beside him.

"Nothing. Let's go."

He lowered her to the bridge then jumped, with an unsuppressible groan, himself. Their luck held: the bridge remained deserted and, even more miraculously, the dyeworks watchman saw them coming and had the door open before they reached it. Richard was in the midst of his thanks when the south spire of Nikolaev erupted in flames.

Alarm bells began clanging from every nearby porch and alcove. The watchman had his job to do and scuttled off to ring his own bells. By rights, Richard should have stayed to oversee the protection of the dyeworks but protection of his family was even more important. With a shouted promise that he'd carry the alarm along the Grand Canal, he grabbed Marina's hand and headed for the dock.

The harbor chop had blown into phosphorescent whitecaps. Had Richard been at Kamat, it would have been a welcome sight—rare was the month that had two First-bath runs—now, with Marina huddled under the torn drapery in the middle of the punt, it only meant treachery on the water and agony on his weakened ankle.

Marina had never been much of a sailor; she'd walk from one end of Merovingen to the other rather than ride a poleboat against the wind or tide. Her ordeal hadn't improved her seaworthiness any and she lunged for the side of the punt just as Richard hit the Ramseyhead race. It was all he could do to keep the punt level in the water; his desperate thrusts and turns caught the attention of the nearest craft coming to Nikolaev's aid.

"Need a hand?"

"A rope?"

"Take the lady for you?"

Richard faced the darkness where the last voice

had been. Huddled and bedraggled, Marina didn't look much like a lady anymore; he was surprised anyone had guessed her sex much less her status. He had a notion to accept the offer and in the next heartbeat reconsidered. At least some of the boats milling around had been tied-up near Nikolaev; some of the boatmen tonight might be Sword.

"Thanks, no—" he shouted instead, skudding the punt away with a hard thrust. "A fare's a fare."

He ached from foot to shoulder by the time they'd crossed the heavy water to the Grand where he could catch the flow of the tide without worrying overmuch about the wind. Traffic was against them; he hugged the starboard pilings, resting more often than he liked but unable to thread the punt through the crowd.

Fire! Fire at Nikolaev! echoed from the bridges and walkways above him. He'd pushed across the Snake, though, before he heard the first shouts of *Assassins* much less the whispered: *'Hare Sword!* here on the water itself. They were under the Hanging Bridge itself when a shout passed down the canal like electricity.

"Signeury's hit!"

Richard shoved the pole in the muck and brought the punt to a standstill. His mind ached trying to comprehend it all and he didn't notice Marina until she fairly shouted his name.

"We've got to tell him!" she pleaded, turning to look across the Grand.

They were just about opposite Ventani; even in his confusion, Richard had little doubt who she was talking about. But there were twenty boats, at least, between him and the tavern and his Househead fears were getting stronger by the moment.

"Please, Richard?"

He shook his head. "Our place is at Kamat—to make sure whatever's happening isn't happening at home. Your Mondragon's on his own tonight; we can't help him if we don't take care of ourselves. Tomorrow's different."

Very different—even if Mondragon himself didn't

make it through the night. It was personal now, transcending business. The Sword had cut through Kamat; had casually meant to kill Marina for god knew what reasons—except a tie to Thomas Mondragon. He and the rest of the family would never have known—never begun to suspect—that Marina's murder was anything but the tragic aftermath of a moment's recklessness. Richard hoped Rod Baritz was brazen enough to come by the residence offering his sympathy. The Sword-man would never leave.

The Sword of God was due a lesson: First-bath meant something more than midnight indigo.

FESTIVAL MOON
(REPRISED)

C.J. Cherryh

A good whiskey swirled into the glass, and Jones
took it up. Mondragon poured one of his own, there
in Boregys' kitchens, in the stony dank underside of
a high Revenantist House the size of the Isle it sat
on. There was whiskey and there was a roast, and
Jones' stomach was not so churned she could not
take to that. She had a cold slice in front of her and
a bit of upDet cheese, and she put both into her
mouth in big, hasty gulps, chased down with whiskey.

Mondragon had just the whiskey. The jeweled collar and cuffs were open. His face was all hard planes
and clenched muscle in the hollows, and his knuckles
were white where he gripped the glass, his throat
working once, twice, three times when he took the
first drink, like it was water.

He stared at the wall. She saw that in the middle
of her own third mouthful, that it was not Mondragon
being mad, it was pain she was looking at.

That killed her own appetite, desperate as it was.
She forced a too-large bite down a throat gone too
small, with whiskey that stung tears to her eyes. She
sat staring at him, because he had said Boregy was
where they were supposed to be, where they were
called on to be; but he lied sometimes for his own
reasons, he lied sometimes when the reasons were
too tangled, or when he did not want to talk, like

now, when there was hell in his face and he had
brought them here to the last place she would have
come.

"Kalugin going to come here?" she asked finally.

"Kalugin won't have left the Signeury."

"You mean it wasn't him on that damn boat?"

"Decoy. He's there. In the Signeury. His agents
are out to Nikolaev."

"And here?"

He slid a glance her way, a stranger's look, all hard
and full of shadows. "*I'm* here. *We're* here."

"F' *what?*"

He did not answer her right away. He stared at
her with the unwavering glow of electrics on him,
and a muscle jumping slowly in his jaw. Then: "Stay
with me now. If something happens to me, go to
Anastasi—"

"Nothing's going t' happen to you!"

"Go to Anastasi."

"T' *that* damn—"

"You'll have something to offer him."

"I ain't. I won't. I'll—"

"He's your only protection. Don't leave it."

"What've ye told 'im?" She hated the coldness in
his voice, hated the numbness in it. She snaked out
her hand and caught his wrist, jolting whiskey onto
the table. "What's he want?"

He made that move of his eyes which reminded
her of listeners—even here, always here, same as
gossip down on the water. The food sat like a lump
at her stomach.

She let go. His fingers curved round hers. His
were cold, for all it was a warm night.

NIGHT ACTION

Chris Morris

Enough hell had broken loose at the Signeury to bring the sharrh's wrath down upon them from heaven, and most of it was Michael Chamoun's fault.

For a while, during the aftermath of the Festival Eve Ball, before the militia would let them leave—before Vega came to get his daughter and prospective son-in-law, enfolded them in the cloak of his power, and swept them away—Chamoun was sure his cover was going to crumble and he'd end up like Rack al-Banna, stretched out neat and dead on the ballroom's marble floor.

But dead, there'd be no marriage, no alliance, no life of lies with the girl shivering under his arm. Cassie Boregy's teeth chattered so hard on the boatride home that he could hear the sound over the launch's motor.

She had the flashlight he'd given her clutched against her breast like some phallic promise and he couldn't get her to put it back in her purse. Her nose was red and her lips swollen and all Chamoun could think about, now that he was safe and on the boat back to Boregy House, was Romanov calling a hit on Nikolaev House—on Kika and Rita.

Chance Magruder's voice kept rumbling in his head: *It's probably Romanov's doing. Trust me, I'll take care of it. That's a promise.*

For one appalling moment, Chamoun wished that Romanov had been successful in killing Rita, as well as Kika. Would have made the rest of Mike Chamoun's life lots simpler. Made the upcoming decisions easier, too.

Romanov still had one al-Banna brother, and Ruin al-Banna was the deadlier of the two. Chamoun found himself half into a plan to get to Romanov despite his bodyguard—get to him before Chance did. And stopped.

Magruder would have his hide; you didn't want Magruder for an enemy. He found his hands were sweating in spite of the night wind whipping his face, sweating well before the launch approached the water gate to Boregy House and the enemy's fortress closed around him with the screech of winching chains and the dull roar of the launch's motor bouncing back off the stone and the claustrophobia-inducing thud of the water gate hitting bottom behind him.

Closed up tight in Boregy House like a lamb in the slaughterhouse, Vega looked at him again with those pale eyes in a marble face and said, "I'll see you in my study once you've said goodnight to Cassie."

Then there was lots of debarkation protocol and milling of servants and household and retainers with hand-held tallow lamps and too many stairs to climb.

Chamoun stumbled through it all with perspiration running down his backbone, his ribcage, soaking the collar of his dress suit because there was no reason for Boregy to give him that look and those instructions—no reason that didn't have to do with the Sword of God hitting first Chamoun's dream lover and later the engagement party *cum* Festival Eve Ball.

"Cassie, Cassie, come on, you'll burn out the bulb. Juice I can replace, but the bulb . . ." Eventually he got the girl to turn off her flashlight, somewhere in one of the ormolu-festooned sitting rooms, and her people took her off to bed.

Limp and exhausted, Chamoun sat staring at the empty fireplace, and tried to order his thoughts before somebody came to take him to Vega Boregy. Or the damned dungeons.

There was no way Boregy could have connected him with the Sword hit on the party, was there? He hadn't even *known* about it. Chance hadn't trusted him enough to tell him. Could Magruder, in his infinite deviousness, have decided to sacrifice Chamoun to save his own cover? The look Vega Boregy had given him on the boat still hovered in Chamoun's inner sight, scouring his soul.

These Merovingians were good people in their way. Karl Fon and Chance Magruder might be ready to sacrifice whatever was necessary to gain a foothold in Merovingen, but Michael Chamoun had never been ready to sacrifice Rita Nikolaev. For all Chamoun knew, the hit on Rita's house had been masterminded by Magruder himself. . . .

"No," Chamoun said out loud to the empty room and shook his head forcefully. And "No" again. Magruder was on Chamoun's side. Magruder had promised to take care of Romanov, didn't want Chamoun getting involved because so many people had gone to so much trouble to put Michael Chamoun right where he was, in this fancy Boregy House sitting room, in the stronghold of the enemy.

Vega Boregy was tight with Anastasi Kalugin, who controlled the militiar blacklegs. Anastasi wanted war with Nev Hettek because it was the only way to put together a bigger force and more power than his sister, Tatiana, had; Tatiana controlled the city blacklegs, the Merovingen police.

Vega Boregy, like Chance Magruder, was too experienced and too smart for Chamoun to handle alone. And Boregy had some tenuous connection with the infamous Mondragon, ex-Sword of God, which probably meant that Boregy knew more about the Sword's long-term goals and perhaps its agents in Merovingen than anybody else. More, maybe, than any of the Kalugins.

And Vega Boregy wasn't real pleased about the way the party had gone. Now he wanted to see Chamoun. The young Sword agent sat immobile, still sweating, his chest heaving as if he'd run a long way.

Chance ought to know that Chamoun wouldn't be able to parry Boregy's probing after something like this, not alone. But Magruder had been last seen with Tatiana Kalugin, and Chamoun didn't even want to think about what that meant.

Over and over, the young Nev Hetteker's mind kept coming back to the certainty that, if Sword strategy demanded it, Michael Chamoun would be sacrificed to the Cause without a blink of Chance Magruder's eye.

Was that what he was going to learn in Vega Boregy's study? That Chamoun was going to have to marry Cassie tonight, so she could become a wife before she was made a widow in the morning—just in case there was any issue from their tryst on the *Detfish?*

Alone on the brocade settee, Mike Chamoun might have been carved from stone. He had a tendency to become very still when he was nervous, to appear lethargic, to sprawl without moving a muscle and stare off into space.

This mannerism had served him well on the journey down the Det, with the al-Bannas and Romanov and Magruder on board, all jockeying for position while Chamoun tried to keep up the fiction that he, Michael Chamoun, was captain of at least the *Detfish,* if not of his own destiny.

Now, the automatic stillness that came over him at times like these was less useful. Part of him exhorted the rest to get up, get off his butt, slip out the front, over the bridges, and find Romanov himself. It was *his* honor, not Magruder's, at stake; his heart that had been pierced as surely as the casualties in the Signeury—as surely as Kika's frail body.

Rita would have died too, if the Sword had had its way. Chamoun had stayed out of the Sword's factional infighting, bent over backward to get along with all the Romanovs in the power structure. And look where it had gotten him, thinking that his usefulness and Chance Magruder could protect him and his parents back in Nev Hettek.

Chamoun was nearly ready to renounce his allegiance to the Sword of God. Despite the lesson of Mondragon, despite what Chamoun knew happened to men like Mondragon especially when they didn't have Mondragon's connections. If Magruder had been there to argue with, to receive an ultimatum, to take his damned resignation, Chamoun would have tried all of those.

But Magruder was closeted with Tatiana Kalugin and Mike Chamoun was on his own. Unless and until Vega Boregy had him arrested.

Chamoun snapped to his feet suddenly, shaking off the lethargy of indecision. He was going out into the Merovingen night, what was left of it. He was going to find Dimitri Romanov and gut him with a fishing knife, then throw his body into a handy canal. He had to, or die trying.

It beat what would happen to him if he disobeyed Magruder's direct order and went to Nikolaev House, broke in there, saw Rita. . . . *Tried* to see Rita.

Rita, I'm sorry. Please be all right.

Rita was just wounded, Magruder had said, or led him to believe. Chamoun was pacing now, and didn't hear the retainer until the man cleared his throat.

"What? Yeah, I'm comin'," Chamoun muttered, forgetful of his diction. He was a riverboater, was all. Less before that. Magruder couldn't really expect him to pull off this charade, not perpetually.

Magruder didn't expect it, then. It was part of the Sword's plan for Chamoun to fail, sooner or later. So it didn't matter what he did. He could slip out a door, if he could just find one, instead of following this velveted mannequin deeper and deeper into the rock of Boregy House, where Vega awaited, probably with hot pokers and saw horses to stretch Chamoun's guilty body over. . . .

Rita, I'll make it up to you.

But he couldn't find a way out, a corridor that seemed to lead upward, or the sand in his craw to bolt and wait for Magruder to find him. Michael

Chamoun would rather be taken captive by the sharrh than by Chance Magruder. He couldn't risk his only friend here, not until he'd made a plan, some sane preparations.

Not until he had proof that Magruder *wasn't* his friend, that Chance had sanctioned the hit on Nikolaev House.

Chamoun didn't realize until the retainer stepped aside and he walked into a rock-walled chamber deep in the lower reaches of Boregy House that he'd come up with a plan of his own. Find Romanov. Torture the truth out of the Sword's tactical officer—whether or not Magruder had had a hand in the Nikolaev affair.

Then, if Magruder was guilty, take Rita and run. Blow the Sword's hand, go for himself. . . .

"Sit down, m'ser," said Vega Boregy in a voice full of guile, with a cultured edge that not even violence could dull.

Chamoun looked up, blinked, and stopped in his tracks. Vega Boregy had company. By the tapestry which hung over what must be a water-level window because the shutters were on the inside and made of steel, another man stood. Chamoun heard the door close behind his back. There wasn't another, no way out of here but the way he'd come in—or the window.

The man standing beside it was blond, aristocratic, and leaning on one stiff arm against the tapestried wall. The face was as pale as Boregy's, but the light hair made it seem fairer.

On that face was a weariness not attributable to the stubble of a day's beard.

Chamoun had studied that likeness, drawings in files, portraits done before men fell out and friends became enemies. His hands curled around his belt, where two emergency stars nestled, squeezing them out slowly.

Then he forcibly relaxed his grip and nodded to the man the Sword wanted more than any other in Merovingen, "Mondragon, isn't it?"

"Done your homework, have you?" said the tired man.

"Don't need none. You're famous in Nev Hettek." Then in cold afterthought: *Does Borey know what he is?*

"I said, sit down, Chamoun," Vega Borey insisted without raising his voice. "And you too, Thomas."

Mondragon obeyed, suddenly meek, obviously taking hold of a frayed temper here before a man who, if rumor was true, had saved his butt more than once because of tenuous blood ties.

Chamoun shifted his gaze from Mondragon to Vega Borey, who was obviously calling the shots. The handsome Borey was barely Magruder's age and yet tonight he seemed ancient. He leaned forward, fingers entwined on his desk, and tapped the joined fists on its shiny wood top.

"We've reached a moment where a great deal can be lost or gained, gentlemen. Michael, you're married into this household as of this moment. Do you understand? When you walked through that door, you passed the point of no return."

"I figured." Chamoun slid a glance toward Mondragon, who'd pulled up a chair cattycorner to the desk and now slouched in it, eyes narrowed so that crow's feet showed around them, as if the dim electrics were too bright.

"This is a fellow countryman of yours, and kin of mine. I'm going to let him tell you what he proposes. Answer as truthfully as you can."

And Mondragon said, sliding down on his spine, propped up by his elbows on the chair's arms, "Anastasi wants a truce with your people—with the Sword, and don't waste time telling me you're not. Even if you hadn't come in here with Magruder, it's written all over you."

Chamoun shrugged as if it didn't matter to him what Mondragon, a traitor, thought. *Does know, then. Now what?*

Borey leaned back in his chair and reached for the single filled wineglass of three behind him, on a chest. Silver pitcher, crystal glasses, all this opulence and it didn't make any difference: when it got down to cases, Vega Borey couldn't buy his way out of whatever he was into, or Michael Chamoun wouldn't be here.

"Anastasi's going to hang me if I can't put together some sort of truce between the Sword and his people," said Mondragon in a hoarse voice. He looked bluntly at Chamoun, with no apology for ruining all these months of planning: Vega Boregy wasn't going to let his daughter marry a confirmed Sword agent.

Michael Chamoun considered the two stars in his belt again: one for each man, and who was to argue if Chamoun said they'd killed each other? Secret safe. Marriage saved. And no Magruder chasing him around the world until he, like Mondragon, ran out of hiding places.

"Not my problem," said Michael Chamoun.

"You're here," Vega Boregy interjected, "because I want you to help us with this. Boregy House has ineradicable connections with Thomas, here. Now we have you. Anastasi has seen your Minister Magruder approach Tatiana. He desires an understanding—a truce or alliance—with your superiors, before Tatiana uses Magruder and what he controls against us. Is that clear?"

"Hell, no," said Michael Chamoun. "Anastasi wants war with Nev Hettek; Karl Fon wants war with Merovingen. What kind of 'alliance' could either Kalugin make under those circumstances?"

"Don't ask those kinds of questions, boy," Mondragon said harshly. "Don't think about what you're not capable of comprehending. There are factions inside the Sword, surely you're aware of that."

"I'm aware that you say your neck's in the balance, is all. And I guess the Boregy reputation, or Vega wouldn't be hosting this meeting." Was it really *the* Thomas Mondragon, public enemy number one, here before him? "But I've got to say, m'ser . . . *Vega* . . . I don't know what he's talking about."

Boregy's face quivered, every plane of it shivering. "My daughter's life, the House as it's stood for so long, my own somewhat privileged relationship with Anastasi Kalugin—all of it rides on you and your connections, Michael Chamoun. Notice I don't say 'guilt.' There are no innocents here tonight." Boregy toyed with the glass before him and looked into it as if Chamoun's answer was there.

"If I were Sword, just supposin', of course—how do y' think I'd feel about yer mixin' in, blowin' me five ways from sunrise, Mondragon?" Chamoun was praying Magruder would approve.

"Your risk; you're paying the price. Am I right? The Nikolaev incident? Sword's showing you how much leash you've got, what the price'll be if you screw up."

Chamoun was on his feet. "You scumbag traitor, I don't know what you're talking about. There's a price on your head in Nev Hettek, for all I know there's one here. If you're Sword, then go talk to *your* Sword friends. If you think Magruder can help you, talk to him. He's our Minister here. I'll set up your meeting. But don't implicate me, or draw me into your games." He turned to Vega, who watched him with deceptive casualness over the glass. "M'ser, I want to marry your daughter, make an alliance with Nev Hettek possible—do everything I said. If *you* ask me to use what little influence I've got with ... whoever, I'll try. I'll get Minister Magruder to help me. But don't believe this liar about who's who and what's what in Nev Hettek. He just flat doesn't know."

"Easy, Michael. We'd be pleased if you could set up a meeting with whomever might be appropriate—Anastasi can't have this sort of incident taking place at random here."

"That's got nothing to do with Chance," Chamoun blurted. "It's that bastard Romanov—" And stopped.

Vega Boregy, putting down his glass, sat back.

Mondragon stood up and went to the window. "But Magruder's making Anastasi nervous. If he backs Tatiana ... Tell Chance," said the fugitive named Mondragon, "I'll help him ... even help with Romanov ... if he'll come in on our side of this. For old time's sake."

Chamoun tried half-heartedly to protest again that he wasn't part of any Sword contingent here, but Vega Boregy cut him off:

"Welcome to the family, Michael Chamoun. It's a family that does what it must to survive. Whatever it must. Right now, that's setting up a meeting between Mondragon or another of Anastasi's agents and an agent of the Sword of God—perhaps Dimitri Romanov, if you're ... unqualified ... and Magruder is unsuitable. Which Mondragon assures me, and his behavior with Tatiana may confirm, that he is."

And from the window, Mondragon said in an undertone, "A family that does whatever Anastasi says it must," but Vega Boregy pretended he hadn't heard it, and so did Michael Chamoun.

Chamoun was entranced by Boregy's eyes, feeling like a fly in a spider's web. Now he understood: they wanted him to turn against Magruder, play factions, play deadly games—games of the sort that had gotten Mondragon into this mess in the first place.

They were offering him Romanov, if he agreed. And telling him that, if he refused, not only Mondragon, but the whole Boregy family, Cassie his betrothed, and Michael Chamoun himself were about to find themselves on the wrong side of Anastasi Kalugin.

People on the wrong side of Anastasi didn't live long.

But people on the wrong side of Chance Magruder didn't live, period.

Chamoun wasn't sure where he was when Mondragon muttered gutter-talk at the skip-boater, and the woman let them off somewhere at canalside between the Foundry and the Fishmarket, somewhere there were fish stands and bars and rough folk staggering blearily down walkways filthy from marathon celebration.

The waters stank here, especially the Grand Canal. The people here celebrating the Festival were a whole different sort of folk from those he'd met in hightown, and the drink and drugs of Festival just made them more surly.

Mondragon was striding ahead, seemingly uncaring whether Chamoun got lost, a pale head bobbing among the shadows of the overhanging tenements.

This was the Merovingen that Nev Hettek wanted to liberate, if it wanted to liberate anything at all. A weird home for a noble like Mondragon, until you thought about his history.

Then it made all the sense in the world. Chamoun avoided three wobbly groups of ruffians, closed his ears to the catcalls coming from waterside and slum flat, and kept on grimly.

To Romanov; Mondragon had sworn to lead him to Romanov. But somehow, Chamoun was getting the feeling that wasn't what was going to happen. The Nev Hetteker might not know Merovingen, but he knew men like Romanov. The Sword's tactical officer wasn't skulking down here, not after tonight's coup.

They should have gone to Magruder; Chance could have seen a safe way through this for everyone. But Magruder was out of the question, at least from Mondragon's point of view.

Chamoun's steps began to slow as indecision and doubt weighed heavier on him. He shouldn't have come. He hadn't been thinking clearly. Whatever Mondragon had in mind wasn't sensible—it was the product of desperation, and perhaps suicidal.

Not until Chamoun had slowed to a shuffle, and Mondragon's head was a pale glint far down the walk did Chamoun realize there were footsteps behind him. Then he heard a voice (high-pitched: a boy's voice, a woman's voice, or a voice heightened by fear) telling him to move along.

And he felt something sharp prick his spine.

There was nothing for it but to move ahead of the sharpness which urged him unremittingly in the path of Mondragon.

Suddenly stairs loomed, steps that Mondragon climbed without a backward look. Steps that led high into the crazy-quilt of the tiers. And at the bottom of those steps, the sharpness jabbed him again, and the high voice said, "Move. Climb. Don' turn round."

He'd heard more than one pair of feet, shuffling

there. In the pause, he could make out the ragged breathing of more than one person, hot puffs on the back of his neck.

Chamoun climbed. And climbed again, past a landing. And looked between the rickety steps on the next landing where the stairs widened and turned, to see two pairs of feet following his up those stairs.

At the top of the next flight, Mondragon was waiting, leaning on a railing where a ramshackle tier began, dark and twisted boardwalks leading every way under the shadows of overhanging warrens. Mondragon said, "Here's good enough, for this kind of talk. Give him room, there."

And the sharp pressure on Chamoun's spine ceased; he could feel, as well as hear, the two following him back off.

"Now," said Mondragon in a voice stripped of all accent and emotion, "let's talk about this, Sword to Sword."

"Romanov," countered Chamoun.

"You're going to find Romanov, boy—by yourself. And give him my message. All this was for you, for your foolish cover, for your game. I didn't force it in front of Vega, you tell Magruder that. That I didn't push it to where anybody's sure what you are. But I am. That's why I don't care who you talk to—even Chance."

Eyes glittered, fixed on Chamoun in the dark. The Nev Hetteker said, "Thought you was goin' to give me Romanov—take me to him, I mean."

"You'll find him, you'll do what your kind always does. Unless you're smart. If you're smart, you'll give him our message—he can't be too thrilled with Magruder right now. But listen here, trash—that's what you are, Nev Hetteker trash; everything else is Sword fabrication and don't think I can't see it: you go to Romanov, or Magruder, and say what you want."

"That won't help you, traitor." Crazy, with hostiles behind him, but Chamoun didn't have much to lose.

"You mean it won't help the family you're marrying into. I'm beyond help, fool. Just going through the motions. And you're wrong: let Romanov know your friend Chance is jeopardizing this whole gambit by Magruder's move on Tatiana—or let Chance know, doesn't matter to me. I need a contact with the Sword of God, and brother, it's you. Is that clear?"

"I'm not in any position—"

"Then get into a position where you can, fool. Your life's on the line." Mondragon took one step backward. "These people'll get you back to your boat, or to Boregy House, which might be smarter. I won't tell anybody the name of my Sword contact, won't give you up. But let this be clear: I'm dealing with no one but you. I need assurances, papers to shove under Anastasi's nose, and I need them quick. By morning, something to show. Or I'll show you and you won't like how it feels."

"Impossible. I can't—"

"—can't fail. That's right. Go on, go with them. You've got lots of work to do . . . traitor." There was a glimmer of brightness, as if Mondragon had smiled a full smile, before the outlaw turned away and slid back into shadows.

Chamoun took half a step forward before those on his track warned him off and the sharp thing was back, tickling his spine.

He remembered little of the trek down endless winding stairs, or of his pole-boat ride that ended where another boat waited, a boat which took him unerringly to the *Detfish.*

He didn't start shaking until he'd swung aboard, but by the time he reached his cabin he was dizzy with reaction.

Maybe that was why, when he unlocked the cabin door and found resistance, he pushed harder, instead of thinking what that might mean.

Inside, the electrics were doused. He stumbled over something, fumbling for them. Then he flipped on the lights and realized what he'd tripped over.

Dimitri Romanov lay sprawled on the cabin floor amid everything that had once been neatly stowed or carefully secured—clothes, provender, charts, maps, books. The blood from his slit gullet was all over everything. The evisceration was so complete that Chamoun barely made it to the window before he heaved his own guts over the side.

Then he sat there, head in hands, elbows on knees, on his bunk, staring at the blue-green-white-bloody corpse of Romanov, thinking that Chance shouldn't have been so sloppy.

And then thinking that Chance *wouldn't* have been so sloppy.

And *then* thinking that, with the exception of Ruin al-Banna and Chance Magruder, Michael Chamoun didn't know another soul in Merovingen by name or sight who was an agent of the Sword of God.

Finally, after too long staring at the corpse of Romanov, Chamoun moved stiffly to begin cleaning up the mess. He had no purpose, at that moment, beyond getting rid of the evidence. He wasn't about to try to explain to authorities here how a man happened to be dead and cleaned like a fish in his cabin, not tonight. Not any night.

After the first fear ebbed, he admitted he needed help and got two deckhands who knew from his face what was required, and from what they saw on the floor that breathing a word of it would get them similarly dead.

Together, they cleaned up the cabin and fed Romanov and his giblets to the fishes. Once that was done, relief washed over Chamoun like a riptide.

But in its wake, clear and sharp, lay another corpse: a phantom corpse, his own—a forewarning in his mind's eye of what was going to happen if he couldn't satisfy Mondragon's demands.

The only way to do that, now, was through Chance Magruder, by whatever means. Deceit might work, or the truth might do it, but somehow Michael Chamoun, agent of the Sword of God, had to bring Mondragon what he wanted by morning.

His own life, and the lives of too many others, depended on it. And Magruder was the only way. But Magruder was in with Tatiana Kalugin.

He couldn't march up to the Kalugin's ancestral

home, demand to see Chance, and state his problem, not when Chance was working on an opposite solution.

And yet, Magruder needed to know what had happened to Romanov (assuming Chance hadn't made it happen). And Michael Chamoun needed to know the name of somebody he could trust with this, some agent of the Sword in Merovingen (assuming that man wasn't Chance Magruder).

Both of those assumptions were made on too little data, on a crest of fear that moved the young Nev Hetteker out of the *Detfish* and back toward town, trying to think of answers.

And all the way there, Chamoun kept looking behind him, waiting for Ruin al-Banna, or one of Mondragon's men, or whoever else it might be who had gutted Romanov, to try the same with him.

FESTIVAL MOON
(FINAL REPRISE)

C.J. Cherryh

It was Raj came scuttling in by the Stair, there by Jones' skip, in this noisy, bloody night. "Over by Factory," Raj panted, dropping down on his heels by the boat. "M' brother still got his eye on him—"

"Which way headed?" Jones asked.

"Tidewater."

"Megarys," Mondragon said, and edged out from the hidey.

"Damn," Jones said. "That'd be."

"What'd be?" Raj asked. "Who we following?"

"Do you have another run in you?" Mondragon asked.

"Yes, ser." A gasp after air. "I c'n do another."

"Get back after your brother. Pull him back. Both of you *go home*."

The mouth stayed open. It was not what the boy had expected. It was advice any fool ought to take.

Jones stood up and unracked the pole, while Mondragon untied.

"Right to the other contact point," Mondragon said when they were clear of the bank and young ears. "Damned nice of him."

"What in *hell* are we going to do about it?"

"Just pole, Jones." He ran out the other, the long hook, and used the butt end on the bottom. "Down by Factory, like the lad said."

*   *   *

It was right down by the dead gates, was Megary.

Slavers. Illegal as hell and still running, quiet-like, which meant someone was paid off. Fined since they ran afoul of Anastasi himself on a certain run after a prisoner named Mondragon. But that was all that happened to them.

Just quieter, this summer, quiet as they used to be, here on this stinking backwater where the sea-gates had frozen dead in a quake and half-drowned the whole damn Tidewater End. No lights here, just black warehouses, the glisten of water, the sometime slink of a cat after something edible.

All shuttered up and not a chink in the windows.

Damn well no back balcony either. Megarys learned.

A skitter ran along Ulger's failing bridge, that was no cat.

"Hey," Jones muttered, and poled down and braced a little.

"Megary," the whisper came down from that bridge.

"Get *home*, boy," Mondragon whispered back. "Get! —Ya-hin. Yoss t' West 'n hin."

"Yoss." Jones eased forward, easy and quiet.

Down to West and stop, right where the canal ran by Megarys.

Bad memories hereabouts. Bad ones. It was a long wait, on the hard slats of the skip at tie-up, and they propped each other, back against back, weight against weight—easiest to watch all ways, like that.

And Mondragon was all tensed up, no give to him.

"Easy," she said. "He's got to come out soon or late. You isn't going in there. No way." She ran that past several times and counted on her fingers. "Ye ar-en't."

"*You* aren't."

"You—" Of a sudden she caught the way he had said it, felt the move, and turned round with a thump on the slats and caught his arm. "Damn, no, ye don't."

"Just get me closer."

"I'll lay ye out cold first."

He pressed her hand with his. "Jones. No arguments. Get me over there. No noise. Remember what I told you. About Kalugin."

"Which side're you on, hey? Mondragon? F' God's sake—ye can't deal with 'em. You ain't Sword." She gripped hard. "Are ye?"

He drew in a long breath. "Whatever pays, Jones. Whatever pays."

"Thought ye'd lost your senses," she muttered, and let go a little sigh. "Ye ain't going in there. . . ."

"Did I say? Go."

"Yey." She stood up and ran out the pole, ever so softly. Mondragon got up beside her on the halfdeck, as she brought the skip round and gently across by the boat-slips on Megary's dockside.

He left at the doors there, just stepped up onto the landing and stopped by the lock.

And yanked the bell-pull.

"Damn!" she yelled out. She grounded the pole in the skip's drift. "Get back here!"

He paid no attention at all. Only stood there, while inside of Megary was probably a whole house in panic; and there was nothing to do with a damnfool who stood there with his arms folded.

Except pull the skip over across the canal behind him, and hold hard with the hook into the rotten pilings there to keep her in place, while she got down into the drop-bin with the other hand for the pistol she kept.

Mama, you told me, you told me, and here I sit with the damn Megarys, and all—

Mama, I ought to have hit him other side of West.

Damn, they're coming—

Light flared on Mondragon's face. The gardeporte had opened. Someone challenged him. He stood fast.

"I'm Chamoun's pickup," he said out loud: she heard that much.

The gardeporte shut, taking the light.

He half-turned then, damn him, and looked at her sidelong, and swung back again to face the door as it opened, as two men with guns beckoned him inside.

"Stand there!" she yelled across.

Mondragon lifted one hand to motion over his shoulder, toward her. He told them something. He sauntered into the doorway and stopped again, blocking it wide.

Lord and my Ancestors—they don't think he's alone.

She waited, her arm shaking so she could hardly hold the boat against the drift.

"Jones," Mondragon called out then.

Oh, thank ye, Mondragon 'less they was in any doubt.

"Yey?"

More figures showed in the light. One was Chamoun. Others had guns. A lot of guns. She got down into the well, behind solid wood.

But Mondragon backed out. Chamoun came out. The door shut, taking the light again.

She started shaking like the fever, till she nearly squeezed the trigger by mistake.

Then she got the hook loose and got up and shoved off across the canal, where her two passengers waited at the corner.

"Name's Baritz," Mondragon said, when he came back to the skip from Boregy's door having delivered Chamoun and a certain paper. "The contact is Baritz. One of Romanov's boys. Megarys are damned worried."

The door inside Boregy Cut had swallowed Chamoun, all in dark. She held the skip by Boregy's canalside door, and Mondragon stepped up on the halfdeck, picked up his pole again. The watergate was still open, this gray dawn with the iron bells ringing across the town.

Day of the Scouring. The solemn day. The day of fasting and thinking on karma gained.

"Ain't no name I know," she said as they eased out the gate.

"The Sword cell here is in a tight place," Mondragon said. The gate-chains rattled and hinges squealed over the Signeury bells. "Now they know they are. They just had to believe it was really Anastasi's offer."

"Damn, damn, how long can we run this thing?"

"Long enough," he said. "Long as any other."

APPENDIX

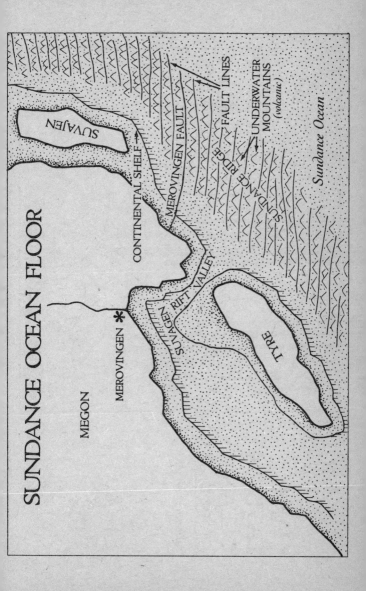

SUNDANCE OCEAN FLOOR

MEGON

SUVAJEN

CONTINENTAL SHELF

MEROVINGEN FAULT

FAULT LINES

UNDERWATER
MOUNTAINS
(volcanic)

SUNDANCE RIDGE

MEROVINGEN ✳

SUVAGEN RIFT VALLEY

TYRE

Sundance Ocean

MAJOR
EASTERN
OCEANIC
CURRENTS
(affecting climate)

N

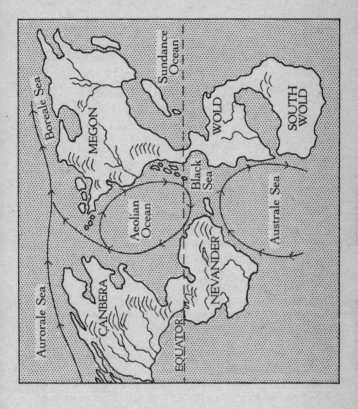

WESTERN

MEROVINGEN ECOLOGY

PRACTICAL MEROVINGEN AQUATIC ECOLOGY 101 OR "WHAT'S TO EAT?"

Mercedes R. Lackey

The aquatic ecosystems of Merovingen and its surroundings are influenced primarily by the following two factors; (1) the cold arctic current that travels down along the eastern coastline and cuts in through the Strait of Storms (which, cold current meeting warm, is why the Strait has so many storms) (2) the relatively narrow continental shelf. These two factors give the area around Merovingen a climate a great deal like Northern California (as opposed to the Eastern Seaboard).

The current is fast and pretty much constant, carrying away silt and sand. As a result the shellfish and crustaceans found in the area around Merovingen are either of the "rooting" variety (i.e., they anchor themselves and let food come to them), or they are large enough (around a meter in size) when full grown that the current can't pick them up and carry them off. They are intolerant of changes in temperature and salinity, hence for the most part cannot live in the harbor or estuary. Because the continental shelf drops off so quickly, their preferred habitat is below ten meters—this makes them nearly impossible for anyone but trained divers to retrieve. This keeps them rare, expensive, and prevents them from being fished out.

The one exception to this is a tiny "crab" of about three inches in diameter that lives among the reeds in the swamp. These are edible only in summer when they emerge from hibernation in the mud. After the 15th of Quinte they have ingested enough insect larvae to give them an extremely disagreeable taste—and worse, very powerful purgative properties. A favorite punishment among the swampy gangs is to force a malefactor to eat a double handful of them after they've gone inedible.

DINNER TIME IN THE SWAMP

Spring (Prime, Deuce, Planting):

Edible are the very young shoots of reeds and marsh-grass (edibility can be judged by the color), either raw or boiled. Fish, of course, provide protein—but the springtime staple is the "mud-pup." Mud-pups are the juvenile form of a remarkably ugly, tough, and vicious oceanic reptile called the "dragonelle." Dragonelles (not entirely reptilian as they are endotherms and do not hibernate, and have a warty hide instead of scales) are sea-going creatures that range from one to two meters in length, and are possessed of a mouthful of needle-teeth, long, tearing claws on webbed feet, and poisoned ventral and tail spines. Their flesh is very unpleasant to the taste, and quite poisonous. In late summer they mate at sea, and the gravid females take to the marshes to lay their eggs in the mud at the foot of reed-clumps. The mud-pups emerge all three months of spring. Mud-pups are plump, stupid, and easy to catch, having only the urge to get to salt water on their tiny minds. Their flesh is fairly tasteless, but nourishing, and most of a mud-pup is edible. And there are *lots* of them, presumably to make up for their stupidity, as one adult dragonelle can produce up to a thousand eggs per season, laying them over a period of one to two months.

Summer (Greening, Quartin, Quince):

Sometime in the beginning of Greening the crabs begin to emerge from hibernation. They are not overly large, and they are not as easy to catch as a mud-pup (they defend themselves) but again, there are lots of them. Fish, as usual, provides the rest of a swampy's protein. Vegetable material is provided by one of the few things seeded by the Ancestors; several varieties of edible deep-sea kelp. By Greening the kelp beds have grown up to reach the surface and long pieces are constantly being broken off and carried in to the beach. A hungry swampy need only stake out a section of beach for a few hours and sooner or later an oceanic salad big enough to stuff him and several friends will come floating in. If he's really lucky, clinging to the kelp will be one of the oceanic crabs, but he'd better keep such a piece of great good luck to himself—

Fall (Sexte, Septe, Harvest):

These are the lean months for the swampy. The kelp beds have died back down, the mud-pups are gone, the crabs can't be eaten, and the reeds and grasses have all gone woody and fibrous. The only vegetable material he can get is the pith of certain rushes; knowledge of those rush-beds is carefully guarded. About all there is for the hungry swampy is fish and river-eels. Things can get very unpleasant in the fall—

Winter (Falling, Turning, Fallow):

Things just got better. The seeds of the marsh-grass and the seed-pods of the reeds have ripened and are now edible, either raw or cooked. As soon as the seed-pods have hardened, the change in the sunlight triggers a chemical change in the reeds, and their roots fatten up with stored starch and go edible. And an oversized marsupial mouse called a "swamp-hopper" makes an appearance, going after the seeds. There are also tart berries something along the line of a cranberry that ripen during Turning. And of course, there's always fish and river-eels.

MEDICINALS AND OTHER RELEVANCIES:

Although most of the vegetation in the swamp is either poisonous or disagreeable in quantity, in small amounts quite a number of the plants have medicinal properties.

Redberry bush bark: contains salicylic acid *and* acetylsalicylate (aspirin). Useful for headache and fever-reduction.

Wiregrass: contains quinchona (quinine).

Knifegrass: root acts as a vermifuge for intestinal parasites; leaf as a laxative.

Marshcress: an expectorant.

Nodding Tom (a reed): seeds produce a mild tranquilizer; root, a sedative.

Numbvine: sap has a benzocaine-like-substance; a local anesthetic; also speeds clotting.

Potchbush: sap has a very powerful antibiotic effect, but only externally.

Rainbow weed: stimulant.

PRACTICAL MEROVINGEN ECOLOGY 102 OR "WHAT'S EATING YOU?"

In sober fact, most of the wildlife of Merovin finds human beings (a) inedible or (b) as poisonous as humans find the wildlife. This is fortunate for the humans, especially those in the swamp. However, there are any number of things out there that are perfectly willing to defend themselves/territory by taking a bite out of you, provided they can spit it out afterwards.

JAWS 3, SWAMPY 0

The single largest dangerous critter a swampy is likely to encounter is the gravid female dragonelle. They are between one and two meters long, have short tempers (you'd be peeved too, if you had up to a thousand eggs to lay), are highly territorial and aggressive, and are possessed of poisonous ventral and tail spines and a mouthful of needle-sharp teeth.

They swarm into the swamp in the winter months, coming in after dark with the high tide and leaving with the ebb (like grunion) before dawn. They have been known to take a whole foot off an injudicious swampy, and will certainly extract the proverbial pound of flesh if they get the chance. The main rule in dealing with dragonelles is, NEVER, EVER, PUT ANY PART OF YOURSELF INTO THE WATER AFTER DARK IN WINTER. While they are amphibious, they don't really like "dry land" and much prefer to grumble down in the mud underwater. They will not climb up on rafts or into boats.

Moving down the food chain, we come to the smaller "reptiles and amphibians." Here the rule is, if it has teeth, it will usually bite. Nature has been a bit kinder to humans here—the poisonous ones advertise themselves with bright, vivid colors. The three most often fatal are:

THE BLOOD-SKINK: about ten to twenty centimeters long, and a vivid ruby red in color, the blood-skink is normally shy except in summer (mating season). Both sexes fight, both are poisonous. The venom is a neurotoxin acting on the autonomic nervous system.

THE ASP: named for Cleopatra's pet, this is actually a legless lizard patterned in brown and bright yellow. It lives in the center of reed clumps. It is normally shy but will bite if disturbed, frightened, or captured. The venom is, like that of the Indian krait, a catalyzing enzyme; it causes euphoria and vivid hallucinations, and death is usually due to heart-failure.

THE KOBRA: this is a true snake, rarely exceeding ten centimeters and pencil-thin. In color it is a vivid emerald green. It is most often encountered because it has climbed up onto a raft or boat to sun itself; it is incredibly quick, and can strike and be over the side almost before the hapless swampy has realized it was there. The venom is a respiratory system depressant; death is caused by asphyxiation.

A variety of other toothy denizens can be an indirect cause of death via infection of the wound.

WHO'RE YE CALLING VERMIN?

Along with cats, rats and mice went to space, made it to Merovin, and unlike the human colonists, throve. How they got here is uncertain; legend has it that they are all descendants of a shipment of lab animals whose cages broke during an earthquake. This may be at least partially true; there is a heavy preponderance of albinism among them; also about twenty percent of the population are piebald (Wistar) rats.

The indigenous critters to look out for are as follows:

SKITS: about the size of a large mouse, these things look like an unholy mating of crab and shrew; they have sharp hairy snouts with lots of teeth, a horny carapace, a long, hairless tail, and a voracious appetite. They are found in the swamp and in town, both. They are omnivorous, and the main reason why no sane swampy will try to store food; if more than ten assemble to chow down, it kicks off a feeding frenzy among them. If stored food attracted a swarm (a feeding group of a hundred or more) to a raft, the inhabitant stands a real good chance of ending up on the menu, literally nibbled to death.

MUDSUCKERS: the Merovingen leech; they will attach themselves to the unfortunate who happens upon them and will create a nasty sore before realizing that they've latched onto something inedible and drop off.

NARKS: the Merovingen cockroach; similar in habitat and indestructibility, they look rather like a silverbit sized insect that couldn't make up its mind whether to be a spider or a beetle.

In addition, a number of the smaller lizards have made themselves at home in the canals and buildings of Merovingen. They're mostly shy and harmless; many of them actually provide a service of eating insects and insect larvae.

For the most part, Merovin insect life finds humans unpalatable; the one thing a swampy or canaler DOESN'T have to deal with is mosquitoes and flies, or the local equïvalent. This is the one bright spot in an otherwise unpleasant existence.

Index of Isles and Buildings by Regions

THE ROCK: (ELITE RESIDENTIAL) LAGOONSIDE

1. The Rock
2. Exeter
3. Rodrigues
4. Navale
5. Columbo
6. McAllister
7. Basargin
8. Kalugin (governor's relatives)
9. Tremaine
10. Dundee
11. Kuzmin
12. Rajwade
13. Kuminski
14. Ito
15. Krobo
16. Lindsey
17. Cromwell
18. Vance
19. Smith
20. Cham
21. Spraker
22. Yucel
23. Deems
24. Ortega
25. Bois
26. Mansur

GOVERNMENT CENTER

THE TEN ISLES (ELITE RESIDENCE)

27. Spur (militia)
28. Justiciary
29. College (Revenant)
30. Signeury
31. Carswell
32. Kistna
33. Elgin
34. Narain
35. Zorya
36. Eshkol
37. Romney
38. Rosenblum
39. Boregy
40. Dorjan

THE SOUTH BANK

Second rank of elite
41. White
42. Eber
43. Chavez
44. Bucher
45. St. John
46. Malvino (Adventist)
47. Mendelev
48. Sofia
49. Kamat
50. Tyler

THE RESIDENCIES

Mostly wealthy or government
51. North
52. Spellbridge
53. Kass
54. Borg
55. Bent
56. French
57. Cantry
58. Porfirio
59. Wex

WEST END

Upper middle class
60. Novgorod
61. Ciro
62. Bolado
63. diNero
64. Mars
65. Ventura
66. Gallandry (Advent.)
67. Martel
68. Salazar
69. Williams
70. Pardee
71. Calliste
72. Spiller
73. Yan
74. Ventani
75. Turk
76. Princeton
77. Dunham

PORTSIDE

Middle class
78. Golden
79. Pauley
80. Eick
81. Torrence
82. Yesudian
83. Capone
84. Deva
85. Bruder
86. Mohan
87. Deniz
88. Hendricks
89. Racawski
90. Hofmeyr
91. Petri
92. Rohan
93. Herschell
94. Bierbauer
95. Godwin
96. Arden
97. Aswad

TIDEWATER (SLUM)   FOUNDRY DISTRICT

98. Hafiz (brewery)	109. Spellman
99. Rostov	110. Foundry
100. Ravi	111. Vaitan
101. Greely	112. Sarojin
102. Megary (slaver)	113. Nayab
103. Ulger	114. Petrescu
104. Mendez	115. Hagen
105. Amparo	
106. Calder	
107. Fife	
108. Salvatore	

EASTSIDE   RIMMON ISLE
(LOWER MID.)   (ELITE/MERCANTILE)

116. Fishmarket	124. Khan
117. Masud	125. Raza
118. Knowles	126. Takezawa
119. Gossan (Adventist)	127. Yakunin
120. Bogar	128. Balaci
121. Mantovan (Advent.)	129. Martushev
(wealthy)	130. Nikolaev
122. Salem	
123. Delaree	

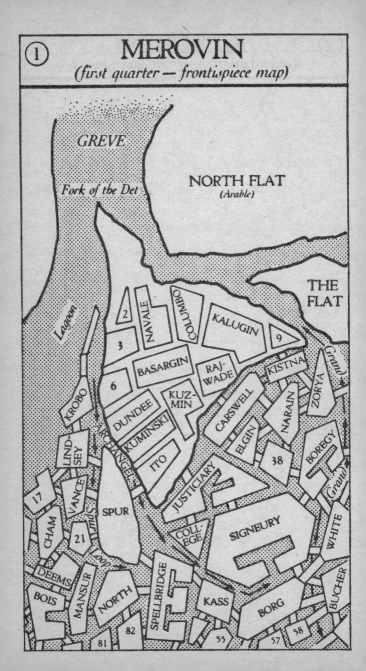

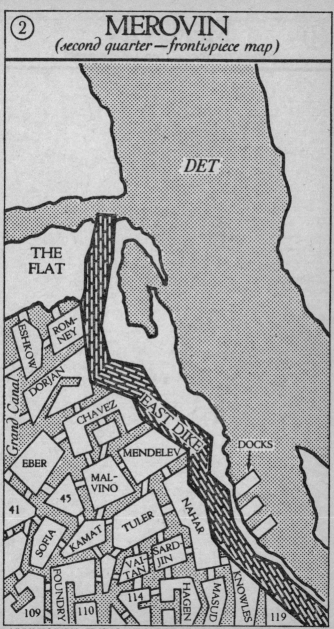

DET

THE FLAT

Grand Canal

ESHKOW

ROM-NEY

DORJAN

CHAVEZ

EAST DIKE

DOCKS

EBER

MENDELEV

MAL-VINO

45

41

SOFIA

KAMAT

TULER

NAHAR

VAI-TAN

SARD-JIN

FOUNDRY

109

110

114

HAGEN

MASUD

KNOWLES

119

✱ NUMBERS INDICATE ISLES AND BUILDINGS LISTED IN INDEX

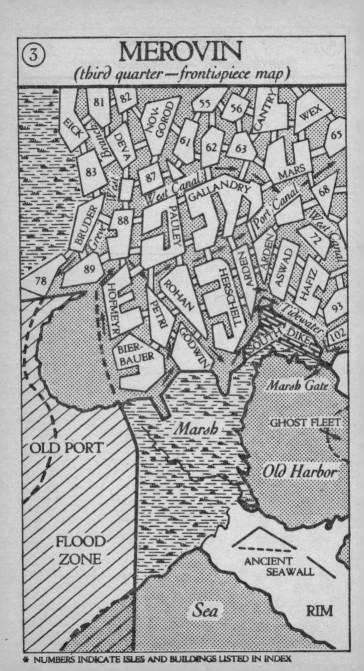

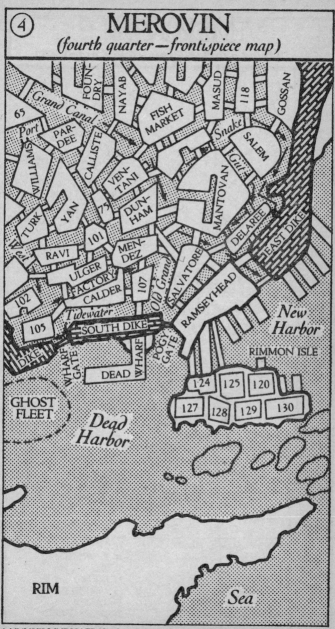

④ MEROVIN
(fourth quarter — frontispiece map)

Grand Canal

65

Port

FOUN-DRY

NAYAB

MASUD

118

GOSSAN

WILLIAMS

PAR-DEE

CALLISTE

FISH MARKET

Snake

SALEM

Gut

TURK

YAN

VEN-TANI

75

MANTOVAN

DELAREE

EAST DIKE

RAVI

101

DUN-HAM

SALVATORE

RAMSEYHEAD

New Harbor

ULGER

MEN-DEZ

FACTORY

CALDER

107

Old Grand

102

Tidewater

SOUTH DIKE

POGY GATE

105

DIKE

WHARF GATE

DEAD

WHARF

RIMMON ISLE

124

125

120

GHOST FLEET

127

128

129

130

Dead Harbor

RIM

Sea

✱ NUMBERS INDICATE ISLES AND BUILDINGS LISTED IN INDEX

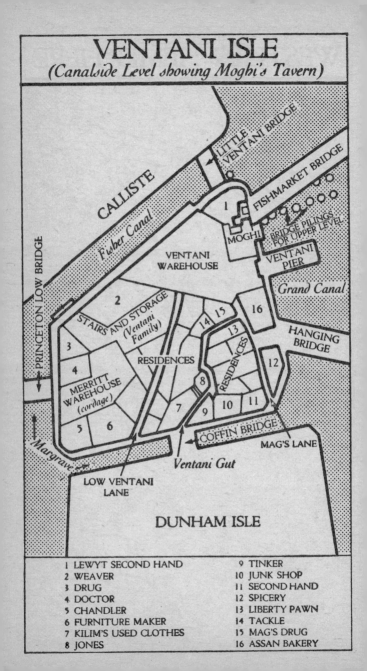

VENTANI ISLE
(Canalside Level showing Moghi's Tavern)

LITTLE VENTANI BRIDGE

FISHMARKET BRIDGE

CALLISTE

Fisher Canal

1 MOGHI

BRIDGE PILINGS FOR UPPER LEVEL

VENTANI WAREHOUSE

VENTANI PIER

Grand Canal

PRINCETON LOW BRIDGE

2

STAIRS AND STORAGE (Ventani Family)

14 15

16

3

13

RESIDENCES

HANGING BRIDGE

4

RESIDENCES

12

MERRITT WAREHOUSE (cordage)

8

5 6

7

9

10 11

Margrave

COFFIN BRIDGE

MAG'S LANE

Ventani Gut

LOW VENTANI LANE

DUNHAM ISLE

1 LEWYT SECOND HAND	9 TINKER
2 WEAVER	10 JUNK SHOP
3 DRUG	11 SECOND HAND
4 DOCTOR	12 SPICERY
5 CHANDLER	13 LIBERTY PAWN
6 FURNITURE MAKER	14 TACKLE
7 KILIM'S USED CLOTHES	15 MAG'S DRUG
8 JONES	16 ASSAN BAKERY

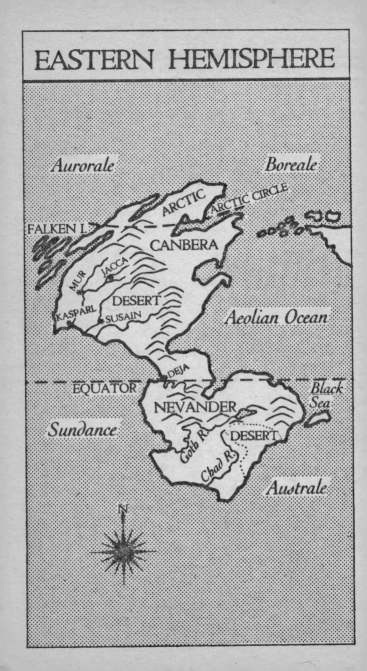

GUARDIAN

Lyrics & Music: Leslie Fish (c) 9/22/83

(rewritten by: Rif)

See him stalking, day or night, the islands of the bay,
Like some veteran tiger[1] come to hunt his chosen
　prey.
He'll never lack for targets here, for scum will always
　rise,
And to the man who guards your walls that comes as
　no surprise.

Chorus:

And who will be the guardian to take your dangers
　on?
Who will guard your sleep at night when ol' Black
　Cal is gone?

For one in ten's a predator who treats the rest as
　prey,
So someone's always needed here to drive those
　wolves[1] away.
We never left the jungle; we just brought it into
　town.
The leopards[1] take on human form, and follow us
　around. (Cho.)

Who will dare deny him there, and say it isn't so,
Must claim there is no street[2] at night they wouldn't
　dare to go,
That charity or righteousness will keep them safe
　from harm,
And if their own front door is shut, the whole wide
　world is warm. (Cho.)

Who will say the job is wrong, and shouldn't be at all,
Must then take up the gun themselves to guard
　each door and wall,

Must spend their nights in sentry-rounds, their days in packing heat.
It's easier to pay the man full-time to guard your street. (Cho.)

Evolution never stopped; we always have to choose.
The thug who waits to mug you is collecting Darwin's[3] dues.
And you can't drive hyenas[4] off by kneeling down to pray—
So who will raise the weapon, then, to keep the beasts at bay?
(Cho.) Last Chorus:

Run like deer,[1] or die like sheep, or take your dangers on;
For you must guard your streets yourselves when ol' Black Cal is gone.

(Available—original form—on tape from Off Centaur Publications, P O Box 424, El Cerrito, CA 94530)

---

[1]Like many songs of Merovingen, this one came down from early ballads of Earth, written by the poet Leslie Fish. It shows its authenticity by the reference to several Terran lifeforms of which only vaguest details have been preserved in record. Likely it underwent several transitions from the original material before it achieved its present form, attributed to one Rif, no other name known.

[2]This reference may have predated the Great Quake.

[3]Darwin is a saint in New Worlder belief, and this difficult verse is possibly corrupt.

[4]The word *hyenas* is of uncertain meaning. It may refer to ancient spirits of disaster.

BLACK WATER (SUICIDE)

(Sung by Rif and Rat at Hoh's)

Black Water, be my lover, for lover have I none
Nor ever shall, and empty ache alone
Black water, be my lover, for all my dreams are done
And you are kinder than what life has shown.

CHORUS:

Black water, final rescue; dark water, lasting peace,
Black water, keeping secrets none may know.
Black water, final rescue; bring silence and release
Black water, through the city swiftly flow.

Black water, hold my secret—my shame I beg you
    hide
I cannot bear to meet a friend or foe
Black water, hold my secret and save my shattered
    pride
And let them never guess and never know.

Black water, I am weary—the days are all the same
The years creep by with never hope to see.
Black water, life is dreary—I'm tired of the game
I'd rather far your quiet company.

Black water, be my refuge—I hear them at my back
My enemies pursue me to a man
Black water, be my refuge—they close upon my track
And better your embrace than what they plan.

PRIVATE CONVERSATION

Lyrics copyright 1986 by Mercedes R. Lackey,
Music copyright 1986 by C.J. Cherryh.

Angel, this is Altair Jones—ye maybe know my
name—
'Cause yours is Retribution an' my Mama's was the
same.
Angel, I got problems, an' I ain't sure what to do—
So maybe I can get 'em straight by tellin' 'em to you.

Angel, there's this feller—oh dear Lord, that man is
fine—
He kinda looks a lot like you; I kinda hope he's
mine.
Now enemies are pretty cheap—I got my share, I
guess—
But Angel, from what I can see he's in one *god-all*
mess.

It seems he maybe likes me, kinda maybe like he
cares—
But when I ask his troubles, well he just sits there
and stares.
An' when I wanta help 'im—damn, he won't take
help from me!
Angel, what's the problem? Is it somethin' I can't be?

Angel, yeah, I hear ye—thinking, 'damn that girl's a
fool.'
But hey, if *I* don't help 'im would ye kindly tell me
who'll
Put their own necks in the noose or give 'im so much
as a hand?
Oh I see ye smilin', Angel—kinda thought ye'd
understand.

Angel, Mama tol' me not t' do what I just done—
T' let my heart go lead my head—hell, not fer anyone.
But Angel, he's a fool, an' I'm another fool, ye see—
An' I hear that ye stayed here to watch over fools.
Could ye keep 'im safe—fer me?

DAW

More Top-Flight Science Fiction and Fantasy from
C.J. CHERRYH

DAW

DAW PRESENTS THESE BESTSELLERS BY
MARION ZIMMER BRADLEY

DARKOVER NOVELS

DAW

DAW PRESENTS STAR WARS IN A WHOLE NEW DIMENSION

Timothy Zahn
THE BLACKCOLLAR NOVELS

The war drug—that was what Backlash was, the secret formula, so rumor said, which turned ordinary soldiers into the legendary Blackcollars, the super warriors who, decades after Earth's conquest by the alien Ryqril, remained humanity's one hope to regain its freedom.

☐ THE BLACKCOLLAR   (UE2168—$3.50)
☐ BLACKCOLLAR: THE BACKLASH MISSION

(UE2150—$3.50)

Cynthia Felice
☐ DOWNTIME

The Decemvirate has ruled the galaxy for ages ... and will rule for ages hence, as long as they remain the sole guardians of the longevity elixir. But a galaxy-wide rebellion is brewing, led by a cunning and determined band of traitors who will stop at nothing to taste immortality.   (UE2170—$2.95)

John Steakley
☐ ARMOR

Impervious body armor had been devised for the commando forces who were to be dropped onto the poisonous surface of A-9, the home world of mankind's most implacable enemy. But what of the man inside the armor? This tale of cosmic combat will stand against the best of Gordon Dickson or Poul Anderson.

(UE1979—$3.95)

Attention:

DAW COLLECTORS

Many readers of DAW Books have written requesting information on early titles and book numbers to assist in the collection of DAW editions since the first of our titles appeared in April 1972.

We have prepared a several-pages-long list of all DAW titles, giving their sequence numbers, original and current order numbers, and ISBN numbers. And of course the authors and book titles, as well as reissues.

If you think that this list will be of help, you may have a copy by writing to the address below and enclosing one dollar in stamps or currency to cover the handling and postage costs.

DAW BOOKS, INC. DEPT. C
1633 Broadway
New York, N.Y. 10019